IFWG Publishing Titles
edited by Deborah Sheldon

*Spawn: Weird Horror Tales About Pregnancy, Birth
and Babies (2021)*
Killer Creatures Down Under: Horror Stories with Bite (2023)
*Spawn 2: More Weird Horror Tales About Pregnancy,
Birth And Babies (2024)*

Spawn 2

More Weird Horror Tales About Pregnancy, Birth and Babies

EDITED BY

DEBORAH SHELDON

Spawn 2: More Weird Horror Tales About
Pregnancy, Birth and Babies

ISBN-13: 978-1-922856-80-7

V1.0

All stories are original to this anthology, except the following: (first publishing instance) "The Tea and Sugar Train" by Deborah Sheldon, in *Dimension6* #18, 2019.

IFWG Publishing Publishing
Gold Coast

www.ifwgpublishing.com

For Allen and Harry

TABLE OF CONTENTS

INTRODUCTION

Birth and death are not two different states, but they are different aspects of the same state.
—Mahatma Gandhi (1869–1948)

IFWG Publishing had a booth at an Australian convention, never mind which one, in 2021. Among the stacks of books for sale were paperbacks of the anthology I conceived and edited, *Spawn: Weird Horror Tales About Pregnancy, Birth and Babies*. A half-dozen writers manned IFWG's booth—including one of my own contributors, J.M. Merryt—to spruik, interact, and sign copies. Posters of various book covers crowded the back wall. A customer strolling the corridor stopped when he saw the poster for *Spawn* and became irate. Red-faced, he railed against this blasphemy and decried everyone associated with the book as evil. How could we treat pregnancy, birth and babies with anything other than reverent respect?

Later, when J.M. told me over the phone about this awful experience, I wondered: Had this angry, triggered man ever been present at a birth? Seen the fear, blood and shit, witnessed how closely the mother and baby kept orbiting catastrophe, how the medical staff were constantly on tenterhooks and doing their best to circumvent the worst? Probably not. Or perhaps he was of an era when men belonged in the waiting room, shirt pockets full of cigars, genteelly hidden from the screaming, puking, splitting, ripping and haemorrhaging that was going on in the birthing ward behind closed doors.

You're holding in your hands the second volume in my intended trilogy. The first volume, *Spawn: Weird Horror Tales About Pregnancy, Birth and Babies*, comprised stories by 23 Australian writers, mostly obtained by open callout, and was published by IFWG in 2021. Critically acclaimed, *Spawn* was shortlisted for six awards and won two of them: the Australian Shadows Best Edited Work Award for myself; and the Australian Shadows Best Short Story Award going to Matt Tighe for his contribution, 'A Good Big Brother'. Matt's work also appears in this second volume.

Since my idea for the trilogy was inspired by my story "Hair and Teeth", I included it in *Spawn*. So, I thought for this volume I'd add my body horror tale 'The Tea and Sugar Train', first published in *Dimension6 #18* (Coeur De Lion Publishing, 2019) and reprinted in both *Year's Best Hardcore Horror #5* (Red Room Press, 2020) and my award-nominated collection *Liminal Spaces: Horror Stories* (IFWG, 2022).

My inspiration for this story was twofold. Firstly, the actual 'tea and sugar train', an Australian relic from early last century, which ran daily along the 1,700 kilometres of desert between Port Augusta and Kalgoorlie. It functioned like a mobile shopping mall for the line workers and their families who lived adjacent to the Transcontinental Railway and kept it maintained. And secondly, the heavy clumsiness of my own pregnancy. Gestation, with all its various weird and wonderful accoutrements, is remembered deeply by her body for the rest of a woman's life.

At the time of writing, the son I share with my husband is 23 years old. Yet I still have dreams of my lone full-term pregnancy where I feel again the knocks and rustlings of his feet, knees and elbows. Even now, I can physically remember my shifted centre of gravity and waddling gait, the constant pressure on my bladder, that stuffed-sausage feeling of my stomach crammed up into my throat. A few years ago, when I was hospitalised for a spinal injury, the nurses kept asking, "How's your pain on a scale of one to ten?" At first, my honest reply would frustrate them. I'd say, "With 'ten' being what? Childbirth?" Depending on the nurse, reactions included an exasperated sigh, a chuckle, a rolling of the eyes or even a storming from the room. I soon realised that the hospital's pain scale ignores the experience of childbirth. The scale is only for "normal" pain levels. Whatever they might be.

Yet my question to those nurses remains a genuine one. How do you compare any other pain to giving birth, which is the most brutal natural process the human body can endure? When ruptured discs press against spinal nerves, it feels like an axe swung into your back, over and over, as if you're a tree and an enthusiastic lumberjack is trying to cut you down in record time. It's an utterly stunning, shocking, screaming agony.

But still not as painful as childbirth.

Not in the same ballpark. Damn, it's not even the same *game*.

When you know, you know.

In 2023, I opened *Spawn 2* to stories by Australasian writers. Just two of the published 23 stories are by New Zealanders; fair enough, given the country's small population, only about the size of Melbourne.

Spawn 2 attracted a great many submissions. I spent a lot of time and angst deciding between stories. The prospect of sending rejection letters was difficult to face. To spare myself, I decided to send them all on one day, then suffered a violent migraine and two or three sleepless nights thereafter. As a writer who has experienced countless rejections throughout the 37 years of my career, I felt the pain and disappointment I'd caused.

Yet my personal response to rejection over the decades has always been: *Tough luck, suck it up.* I've tried and failed to maintain this attitude in my role as editor. How can I be a hard-arse when I know how much rejection can hurt? As my publisher, Gerry Huntman of IFWG pointed out, sending rejection letters is an occupational hazard.

From the slush, what struck me in particular was the sheer number of first-person narratives. Generally, most short stories, novellas and novels are written in the third-person. My Table of Contents happens to reflect the slush ratio, since 15 of the 22 stories in *Spawn*

2 contain an 'I' character. Interesting.

Submissions from female writers outnumbered those from males by about two to one. Coincidentally, that ratio is reflected in the Table of Contents, with 15 stories by women compared to seven by men. (While the numbers match, no, the seven men didn't write all the seven third-person stories.)

I'm sure a psychologist with a penchant for statistical analysis could posit a few theories on the above. As it is, I'll leave you, the reader, to come to your own conclusions.

But across the board, regardless of narrative point-of-view or the author's sex, these stories share and expose intimate and relatable thoughts and feelings. Expect emotional or physical reactions. Plenty of these stories made my heart race. Brought tears to my eyes. A couple even nauseated me. Clearly, your responses will vary according to what rings your bell.

Yet here's something I *can* promise: as you read this anthology, you'll be constantly on the back foot. While I asked writers for "body horror" stories, I left the subgenre open-ended and encouraged a loose, free-form response to the theme. And what a cornucopia of stories I got in return! From space opera to cybernetics to historical to phantasmagorical to realism to folk-horror to Aussie "ocker" to the occult and more, *Spawn 2* delivers an eclectic mix. This second anthology in my series interprets and reinterprets pregnancy, birth and babies in a myriad of unexpected ways that I hope will surprise, frighten, shock, disgust, horrify and move you.

Please enjoy. And share the word.

Deborah Sheldon
Melbourne, 2024

BODY OF WORK

LILY MULHOLLAND

They are beautiful, preternaturally so, these aliens who have come to save us.

Most call them angels, as though descended from the heavens to purge the planet of our sins. Only they're no creation of an omnipotent god; instead, they came to us from the Small Magellanic Cloud, beyond the Milky Way.

"We come in peace," they'd said, that first tumultuous day when they'd arrived in their space flotilla, relaying signals to all earthly receivers, seeking permission to land on each of the seven continents. What a cliché. And yet, so they had proven in the fifteen months since their arrival, rolling out delegations across the planet, charming their way through population after population. And yet.

And yet, some of us had not believed their presence was unconditional. We surged, gathering activists from all countries and cultures. We organised, marching in the streets, dominating the airwaves, pushing back on the elite's embrace of the extraterrestrials. But as the angels shared their planet-saving and disease-curing technology, our numbers dwindled, so much so that we, the last remnants of resistance, were openly derided as crackpots by the commentariat and a newly invigorated mainstream media.

The world succumbed to the angels.

I had done my best, of course, to avoid contact, observing from my self-imposed distance the ease with which they'd charmed the planet's inhabitants. From the elite to the working poor, the global community had coalesced around the promises of a controlled climate, the end of dangerous weather events, diseases cured, and peace brought to all. The lure of joining an intergalactic coalition of sentient beings who sought to share knowledge and resources for the greater good of the universe had ensnared every man, woman and child.

I mean, what rubbish—they clearly wanted something!

But the whole planet had bought it. In an era of mis- and disinformation, the angels had proved to be masters of charisma and communication.

What was even more astonishing was that their arrival and promise to save the planet had sparked a baby boom. Millennials like me, who swore they'd never have children, were reproducing like rabbits.

I'd be full of admiration if I wasn't so full of fear and foreboding.

Especially now, as I'm stuck in this most gorgeous of prisons. A holding cell, full of my favourite things, but with no way out. Since I was brought in last night by the Feds—under warrant from a freaking magistrate, no less—I'd been fed, bathed, and slept (badly) in this fully automated apartment somewhere in the depths of the facility the aliens had built outside Canberra.

All night, I'd tossed and turned, trying to work out what they wanted from me. I'd come up blank. And now I had nothing to do but contemplate my first moves and conjure what my first words would be when the angels finally deigned to reveal themselves. A born overthinker, this wasn't going well. In actual fact, in response to my worst imaginings, my breakfast of scrambled eggs and dill was rolling in my stomach like wet clothes in a washing machine. Was my face as green as my gills? Unsure, but I wasn't game to move in case I sparked a new wave of nausea. I had to focus. Get my thoughts together so I could find out the truth: Why had they come to our planet and what did they want from us?

A sudden shift in the intensity of the ambient lighting presaged the smooth hum of a wall panel starting its slide into a recess. So, the walls are doors. Clever. This admiration of architectural form and function is, of course, my brain buying a few precious seconds to—

I'm hit by a sudden shock of adrenaline, which courses through my limbs and out to the tips of my fingers and toes. The back of my head tingles. My stomach churns. My body is heavy with anticipation. I close my eyes for a second, breathe, prepare.

I am ready to meet the angels.

I have disassociated. I know this because I can't move my body, and somehow my brain is going in reverse. I scramble, scrabble, slide off my intellectual footing into a place where I cannot think.

The alien who stands before me is beautiful. He is tall, his jet hair offsetting eyes the colour of my mother's kyanite bracelet. He regards me through these crystalline eyes, sending a chill through me from crown to heel.

"Doctor Grainger. It is an honour to meet you."

I haven't used my doctoral title in years, not since social media activism lured me away from medical research. Looks like the aliens have done their own on me. He steps forward.

I want to step backwards, but my feet do not oblige.

He extends one hand, and somehow my own reaches forward to clasp his, the cool of his hand thrilling against the heat of my own. We shake, and the release of our grasp brings me back into my body.

"Welcome to Orroral. My name is Mark Quicksilver, and I am to be your companion."

He ushers me down the open corridor, diffused light flooding the atrium. I cannot see the sky because the panels of the dome are filtered, but I know it is a beautiful day.

We reach the far side of the atrium. A panel glides left to reveal a new corridor leading into a lovely, light-filled open space with tables, chairs and reading nooks.

My mercurial friend turns to me as we walk together. He pours me a glass of water from a drinks station. "Thank you for coming."

Despite my best efforts to remain calm, my cheeks burn pink at this game of disingenuity. "Like I had a choice. Why don't you tell me what I'm doing here?"

"Dr Grainger."

"Penny."

He smiles at me, a facial gesture that is equally awkward and disarming. It's like he is only just learning how. "We admire your work, *Penny*, on body positivity, the harms of social media and the rise of the influencer."

The back of my head pulses, my cheeks tingle. Big breath in. They have read my research. How? I must've said this last part out loud, because he answers me.

"We accessed every research database on your planet to understand how your species functions, communicates and procreates. We found your research on the effects of misinformation on primal fears particularly enlightening. You could say we used it as a blueprint for our successful…I believe you call it colonisation…of your planet."

The planes of my existence shift for the third time today. *Colonisation?* I gulp at my drink, trying to hide my confusion.

"You have resources not available to us on our home planet, or in our other colonies."

Other colonies? I still my face as my mind whirs.

"As we have discussed with your world's leaders, we require space-link facilities on Earth. So that we can project further into the universe than we are able to from our own galaxy."

"Which we have given you in return for access to your climate tech and medical knowledge. Mr Quicksilver, I would much prefer you be straight with me. What are you really doing here?"

He licks his lips in a way that makes me uncomfortable. It's not lascivious exactly, but neither is his tongue movement human. The hairs on my forearms stand to attention, and my jaw muscles tingle.

"Penny, you know of our chromatophorous physiology." It's a statement, but I must look blank, because he elaborates. "We are able to change our appearance to match that of the predominant species. That is how we are able to appear to you as humanoid."

Like a chameleon or octopus. Clever.

"Similar, but not quite. In addition to being able to change our colouring, we are also able to control our radial musculature."

"Hold on. You answered a question I didn't ask."

"Oh dear." One eyebrow raises and his mouth quirks. "Yes, the secret is no more; we are able to communicate with you telepathically."

I don't buy it for a second. No doubt every other scientist they meet has the same thoughts as me when they first encounter these shape-shifters.

Most of them, Dr Grainger, but we are rather taken with the way your brain works.

Okay, fuck, I can hear his voice in my head. La-la-la-la. My favourite snack is coconut yoghurt.

You must be tired, Doctor. I will return you to your apartment now and answer any questions you may have. Tomorrow, we will show you why you are here.

As I awake and stretch, the light in my room brightens until it resembles daylight. The niche in the wall opens to reveal a small insulated flask of coffee, a mug, and a bowl. I'm famished and I've consumed the coconut yoghurt, berries and flaked almonds before I even realise what I've eaten. It seems every whim is catered for. If I wasn't imprisoned by aliens, I'd probably quite enjoy being pampered like this.

After a shower and a change into a new set of clothes from my wardrobe at home—apparently, I've been moved in—I am ready for the day. Well, as ready as one can be when one's world has been inverted.

Shall we? Mark's voice slides into my head.

How long have you been listening to my thoughts?

Long enough to know you enjoyed your breakfast.

I am going to have to be careful.

The door slides open, the very beautiful Mark standing in front of me.

Thank you. We worked hard to perfect my appearance.

He takes me back to the first atrium from yesterday, diverting from our previous path as we cross the room. Another door opens to our right and we proceed into some kind of elevator.

There are no buttons, but we descend.

We step out into a sanctuary of verdant foliage, butterflies, ponds and plush seating. Light streams from above. It is divine.

"Mark, what is this place?"

"Garden of Eden, Avalon, Goloka, Tír na nÓg, Emain Ablach, the Grand Seraglio of the Ottoman Sultans. Paradise."

It looks like something pulled from my Pinterest "dream garden" board. It's perfect.

Wait, why does this look like my mood board?

Penny, everything in this facility is designed to meet your practical and aesthetic needs.

A sudden headache grips my skull. Mark leads me to a bench seat, lowers me gently. He kneels before me and takes my hands.

"Sorry, Penny, telepathy can take some getting used to. Let's speak out loud for now. There's a lot I need to show you today before we get started tomorrow."

I slow my breathing, close my eyes, still my thoughts, searching for clarity. His cool palms on my warm hands are soothing. I open my eyes to find his gaze fixed on my face. He is a picture of warmth and concern—these creatures are so quick to adapt to our social cues, I wish I had the time to study them. But I need answers and I need to get out of here.

"Penny, I'm going to try to block your thoughts so you can have some privacy, but I just heard what you said. Yes, we are fast to adapt. Our survival as a species depends on this agility. I will be happy to answer all of your questions—you will be our guest here for the next six years. I take it this is long enough for a research project?"

His smile is tinged with sadness. I am not yet ready to ask him why.

He stands, pulling me up with him. "Let us begin."

We wind our way through this oasis, through to yet another part of the complex. I'm stunned at what they have built inside two years.

"How many humans have been down here?"

"One hundred and sixty-seven. Before you, that is."

We are in a tunnel suffused with light, neither warm nor cold. It's comfortable. Usually I'd feel a little claustrophobic, but somehow this feels spacious, and out of time and space. I certainly don't feel like I'm—

"How far underground are we?"

Mark smiles as he answers. "I'm regretting my decision to tune out your thoughts. It was easier following your logic when I knew what you were thinking."

Ah, yes, the good old ADHD brain. I stop. I haven't taken my meds for the last two days, and yet I feel calm. And I really shouldn't, given the situation. "Why am I feeling so well?"

He backtracks. Takes my hand. "We have adjusted your nourishment. Our technology enables us to provide everything you need for your brain chemistry to remain perfectly balanced for your individual needs."

Jesus. "Are you telling me you can fix our mental health crises?" The pressure of his hand in the small of my back propels me forward as I contemplate the enormity of this revelation. "What else can you fix?"

"Everything. You see, our lives are short and our reproduction rate is significantly lower than yours. So, life is far more precious to us than it seems to be to humans."

I halt. Again. There is so much to take in.

"Wait. Did you say I was going to be here for six years?"

He places his hand against the wall and a bench seat appears. We sit.

"Okay, let's take a minute. First, I am sorry that this is all coming at you so quickly. One of the reasons you are here is that your ability to comprehend significant volumes of data and information from multiple sources across many disciplines far surpasses that of most humans. But I should have realised that even for someone with your capacity, this is likely to be quite overwhelming."

He could say that again.

"But I won't."

I look at him sharply. "I thought you'd tuned me out."

"I did, but I'm back in your head again. We have so much to cover, we need to be as efficient in our information-sharing as possible."

I shake my head, corralling my thoughts, which is surprisingly easy to do now my brain chemistry is better supported. "Six years? What makes you think I'm prepared to stay here for that long?"

He doesn't meet my eye. I wait. Finally, he turns his gaze to me. His face is unlined, his eyes bright. How old is he?

"Well, one, that's how long we'll be here for and two, we cannot allow you to leave."

My mouth hangs open. I can't decide which revelation I'm more shocked at.

"Why six years?" My intellectual curiosity outweighs my personal freedom, apparently.

"That is how long it will take. We have matched our requirements to your time patterns, and we will have the resources we need from Earth within the next six years."

"And then you'll just leave?"

"Yes, but the space-link will remain, and humans will be offered the technology to develop vehicles for intergalactic travel if they still wish to join our community."

I know I am missing something but with so many facts and new information coming at me, I can't think my way clear.

"As for how old I am—the equivalent of thirty-three human years."

Equivalent?

"I have been alive for eleven Earth years."

Is this like a dog thing, where they reach full maturity within a few years but then have a long adult life?

"Do you like dogs?"

"Yes, why?"

"I was trying to understand whether that was a complimentary comparison."

"Better than a cuttlefish."

His cheeks turn pink.

"Ah, so you were listening in while I was trying to make sense of you, uh, um, angels." I had no idea what to call them.

"'Angels' is fine. Part of our brand now. As I said, I need to get to know you as quickly as I can, because we will spend the next six years together, and I need to be able to look after you while we harvest what we need."

We? "Okay, back to me. I'm here because I'm a brainiac and my research taught you everything you need to know about human failings?"

His laugh is rich, deep, magnetic. "I would not put it like that, but yes."

I've walked onto the set of *Westworld*. Or at least that's what it feels like. Glass-walled room after room spiral around a central core. In each room resides a woman, lounging on a settee and speaking animatedly into a camera, a smile stretching her face under a frame of perfectly coiffed hair. Behind each tripod stands an angel, although none like those I've already seen. These are taller, more slender, somehow more beautiful.

Other ethereal angels push carts from room to room, adjusting hair, makeup and wardrobe, ensuring each of the women looks stunning.

As we walk, I lose count of the rooms somewhere past forty-three.

There are one hundred and sixty-seven. All here voluntarily.

A shudder passes through me as I imagine I will be number one hundred and sixty-eight. *Is this where you're leading me?*

Mark shakes his head. *We need your brain, not your body, remember?*

I do not remember the second part. We continue to work our way to the centre of the spiral. Who are these women? My heart thuds in my chest as I recognise one of them.

Is that Krystal Chance? The Real Housewife?

I stare at her as we keep walking. She doesn't break her monologue as we move past her room. I pay more attention as we walk, counting off seven Instagrammers, eleven Tik Tok stars, and eight models and actresses.

"What the hell are they all doing here? And what are they recording?"

Social media posts encouraging human-angel cooperation. We're banking them for release over the next few years while they are busy having…I mean…helping us with the harvest.

We reach the end of the spiral, where Mark ushers me into a large, circular room with an opaque skylight that brings in enough natural light that we can see clearly, but not so much it interferes with the imagery appearing on screens that line the walls.

Mark gestures to the angels working along one wall. They appear to be operating dials and switches built into desks below the screens. *They are monitoring human sentiment. Wherever we detect anomalies, we insert additional material into social media feeds that is designed to foster positivity and suppress negativity. We also roll out our spokespeople to engage with traditional media and to dominate talkback.*

All strategies proven through my research to be effective in subverting attitudes and behaviour in populations the world over. "You've built an influence factory? But why did you need to bring the influencers here? Since the pandemic, we've all learnt how to work remotely."

There's more to see that will explain why we need them to be collocated. But you must be hungry. Let's get you fed before we move through to the nursery.

I'd hoped, rather than believed, that the nursery would be for the plants we saw in the garden. What I did not expect was to find myself in a room filled with dozens of heavily pregnant women. There must be a hundred at least.

Seventy-four to be exact.

Each woman reclines on an inclined bed connected to a monitor. Angels move among them, bringing them cups of tea, plates of sandwiches. Others push the hair and make-up carts, fussing over and primping the women.

One of the women spots me and waves me over.

My feet carry me forward.

She has the same grin plastered on her face as the women who'd been recording their videos. There must be some serious happy medication in their tea.

"Darling! Hello, you must be new here. Welcome, welcome, it's so lovely to see a fresh face!"

"Hi, I'm Penny." I lean forward to shake her hand and see that underneath the hair and make-up she is haggard. Her skin looks like plastic wrap stretched over Caesar salad. "It's, ah... great to meet you too." As our hands connect, I am revulsed by the clamminess. A sweet scent reaches my nostrils, turns foul. Hydrogen sulfide. What the hell?

"Oh, forgive my preggy brain! I'm Lucinda."

Boom. *"Dancing with the Stars* Lucinda Denton?"

She is almost unrecognisable. This skeletal, gaunt woman in front of me looks like a famine victim.

She flaps her withered hands at me. "The very one." The blanket covering her body shifts, drops away, and, for the first time, I notice how gigantic her belly is.

"My goodness! Twins?"

She follows my gaze, runs her hands over her belly. The gesture is loving, maternal. "Sextuplets!"

No wonder she is so engorged. "When are you due?"

She looks to her angel. His smile is only for Lucinda.

He says, "We've just entered the third trimester, so three weeks."

He must mean months. I look around the room. Every woman has the same distended belly as Lucinda. I try to do the maths in my head.

"Penny, we must continue with the tour." Mark's hand has returned to the small of my back.

"Lovely to meet you, Lucinda, and good luck with the birth," I manage to say as he leads me away.

We pass sunken face after sunken face, and my mind tries to grapple with what I've just seen. Before I can get anywhere with my thoughts, we leave the nursery and after a short walk, enter another part of the complex he tells me is the school.

I pull up short. "Children. You're harvesting children?"

Yes, and no. Come, I have more to show you.

"No, I won't. Not until you tell me what's going on."

Fine. Come with me.

This time his touch is not gentle. He all but pushes me through the school. I catch glimpses of classrooms full of babies and toddlers. Further down the corridor are empty classrooms. I have completely lost track of where I've been. I will never be able to find my way out of this place. My chest tightens as my throat closes. My lunch threatens evacuation.

Mark scoops me up and carries me the rest of the way. I close my eyes and turn my face into his chest. I can hear his heart beating.

I am alone.

Mark returned me to my apartment, put me into bed and told me to sleep. I pressed him for answers, but he refused, saying he'd overwhelmed me and that I needed a break. He left and I lay fuming. Somehow, I slept and when I woke, he was gone.

God knows how long ago that was. I have lost all sense of time down here.

I call to Mark in my mind, but there is no answer.

I stretch. Although my body aches, I am no longer tired. I pull back the covers, and the niche opens. I eat, I drink, barely paying any attention as I rehash the day and try to piece together what is happening here.

Influencers, reproduction, an oasis, an angel for every human. I cannot make sense of it.

I shower. Dress in fresh clothes. The door opens.

"May I come in?" Mark has also showered and changed. This alien man, who contrives to look admonished and attractive all at the same time.

Only if you are going to put this puzzle together for me.

Shock registers for a moment before he hits me with his dazzling grin. *Very good, Pen.*

He strides through my apartment, places his hand on the far wall, which opens to reveal a library.

Drink? He points to a fully stocked bar nestled into the bookcases along one wall.

G&T?

He nods and motions to a Chesterfield sofa.

Mark hands me my drink and sits on the opposite sofa.

We talk and drink, drink and talk. Hours pass by, but I am enthralled and no longer care about time.

I think I've just about got it. I take a large gulp of my third—or is it fourth?—gin. *Your race cannot reproduce fast enough to replace itself so you need to buy in some help? And you colonise dominant species, using their female gametes as carrier cells for your male gametes and DNA. So, you are creating cloned angels, using the dominant species as surrogates?*

My head is spinning. It could be the gin, but the science is blowing my mind.

Almost. We can't just whack our gametes into another species' reproductive cells. What we do is blend our DNA with that of the host clone.

I parse this new information against my knowledge of reproduction. *But...that would...create a new species. How does that work?*

He gets up, goes to the bar, and makes us each another drink. *It's complicated, but you remember what I said about being chromatophorous and able to change our physiology? We include that genetic information in the DNA we blend. The babies being born here will carry those genes and so be able to adapt to the next species we colonise. Our next target galaxy is Segue 1, a satellite of the Milky Way. We've identified a species that is intellectually advanced and highly likely to be a compatible host.*

I hold up my hand. *Wait, wait, wait. You said you are only going to be here on Earth for six years. You can't colonise a planet with babies...can you?*

No.

A few more cogs rotate in my brain. *Hang on. You're thirty-three but actually eleven. The angel in the nursery said the third trimester would go for around three weeks. How is this actually possible?*

Angel DNA. Our lifecycle is three times faster than yours. Gestation is therefore reduced to three months. Each mother gets a three-month rest before she is re-impregnated.

My brain is aching. *With another six babies?*

Yes.

Every six months.

Yes.

For six years. But that's… I scramble to do the arithmetic.
Seventy-two babies each. Yes.

"But that will kill them." I feel the heat rising in my cheeks, the backs of my hands. My heart thumps.

Eventually, but we will keep them alive until their last brood. Remember I said they are here voluntarily? Well, using your research, we have convinced them that these babies will be their legacy. They are being paid millions of dollars. Their videos are garnering them hundreds of thousands of followers. We are making their dreams come true.

I awake the next morning. I expect a hangover, but I feel fine. I open my eyes and there is Mark, watching, waiting.

"What happened?"

"Before or after you passed out?"

I groan, pull the covers up over my head.

He leaves me to wash and dress and then returns while I eat my breakfast. This time of bacon, eggs and hash browns. I may not have a hangover, but I welcome the grease and protein. As I chew my food, I chew over everything I've learned.

The new human hybrid species you're creating here is going to be colonising the next planet? One good thing about speaking with your mind is it doesn't matter if your mouth is full of food.

A self-satisfied smirk edges his lips. *You are as smart as they said you were. Yes, Penny, we're taking humans intergalactic. Well, half-humans. We'll have to come up with a better name than that, won't we? What about Graingeans?*

I scoff. *After me. I hardly think that would be appropriate.*

He raises his eyebrows at me, lowers his chin.

No. It can't be. I put my knife and fork down on the plate.

He nods, salutes me with his coffee mug and takes a sip while the truth hits me.

How did you get my DNA?

Your blood test in 2021.

I think back. It was during the pandemic and I had to go to that other clinic because my usual lab was…closed. Oh fuck.

How many babies did you say are planned?

We need two thousand.

I choke on my drink. I can't even imagine more than one of me, let alone two thousand clones.

Wait, you said my DNA was blended.

Mark stands up and crosses over to my sofa. Sits next to me, puts my drink on the table. Takes my hand in his. *We make beautiful children. Would you like to come and meet some of them?*

I push back from the computer and stretch my hands above my head. The report is finished. The angels left eight weeks ago, and I am finally free to leave what remains of the facility, to share the findings of our research.

I look over at the Chesterfield to where Mark is having a nap. He's fifty-one now, although he's only been alive for seventeen years. He's still as beautiful as ever, but I know he will soon far outstrip me in age, and leave me a widow in a handful of years.

I lever myself up out of the chair, my heavy belly making movement difficult. The human population thinks the angels have gone, none the wiser about the two thousand Graingeans that were uplifted with them when they raised the pods from their subterranean incubators and transported them through the space-link. I never saw them as my children, those cloned drones destined for far-off worlds, and I was happy to see them go.

The only Graingean child I care about grows within me. When I look back at the body of work that's been done since I first set foot in Orroral, it's this new life I'm most proud of, this childling, who I thought I would never have but who will be as preternaturally beautiful as her father. I'll never be able to share this miracle with anyone though, and she must never know that she, too, is an angel.

TOO FULL

DERYN PITTAR

It began the night I swiped right one time too many. Single, lonely, late-thirties, and craving attention, I didn't want much. Just some admiration and perhaps a bit more if we physically clicked. That night we did.

Such a cool dude. Swarthy complexion, thick black hair, golden eyes, strong jawline and a physique that looked as if he hit the gym regularly. My blonde, blue-eyed genes just love the opposite, and I clung to him like iron filings to a magnet.

He must have left my bed before dawn, because I woke to the first chirps of the birds that roost in the old oak. His side of the bed was still warm to touch, but empty. I staggered to the kitchen to gulp water and ease the dust in my mouth. "Sore and satisfied" would be how I'd describe my physical being.

The afterglow lasted for weeks, compliments of Mr Nameless. My body fizzed with energy and contentment until I began to vomit—and vomit, and vomit yet again. My boss, ever accommodating, said I could work from home. I cursed the stomach bug I'd caught, except it never went away, and I had to take medical advice.

Pregnant! What a ghastly diagnosis.

Not that I hated kids. Being a mother had never come up on the radar. It wasn't on any bucket list, and I set about trying to shift the diagnosis from pregnant to not pregnant. Nothing worked. Hot baths, drunken nights, physical exercise until I dropped, more hookups. Everything except abortion. That option was a step too far for my abandoned religious upbringing, but any old wives' tale you've heard, I tried. Nothing budged the little critter. I continued to vomit unless I stuck to proteins only, and stopped eating vegetables and fruit. Crumbed brains, savoury sweetbreads, spicy tripe, all stayed down.

I changed my workload to "agile" and once my little clone arrived, I worked around her sleeps and feeds, as you do. A picture-postcard child, the image of me except for her eyes. I wondered, where were the rest of her father's genes? The only medical problem seemed to be her anaemia. My mother solved the problem by telling me about an old doctor who recommended giving raw liver, wrapped in a piece of muslin, to get folates into a weak child. Polly loved it. Sucked it like fury. Demanded it every day. Anything to keep her happy.

Lots of toddlers eat sand, and mine ate soil by the handful until she discovered slugs, snails and worms. Munch, munch… and then she became fussier as to where she would dig. Such a carnivore! I used to laugh at my daughter's cravings until the day her daycare teacher rang.

"Ms Prideaux?"

"Speaking." Apprehension tightened my throat. What now?

"You'll need to come and collect your daughter. She's injured another child. Bit him, rather badly."

"Lots of children bite. I've read about it. She'll grow out of it." I had the day planned, work to sign off, goals to achieve—a stroppy three-year-old I didn't need.

"We'll discuss it when you arrive, but you must come and collect her."

Frosty smiles and stiff backs met me, with few explanations except for the insistence that the child—go—*now*, and "don't bring her back."

As we left, one of the helpers followed me out the door and quietly said, "Polly didn't just bite, Ms Prideaux, she drew blood. Held the boy's arm and sucked the blood. She screamed with rage when we pulled her off. Then she tried to clamp onto me," and she held out her arm. The small crescents of teeth marks were still red. "It was very scary."

"She suffers from anaemia," I offered, but my stomach turned at the description of her attack. Images of vampires came to mind.

I dulled my imagination and concentrated on finding another childcare centre.

The biting continued, as did my constant search for daycare. I suspected she'd been blacklisted, as eventually I had to hire a woman to look after her at home, and any play date with children met in the park never triggered a return invitation.

My little girl was different.

She grew, all childhood markers achieved and passed. Still friendless, I bought her a cat for company. A big stripey ginger fellow. Big enough to stand up for himself when she tried to steal the mice he caught, although he generously allowed her to take the odd rat. I don't think he liked their flavour. Polly did.

I took her to a neighbour's one day to see a batch of kittens. The neighbour had told me of their arrival, citing my ginger tom as the father. I thought a lesson on where babies, or kittens, came from was in order. Polly loved them and begged to be allowed to stay for a few more minutes while I said our goodbyes. The neighbour rang later, distressed. One of the kittens had disappeared. I checked the house, looked outside, but nothing. Only thing different was Polly had cleaned her teeth before we had dinner, which seemed a bit odd.

I wondered about getting a dog, and our visit to the Rescue Centre caused a total meltdown. Polly wanted to take a puppy home.

"It smells delicious, Mummy. I want it, I need it." Such a sweet plea, although I did wonder later on if I'd read her meaning correctly.

School days arrived. Quieter working time for me. Schools aren't allowed to send children home for biting—but there is expulsion— and I'd threatened Polly with a meat-free diet if she caused harm enough to be expelled. Instead, she kept bringing home roadkill and putting it in the freezer. To my objections, she pointed out that people did eat possums. There were even places which sold possum pies, and why couldn't we make our own, or at the very least, go and buy some?

This daughter of mine loved to argue the point. I could see her on a debating team by the time she reached secondary school, if she lived that long. Her disgusting habit of eating raw animals began to wear thin. Who does that? They carry diseases, and she'd be bound to catch something if she kept it up. No one in my family had these disgusting traits. A few nymphomaniacs, a couple of religious nutters and at least one marijuana grower — but no one ate raw animals. Must be from her father's side.

So that's the back story to my present-day conundrum. Now things are getting even scarier. Two weeks ago, old Ginger, our cat, went missing. I called, I banged his feed bowl, searched the garden and stumbled around the neighbour's yard in the dark. Nothing. Nada. Nil. No cat. I'm not the greatest of housekeepers, but I occasionally make the effort and spring clean, room by room. Last Thursday, I cleaned Polly's room and under her bed I found smelly bones and one long, fluffy, ginger tail. I'd know that tail anywhere.

I think eating our cat was the ultimate betrayal.

When I accused her of it, her golden eyes flashed. She bared her teeth and threatened me.

"Watch out, old hag, or I'll eat you next."

Fear gripped my heart in a vice. She wouldn't, would she? Not her own mother.

Her tight lips slid into a forced grin. "Just kidding, Mother, but you're temptingly plump."

She'd been poking fun at my weight increase for some time, never mind I'm hormonal and pre-menopausal. "I won't taste nice," I said, once I found my voice.

"Nothing that a bit of tomato sauce can't fix."

She stalked out of the house, going on one of her nightly "health" walks. I wish that she wouldn't. She always comes home smirking, and I know she's been up to evil, but I'm too scared to ask what sort.

Yesterday evening, the worst possible news flooded the radio and social media. A child is missing, last seen playing in his back yard. The house is on the route Polly takes on her way home from school. She's good with children when she's not biting them. Knows how to make them laugh and often engages them in conversation. I watch her, but I can't be there all the time. Often, I have work commitments. Sometimes she walks a different way home. I know, because I follow her at a distance and watch. I don't think she suspects.

Yesterday, I didn't. I couldn't. Now I'm wracked with guilt, torn between my love for my strange spawn and my duty as a citizen. Should I go to the police with my suspicions? Who would believe me? I've destroyed any evidence of her animal-eating whenever I've found it in the house; even gave Ginger's tail a decent burial. I'm taking deep breaths and trying to act normally, but she's wary.

"Stop staring at me, Mum," and I slide my gaze away. What am I looking for? Bloodied teeth? A small finger sticking out of her top pocket?

I peep under her bed when she goes out. No detached little foot in a small shoe. I've written down what the missing child was wearing, and I've wandered around the yard, supposedly looking at the roses and vegetables, but really looking for little boy's clothes. So far, it's all clear. I'm probably overthinking things.

Now, I'm standing outside her room.

I have a piano wire in my hands, and I've been practising what I have to do. The late news bulletin released the little boy's name, and said his body had been found nearby, minus one arm and a foot. Fear punched me in the stomach and I retched. I'd rather rot in prison than have my daughter's proclivities revealed. The media circus would be cruel. She's only eleven.

I need to be strong. I have to end this nightmare, because Polly refused to eat dinner tonight.

She said she was too full.

MOTHER OF HORRORS

EMMA ROSE DARCY

Mother tends her garden
she harvests everything she sows
and what she reaps she always eats
down to fingers, beaks and
bones

When I opened my eyes, the dawn was watery and mild. With the window open, the room had gone damp and tepid, like the cup of tea someone had left me on the bedside table and I did not wake up in time to drink. I sat up and examined the cup. It was a pretty, delicate piece of work, and I put it down again immediately as if merely the proximity of my rough hands was enough to crack it. It clacked back onto its saucer with an alarming tinkling sound, and spilled tea onto the wooden surface of the bedside table. I cursed. It's not as if I wasn't raised well, I have just always been clumsy. I gingerly touched my head. It hurt.

Out of the corner of my eye, I saw the girl. She was watching me from the doorframe, hiding, so I pretended not to have noticed her. Feigning nonchalance, I continued to explore my surroundings: the bed, the corners of the tiny room, the peaked roof. It was made comical because I am enormous relative to the space.

"Whose curtains are these, I wonder?" I said, as I twitched the lace about. Through the open window I could see it was a secluded place. The house had a beautiful garden and there was a road of a sort, but in either direction in the distance were woods.

"What a tidy little attic room," I said with great exaggeration. "How curious, I wonder how I came to be in it."

I heard her merry voice giggling and turned to the door at last. She had presented herself and was smiling up at me with a shy, freckled countenance.

"Hello." Kneeling down so I was face to face with her, I said, "My name is Tom. Who might you be?"

"Nell." The girl had gapped teeth, and the most charming smile I had been blessed with in quite a while. "We found you out in the woods, by the elf door. Mother said I mustn't let my hopes carry me away. She said you had been dancing with the fair folk for hundreds of years, so you mightn't wake up."

"Did she now?" I rocked back on my heels. It was an interesting theory, I would give her that, and a more palatable alternative to explaining to a child that sometimes men went into dark places to carry out dark business. "Where is your mother? Can I talk to her?"

"She is downstairs."

I followed the girl down a narrow set of stairs worn in the centre, with a smooth shallow groove, by constant use. The stairwell was dark even during the day so I felt my way down carefully. We found Nell's mother in the kitchen, already at work over a cook pot, though I couldn't say I recognised what was bubbling away inside. In the process of being taken apart under her knife was a hare, its wet eye looking all too still living for my comfort. To my surprise, it was the reject pieces of the hare—the skin, bones, eyes, the entrails—which went into the pot.

Mother watched my face on her tipping in the slop, and erupted with a throaty laugh. "Waste not, want not."

The meat she set on a pan to roast. I couldn't help but gag at the thought of the contents of the cooking pot. The smell had certainly not improved with the addition of the offal.

"Nell tells me you found me in the forest," I opened, my tone conversational but perhaps a little too forced. Between us, Nell was oblivious to the wary exchange of body language going on above her head. "An uncommon kindness, surely, for a woman alone with a small daughter to care for, to take in an unconscious stranger?"

Mother smiled at me, exposing one long wolfish canine. "Nell always knows the good ones, don't you, Nell?"

Nell nodded enthusiastically; her small chest puffed up with pride.

"Besides," Mother added, "I really didn't think you were going to wake up."

She tapped the crown of her head, signifying the place on my own head where I had taken the wound. Likely the one that laid me out before Nell found me. I had always been clumsy, but it takes a special kind of oaf to knock himself out on the *back* of the head. No, something had gone wrong in the deal, someone had changed their mind. The wound wasn't bleeding any longer, but the dull ache of it was a sobering admonition of the dangers inherent in relying on a partner.

Furnished with a plate of bread, cheese and hot, wild hare meat—which I discovered I was to share with the dog—I ate my breakfast with the leisurely indulgence of a guest, while about me the household bustled. I judged Nell to be between eight and ten. Admittedly, I was not well schooled in what children in general went about doing, but she struck me as a marvellously capable little creature and followed her mother doing all tasks in miniature without complaint.

It was to my great relief that they moved the cook pot outside, into the back garden. I do not know what they did with it there, but the smell inside quickly dissipated and that was all that mattered to me. For that small while, at least. We passed a very pleasant day together. There were many things around their modest farm Nell was eager to show me, although I was gently steered away from the back garden more than once. At dinner, once again the dog and I dined heartily, but I noted that Mother and Nell had nothing on their plates.

"We ate earlier." Mother smiled her toothy smile.

"Tell me about the fair folk," Nell asked, her eyes bright and shiny with curiosity as emeralds.

I looked at Mother, who was smothering a chuckle, and cleared my throat. After landing me in this pretty pickle, she clearly intended to be no help. I couldn't tell a child the truth— what had started out a simple in-and-out bag job had ended in blood and betrayal—so I struggled to remember the little lore I ever knew.

"Well, they caught me unawares when…I suppose I was just your age. And I snuck away from my parents while they were fight—sleeping. While they were sleeping. I couldn't see where I was going in the dark and stepped into a…"

"A fairy ring?"

"That's right. A fairy ring," I said, and patted her cheek with an affection I was unaccustomed to feeling for anyone. "And they got me straight away. And from then on, it was just dancing and dancing and dancing."

"And music?" Nell added in raptures.

She had her chin in her cupped hand and her eyes were round and faraway with imagining it all. In her plain little homespun dress and bare feet, I thought it likely Nell had never been more than a day's walk from this farm in her entire life. What would she make of a city the likes of which I had just abandoned?

"You never heard such music."

"Were you happy?"

I swallowed the unexpected lump in my throat, as I found something about this child very moving. I had not felt like this in a long time. Despite my best efforts, my story had more to it of my life than I had intended, and I felt strangely bare before my hosts.

"No. Even though I was dancing and laughing faster and louder all the time, I wasn't happy."

Nell looked upset, and put her tiny, milk-white hand on my calloused and scarred one. Something inside me clenched tight.

"That wound on your head must be hurting you, Tom," Mother said, with her voice that sounded like the deep woods and charcoal and storms brewing. "Let me clean it for you. I have something that will sooth the ache."

She ignored my protests and gathered her materials at my elbow. I expected it all to smell and look foul like the hare soup, but it was all fair and fresh flower and leaf that she crushed in a bowl and slathered on my scalp. It burned at first where the skin was split, then it went blissfully numb, and I felt a heady rush of pleasure down to the root of me.

After Nell was asleep and everything was quiet, I could

finally go and sit where Mother was placid by the fire. The air in the room was heavy and smoky. I was drowsy and Mother was blinking slowly, but we had business to conduct.

"Where are my things?" My voice had an echo, like I was muttering into a well. I felt drunk. I hadn't drunk a drop.

Mother looked unruffled "What things?"

"If you found me," I said, "you would have found certain items with me. It's very important for me, and therefore for you, that I have them when I leave here."

Mother stared me in the eye and said, "But Tom, you're never leaving."

When I opened my eyes, I was back in my attic room. The window was locked. It could only have been to bar my escape, it certainly wasn't to maintain any heat or keep out any rain. No longer did my little bed seem so charming and inviting. The attic had become a cell. Although, when I looked at the bedside table and saw the terrible damage my spilled tea had done to the wood, I realised this attic was meant to have been the place of my death. I had never before been so grateful for being clumsy or oversleeping.

The door to the attic was also locked, but brute force solves most problems. I found the little house deserted. When I opened the door to the small chamber that served as the Mother's bedchamber, my breath caught in my throat. The floor appeared to be strewn with small bones. As my eyes adjusted to the gloom, I saw that, in fact, the floor was littered with limp apple cores, dried and twisted with black seeds exposed.

Hidden under the bed, my things were in a wooden crate of withered root vegetables that bore a great resemblance to severed feet, dried to leather. I took my stuff and tried not to think on it too much. I had risked my life to obtain these things and would certainly forfeit said life over the loss. The door to the back garden was open, and I crept out, hoping to take my beautiful but villainous little *mesdames* by surprise, but they were not there.

There was an apple tree in the garden, laden with fruit, but as I drew closer, I recoiled from the rancid stench. The fruit was already rotting on the branch; soft fruit that wept a sticky, pus-like juice, giving off the sickly-sweet aroma of decay.

At the foot of the tree, tangled among the exposed roots, were the corpses of several men.

These, by contrast, did not give off the rank smell of the apples at all. Buried up to their chests, they were earthy and benign things, seemingly inert. Mixed in the dirt I could see the small bones of rodents and scraps of fur; obvious leavings of the foul stew that the Mother was using to water the tree. Was there a space here for me? I was perplexed. What purpose did the Mother have planned for me that she let me live now, when she had laid out the tea yesterday morning to poison me?

I heard music. Strange music. I let it draw me out of that terrible garden and into the woods where I followed the beat of drums, a rhythm that pricked at my senses, maddening. It would turn me one way and seem louder, so I would discern perhaps a flute, but then I would lose it again. I would turn another way and find it louder still, now with a harp. Only then to have it lead me back the way I had come. I did not like the music, that I knew; it frightened me more than anything I had heard before. Every hair on my body stood on end. Yet I knew I could not rest until I had found the source of the music. I knew to see would be loathsome, but to never see would be to never be free of it, and the music would play in my head forever.

As I wandered through the woods, lost and half mad, I saw the firelight, and smelled the blood and smoke, felt the thrumming of bodies chafing and stamping and panting. I could see them all, gathered in a circle, so many different shapes and sizes, terrible to behold each and every one of them. Furred backs, mismatched eyes, cloven hoof, talon and claw, the scaled skin of serpents, the quills of hedgehogs, beaks and maws, in every combination. I drew as close as I dared. It was their music, and it was for her that they made it. Their mother, the Mother. She lay in the middle of the circle, lit by the firelight, and painted in blood and some foul green muck she had no doubt concocted. On the ground she writhed, surrounded by her children, and I watched horrified as they howled and she shrieked, and from between her legs another monstrosity clawed its way into the world.

I stifled a scream of my own as a small hand slipped into mine. I looked down and found Nell at my side. I seized her.

"Nell! We must run while these monsters are distracted with this hellish business!"

Nell only smiled at me as I drew her away from the torches and the drums, into the cool air where we were surrounded by indifferent trees, all anonymous in the dark. Her smile wavered, uncertain, as if not wanting to upset me more. Didn't she understand my fear? But what was not to understand, who could not want to flee this?

"What do you mean, Tom?" she said at last. "This is how I was born."

"You, Nell?" I cried, aghast.

She was in every way a perfect little girl, like a doll. I gathered her up in my arms, refusing to believe it, determined to take her away from that place, that music, the obscenity of it all. She felt different when I held her, unwieldy, like she was made of grease and was melting against the heat of my skin.

"Careful," she laughed, as she wriggled in my arms, slick enough to turn my stomach. "It took a lot of tallow for me to make this body."

But to show me, perhaps so I wouldn't damage her any more, she stepped out of her body as neatly as a girl would slip out of her dress. The wax doll she had inhabited slumped to the ground, empty and eerie. Before me stood a flickering sprite of fire, insubstantial, a living candle flame. She swayed about, long and lissom and hot, and then back into the wax doll and was suddenly Nell again.

"You're not like them, Nell, won't you come with me?" I pleaded.

"What am I like?" Nell asked, her voice the very measure of childhood innocence. "Won't you stay here, Tom? Mother was going to plant you in her garden, but when you woke up, I asked her if I couldn't have you instead."

She slipped her small hand back into mine and squeezed so

sweetly, I was overcome with relief and a strange paternal love for this child who had saved me from a restless sleep beneath that awful apple tree.

"Thank you, Nell."

She leaned into me, adoring, and I embraced her. Behind us in the woods, the infernal drumming of her monstrous siblings had become like a second heartbeat to me. I scarcely noticed it anymore but it was within me all the same. Not wanting to melt her delicate body, I tried to let go as she grew hotter and softer, but she wouldn't let go. Instead, Nell held on tighter.

"Thank you, Tom," she whispered in my ear, the boiling tallow burning me, melting against me, into me. "Now I'll have enough tallow to make myself be a woman."

THE TEA AND SUGAR TRAIN

DEBORAH SHELDON

The railway tracks outside Cecelia's door began to vibrate and hum, signalling the approach of the Tea and Sugar Train. She put her darning aside and took up her shopping list.

The door of their four-room shack opened onto the Nullarbor Plain, a flat and endless expanse of Australian desert in the middle of a godforsaken nowhere. The red soil, red-hot as a fever, sprawled level and unbroken from horizon to horizon while the cloudless blue sky glared above it. Blue over red in every direction, resembling a flag. Sometimes, especially if Cecelia felt tired — as she often did at this stage of her pregnancy — the lack of trees, shrubs or grass played tricks on her vision: the sky and earth appeared to press up close against her nose. She had to blink and focus on the railway tracks before she could regain a proper perspective across this wide, dead, barren world.

Cecelia shut the door against the dust and eased herself into one of the veranda chairs to wait. The other chair, next to the pile of old railway sleepers they used for firewood, was empty. As usual, Henry had left early this morning on his handcar, trundling west to join his team of gangers and fettlers. The Commonwealth Transcontinental Railway spanned 1100 miles from Port Augusta to Kalgoorlie, and some 300 men strung along those miles took care of the tracks. Warped or rotten sleepers had to be replaced, recalcitrant lines kept to the required elevation and gauge, lineside equipment maintained. Henry's job prevented derailment. Too bad the pay didn't reflect the importance of his work. Some weeks, Cecelia's shopping list for the Tea and Sugar

Train took most of Henry's wages. Last week, dear Lord, he had *owed* money to the company.

She must be even thriftier. Count every shilling, every sixpence. Every ha'penny.

From the east, the train appeared as a black dot, growing larger. Cecelia referred to her shopping list and licked the tip of her pencil. *Half pound lamb chops*. She crossed out the item. Two bags of flour instead of one, she decided. Wilting fruits and vegetables were cheap. She would bake sweet and savoury pies, and pasties; rely on damper and scones to bulk out their meals…

She placed a hand on her belly. Soon, another mouth to feed. And when the child was old enough for learning? Why, they would have to leave this dirt-raddled shack and move to a railway stop with a school. The company's rental fee would be high. Textbooks, pencils, stationery, proper clothes. And shoes! Lord, a child is always outgrowing its shoes. Cecelia recalled last night's argument, a fight they had played over and over since her monthlies had ceased. *How are we going to live?* Henry had shouted. *I don't know*, she had replied, as always. Weeping, as always. *I don't know.*

The plume of steam from the locomotive was visible now. Perhaps ten more minutes and the train would be here with its hotchpotch of carriages. From habit, Cecelia glanced at the dead-end siding. Yes, the switch was in the correct position. The Tea and Sugar Train would not derail.

On the siding sat her own little handcar that Henry had scavenged from the scrap heap. Its seesaw pump-lever, platform and battered iron wheels meant the world to her. It was supposed to be for emergencies only. Some mornings after Henry left for work, she would double-check the train schedule—even though she knew it by heart—switch the tracks and take the little handcar, squeaking and rattling, onto the main line. She would work the pump-lever up and down, up and down, the wind in her hair, eyes closed to imagine the hubbub of Melbourne, Adelaide, or even the dusty streets of Kalgoorlie. She always saw herself on a promenade. In her mind's eye, she wore a dress with shoulder pads, a homburg hat topped with an ostrich feather.

But her arms would soon tire. When she opened her eyes, there was nothing but the blue and red flag of this blasted Nullarbor. Puffed from her exertions, she would swap sides and trundle back home again.

Home...

When Henry had returned from the war, morose and aloof, empty as a cored apple, he had wanted to live in isolation. As his wife, Cecelia had followed him out here. Out here into this wide, dead, barren world. No neighbours for two hours by handcar in either direction. No telephone. No radio—

The baby thrashed its limbs, breaking into Cecelia's thoughts. "Hush," she murmured, patting her belly. "Hush, now."

It would be a relief to visit Dulcie, the nurse on the Tea and Sugar Train. At six months, should the baby be so restless, so agitated? This morning, the child seemed to be fighting against the walls of Cecelia's womb. This was her first pregnancy. No one had told her what to expect, not even Mother, who had kept a dignified silence on such matters despite undergoing seven births herself.

The train puffed and wheezed, brakes grinding.

Cecelia stood up with one hand on her aching back. She waved. Ollie the engine driver, a giant Irishman, waggled his arm out the window in return. Cecelia's heart lifted.

People!

For a few minutes, she would chat with Ollie, and Nick the greengrocer, Wilfred the livestock handler, Albert the butcher, George the dry goods man, Reggie the water man, and share a laugh with them, hear the latest news from towns and cities. Dulcie was good for a yarn... *I'm so lonely*, Cecelia sometimes whispered to Henry over dinner. *Please talk to me.* He would only bend his head over his plate and attend to his meal.

The train, growling and heaving like a beast, came to a stop.

"Hello there!" she called, waving and smiling. "Good morning! Good morning to you all!"

"Are you grand today, Mrs Young?" Ollie shouted out the window. "I'll be down in a sec. How's your sweet tooth?"

"As sweet as ever!"

Most weeks, Ollie the driver gave her a box of chocolates. She didn't know why. It frightened her but she always took the gift, hiding it in the pantry, scoffing the treats while Henry was gone, burning the box in the fireplace. What did Ollie want in return? He hadn't told her yet. She hoped her smile was enough. Occasionally, though, she wondered what might happen if, one day, she packed her suitcase and climbed into the locomotive's cabin and went with him all the way to Kalgoorlie. The Indian Ocean must be as green as jade.

The frantic bawling of ewes spun her around.

From the livestock carriage some yards distant, two sheep fell onto the ground. The screeching animals couldn't get up. Instead, they rolled and bucked in the dirt. Cecelia saw the blood. It squirted out of each sheep from where their four legs should have been, and yet were not. Cecelia's stomach turned over.

Where were their legs?

She called for the livestock man—"Wilfred! Wilfred!"—and the ramp emerged, teetered, and touched down on the dirt. About a dozen sheep, bleating and jumping, fled from the carriage and ran in panicked circles around each other. Close behind them hurried a few shrieking pigs. Out tumbled the flapping chickens. The birds scattered and ran into the emptiness of the desert without hesitation, as if the Devil himself were on their heels. The sheep and pigs rushed after them. There was no water in the Nullarbor Plain. The animals would die. How had they escaped their cages? And why hadn't Wilfred left the carriage yet?

What was taking him so long?

Cecelia held a palm to her throat, the keening of the mutilated sheep raking her nerves. She was about to call for Ollie when Wilfred's arms finally appeared, hands groping at the ramp, followed by his head and the rest of him.

But how in the world…?

He was descending the ramp on his hands and feet, arched over backwards, spine bent at an impossibly sharp angle. His head dangled loose on his neck, grey hair sweeping the boards. Shock and dread fired through Cecelia, freezing her to the spot. Wilfred shuffled like a broken spider down the ramp. Blood smeared his cheeks.

When he reached ground, he worked his jaws and turned his face to gaze at her.

They locked eyes.

Cecelia couldn't breathe.

What kind of hellish vision was this? Could she be dreaming?

Like a rusty flywheel, Wilfred's head began to rotate, slowly, jerkily, notch by notch, until it was the right way up. Even from this distance, Cecelia could hear the bones in his neck cracking and splintering. His mouth opened, releasing a glut of blood and raw meat. From the sheep's missing legs, she knew.

This couldn't be happening.

Had she lost her mind?

Wilfred scuttled towards her at great speed. Cecelia drew a lungful of air and screamed.

"Saints preserve us!" Ollie bellowed.

She glanced around. Ollie dropped the box of chocolates and launched himself back up the ladder and into the engine's cabin. *Dear Lord*, Cecelia thought, heart pounding. *He's going to leave me here with this monster.* But the next second, Ollie leapt out with a coal shovel.

"Stand clear, Mrs Young!" he cried.

The monster that had once been Wilfred yawned open its maw and picked up its scrabbling pace as if to attack. Ollie swung the shovel two-handed like a cricket bat. The blow against Wilfred's head made a loud, slapping, wet sound as it caved in the bones. Cecelia squeezed her eyes shut. The blows went on and on and on.

Thud. Thud. Thud.

Ollie meant to smash the monster's skull into pulp. Her racing heart fluttered and skipped. The maimed sheep kept bawling.

Thud. Thud.

And then, one final time.

Thud.

She opened her eyes. The monster that had once been Wilfred lay in the dirt, limbs twitching spasmodically, blood and mush spattered around him in a curdling puddle. Ollie strode towards the sheep. Before Cecelia could look away, he had dispatched both animals with the shovel, bringing the blade straight down, first upon one neck and then the other.

Now, all was silent apart from the soft, billowing breaths of the train.

She tried to gather her fractured thoughts.

A demon.

Wilfred must have been possessed by a demon.

Oh Jesus, she thought. *My Lord, Jesus Christ, remember that I am a sinner. Most Holy Virgin, pray for me. You shall always be praised and blessed. Pray for this sinner—*

"Mrs Young?"

Ollie had turned to her. His chest heaved. Blood covered his bib-and-brace overalls. He took off his billed cap, wiped his forehead with the back of his hand and walked over, unsteady, trailing the gory shovel through the soil behind him.

"Mrs Young, are you unharmed?"

"Yes. And you?"

"Sure." He gestured at his overalls. "Ain't none of this blood's mine."

She locked her knees to stay upright. "What in God's name happened to Wilfred?"

Ollie's face was blanched, eyes glazed. "Damned if I know. He was fine at our last stop. Taking the piss as usual, playing the fool." He whistled a reedy note. "Damned if I know."

They stood together for a time, panting, trembling.

"We'll have to send for the constables," Cecelia said at last.

"I suppose you're right."

"I'll be your witness."

"If anyone believes us." He groaned, seemed to droop. "Oh, shite. I killed a man."

"No, not a man. A monster."

Ollie blew out a breath. "How do you suppose he...*twisted* himself in that way?"

"I've no idea. I've never seen anything like it."

Ollie put his cap back on his head. "Well, I'm not leaving you here. You can't stay with him looking...like *that*. Hop in the cabin. You can ride with me, sure enough."

"Oh, thank you, Ollie. Thank you so much."

"Right. Let's crack on."

He started for the engine. And then it occurred to her, in a sick and panicky rush, that the other train workers had yet to appear. Surely, they had heard the commotion: the shouting, bleating, smashing and slaughtering... Why hadn't they shown themselves? The possibility felt too ghastly to contemplate. Her teeth started to chatter.

Carriage doors rattled open. Simultaneously, Nick the green grocer and Albert the butcher showed themselves, alighting from the train wrenched over backwards.

"Ollie!" she wailed. "Ollie!"

In unison, the heads of Nick and Albert turned right way up, bones snapping.

Brandishing the shovel, Ollie ran past her at the abominations. "Get in your house and lock the door!"

Cecelia staggered on rubber legs towards the shack but took in the danger of it within a moment: one way in and out, a flimsy wooden door; thin panes of glass in each of the four windows and no shutters. If a monster got inside, she'd be finished. A monster would do to her what Wilfred had done to those poor sheep.

Gnaw at her limbs.

Eat her alive.

With a sob, she veered towards the woodpile. Images of Henry flashed through her mind. Henry's shoulders rolling as he chopped the sleepers. His affectionate smile, rare as it was. The calm, unhurried way he packed and smoked his pipe after dinner. His sombre hazel eyes gazing across the Nullarbor Plain as if he could see for a thousand miles or more. Sometimes, he would take her hand and kiss her fingertips. Henry. *Oh God, Henry.*

Cecelia grabbed the axe.

The blasted thing was so *heavy*.

Her baby jolted and kicked. Could it sense Cecelia's fear? She had to be strong. Had to fight like a man if she hoped to save the child and herself. She wrapped an arm about her belly and, breathless, faced the melee.

Nick the green grocer was down, a broken and bloodied heap in the dirt.

Ollie, swinging the shovel, was defending himself against Albert the butcher.

Albert darted around Ollie's legs with the speed and agility of a huntsman spider, gnashing his teeth. In life—for surely, he must be dead and somehow reanimated?—Albert had been a stout and strapping lad, unlike Wilfred and Nick, who had both been thin, elderly, frail. Cecelia *must* help before the monster overwhelmed him.

Except her legs gave way.

Dizzy, she stumbled against the pile of wooden sleepers. Good Lord, she almost dropped the blade of the axe straight into her own thigh. The scare of it cleared her head. She struggled to get up again.

Ollie's shovel broke in two.

Cecelia stumbled towards them, axe held out from her body in one hand, the other cradling the weight of her belly as the baby struggled and flailed. Ollie dodged the champing teeth and sprang into the butcher's carriage. Albert went to follow.

Unseen from behind, Cecelia swung the axe sideways into his knee.

To her surprise and horror, the heavy blade went straight through his leg. Unbalanced, Albert toppled like a three-legged table. She lifted the axe to chop again. Ollie bounded from the carriage armed with meat cleavers. His flurry of blows on Albert's head and neck released fountains of blood. Hot droplets spattered her face. She turned away and gagged.

"Mrs Young," he yelled, "want a bollocking? Get yourself indoors."

She shook her head. "They've all changed. All of them. Look."

Out came Reggie the water man, George the dry goods man. On the landing of the Health Centre Coach, grotesquely arched and distorted like the others, face upside-down, was Dulcie the nurse in her starched uniform, the triangle of her veil hanging loose.

Their three heads rotated. Three necks cracked and broke. Three mouths stretched open.

"*Nách mór an diabhal thú,*" Ollie murmured, but Cecelia didn't know what that meant.

He stepped back. Cecelia moved closer to him.

"Let's go," she whispered. "Can you uncouple the engine from the carriages?"

"I can, but not before these devils attack us."

She swallowed. "Are we to die?"

"More than likely." Ollie reached out and squeezed her hand, briefly. "I'll do my best."

The monsters rushed them.

Ollie lunged forward to intercept Reggie. George, stocky as a hog, lumbered at Cecelia with his teeth bared. Terror shot through her arms and gave her strength to swing the axe two-handed in a sweeping arc. She brought the blade down on the monster's skull. The blade cleaved the head in two and lodged itself in the jawbone. Cecelia gasped. She had expected the skull to be tough, as hardened as a length of sleeper, but it had offered no more resistance than an eggshell. George collapsed in an untidy heap, bleeding, fitting and spasming.

Dulcie was still picking her way down the steep ladder of the Health Centre Coach. Cecelia tried to free the axe. Impossible. Stuck fast. Her efforts only managed to tug and shift George's twitching corpse in the dirt.

Behind her, Ollie and Reggie struggled, tussling like wrestlers. Ollie had lost one of his meat cleavers. She had to defend against Dulcie and then help Ollie. But how? She couldn't pull this blasted axe from George's head.

Dulcie reached ground and came at her in a spritely, loping gallop.

"Come on, goddamn it!" Cecelia shrieked at the axe, yanking with all her might.

The axe wouldn't budge.

She turned and fled towards the house, Dulcie's teeth catching at the hem of her dress. Could she stove in the monster's head with a sleeper? No, no, Henry had not yet cut these ones to length. How could she lift a sleeper the size a of a tree trunk? Henry had taken his pick, shovel, ballast fork and lining bars with him. Vaulting across the veranda, Cecelia bolted inside and went to slam the door.

Too late.

Dulcie's head was already over the threshold.

Grunting with effort, Cecelia leaned against the door and shoved, shoved, shoved. No good. Her shoes lost purchase, began to slip and slide as Dulcie shouldered further and further inside. The toe of Cecelia's shoe found a knothole in the floorboards. Now she could push back. A stalemate for a few moments; equal force against equal force. Praise God, was the door closing? Yes, it was. It *was* closing.

The monster's tongue unfurled and whipped about.

Cecelia yelped.

The tongue elongated. Soon it would be long enough to wrap itself around Cecelia's ankle and pull her into those teeth that were growing, sharpening, extending.

"In the name of Christ, get away from me!" she screamed.

Dulcie burst open the door, throwing Cecelia against the table.

They faced each other, motionless, for what seemed like an age. The hideous mouth opened wider. Its throat convulsed. The tongue roped onto the floor, its tip switching back and forth like a snake's tail.

A weapon. Cecelia must find some kind of weapon.

The cast-iron pan?

She took a single step towards the woodstove. Hesitated when Dulcie shifted on four limbs. The distorted body started to tighten and pull itself together as if preparing to jump.

Cecelia lunged for the pan. Dulcie sprang. The flat of the pan caught the monster across the face. The nose broke away cleanly and drooped alongside one cheek. The monster didn't appear to notice. The tongue intercepted the second swing. Prehensile, it lashed itself around the handle and ripped the pan from Cecelia's grasp. The tongue had touched her for a split-second, the texture of it dry and scaled, and Cecelia howled in revulsion and terror.

The pan clattered to the floorboards.

The tongue retracted.

The advancing jaws snap, snap, *snapped*.

Cecelia grabbed the skinny little poker from the fireplace and held it out just as Dulcie leaped, all limbs in the air at once like a spider. The poker entered the gaping mouth and Dulcie's impetus drove it straight down the gullet. Cecelia felt it punch and lodge somewhere deep inside. The monster dropped, short-winded and retching, tongue lolling.

Cecelia wrenched out the poker and brought it down on the grotesque head over and over, crunching the bones, staining the gauzy white veil first with blood and then with brains. At last, Dulcie teetered and fell.

Strength ebbed from Cecelia. She leaned against the table and wept. The baby, oh dear Lord, the baby started to thrash in what felt like a wild, animal panic.

"Shush, my darling," she whispered through quivering lips, patting at her belly with one bloodied palm. "Hush, now—"

Was that a contraction?

Shocked, Cecelia stopped weeping.

That quick, vice-like sensation in the cradle of her pelvis? *There it was again*. She knew what that meant. No, she was only six months along. She had to get to a hospital.

"Ollie?" she called. "Can you hear me?"

No answer.

She cocked her head to listen.

Nothing but the huff and respiration of the Tea and Sugar Train.

Her heart started knocking again. Lifting the bent and crump-led poker, holding it out like a sword, she stepped around Dulcie's corpse and approached the open door. The fight with Reggie the water man, the monster that Reggie had become... had Ollie won?

"Ollie, please say something," she cried.

No reply.

She peeked around the jamb.

And there was the Irishman, standing over the remains of Reggie. She sagged and shook with relief. Every monster was dead.

She made her way outside haltingly, painfully, groping for support against the doorframe, the chair next to the woodpile, the nearest veranda post.

"I killed Dulcie," she said.

Ollie turned. The sight made her flinch. He was covered in gore from head to toe as if dipped in a vat. Eyes shining white in his bloodied face, he stared at the meat cleaver in his hand and dropped it, raising a puff of red soil.

"Can we leave right away?" she said. "I think the baby is coming."

He didn't reply.

She hugged the veranda post, watching him. Her womb clenched and released again.

"I need a hospital," she said. "Will you drive me?"

The closest hospital was four hours away. And if she got there in time, could the doctors stop her labour? Save the baby? She had names picked out already: Douglas Ross for a boy; Maureen Joy for a girl.

"Ollie?" Tears rose. "For God's sake, answer me."

He coughed. Brought a hand to his throat and coughed again. It was an alarming sound, a choking sound. Cecelia pushed off from the post, stepped from the veranda and managed a few paces on unsteady legs. Woozy, she had to pause. Ollie started wheezing. It worsened into a strident, whooping sound.

"What's the matter?" she said, frightened. "Where are you hurt?"

Ollie hacked and barked, clawing at his throat. Dear God, how could she help? No medical training, no medical supplies... Then, as if punched by an invisible fist, his head flung back with a loud pop and stayed there.

Cecelia froze.

The coughing and wheezing ceased. Ollie's knees started to bend.

"Dear Lord," she whispered. "No. Please no."

Ollie swung his arms overhead so violently that both shoulders cracked. Methodically, steadily, he bent over backwards, lowering himself inch by inch until his palms lay flat on the ground. He shook himself with the vigour of a wet dog. Shuffling, he faced her with his upside-down head.

Cecelia lifted the crooked poker. "Stay away. Can you still understand me? Stay. Away."

Neck bones cracked and broke as his head swivelled the right way up. He bared his teeth.

The fight left her with a sob. How could she defend herself against this giant of a man? Ollie must be three times her size. She had nothing but a flimsy poker. What now? What?

She would kneel and pray.

There was no other recourse. And while this monster that had once been Ollie murdered and defiled her, she would hold the love of God our Father in her heart. Lifted into Heaven with her unborn child, she would wait there for Henry until his time on Earth came to an end, until they would be a family once more, together again for all of eternity.

And then she remembered the handcar.

With a spurt of fresh energy, she dropped the poker and sprinted.

Ollie shuffled noisily through the soil behind her in pursuit. Her lead was only a few yards. She hauled the switch to move the tracks, checked over her shoulder.

Ollie was too close.

Jumping aboard the platform, she grabbed the pump-lever and worked it. Shuddering, creaking, the handcar began to inch along the tracks.

Faster, faster, she had to go *faster*.

She looked back. Saw the open mouth. Instinctively kicked out, once, twice. The sturdy heel of her shoe broke his front teeth. Panting with exertion, grunting, she wrenched on that damned pump-lever as quickly as she could. The handcar gained speed. It bumped onto the main track, began to zip along. Negotiating the wooden sleepers would slow Ollie down.

Unless he retained enough human sense to run alongside on the dirt.

She looked back again. He was stumbling over the tracks, almost upon her. She kicked out again. Yet she couldn't kick and work the lever both.

"God help me," Cecelia yelled to the heavens.

Shutting her eyes, she focused on the lever. *Up down up down up down up...*

Her muscles burned. The flesh on her legs crept as she awaited Ollie's bite.

A flurry of contractions buckled her. Stars danced in her vision. She lost the pump-lever's rhythm. Was Ollie close? No time to check. Near, too near, she heard him clattering over the tracks. Panic would be her undoing. She brought to mind the padded shoulders of a new dress, the ostrich feather in a homburg hat. The promenade, the promenade. She would be strolling the promenade with Henry while he pushed the perambulator with their child sitting inside, a chubby little girl, Maureen Joy, with her waving arms and strawberry blonde hair...

Cecelia glanced around.

Ollie, some yards back along the tracks, had stopped. Had given up the pursuit.

Thank you, God. Oh, thank you.

Shaking, Cecelia slowed the pace, arms on fire. How far was Henry and his gang? Surely, no more than an hour. If she spared her strength, she could make the distance in good time.

Up down. *Breathe.*

Up down. *Breathe.*

The wind dried the tears on her cheeks. Willpower stopped her legs from folding. All she wanted now was to feel Henry's arms about her, his kisses on her mouth. How to explain the horrors from the Tea and Sugar Train? The events defied description. She glanced back. The locomotive lay far in the distance. She was safe.

But what had changed everyone? What had changed Ollie?

Something from the sky, perhaps, something out of the air...

A cold fist closed around her heart.

What if she, too, were doomed to turn into a monster?

Unnerved, she took one hand off the lever to knead at her neck. Did she feel all right? Any different? It was hard to tell, her body wracked with pain, cramps, fatigue... Yet she didn't need to cough. No choking sensations. That meant she was okay.

Didn't it?

She put both hands on the pump-lever. Focus. Up down, up down. Her mind raced.

What about Henry? She might come upon him and the other fettlers and gangers, only to find them contorted upside-down. Could the whole Nullarbor Plain be infected? Or even the whole of Australia?

Another contraction took Cecelia's breath.

A contraction…or was it a *bite*?

The baby stretched as if trying to arch itself.

Arch itself backwards?

Cecelia screamed into the empty blue sky. Her screams rolled out without answer or echo across the wide, dead, barren Nullarbor Plain.

CHOP_SHOP

SAMUEL M. JOHNSTON

//Warning. < system failure >
///Query: < check pulse >
//working…
/Log-???-01
///System Reboot.
//Alert: < Respiratory system online >
//Alert: < Ocular system online >
///Response: < Commence defibrillation >

Reality comes crashing back into my body through several violent shocks, throwing me into a blinding white light that pierces my eyes. I adjust the focus of my ocular sensors, but it's all a blurry haze. I try to shield my eyes. My arm won't raise. There's only slight feedback from my fingers. What about my other arm? Nothing. My legs won't move either. Oh God. Nothing's working. I attempt to analyse the root cause of the problem.

//Warning. < motor functions offline >

My system is in deadlock. I'm trapped. Trapped inside myself. The rhythmic beat of my heart fills the silence. I can feel it wanting to break free. Calm down. Remember what She taught you. You need to breathe. Count to three. Breathe. Repeat. Count to three. Breathe. Repeat.

My heart rate begins to lower, enough for me to think anyway. The probable cause is concentrated trauma to my spine or head. But where did that happen? *Think.* I was…walking down Central Road…Connere District… Why was I there? Shit, if I'm gone for too long, She'll detect it. I need to have my check-in. I can't be off program.

Bang. A metallic crash ripples through the air, bouncing from wall to wall like a never-ending drum. I'm not outside, so that's a start.

I can feel some function in my neck. I slowly tilt my head, trying to gauge where I am. The brightness begins to fade, and I adjust the aperture of my eyes to the room. The off-white paint shimmers under the light. Chains with large, rusty hooks droop from the ceiling and sway overhead. They are perfectly aligned with my body. A few security cameras monitor the room, every so often panning left to right with a soft hiss. A collection of oxidised hybrid tools rests on the ornate shelves lining the walls, each tool splintered at the tip. What is this place?

A stench violates my nostrils. If I was standing, it would have brought me to my knees. What the hell is that smell? I turn my head.

Hollow eye sockets stare back.

The remains of the man want to scream, I want to scream, but both are impossible. The mouth is contorted, broken open with force. The body is crudely strung on the table next to me. The thick, wire-meshed tubing that are his intestines are still convulsing as they slump to the floor through an incision in his abdomen. Red and black liquid oozes out of the orifices where his limbs once connected, and a dilapidated machine sits below, filtering the nutrients into a frozen jar. Within lies a small shadow. I can't make out the details due to the severed cables protruding from the man's gut.

You can barely recognise that his body used to be human, except for the hints of dull grey skin on his flanks. A pile of beautifully sculpted golden limbs lies on the bench next to him. He's a Class-Two...*was* a Class-Two. Now he's just a hunk of flesh and parts.

I need to get out of here.

The clunking of metallic boots breaks the silence, growing louder with each step. I shift my head to resting position, closing my eyes. I begin to slow my breathing as the figure limps past my body. *Keep it together. Don't make a sound.* Every step a dragging thud. I open my eyes slightly. The hulking mass looms over me. The light masks his appearance.

He raises my arm to his face, inspecting it. I try to squirm free. I can't. I can feel his breath on my fingers as he sniffs each digit and places them in his mouth. Each one slides deeper into the moist cavern as his tongue wraps around them. My stomach turns as he plays with them. He drags them back out, the saliva dripping onto my body as he drops my arm back to the table.

"Man, you are one pristine model," he chuckles to himself through a low, husky cough. He leans in closer, grabbing my head, shifting it to all angles, eying up my implants. He licks his metallic lips. "These must be those new augments everyone's been hounding me about. I must say, they are gorgeous."

His fingers slide down my thigh, softly, caressing the grooves, caressing my sensors. *Stop. Get off me.* System, please restart.

"Platinum engraved metal and everything, they are truly beautiful."

The figure steps away from the bench, scanning the small table latched onto its side as he throws various components to the ground, searching for something. While he's distracted, I inspect my surroundings. There's got to be a way out of here. I can't let Her know I was gone. I have to reach the check-in. She'll decommission me otherwise.

What would Boss do? Where's the exit?

//Alert: < location data unrecognisable >

///Query: < where are you? >

No. Not now. Don't check my status. Once She sees my brain activity, it's over. I can get myself out of this. I just need time. They can't know. I can't lose the rest of me.

//Response: < tracking data manually disabled >

My eyes jump from wall to wall. I can only keep my trackers offline for so long. I feel the internal countdown inside my mind commence, Her fingers hovering over the reset switch back home. I can't become a lost one. I just need to remain within optimal stress. *Focus.* Come on, there must be something.

He turns back and slams a prism on the table. I force my eyes shut.

The prism begins to hum as the holo-data loads. He unlatches the device, dragging an extension lead over to me, forcing my head to the side as he jams the probe into my neural dock on the back of my neck.

//Warning. < foreign probe detected >

Where did he get an invasion program like that?

//Warning. < Invasion program activ4tion ins1de h0st >

//R??B/O/>>

The probe drills through the dock, slicing through the skin. If it reaches my core, I'm fucked. The figure fixates on the screen, the numbers detailing all my specs, detailing all my *active* functions. The numbers detail who I once was. What I had done.

He leans closer. His eyes widen.

Stop looking at them. Stop looking inside me.

Please. He'll know. He'll see I'm awake. Come on, System. Fight back. Help me.

//Anti-Inv4si0n < act1ve >

If I could muster a sigh of relief right now, I would. He slams his fist into the prism and curses under his breath. A metal rod slides across my face and latches onto my eyelids, spreading them open. Black, rotating eyes inspect me. His face is malformed, skin loosely hanging from his augmented skull, nails holding it all together towards the back. A Class-Eight build, they never leave the slums. That means I'm at least twenty-five kilometres away from the Boss. I could make it back in time.

His face contorts with disdain. "You're supposed to be dead." He hovers over me, eyes unwavering. "Oners can't self-reset like that. How'd you do it?"

I remain silent. He grabs my mouth, shoving fingers deep. Choking me.

"That's not what I want to hear." He pushes my head to the table and steps back. His eyes bolt side to side, analysing me. "Those Fivers fucked me over," he mutters as he checks on the feeding machine. Placing his hand on the sealed jar, his smile is solemn.

///Query: < check motor functions >

//Response: < reboot in progress >

"Never mind that, you are divine. You've made my day. It's a shame you're a Class-One, everyone would have loved a premium servant like you." He grabs a container from the tool shelf and sets it down next to my body. He flicks a switch hidden under the bench, and an elongated tube descends from the ceiling and stops just above my abdomen. "But your kind sells well on the market." He drags the hanging chains down to eye level. "Could feed one of our towns for six months," he says, stroking my shoulder, "and that liquid slop they pump through you can make miracles happen for others."

The strokes turn into a hold, and he drives the hook into my shoulder. I shriek. He grabs my other shoulder and burrows the other hook. My wailing continues to pierce the air. The chains hoist me up to the nutrient tube. A sharp, hot sensation spreads throughout my stomach as the machine begins to extract.

//Warning: < external nutrient syphon detected >

The chains suspend my body above the table. My shoulders spasm, wires sparking as blood drips down my arms. I can feel something, a burning sensation in my arms I couldn't feel before. A thousand fiery needles splinter throughout my fibre nerves, piercing down my body.

//Alert: < lower body motor functions restored >

"Us Eights are on our last legs. All you new-wave hybrids trying to replace us," he says grabbing my body. "We can't replace our augs like you, we're designed to rot away because we couldn't afford the good shit like *you*," he says as he pushes me away.

I lightly sway in place. I tilt my head up, scanning the walls with my height advantage. There! Along the back wall, behind the Class-Two's body, next to the lever, is the exit door. He taps an out-of-place button on his wrist brace. The hooks groan as the chains start to retract into the ceiling. My shoulders continue to burn. I grit my teeth, hold back my cries. I must...hold myself together. I can almost slip free. If I can get one more push...

"So, you all live like this?" I ask.

The Eight stops. "Some do, others aren't so lucky."

"Pity you're not made to last, like us."

The Eight turns around, his eyelids twitching as he hobbles towards me, dragging a tool along the ground with each footfall.

Look for an opening. Just like Boss taught me. I hold my leg in position.

He stops in front of me, tears welling as he attempts to speak. "You're not special. Take one step outside, and they would rip you to pieces. Hell, your 'handlers' will kill you anyway for leaving the city. I'm doing you a—"

I kick him in the chest with all my might, propelling him into the wall, launching myself backwards from the force of the strike. The hooks shatter, sending the rusty bolts barrelling like bullets through the tin wall as I topple over the bench. The tube tears itself from my stomach as my head slams into the floor.

//Warning: < optical damage sustained—adjustment in progress >

The world spins. I try to stand but I'm brought to my knees by intense nausea. I slump against the bench as my eyes regain focus. I peer around the corner. The Eight drags himself behind the opposite bench. The wall I kicked him into is indented, shelves split in half, a trail of leaked blood across the floor. The exit doorway is clear. There's no way he could stand after such a blow. My arms are still unresponsive. I will have to make do with just my legs. Luckily, that kick didn't break any gears. I creep past the bench, towards the exit door, still no sign of the Eight. I break into a sprint.

///Query: < check upper motor functions >

//Response: < upper motor functions disabled >

The door is within my reach. One more kick and I'm—

A saw flies past my head, scraping the top of my shoulder and penetrating the wall. I drop to the ground. The Eight limps towards me, wheezing with every step.

"You..." He clutches his chest, coughing violently as he adjusts his stance, straightening his back, towering over me. "You...Oners are deceptively strong."

He drags a different tool off the shelf, this time a barbed hook with a translucent-blue inner blade. He charges. Each swing slices through the metal shelves around me like butter. With sheer brutality, he drives the blade down as I throw myself to the side. The hook cuts through the door, snapping it from its hinges. Then he clutches his chest. Overwhelming wheezes force him to his knee. While he isn't looking, I slide back behind the bench. I attempt to catch my breath. My heart won't shut up. He'll hear my heart before he hears me. I breathe deeply, but it's no good. I feel like I'm going to explode. I need a way out. I don't know if I can keep this up.

The Eight lets out a strained roar. "I told them. To send me a dead one. You're supposed to be dead. They know I can't handle a live one…" Staggering to his feet, he walks over to the wall and grasps a lever.

The lights go out.

Come on System, fix my arms. Please.

//Warning: < individual functions unresponsive. would you like to perform a full body reset? >

Reset all functions except ocular and auditory.

//Alert: < segmented reset in progress >

Even with my aperture at maximum, I can't see anything except what he's holding. The dim blue glow of the blade reflects off the metal awnings. My body remains motionless. Any further errors, and I'll have to force external reset programs. Which means he'll hear me.

The Eight patrols the room. *Thud. Thud. Thud.* An oppressive rhythm that bounces from wall to wall. His animalistic panting fills the rest of the void. The sound creeps closer to the bench. The metal boots stop right next to me. I can feel his breath. I think I can feel it.

//Alert: < torso and upper vertebrae functions online >

Don't turn. Stay still. He'll go away. A soft hiss releases from a joint in my shoulder. There's some sensation returning to my hands, and they start trembling. As the ventilation grows louder, I press the hole against the bench to quell the noise. I try to control myself. The Eight does not move. I begin to brim with tears. *Don't see me.* His breathing persists like it's flowing down my neck, and he'll wrap his hands around me at any moment. Dear God… The breathing stops and he limps away. I let out a breath.

A metal clamp grabs my throat and throws me through the air.

The room explodes with light as the Eight slams me face-first into the bench, forcing it to bend under my weight as he holds me down by the neck. Blood pools around my mouth. The Eight stumbles to the other side of the room to grab his blades. I lie there motionless. No…everything's…fading… I…can't stop now…

Get up. Move.

I slowly force myself off the bench, plummeting to the floor.

System, I need you to force ocular and motor reset.

//Alert: < ocular and motor function reset >

I try to drag my body across the ground with my head and shoulders.

//Warning: < please wait until function is reset >

I…just need…a moment. The world is fading from my eyes. I probably have a concussion. I hope that's all I have. I'm feeling faint. I need to stay awake. For the reset. I must get back. I can't be declared missing. I can still reach the checkpoint in time. They'll tell the Boss if I don't. She'll take *the rest* of me away if I don't. I can deal with the pain. I need to reset. I need to…

//Alert: < ocular reset complete >

The light returns and so does the Eight.

His hand crushes my neck as he lifts me into the air. I struggle to make even the slightest breath. I try to fight back, but my body is still in reset. His black rotating eyes stare into my soul, blood seeping from his nailed-back facial flesh.

"I didn't think I'd manage to beat a Oner like you," he says through husky wheezing. "They said it'd be impossible." He coughs again. He raises the hook to my eyes. "No last words? Are you even afraid? They probably built in some inhibitors to remove all that shit."

The Eight lowers me to my knees, tightening his grip on my throat as he holds the hook above my head.

System, help me.

//Alert: < remaining motor functions online >

CRACK. With one final strike I shatter the Eight's knee. He lets go of me. Air rushes back into my system. He crumbles to the floor, screaming in agony, his leg contorted in the opposite direction. His hands try to squeeze the severed tubing shut. Blood and simulant liquid leaks out of the freshly exposed iron tibia as it hangs by a thread to the silicon skin.

//Alert: < retaliator mode active >

My body launches me to my feet. A sharp buzzing sensation ripples through my hands as my fingers flex back and forth. Every arm movement is lighter than the last. The discs in my knees spin in place to reset the tension from the kick. I can feel the air circulating throughout my system, a bliss I had not felt since I gave up my body.

I take a back seat as my body steps towards the Eight.

Every step is heavy; my feet partially slip to the side as it learns to walk again. It holds out my hands for balance as the motor functions return to normal. My fists open into claws ready to thresh.

The Eight starts to shuffle away from me towards the leaking nutrient machine, damaged from when I kicked him into the wall. His degenerate smile has vanished. He doesn't look at me. My body grabs the jar. He begs me to stop. My hand rubs the frosted glass, revealing a small, partially-built embryo inside.

"You're making some sick little experiments out of us? What the hell are you?"

My body shatters the jar. The Eight screams as the remains of the embryo stain his legs. A tear glides down his sagging cheek as he looks up at me. His face is almost entirely dislodged from his skull. My hands caress his rubbery skin, stroking his very defined cheekbones as I wrap my hands around his head.

And squeeze.

I stumble out of the exit door and find myself in a hallway. Blood smears the wall whenever I push against it to maintain balance. My vision is fading. I guess even a Class-One like myself can only handle so much damage. It's just a little bit further, surely? I fall against another door, clutching the handle and shoving it open.

The cold breeze wraps itself around me as I take my first step into the night.

The street is empty. Abandoned buildings line both sides.

There's…a figure in the distance, hunching over an oil drum that has been set alight. I try to call for help but I cannot speak. I have to reach the check-in. Boss…don't take me away… My feet sink deeper into the muddy ground. Everything turns into a blur as my body lets go. I fall to the ground.

And the world goes dark.

In the darkness, I can see the Boss standing over me. She reaches her hand out towards me. Her displeasure is immeasurable. I pretend She's not there, but I can hear her approach. *I tried to come back, Boss. I tried so hard. It's not my fault. Please believe me.* Her hand finds its way to the back of my neck. *Don't do this.* She peels back the skin over my external ports. *Stop.* And She pulls out my memory chip.

I scream into the void.

//working…

//Alert: < sensory systems rebooted >

Whispers fill the air. Muffled voices attempting to communicate. With me? I'm not sure, but I can't respond, regardless. The voices grow clearer. My body jerks back and forth as a pair of rubbery hands drag me along the ground.

"What are you doing?" says a voice.

"We can't just leave it here," says another. "Do you have any idea what they'll do to it?"

"Do you have any idea what they'll do to *us* if they know we helped a Oner?"

"I'm not having this argument. Just shut up and grab it."

Silence returns. It's peaceful… Something I haven't felt since I became a Class-One… I wish I could return to that time. A time where I can feel whole again.

//Alert: < system online >

Two figures stand above me. They're covered in tattered clothes, dust flaking off them as they move around. Underneath their sleeves are some rusty augmentations, nothing as crisp as you would see in the upper ends, but sleeker than the Eight. I slowly sit up, giving them a fright.

"Shit! You're finally awake," the male aug says.

He holds out his hand. The fingers are cracked, the metal bones sticking through the rubber tips, but they are new compared to the rest of his arm. I accept the offer; he lifts me to my feet.

I feel...surprisingly fine. I inspect my body. No probes, no forced entry, and only a few rudimentary bandages around the holes in my shoulders. Torn pieces of old wool scarves are pinned to the tears in my sleeves, wrapping around my platinum arms, keeping them hidden beneath the beautiful purple colour now draped in dirt and blood.

"That's good and all, but can you just, you know, be on your way now? We don't want no trouble with the people," the short female aug says.

She stands before me, stern. She would be imposing if I weren't taller. Her augs are entirely brand new. They look Class-Five, but she doesn't. Scavengers? I keep my mouth shut.

"We found you lying outside Doc's shop. You were in deadlock... We couldn't leave you out there," he says.

"If anyone else found out *you* were free for the taking, you would already be dead," the other says.

We're in a small place, tables littered around the room, old brown wallpaper peeling off the walls. No one has touched this place in a long time. The weak fragrance of mouldy wood fills the air from a damp hole in the ceiling. The augs seem about as worse for wear as this town.

"Who are you?" I ask.

"I'm Dylan, and this is my wife, Maria."

"What's a Oner like you doing here?" asks Maria.

"I was taken from Connere District," I say.

They stay silent. Maria glances to her husband, who struggles to contain his panic. They don't say anything for some time. Did they know that monster?

"What happened between you and Doc?" Dylan asks, carefully.

"What happened?" I move towards him. "I was nearly sliced for parts and fed to a jar by your 'friend', Doc. That's what fucking happened."

Maria stands between the two of us. "*You* need to take a few steps back," she says, holding her shaking hand against my chest.

"Where is Doc?"

"Dead," I reply.

"And the 'jar'?" Her voice quivers.

"Destroyed."

Their friendly demeanour vanishes. Dylan paces over to the window, scouting out the area across the street. The workshop door swings in the wind. A few locals walk by and start to take notice of the trail of blood leading out of the workshop. Maria's eyes widen and she drops to her knees. She whispers a prayer to herself, over and over, clutching her heart, then her stomach. Dylan goes over to comfort her.

"You need to leave now," he says, pushing me towards the door.

I unconsciously plant my feet. My hands flex into claw-like grips. He begins to step away from me slowly.

"The other Eights won't be happy if they find out their only fixer is dead. You've basically ended their lives," Dylan says, pointing to the growing crowd.

"He nearly ended mine!"

I grab him by the shoulders and slam him into the wall. Maria runs to hit me, but crashes into the floor. I glance down to see my leg lowering. When did I kick her? Dylan tries to fight me, but his arms aren't long enough.

"Look around you!" he insists. "You see this town? This is where everyone under Class-Six goes to die."

"People like us *come here to die*," Maria says, her eyes glistening with tears as she points to the rotting hole surrounding her heart casing.

//Alert: < retaliator mode disengage >

I avert my eyes from her open heart, and let Dylan go. He drops to the ground and rushes to his wife. They hold each other close as I step away.

"Why kill Ones like me?" I ask.

A silence that could last a lifetime.

"Because we need parts like yours to survive," he finally says.

Maria stares at the red and black liquid leaking from the tear in my stomach, as if it means something.

"If all you needed was parts, what's with Doc's experiments?" I demand.

Maria buries her head in Dylan's chest, her hands digging into his shoulders as she fails to maintain a steady breath. She says, "Our rotten parts kill everyone's future for a family. Your nutrient systems are the only way we can have—" She stops.

Have what? I don't understand.

Dylan shakes his head, knowing I won't listen. He lifts Maria to her feet and hobbles towards the door. "You'd better leave. Before they discover what you did."

Maria turns back to me. "I pray for your future, Oner. That it's ripped from your grasp, just like ours."

They walk into the darkness.

I follow suit in the opposite direction, leaving this decrepit place behind. As I stumble through the empty streets of the town, I hear a scream in the distance. More incoherent yelling follows. I pick up the pace, holding the cloths tighter over my arms.

Eventually, I reach the border of the town. A broken sign hangs by a thread on the post. *Welcome to Outer Hell.* Fitting name. The cool midnight breeze is my only company, along with my thoughts.

I'm almost home. Boss. I'm okay, I swear. I'll be there for the check-in. I'm only ten kilometres away now. There's nothing to worry about. It's just an extended midnight stroll, I tell myself. They won't know the difference. My walk turns into a light jog through the starless night.

//Notification: < tracking data re-enabled >

Forty minutes pass and I can start to make out the city lights in the distance. But I can feel someone following me. A shadow. I turn to face it, but there's nothing, only a sound. Screams. *My* screams. They echo in the wind. I can feel a hand tighten around my neck, but there is no hand. This feeling...I can feel him. I can feel him choking me.

I drop to my knees. My breaths become sporadic.

I gasp for air as his presence looms. His grip tightens. But I'm free, aren't I? He's not here. Where is he? I can't stop feeling his grip. *No.* If I think about it too much, Boss will know. *Shut up.*

Just shut up. I cover my ears. My laborious breathing shudders at my exposed wires. As their ends touch, a shock spikes my heart rate.

///*System: < unnatural brain activity detected >*

I need to calm down. They can't know. Heart, please shut up.

///*System: < external access detected >*

Boss, I can explain. You need to give me a chance to explain.

///*System: < data erasure commencing >*

Stop. Please. Boss, you can't do this. I was attacked. It's not my fault. I like my life. I'm a hard worker. I'll return to normal. I swear.

///*System: < request denied >*

Please. My memories are happy ones. They're all I have left. Don't kill me.

///*System: < I'm sorry, but Protocol dictates that I must. I'll take care of you. Like I always do. >*

That's not what I want. Mother, please don't take me away. I—

///*System: <It's over now. Don't worry. You won't remember anything. >*

///*System: < erasure complete >*

////*System: < I'll see you when you're born again, my child. >*

A comforting sight appears. Beautiful displays of pristine white lights line the glass buildings as I limp down Central Road. My body is on autopilot. It's time for my nightly check-in. The thunderous roar of flying cars replaces the silence. Rich drunkards ask strangers for credits, and the upper echelon of Class-Ones stroll without a care in the world. They give me disturbed glances as they pass by, stepping away to avoid touching me. Why? I'm not an Eight.

I turn to see my reflection in a shop window. I see a ghost staring back.

A ghost with its clothes completely torn, cracks down their platinum arms, contorting metal and wires sticking out of their shoulders like party decorations. I look down. Some shabby scarves are wrapped around my wrists, the excess swaying in the breeze. Why would I tie these ugly things around my arms? I look closer at the reflection. The silver metal around my eye socket peeks out of my bottom eyelid. The skin sags slightly as if my eye had been recently dislodged. Blood is lathered over my chest and hands. Where did it come from?

I stare at my trembling hands; they clench as if they're squeezing something. A distorted image flashes between my hands. A fuzzy, round shape compounds in thin air before bursting into nothing. But the pressure exerted from my fingertips remains. My chest begins to tighten; tears roll down my cheeks. I feel a hand caress my neck, but there's no one here. I want to throw up. I try to get the System to recall, but all I see is a haze of incomprehensible data. What happened to me? Where was I?

I...I don't remember anything.

STALE

EM STARR

The fridge calendar is marked, and the clinic is on the other side of town, but Travis reckons he's dropping a 308 engine in the Torana today, so I guess I'm walking to my appointment.

It's not even six blocks, he says, perched mid-shit with the toilet door open—reminds me I'm only in my second trimester, not incapacitated—and I know he's offended by my thickening body, so I don't tell him that my thighs have started rubbing together, about the chafing rash that makes these journeys so painful. I just lather up with discount Vaseline and crab walk out of the house, alone.

Pregnancy sucks. I wish Mum had told me that before she left.

The flyscreen door is angled and off-hinge and doesn't close properly at the best of times, and it's always worse on a dry-as-dogshit day like this, when the dirt is thirsty, and our fibro cottage has fallen a few inches. I give the flyscreen door a couple of extra slams against the rusted frame to let Travis know I'm not happy.

"Laura?" he calls out.

Maybe he's changed his mind about giving me a lift. I yell back. "What?"

"Get me smokes!" he says.

I slam the door again, and wave to Mrs Collins next door as she dry-mows her dead lawn.

Then the searing pain across my abdomen starts up again, and I know it's time to go.

Dr Simmons has seen more vaginas than anyone else in town. Six decades of delivering babies means he knows a thing or two about generational and genetic anomalies, and that's why I'm here today. He knows my family. He knows our gynaecology.

He whistles a Hunters and Collectors tune as he takes my blood pressure, and checks for bacteria with a quick urine test and a coloured stick. Gives me the all-clear. I show him the chafe rash on my inner thighs, and he prescribes some simple zinc oxide—no big deal.

"Everything is progressing nicely, Laura," he says, jotting notes of approval. "What brings you back so soon?"

I'm scratching at my abdomen when he asks. The pain comes and goes, like an ice burn, but the itching has been relentless lately, and sometimes I scratch so hard it draws blood. I peel back my t-shirt and show him my belly. Brace for the judgement.

"They're stretch marks," he says.

I nod. "And?"

He stares at me. "And what?"

"What can you give me for them?"

Dr Simmons laughs, sees that I'm serious, and clears his throat. "Laura, there's nothing I prescribe to get rid of stretch marks. It's quite normal for this stage of pregnancy."

I stare at him, horrified.

"Some women see them as a badge of honour," he says.

"Badge of honour? My stomach looks like a fucking roadmap!"

He makes a small-town joke about not having to worry about getting lost, adjusts his bifocals, returns to his notes.

"Did my mother have them?" I ask. "I can't remember."

And he falters, but I'm not sure if it's because he doesn't know, or because he can't remember either. Six decades is a long time and a lot of vaginas. He suggests I try some cocoa butter for the scarring, but doesn't whistle any tunes after that and, when he gives me a strawberry lollipop, it turns to dust in my mouth.

The good brand of cocoa butter is on special at Drakes, so I treat myself to a large tub, and line up at the counter with a discounted chook and the 500 grams of stretch-mark remover.

The checkout worker, Becky, scans the goods. She eyeballs the cream. Asks for a price check. While we're waiting, she assesses my swollen belly, eyes heavy-lidded, as if the layers of black liner have done their worst.

"It doesn't work," she says.

I'm confused. "Sorry?"

"Cocoa butter," she replies. "My sister used it—still got stretch marks."

I smile politely. Wait for her to confirm the discount as the local radio station leaches classic hits through the speaker system—another song about the dry, as if people need reminding.

"Does your mother have them?" she keeps on. "If your mother has them, you'll get them, for sure. It doesn't matter what you put on your skin."

"My mother is dead," I tell her. I pay for the chicken and half-price cream, and flip Becky a departing death stare.

Return, moments later, for a packet of cigarettes.

The walk home is a painful one, despite the zinc ointment that's slapped between my thighs. I make my way down Fork Street, hips splayed to avoid an accidental meeting of friction-burned skin. The footpath is crumbling and infested with bindi weeds that bite at the soles of my rubber thongs. I stop to pull out the burrs and prick my fingers. Tiny droplets of blood cook like gravy on the asphalt.

"Fuck you, Travis," I yell.

Nobody hears me because the streets are empty, like they always are when the northerlies are blowing. That northern wind burns like hot smoke in your lungs, leaving air sacs scorched and scabbed over when you breathe it in. Some folks will be home with the water cooler blasting; some will be camped up at the pub where the lines are yeasty, but the beer is cold; others will have made the hike to Spencer's swimming hole, only to find that the riverbed is long parched.

Spencer's has been dried up for years now, but it seems like only yesterday I was tanning by that poo-brown water, floating amongst the ghost gums and cow carcasses, svelte and confident in my childless skin. Maybe it *was* yesterday... Things tend to happen that way around here. One minute, you're marvelling at your womanly curves in the reflection of the water as the farm boys fight for your attention—the next, you're pregnant, the swimming hole runs dry, and the farm boys never look at you again.

I pass by the old Catholic school, its outer husk of classrooms and hallways that once housed me, my mother and my grandmother, now hollow. I hate that the school takes up an entire block. It looks haunted. Hard to believe it ever looked any other way. In my memory, it's shinier, the trees greener, and I hate the reality of convent windows that are barred and broken, the once-manicured gardens overgrown with Paterson's curse. The place has been condemned for a few years now. Travis reckons the nuns all turned to dust in their beds; he heard it from a squatter who made it his home for a night, and never got the smell of death off his skin.

"*Oi!*"

An orange panel van with P-plates skids by, local radio station blaring from tinny speakers. The driver is sweaty, and his passenger is sweaty, and they are looking me up and down like they're judging a wet t-shirt comp—then they notice my swollen belly, my fingers scratching at fresh scars.

"Nah, she's pregnant," the passenger says, and they speed away with the muffler rattling.

"Thanks for the ride," I call after them.

They turn right, down Rafferty, and take their tinny tunes with them. They'll be back in ten minutes if they cut a full lap of town. An hour, tops, if they're doing burnouts in the backstreets.

I keep walking, fingernails digging into my abdomen as the searing pain starts up again.

Travis is in the shed when I get home. He and Micka are in matching blue Bonds singlets, gaping over the Torana's empty engine bay and swapping diagnostics. There's an industrial fan in the corner blowing hot gusts of tobacco and BO through the open roller-door.

"Did you get smokes?" Travis rummages through the shopping bag, finds the cocoa butter. "What's this?"

"It's for stretch marks," I say.

He locates his cigarettes, gives me the bag back. "Gross."

"You should try Vitamin E." Micka's chiming in now. "My missus used it every day. Never got a mark on her."

"Laura's already got 'em everywhere," says Travis, his disgust obvious.

He lights up, breathes nicotine clouds between us. Offers me a drag.

"I quit, remember?"

He doesn't. His attention is back on the car, and Micka's lighting up, and the tobacco cloud is expanding, so I head inside where the air is still hot but at least it's smoke-free.

I refrigerate the discount chook, find a shaded corner, open the cocoa butter. It smells like the tropics, somewhere with humid breezes and more than one radio station. I apply the cream to my belly, and it cools the welted lines that crisscross into forks and bend from my navel to my groin.

It really does look like a roadmap.

The pain wakes me from sleep, and I'm standing on a deserted road wearing the old AC/DC top that Travis lets me borrow sometimes. There's a T-intersection ahead. To the left are the familiar lights of town, to the right a bridge that crumbles away into nothingness.

I walk to the edge of the bridge, teeter over the vortex, and think I can see something down there. A glint of colour in the moonlight and—shit! It's an orange panel van at the bottom of the ravine, split against the cragged rocks, top peeled back like a sardine tin. The driver is in there, his passenger too, and they are wide-eyed, and leering, and oh-so-unmoving. The radio is still spitting intermittent bursts of classic rock. Singing about *the dry, the dry, the dry*—

Then the northern wind blows, and the car turns to dust, and I'm awake in my bed.

The room stinks of death—of the cancer that took my mum— and I realise I never did see that panel van make its second lap.

And the pain starts again, and my abdomen burns, worse than before, like I'm being branded from the inside. I roll up my shirt, fingers trembling. There's a new stretch mark etching its way across my belly and it's veering towards a hard right, arrow-headed and pointing.

Like an exit sign.

It's cooler outside than it is in the house, so I take my jar of cocoa butter to the front doorstep and apply it by moonlight. The night sky is dotted with constellations, and I wonder if anyone ever used them to find their way out of town. Maybe that's what happened to those nuns.

Mrs Collins's porch light is on, which means Sheree isn't home yet. Probably at the pub. Sheree is always leaving the kids with her mother these days, even though old Mrs Collins mows dead lawns and dozes off on the front porch while they play. Sometimes those kids are out at midnight, horsing around in the dirt. I've thought about reporting it, but Travis says I'm just jealous that Sheree still has a mum.

The kids aren't playing outside tonight, but there's someone else in Mrs Collins's yard.

A stranger crouched in the shadows of her dying desert oak.

I stop the circular motion of cream on skin. Stop breathing.

The stranger hasn't seen me yet. He's not even looking my way. He's staring at Mrs Collins's house and he's grinning with skewed teeth and everything about him is wrong. Neck too long. Jaw too twisted. Skin crumbling like a badly kept footpath. He starts to crawl towards her front porch, reaching with arms that are cracking and stretching; he's crooked-mouthed, and stinking of smoke...

"Travis," I whisper, but I already know he's passed out on the couch with a tinnie in his hand, and won't be in any state to help.

The stranger pauses at the sound of my voice. Scours the night with blackened eyes.

He sees me. Smiles. Waves. I stay deathly still. Hold my breath till my lungs are burning.

"Laura?" Sheree is home, and quick as a brown snake, the stranger turns to dust. "Why are you out here staring at my house?"

She's standing on the nature strip by the open door of a banged-up Camry, and there's classic rock on the radio, and I haven't even noticed. I pull down my t-shirt, embarrassed by my scars.

"Fuckin' weirdo," she says, voice all slurry. She heads inside, walks right through where the stranger just was, doesn't notice the dust.

The front porch light is barely off, and I can already hear her yelling at her mum.

I follow the stretch-mark map. Walk as far as it will take me, despite the chafe rash that still smarts between my thighs.

The broken bridge is right where it was in my dream, but there's no orange panel van at the bottom, no T-intersection, no other road but the one that leads back into town.

I'm exhausted when I get home, and my feet are raw and swollen. Rubber thongs are not designed for long-distance walking. Mrs Collins is on her front porch, drinking lemonade with the grandkids, and waves for me to join her.

"Would you like a shandy, love?" she asks, cigarette burning with an inch of ash that refuses to fall.

"I'm pregnant," I reply. "But I'll take some of that lemonade."

She clucks and pours from the pitcher. "I don't buy into that crap. A little tipple never hurt me none when I was pregnant with Sheree."

I sip the lemonade, and it's cool and sweet against my sand-paper throat. I consider telling her about the stranger in her yard, but if there was no panel van, maybe he didn't exist either.

"You look tired, love, come and take a seat." She pats the rusted chair next to her, coos over a mud pie that her granddaughters are making—and it makes me miss my mum.

I ask Mrs Collins if she remembers her.

"Oh yes," she smiles, eyes wet with tears. "She loved you so much, Laura...but she's dust now, and nobody talks about dust."

I stop, mid-sip. "What?"

"She's in the ground, love. Where we all end up. Just bones desiccating in the dirt. No use talking about it. She's just a bag of flesh that's rotting and festering and turning to dust." Her eyes bulge as she speaks, pupils so dilated they're almost black.

I touch her hand. Her skin is dry, like crepe paper. "Are you all right, Mrs Collins?"

She grins at me, and it's all twisted and wrong and yellow-stained. "You're going to die here, Laura. You and your baby."

I put down the lemonade. "Fuck you, lady."

"Um, what did you just say to my mother?" Sheree is coming up the steps behind me, eyes wide.

I look back and Mrs Collins is staring at me like she's been slapped. I mumble apologies, push past Sheree, stumble out of the yard.

She leers on the doorstep, waving smoke clouds over her kids, who are still making mud pies. "If you weren't pregnant, I'd kick your arse!"

I hurry towards my unhinged front door and, right on cue, the searing pain starts.

I wake from a dream about the stranger in Mrs Collins's yard—he was creeping through the convent halls of the old Catholic school, and the nuns were all screaming and turning to dust.

But I'm not asleep now, and the screams haven't stopped.

And I smell smoke.

Travis is on his usual spot on the couch, ashtray beside him. I shake him awake and he sits up, groggy. Sniffs at the burning air.

"I can smell it too," he says. Then, "Shit, the Torana."

He's still out in the shed when the fire truck pulls up to save Mrs Collins's house. The fibro cottage is in flames with black smoke that blankets the stars. Sheree and the kids are standing on the road, and they're screaming her name, and she's not coming out.

I can see her at the kitchen window, charred and dazed. She's pressed against the glass, and chunks of burned flesh are sticking to it. And behind her is a crooked face with blackened eyes and it stares at me, grinning and smoking, till they both turn to dust.

I sit on the front doorstep in my old bikini top, sipping iced water, as they remove the last of the rubble from Mrs Collins's block. Sheree is overseeing the cleanup. She reckons her mum was partial to a cheeky smoke at bedtime—probably fell asleep with it between her fingers, and set herself alight.

"Once the insurance pays out on the house, I'll build another one just like it," she tells me, one kid on her hip, the other one tugging at her shirt.

"You could always take the money and go. Start a new life for you and your daughters," I say.

She stares at me, unblinking. Lights up a cigarette. "Why would I want to leave here?" She takes a long drag. Eyes my exposed belly. "You know they've got creams for that."

Before I can reply, there's a sputter from the back shed, and the Torana engine roars to life. The scream of the 308 sounds fresh and fiery, like a newborn baby, and I suddenly remember that my Mum *did* have stretch marks—she used to say that I drew them, in utero.

I smile through the pain and wait for the roadmap to finish.

PUNCH IN HELL

DMITRI AKERS

.

I: Baby Judy

Doctor Guan moved the white transducer across a swelling belly. He tried, hard as it was, not to look up at the bearded face. On the wall, a screen eddied with tenebrous forms that danced around ghostly whites. Across the room, Ahab the clown wore puffy pantaloons, hued with every wavelength of the light spectrum. A little man, carved and lifelike, bounced on his knee.

"The baby's right there," Doctor Guan said, pointing to the screen. "A girl."

"A girl," Jezebel Sand gasped. "Did you hear that, Ahab? A beautiful girl... What will we call her?"

A head swivelled and squeaked, wood against wood. A maw of worn rouge curved into chipped, blushed cheeks. Doctor Guan side-eyed Mr Punch, the puppet of weirdness, bent and humpbacked. Below azure eyes, an obscene, drooped nose of yew hung—a tree knot, ever crude and ever raw.

With pursed lips, the paediatrician said, "She's quite small. I'll make the next check-up sooner."

"Oh my God. Is it anything to worry about?"

"No, Mrs Sand. But I may have to ask you questions if it's okay, and your husband can stay if he wants."

Across the room, Mr Punch told Ahab Sand what to say.

"I'll stay. But, muffin, let's call our daughter Judy," Ahab said. "Judy Junior."

"Judy Junior? I love it!"

"Judy'll love it. Mr Punch already does."

The painted head spun inside that black hole where a neck should have been. Wood rattled, a morbid maraca.

"Yes!" Jezebel Sand said. "We'll make her part of our plays for the travelling *Cirque de Sable*."

Vermillion lips twisted into an unnatural grin. Hedgerows of teeth exposed, white if not for remnant marks of lipstick. Behind them, a sable void contained no light. Mr Punch whispered. He always whispered. But not everyone heard it.

"When's the next appointment, Doc?" Ahab asked.

"**W**hat is it, Doc?" Jezebel queried.

"It seems to me that Judy Junior has a growth."

"A growth!"

"Yes, Mrs Sand."

"What growth?" Jezebel gasped.

"We'll take a closer look. But you'll have to come in more frequently."

Tears fell across the black beard that forked from a porcine face; runnels fell with chunks of mascara sediment; the streams meandered down like black adders that slithered towards some cavern. Wood scraped. Unblinking, Mr Punch's opal-like eyes took in the entire room. The Near East had the Evil Eye, whereas *Cirque de Sable* had Mr Punch. Whispers. Whispers.

"I'll make sure to put off the *Cirque de Sable* until we get this sorted."

"Oh my God, Ahab. I'm scared!"

"**T**he baby's safe."

Jezebel Sand sighed. "Oh my God. Thank you, Doc."

"The ultrasound images had me worried, so it's safer to run tests than to be sorry. But we mightn't need to check up any further. The growth on the baby's back isn't malignant at all. It's benign."

What's that, Mr Punch? Mr Punch spun, a curved hump on

his back like a backward fin. Sparkled scarlet silk, which adorned the arms, the torso, the hump, shimmered. The puppet splayed its legs out like some squatting cat licking itself.

"*Me line*? Oh, me line's gotta be told before it *be nine*."

White teeth clattered. Somewhere, a void bubbled. A giggle came.

"So, we've got to the second trimester, safe and sound. There, see? That Judy Junior's a kicker."

"Oh my God, Ahab! Look!"

Ahab's dark brown eyes, dark enough to be black, widened. Emanations of a swelling sea, that white noise, washed in wave after wave of hisses and sprays.

"Judy Junior's a lively one. She's just like you, muffin."

The puppet's yew-hewn jaw dropped. Clink, clank, clunk. What's so funny, Mr Punch?

"*Cirque de Sable* will open once again with a new exhibit, but only for a limited time. See for the first time in our emporium of the weird and wonderful, the freakish and the forbidden, a pregnant bearded lady!"

Ahab the clown held the sign above his amber wig. Cars rushed past gaggles of tourists and salt-encrusted shopfronts. Seagulls squawked on high, as the bovine crowds limped forward with groans or sighs, like pilgrims at an unholy site, some licking ice creams, others walking around, mouths agape. Flies, perched on lips, sucked on drool.

"A bearded lady with my baby inside her! Wouldn't you like to see what happens when a silly clown and his hirsute wife get together to make a baby? She's due in a few months, so come see our baby bump, that hump, that lump. Or see our famous rendition of Punch and Judy!"

Some kids rushed, or tried to. With harnesses around their torsos, they were pulled back on leashes, like overexcited dogs. One boy flailed his arms and groaned, unable to break the adamantine bond.

"Stop pulling, Matthew! You'll get hit by a car!"

"Come on down. Good, old-fashioned Punch and Judy, everyone. Little boy, what about you?"

"Stop pulling, Matthew! I'll never take you to the beach again!"

"**P**ush, Mrs Sand. Push!"

Nurses' hands already held Jezebel's legs apart. There, a doctor inspected the progress. Ahab the clown had never heard such anguished screams, other than at carnival shows.

"Push, muffin. Push!"

With silken gloved fingers, he squeezed Jezebel's tensing palm. Her hairy knuckles whitened. She squeezed back, a vice grip. Screams, ululations, caterwauls. The mouth between her legs opened; the soles of little feet poked out, bloodied; the nurses and doctor yammered; Jezebel contorted and twisted in her new rites as a mother.

"There, almost there," Ahab said. "You can do it for me, muffin."

With gloves of plastic, the masked doctor and nurses pulled the baby out, its sanguine head held up to the fabric of theatre blues. A slap. A slap. Not slapstick, but still a slap. Mr Punch's voice came, but no one heard it. Not even Ahab the clown. There, there, child. Welcome to the world. It is your stage now.

A nurse handed the crying babe to Ahab. He held the ball of bawling. Ahab, bemused and wide eyed, could not help but notice the stumpy growths on the child's back. They felt like tailbones, long lost remnants of a primate past.

Creased and gargoyle-like, Judy Junior's face resembled an elder oak's rings. A toothless mouth gaped, a yawning void. How could something so small scream so loud? The clown rocked her. Blood soaked his pinstriped shirt. Deep down, he wanted to scream, too.

II: What's the Way to Do It?

In the mad dreams of another world, a troupe of shadows danced along strings. Crooked puppets bounced about. Their lines, written and predetermined by some supreme yet unknown being, had never been heard by a living soul.

"You're a bastard, Mr Punch! A rotten bastard, you are! I should've never married into filth."

"Who loved you, Judy, when no else would? Who fed you and brought home the bread?"

"Put down that slapstick, Mr Punch. Or I'll call the bloody constable, I will."

"Take this!"

Marionettes, more like rag dolls governed by certain laws of a chaotic universe than any hand of an unseen god, twisted and fell and danced. That drooping, red nose sniffed the air. The mouth clicked and clacked. Frilly fabric over stuffing flailed, flopped, flew. Separated by black lines, the painted white teeth were held inside crescent, wine-red lips. A cetacean's fin cut through the air to the sound of dolphin laughter.

"Mr Punch, Mr Punch. What's all this then? I got a call for a domestic disturbance, Mr Punch." The tithead rose from those depths that must exist below. A billy club held aloft. "Mr Punch, I'm taking you in, you ruddy murderer."

"Catch me if you can, Officer!"

"Mr Punch, come back. I'll be putting you down as resisting arrest on top of that awful murder, Mr Punch, I will."

A flapping, not of batwing that took flight, but a descent of silk over wood. Maybe that is what the Dawn Star, the Angel named Lucifer, sounded like as it disappeared into that murky well of Dis. Beneath the stage, the laughter echoed out. Tenebrous realms yet to be conquered by light. The stage, like the world itself, had a horizon. And what unseen hell had lived beneath that last horizon?

There be limits to a universe, or at least the mirage of limits. A stage must have physical limits. That booth, more like a grand temple, possessed dazzling pillars and a high roof painted by some master painter, swirling tapestries of stars and constellations. So many masks, or so many thespians, played paupers and kings. Along the bottom of the booth, there hissed and raged waterfalls of bony white and waterfalls of blood as far as the eye could ever see. Pinstripes, *ad infinitum*.

"**H**ow do you plead, Mr Punch, sir?"

"Guilty! Guilty! But is a man not entitled to passions and is not every man guilty of pain and pleasure?"

"Silence, Mr Punch!"

"But man's a beast. Who among you's not guilty of pain, guilty of pleasure?"

"I'll not have you sully my court with balderdash, Mr Punch!"

A hammer struck the pointed cap of scarlet; a thunderbolt never struck the same place twice, but it did not need to. The doll bounced on the edge of the world. The mouth opened, shut, opened again. Chattering teeth of wooden, painted falsity. Guffaws. Chuckles. The laughing stoic, Chrysippus, might have laughed like that. But Chrysippus died that way. Madly, he laughed at the donkey eating figs. Bellies exploded from escaping laughter; escapists were mirages, as laughter is a mirage. Froth and foam lingered on the smile. Death had so many frantic faces.

Mr Punch's smile never died; he pushed himself up from the windowed horizon, at that edge of hell and heaven; he jerked up, threw his arms wildly, and danced a mad dance. Arms swung and shivered.

"Ouch, your Honour. That hurt!"

"Pain might teach you a lesson, Mr Punch. A lesson in how one should conduct oneself. Do not inflict pain if you do not want pain back. I might dole it out to you, tenfold!"

"Tenfold, your Honour? But pain is a state of life, and pleasure can come from pain, don't you know, your Honour? There has only been the same amount of pain, the same amount of pleasure, since the world began."

"Nonsense!"

"Why, your Honour?"

"Pain and pleasure are created by actions, Mr Punch. Pain is to be avoided; pleasure is to be welcomed. And that's about the long and short of it, Mr Punch, sir."

Mr Punch threw his head back. What was so funny about that now, Mr Punch?

"**T**en thousand consecutive years in the slammer, Mr Punch! No possibility for parole. No right to bail, you foul murderer and danger to society, you!"

"Danger to society? I'm what society *is*, your Honour!"

"Not this again, you scoundrel. You stalled proceedings, Mr Punch!"

"What are you, a king? And is this very courtroom not your royal demesne, where you sit on your god-blessed arse upon that toilet throne of yours?"

"That's it, Mr Punch. That is it!"

Pounding, pounding, pounding. Thunderous quakes. Mr Punch's head spun; blue eyes wept a mime's tears; a mouth, so nonliving yet undying, opened and shut like the movement of a butterfly's wings when sat in the sun. Life was so funny, Mr Punch thought, but death was even funnier.

"**H**ow's a million years in the nick sound, Mr Punch? I'll make it two million in the chokey if you don't shut it!"

"Your Majesty, don't you think a million years too harsh? Hasn't man murdered so much already? Who cares if I did? My wife was a pain in the arse, Mr Majesty, sir!"

"That's it, Mr Punch. One billion years in the eternal gaol for murder in every degree imaginable. And you will spend those sentences consecutively. I'll make sure you'll never see the stage again!"

"The darkness is a stage like any other stage, your Majesty."

"I'll make your sentence the age of the universe. Spend all time in the brig!"

"Excellent. Excellent. All the time in the universe and then some! I'd make the play of the century every century, for centuries of centuries."

The hammer came down, a rain of sulphurous fire. Calamity. Mr Punch no longer bounced on the stage's horizon; instead, he fell beneath it, towards unseen depths where ancient currents raged. Sirens called as whales whined. Krakens slept in eons-long slumber, stuck inside the reveries of universes outside of our own.

The midnight yawned. Obsidian paint caked on obsidian paint created alien landscapes. Perhaps this place was never supposed to be seen the right way up, as though camera obscura.

Mr Punch wondered if there was another stage like darkness. Actors worked as shadows, cast by the flickering flame of some candle that men do not verily see, nor truly ever come to understand. He would have likened his prison to a cave. Where a cave could be crawled out of, he could crawl out of this place too. The only thing a puppet needed in a time like that was a set of strings to pull him up. A fishing line could have taken the leviathan from the roiling ocean of infinitudes, those shadows cast by a cosmos of uncountable suns.

"If the world's a stage," Mr Punch began, "then I guess some of us have to exit stage right. But I'll be there when the curtains fall just as when the curtains draw."

The show had started just as it ended. Showtime!

III: Where's the Punchline?

The nursing room hummed. Fluorescent tubes, ghost-lights for some purgatory, glowed. The babies would die one day, to be sure, either stolen in youth or turned to dust in old age. Judy Junior differed. Something, or someone, stirred inside those eyes. An admixture of greys and blues. A newborn pup that might turn into a hound of hell.

"The child seems healthy," Doctor Guan said. "These growths will have to be examined. I'll just need a tissue sample."

He held the baby's head with the small of his hand, the forearm felt the grooves on her back, those strange and eerie grooves, as she dribbled against those theatre blues. The hairy woman leaned against the wall, dishevelled. Jezebel's face, apart from the beard, seemed like melted wax. She nodded, slowly.

"Judy Junior," she whispered. "My baby girl."

Ahab the clown rubbed his hands. Sweat gathered like dew on his white face. Whisperings lingered in his ear. Do not say that Mr Punch, not in the hospital.

The Sand abode was not much, but it was home. Inside the lounge room, strewn with party supplies and boxes worth of balloons, Jezebel lazily laid on a divan. Ahab walked in. He tried to avoid the plastic prank dogshit; he slipped. His bearded wife wheezed. He looked up, smiled, and crept closer in those outrageous clown shoes. Invisible strings forced him forward. They were connected to some hand outside of time. At least, he dreamed something like that.

"Don't go to the hospital again, muffin."

"Why, Ahab?"

Hush now, Mr Punch, she might hear.

"It's just that our baby daughter's fine. Aren't you, Judy Junior?"

"Oh my God. She's so beautiful, Ahab. I think she's going to say her first words, and they're going to be *dada* or *mama*."

The white crib sat in the corner. Within, the baby jiggled her arms in erratic bursts. Little hands, more like misshapen claws, grasped at air.

"She can hear us, Ahab! She can hear us talking about her. Our baby daughter is so beautiful. Oh my God!"

"Muffin, let's see what she thinks of Mr Punch and Judy."

"That's such a good idea! I'll set up the booth."

Stars, speckled with pigmented dust and blobs, spanned the pillars of the booth. Spiral arms inevitably must have collided. Drapes of claret silk fluttered; wings of some butterfly doomed to die in a supernova.

"Gather up. Gather up. This is some good, old-fashioned Punch and Judy, ladies and gentlemen."

The microphone, held beneath Ahab's red nose, quavered. The

tiny speakers upon the booth's pillars barked the command of some dictator of fun and fury. Welcome to *Cirque de Sable*, kids. No refunds.

"Oh my God, Ahab. I haven't seen you do it in ages, baby. I'm so excited. Look Judy Junior, it's your godfather and godmother, Mr Punch and Judy!"

Mr Punch rose. His bent nose mimicked his back's hump, a coiled fin that had been sewn on backwards. The wigged doll came next, inside a sultry dress that brought out her features: those almond-shaped eyes, those full cheeks, those luscious lips that spoke sweet nothings. Judy the puppet turned and turned; her dress lifted.

"What are you smiling about, Mr Punch?"

"Oh, nothing, deary. But have you made dinner yet, love?"

The marionettes danced around another, floating masks. The voices—not affected but adopted from some unseen portal beyond—loudened and rose over the sound system.

"Do you see Judy, little baby girl? That's your godmother, your namesake!"

The pale baby giggled within the crib. Bluish, greyish eyes stared at the display of extravagance and otherworldliness. It went on and on. Giggles, groans, slapstick, silence. When the curtains fell, Ahab the clown walked out from behind the booth in a daze; he staggered towards his wife and slumped beside her. Sweat collected on his brow.

"What's wrong, baby? Oh my God. You look sick, even beneath that makeup."

"I'm fine. It's just…"

Something rustled behind the booth, which sat like an unhallowed obelisk. The curtains drew. There, the little puppet, Mr Punch, grinned and stared with blue eyes; he hovered above the horizon, a ghost brought to life from some unknown crypt that should have been shut with a holy seal.

"Ahab! How did you move Mr Punch when you're over here?"

"I didn't, muffin."

"Oh my God! Look at Judy."

They watched, either in terror or fascination, as the marionettes waltzed on the stage, hand in hand, their heads thrown back. Mad laughter resonated inside the lounge room. In her crib, Judy Junior let out a cacophonous cackle herself, unlike anything a baby should be able to produce.

Jezebel cast her head to the crib; she screamed at what came out. Dread overtook her.

Ropy masses surged from the crib. Were they snakes? They slipped and wriggled there, an orgy of writhing horrors.

The lengths of flesh hung from the roof; some crept up the walls. They looked like cords or maybe ropes. A hangman's noose without a noose. Was this a gallows for the undead? Mr Punch and Judy, still in a strange waltz, looked into another's pale eyes, carved into wood, as simulacra of this ephemeral world.

"Oh my God, Ahab. I can't stop watching…"

Jezebel sat up from the divan. A pulsing rope was wrapped around her abdomen, a harness that might have pulled her up for some theatrics, some acrobatics, some deadly good fun. Ahab lay prone on the floor, his pinstriped shirt ripped open to expose a hairy back. Tethered, those ropes sucked onto his back like leeches.

Mr Punch whispered something, but Ahab barely heard it. Only the blood filled him; it incensed passion, created feeling, caused pleasure and pain. He turned over and pulled down his pantaloons of rainbow hues; there, an erection stood from a mass of hair, grown underneath a flabby gut.

"Let's make another baby, muffin," he groaned. "I love you so much. And we can call the next one after Mr Punch. He told me so."

The entrancing spell over Jezebel evaporated. She turned her head. Gazes locked into another. Eyes flickered with something between lust and love.

"I just popped one out. And you want another one. I love you so much, Ahab."

Panpipes blew somewhere. Drums loudened into a warlike beat. When Ahab entered his wife, he groaned with ecstasy; some rapturous rupture overcame him, as the ropes filled him with more blood. Lips met. The world shook. A sigh, a sigh, a pant, a pant. Eyes rolled into ecstatic shudders.

"That's the way to do it," Mr Punch yelped out.

Ahab climaxed with the best orgasm he had ever felt. Then the sharp pain met his throat. When he looked down, he saw Jezebel had stuck a butcher's knife into his neck. Wood rattled. Teeth chattered. A baby giggled.

Mr Punch never forgot the entertainer's duties: keep the audience happy and fed. Guzzling chocolate milk, Jezebel drank and sobbed and drank more. Rivulets of dark brown stained her face, by the sides of an insatiable mouth.

"I'm so hungry," Jezebel cried. "I've got cravings!"

The animated corpse of Ahab glided through the air on white harnesses. Leech-mouthed veins throbbed to the high sound of panpipes and rhythm of drums. Cleaver in hand, Ahab swung and swung, a circus freak suspended above a giggling, hooting audience.

Who knew that food knew how to prepare itself? He held the meat cleaver up with his right hand, swung it down into his left hand, hacked off a few digits. Treats for the mother of his child, or children… Pan-fried with truffle oil, served in a bowl, and garnished with pepper, salt, paprika, and allspice, with a pinch of curry powder, who knew that death tasted so good?

"Oh my God, Ahab. This is delicious. You know just what I want. I wish Judy Junior could try… But she's still on milk."

Jezebel's eyes stared at nothing. Eyes hidden within sallow flaps. Skin rolled over skin, sweat-drenched, oily, foetid. A flash of delirium danced upon the corneas, upon the pupils. Shadows swung and kicked in a ballroom of blackness.

Veiny vines, risen to the ceiling like puppet strings, pulsed. They clung to her back of folds. Her unkempt beard almost grew past her engorged tits. She lay on the bed and watched her monstrous daughter grin at her. Blue-grey eyes stared and stared, like horrid marbles inside a head of white clay.

A network of stringy appendages, like umbilical cords that bordered on phone lines, hung down from the roof. Did they originate from Judy Junior? Jezebel half-thought they were all over the room, all over the universe. A living, grotesque theatre. In the corner of that theatre, Judy the puppet threw her hands up and pirouetted—a dreadful ballerina. Beside her, Mr Punch turned his head like an owl.

"When's the baby due, Judy Junior?"

Goo goo. Gaga. Giggles.

"If the new son's not dressed and ready yet," Mr Punch went on, "I'll have to rip him out, love."

Jezebel shook like a beetle on its back. No scream came when she opened an oily mouth. Bloated belly fat, ribbed with weeping buboes and layered with pus on pus, writhed for a moment. Beneath the expanse of skin, something tried to kick and claw its way out. Mr Punch laughed.

The puppet flew upward and pounced on her.

Hunched over Jezebel, that immensity of obesity, he placed his wooden palms on her rotted stomach. On the pregnant dome, fingertips dug into flesh. Those fingers, such little puppeteers, entered that womb. Or was it a chrysalis?

Pallid tentacles surged with blood. Jezebel choked on a scream that did not come. Deep, deep, the fingers went in. Judy Junior screeched or laughed. It was hard to tell. Gore and lifeblood soaked the sheets. Despite his usual affinity for red—blushed cheeks, vermillion attire to match those lips, and drinker's nose— Mr Punch had never been so very red.

"You're a bastard, Punch Junior!"

"Who loved you, Judy Junior, when no else would?"

"Put down that knife, Punchy."

"Take this!"

A child's pallid hand swung a toy knife. Too comically large for a squamous pseudo-hand, the knife was also blunt. Judy Junior caught the wrist before the blade connected. That wrist, if it was one, had shed layers and peeled into transparent husks which crinkled in Judy Junior's palm. Only a year old, she stood as tall as a girl of nine. Little brother, little brother, sometimes a big sister is too big to play with you.

They grow up so fast, do they not, Mr Punch?

Punch Junior gasped as his sister pulled him up like a fish on a line. The tiny crocodilian arm cracked and tore: burst tendons, black blood, tender muscle like a lamb, intertwined capillaries. Jerked up, the little leviathan dangled over her red-lipped sucker, that leech-like mouth, a fleshy tunnel lined with rows of chiropteran fangs.

Long ropes of something, between living flesh and corpse rot, hung from the dark ceiling like meat hooks, like fishing lines. A theatre of shadows possessed a deathly stage of sepulchral spillage. Thespians' bodies lined the wooden boards to the point the floor was obscured, so utterly hidden. That is the way to do it, Mr Punch. The two puppets—alive or dead, it need not matter— danced and danced. Laughter, applause. The curtains fell. Or they drew open. Who knew?

Spun like spinning tops, multitudes of nameless planets erupted with cosmic laughter. Magma metamorphosed into lava; worlds blackened into cemetery chrysalises that harboured beautiful chimeras.

The best cosmic joke was told on a planet, once alive, but which lived on through death. Puppets danced there—wild, mad, gay. Lunatics basked within lunate glow. Long tongues, like red ribbons, lolled low from ancient mouths. Below, in that murky meadow, and beneath the milky light of a pallid moon, a spectre wailed. The ethereal, bluish spirit slithered into the turning spindle. There, inside a meadow of black hemlock trees, more dead souls joined the charnel hymns.

Mr Punch's silhouette danced against a white halo. In that firmament beside the moon, long-dead stars twinkled like ghosts of time, votive candles that blew out long ago for souls that sleep and dream mad dreams.

So many shows to be had, Mr Punch. So many moons and stars to see.

RESPECT

CAROLE KELLY

It wasn't until the third night, after Sam quietly left our bed and didn't return until sunrise, that I became suspicious. Sam had always suffered from insomnia, and nocturnal wanderings were not unusual for him. Our small, rented weatherboard cottage was only a short walk to the shore, and I assumed that he'd been exploring the long stretch of black volcanic sand and rocky cliffs, for which the area was well known. This stretch of coastline was also acclaimed for its seafaring history of shipwrecks, daring rescues, and dark stories of uncanny encounters.

A twenty-minute drive to the nearest town meant that our cottage was isolated, tucked under the brooding basalt cliffs with an unobstructed view of the moody, restless ocean. The lack of distractions suited us both well, having determined to use this precious holiday time to work on our tattered marriage. It's not that we didn't still love each other, but years of failed IVF treatments and multiple heartbreaking miscarriages had broken us both. Accepting that I would never be able to have children meant I had also turned away from Sam, and although we still shared a bed, we'd not had sex in months. Sam, typically, refused to discuss his feelings about our childlessness or our sexual desert.

I think it was the unfamiliar smell that first caught my attention. Overlaying Sam's familiar woody scent was something both salty and spicy, yet also fishy. When he returned, seemingly exhausted from his beach stroll, he quickly fell asleep, but the unfamiliar smell lingered on the linen sheets and pillows of our conjugal bed.

When I queried him, he laughed it off, saying it was just the tang of the night sea air or my imagination.

The next evening, I made a point about being tired and needing an early night. Sam was also agreeable to turning in early and, by 10:00pm, was snoring gently while I lay feigning sleep and waiting for him to stir. By 11:30, he was tossing restlessly. After a while, he sighed in a resigned fashion and slipped silently out of bed. Pulling on his old tartan dressing gown and battered runners, he quietly opened the bedroom door, after checking to see if I was still sleeping. Then I heard him leave the cottage.

As soon as his footsteps couldn't be heard on the gravel path, I leapt out of bed and quickly dressed in the dark pants and top I had left artlessly on the chair. Stopping only to grab my runners, I was out of the cottage in moments.

A full moon and a sky full of stars meant I could easily see Sam, but then, he could just as easily see me. I was careful to keep within the grey shadows of the rocks and ancient boulders that formed a natural barrier between our house and the shore. The moonlight caressed the sea that never ceased its gentle susurration, as I watched Sam pick his way through the rocks and then make his way confidently along the beach.

As I waited, I became aware of an elusive lyrical singing that drifted in and out of my consciousness. It teased, tantalisingly just out of my reach, yet Sam stopped to listen before suddenly breaking into a run. Caught by surprise, I hastily ran after him, keeping to the shadows where possible, but he seemed unaware of anything except the singing and its seductive call.

After a few minutes, I lost sight of him as he began to scale the rugged cliff face. Swearing to myself, I carefully climbed across the slippery rocks that Sam had traversed with the ease of practice.

A scary half-hour climb brought me to a vertiginous ledge, overlooking a small natural cove and a beach with glistening ebony sand. I realised that I must have climbed too far and was already turning back when a flash of silver caught my eye. Pausing, I peered more closely at the narrow beach, realising at the same time that the singing had stopped.

The silver flash belonged to a beautiful naked woman with

long, cascading ash-blonde hair, whose translucently pale limbs appeared to have a fine tracery of silver scales. At first, I thought she was alone. Then I saw Sam's familiar body entwined around hers.

As I watched, she climbed on top of him, her generous breasts bouncing with unfettered enthusiasm as she took him into her tight body and started to milk him dry. Even as Sam ejaculated with a roar, she began to pump him again. Paralysed with horror and disbelief, I observed helplessly as she managed to bring him to release another four times before rolling off his comatose body.

Standing, she raised her pale arms and stretched, and the moonlight highlighted the strange silvery markings on her long shapely legs. For the first time I saw her face and noticed her exotic pointed chin, full lips not quite concealing sharp white teeth, and a pair of slanting, impossibly cobalt-blue eyes. I knew then, with certainty, that I was not looking at anything human.

Sam was stirring now and had managed to weakly stand. The woman casually kissed him on the forehead and then ran into the water before quickly swimming off. In moments, there was no sign of her, yet further out, where the natural harbour met the ocean, I thought I saw a flicker of a silvery tail, too large to belong to a fish.

My head was still spinning with the impossible sight I'd just witnessed, but I retained enough survival instinct to realise that Sam shouldn't see me.

My trip back to the cottage was a blur and I found myself in bed, but unable to sleep, long before Sam returned. Once he arrived, he dropped heavily to the mattress and immediately fell into the deep sleep of exhaustion. I lay awake, watching the sunrise through our billowing net curtains, and made plans.

My first reaction, to blame Sam for his infidelity, was overruled by accepting that the mermaid or siren—I was hazy on the difference—had almost certainly seduced him with her enchanting voice, and he was completely in her thrall. "Legends & Myths 101", studied when I was doing my arts degree, had been quite comprehensive about such creatures and their captivating skills. One story I remembered told how mermaids

CAROLE KELLY

were unable to procreate without human seed. The irony of my similar barrenness was not lost on me, as I contemplated how to release Sam from his unwilling sperm donations.

When Sam slipped from our bed that following evening, I was quick to follow him but this time, I was prepared. The siren song sounded plaintive—and even desperate—to my unreceptive ears, but Sam responded with frightening eagerness. From my shadowy concealment, I could see his face lit up by the brilliant moonlight, almost unrecognisable from the distant, detached man I had been living with for so long. His face was alive with a raw passion and lust that both terrified me, and yet sent an answering thrill through my frozen core. Surprised by my reaction, I almost lost sight of him, but I knew where he was headed and made good time climbing the slippery rocks to yesterday's vantage point. I carefully noted the way down to the cove and waited for Sam to arrive.

The mermaid was decoratively arranged on a large mollusc-covered boulder, combing her long wavy hair as she continued to sing her enticing song. Pearly scales glimmered on her impossibly thin, naked limbs, and I idly wondered if Sam could have ever thought she was human.

Sam tumbled into the cove and threw himself on his knees in front of the mermaid, taking her delicate feet into his hands and kissing each of them tenderly. A jolt of jealousy shot through me, and I gritted my teeth as I continued to watch. The mermaid slipped gracefully from the rock and stood in front of Sam, who hastily stripped off his ratty robe and incongruously striped pyjamas as his mouth continued to worship her body.

His eager tongue found her hidden cleft. She threw her head back and made a strange caw, almost like a seagull. I could see that Sam was already erect, and his face was drawn tight with lust. The mermaid drew him down onto the sand and smiled at him, with surely too many teeth, before using those lips and teeth on his stiff penis until his breathing signalled that he was close to climax. She then lowered herself on his painfully erect member and, as she had the previous night, quickly rode him to completion. As Sam cried out, the mermaid made her strange caw again, throwing back her head and caressing her large globular breasts. Allowing Sam no respite, she was somehow able to arouse him again, and continued to milk him in an unending cycle of lust and completion.

I had seen enough. Fuelled with anger and a strange sense of violation, I crept carefully down the rocks to the mermaid's cove. Blessing my old runners that kept me steady on the loose scree, I tried to keep undercover on the way along the treacherous slope; regardless, the couple lasciviously entwined on the sand below remained unaware of my approach.

Once on the beach, I stopped and quietly took off my backpack. Keeping a wary eye on the mermaid, who was still locked in passion and remained oblivious to my presence, I took out my best carving knife that I had carefully honed to a lethal edge. Inching my way closer, I took in a deep breath before stabbing the knife deeply.

Her slender back seemed oddly cartilaginous, and then I dragged the knife down, filleting her like the fish that she was.

The mermaid gave an eerie scream, like the sound of gulls far out at sea. Green-tinged blood ran down her back, and she disengaged herself from Sam before turning to face me. I held the knife in trembling hands, unsure if I would be able to use it again. For a moment, those beautiful cobalt eyes met mine, then she lowered her head—in what seemed to be a gesture of respect—before running into the ocean, where she was immediately swallowed up. This time, I didn't look for the tail.

Sam lay almost unconscious on the dark sand now stained with the mermaid's blood. I knelt next to him and whispered his name. Slowly, he opened his eyes and gazed at me in confusion before reaching out to me with trembling hands. Strangely raked with unfamiliar lust, I kissed him as though he were air and I was drowning. Then it was easy to slip down my track pants and underwear to take the mermaid's place on his ready penis. It took only moments for my overstimulated body to find the desperate release it needed, and for Sam to reach an ejaculation that seemed to fill my unfruitful and parched womb.

Afterwards, there was little to say. I helped an unsteady Sam back to the cottage and lovingly tucked him into bed. By silent agreement, we never discussed that night. The next day, we packed up and went home. Sam's insomnia never returned.

One year later.
I had thought to avoid the cottage and the unspoken memories hidden there, but Sam had an unexpected week free from work, and I was ready for a break. After unpacking, we wandered down to the shoreline where the sea was slatey and agitated.

Cradling our baby Ariel in my arms, I gazed out further to the rolling swell of the ocean. Suddenly, the stormy clouds parted. A ray of sun caught a flash of two silvery tails, one smaller than the other, but both too large for a fish.

I held Ariel up in my arms for a moment and then, passing her to Sam, bent my head in a gesture of respect.

LATCH

H.K. STUBBS

"**W**here am I?" I asked, groggy, like I was drunk, or... *swallowed*, trapped inside cream-coloured walls, inside some kind of system. The narrow bed squeaked as I sat bolt upright in the small room, so quickly that my head spun.

"Your parents weren't impressed with the news."

The stranger wore a jet-black dress with her hair in a slick French roll. She stared out the window of strong glass. Outside, grey sky, and hills far below. The window looked too thick to break, and too narrow to squeeze out, if I tried. Too high to survive the fall, if I jumped.

She walked over to me, high heels clacking. She was young to be in charge, just a little older than me. Eighteen? Sharp nose. Sharper eyes. Too blue. Fake, for sure.

"They sent you here."

They'd threatened a million times they'd send me away—when I dropped out of school, when I stayed out all night, when Damo tooted the horn to pick me up, late.

"Where's *here*?" I scratched my knotty bed-hair.

"Vilque Organics. You know the brand?"

I leaned forward. Outside the window, the hills were pebbly with brown grass. I shook my head. "Nope."

"We're a working dairy."

No crops or flowers, no trees. Looked too cold.

Her "dairy" sounded like bullshit.

"You would have had our products. They're green, eco, cheap. We give girls like you a second chance, and options. Do you want to keep it, or no?"

My hand went to my belly. "Oh, my parents are Catholics. They would never—"

"Your parents are done with you. That thing would've ruined them. Unwed mothers—"

"Mary was an unwed mother."

"No wonder they didn't want you." She grinned like a wolf. "I'm your legal guardian now. At seventeen, you're too young to make choices, according to the government, but I'm giving you a choice because as much as we need you, the texture of aborted foetal matter is delectable. Similar to pâté, just a little softer. Served fresh from the womb, it melts on the tongue—"

"Enough!" I held up my hand.

"You should try it, some day." She clucked her tongue. "Maybe not your own."

She leaned down and took my chin in her hand. Gored me with cold eyes. "Do you want to read the fine print before you choose?"

Stale coffee and a recent cigarette fouled her breath. Her teeth were small, slightly crooked. I read the situation plain enough on her face.

"What I want," I said, leaning in, never good at playing nice, "is *out* of here."

"Then abort it and go." She released my chin, shoving my face to the side. She stepped back, narrowed eyes drilling me.

"I want my baby."

"Then stay. You'll come around. Our girls are happy. Maree will be your guide sister. Eat your nutritionally balanced dinner, and rest. No alcohol. No smoking."

Hadn't had a fag since the second blue line showed up. I craved one now, and freedom. I *had* to get away. She opened the door and the chance to escape yanked me up like a puppet string. *Get out!*

I shoved past her, thumped her out of the way, slid on the polished cement. Both directions were the same. Heavy black doors lined both walls. Left would do. I ran, long blonde hair flapping against my shoulders, white shift catching between my knees, bare feet slap-slapping on the cold cement, breath ragged, fast—

Lips smacking, locking on, pressing close, sucking back, swallowing. Gulp, gone.

Ahhh…

That satisfied sigh did not belong to me.

G roaning as I sat up, rubbing my bruised back. This bedroom, again… *Crap!* The thick glass in the narrow window. This time, leaning against the antique cupboard, a girl with dark eyes and curly hair. She had one knee cocked up, foot in a brown vinyl slipper resting on the cupboard door. Sizeable bump on her belly.

"Brang you a coffee." She offered me a lukewarm mug, staying back, reaching out her hand cautiously like I might bite.

"Thanks."

"How far gone are ya?"

I shrugged. "Couple months."

"I'm five. The G-maas tased you." She grinned, a tooth missing. "You made a good run for it. Knocked old Fiddlesticks on her arse. Middies'll be checkin' you over, make sure you're not gonna lose it. The baby. 'Snot good for bubs, tasing. I'm Maree," she said, offering a skinny hand.

"Amber," I replied, shaking it weakly. "What the fuck is this place?"

"Home now, so love it," she said. "I'm your guide sister. Old Fiddlesticks tasked me to show you round. Get you somethin' to eat first?"

She ran her fingers once though a long lock of my hair, teasing out the knots. Her nails were nice. Blue acrylics.

"Dunno." I was a bit hungry but rubbed my tummy. "Baby won't let me eat much."

"Morning sickness? Don't know why they call it that. 'Smore like a twenty-four seven sucker, innit?"

"Yeah." I watched as Maree twirled one of her ringlets around her finger. "Fiddlesticks—not her real name?"

She punched me on the shoulder. "You're a quick one. It's *Fiddington.* Get your tracky-dacks on." She waved at the grey tracksuit, folded, on the edge of my bed. "And don't try'n run again. G-maas'll tase you. You can't get out." She ambled back to the doorway and stood with her back to me.

Can't get out made me want to scream.

I pulled off my nightie and changed. The tracksuit was worn, with little tufted balls, but comfy and warm enough. How many girls wore it before me? What happened to them?

"No bra?" I asked.

"You won't need one." Maree ushered me into the hall, which was still wet from mopping. It smelled like a wet dog. My slippers left marks...they'd been worn before.

I had a flashback to slipping yesterday, landing on my butt and my head. That feeling of going down, deeper than just hitting the floor. Crashing through normalcy into...

Gulp.

"A hundred girls, give or take, live on this level, all knocked up, like us," Maree said. "Remember your room number, fifty-seven, on level seven. Seven-fifty-seven."

The doors were open, no one home, and the rooms all looked the same. No special things, not even magazines or flowers. No TVs or phones.

"Where's everyone?"

"Factory on level two, laundry on level three. Doin' their jobs. The mess hall's on the ground. We'll head down there. Seven flights of steps is not too bad now, but wait till you're ready to drop your bundle. Keeps us fit, hey."

Factory level. Laundry. Mess hall. Dorms. A hundred girls per level. At least three dorm levels...300 girls.

"What happens to us when we've had our babies?"

She shrugged. "We stay here."

"And the babies?"

"They're adopted into proper families."

"Proper? How do you know? Fiddington wanted to eat mine." I cradled my belly.

Maree laughed. "Don't believe that, do ya?"

It sounded nuts, but so was this place, in the middle of no-where. No town, no crops, no animals (or men), far as I could see, and several floors of girls and women who were knocked up.

"What do they make in the factory?"

"You're *full* of questions." Maree stared out the window, bored, walking down the wide flight of stairs. "Bottles, labels. Cheese. Yoghurt."

"Vilque Dairy." I scratched my head. "Are the cows around the back?"

"Nope."

"Sheep, then. Goats. Donkeys?"

"Cows are in the barn." Maree muttered, far away, then snapped out of it and smirked weirdly. Nothing was funny, far as I could see.

In the big mess hall, she led me to the counter.

"Amber has morning sickness, Brigit. Do you have something she might like?"

Brigit smiled, with a gap between her teeth, and lumpy red cheeks beneath her cook's cap. "A bit of chocky cake?"

Thick icing on top, it looked tasty. I hoped I could keep it down, as I carried my plate to a table by the window. Maree poured us orange juices. We sat. I sheared off a thin slice of cake and nibbled.

"How cold is it outside?"

Maree shrugged. "How would I know?"

"Looks like there's ice on the glass. So prob'ly colder than zero."

"You *can't* get out. But it's so cold, you wouldn't even wanna."

"I *do*. Cold means I'm a long way from home. I want to get back home. Where's the doors?"

She snorted. "Even if you find 'em, there's double manual locks on 'em, as well as tech-locks. Admin and G-maas have special keycards."

I sipped the sweet juice. More girls and women filed in, most in grey tracksuits like mine, but some older women wore blue cotton scrubs, and a few wore black denim. The blues looked like nurses and apparently the black were G-maas, like security or police. Brigit was one of them. More servers popped up behind the hotboxes in the kitchen, most in grey tracksuits.

Hundreds of women came to eat. About a quarter were obviously pregnant. Women of all different heights and colours. Breeding age. Fertile. Pretty happy-looking, most of them, talking to friends or girlfriends. Some of them held hands and hugged or kissed.

Not one guy.

What the hell was going on? What was the game? I didn't know, but it made me jumpy, jittery, sick. This place was out of balance. I had to get out.

Maree had been frowning at me on and off. Staring at me like crazy.

"Is there a dick growing out of my forehead?" I asked.

Finally, she spoke. "Troublemakers don't last in here. It's not worth it, trust me. Just do what's natural." She pointed to my belly. "Keep your head down, and everything's alright. You can be happy. I'm happy."

She showed her teeth. Oh right, that was supposed to be a smile.

"Where's the toilet?" I asked.

I ran where she pointed. Made it just in time to blow chunks.

"Sorry you feel so bad." Her voice was soft and echoey in the tiled bathroom. "We're on folding duty, reckon you can manage? Work takes your mind off things. Earns a few pennies toward your board. Or I can take you back to your room. Admin said to keep an eye on you, or lock you up."

"I'll manage." I flushed the toilet and rinsed my mouth, glancing at my miserable reflection in the mirror. My face was almost as grey as my eyes. "Let's go."

"The laundry's on level three." She smiled cautiously. "I hope you're coming round. It'll take care of you, Vilque will. I'll take care of you, too." She threaded an arm around my waist and squeezed. "If you let me."

Two months on laundry duty, washing, drying, pressing linen; stripping beds, making beds—earning pennies I never saw, that added to a tally kept on blackboards in the mess hall.

Two months in the kitchen, feeding 300 girls and women, eating as many hashbrowns as bub wanted. She started to kick inside me. I wanted a good life for her. But her life—and my life—no longer belonged to us. I didn't know the sex. They didn't do any scans. But I talked to *her*.

"I've failed you, bub," I whispered in my dark room, cold seeping through the thick glass. "I'm not giving you nothin'. I'm not giving you away, though. They're stealing you."

Tears burned my eyes. This whole thing was worse than a nightmare. No hero was riding in to save us. Damo didn't even know about bub. Who knows what he'd have said? I'd been gonna tell him that Sunday night. We weren't even dating, more like better'n'better friends who fucked like rabbits.

Would probably still be doing it, if I wasn't locked up in here. Damo.

What I'd do to have him light me a ciggie or spit a mouthful of red wine into my mouth again, in that kinky way he'd done it, straight out of the bottle. A bit gross, but super sexy. He did it quick, so there wasn't any spit in it.

"**G**etting used to the place?"
I jumped.

Fiddlesticks had snuck up behind me while I was studying the car park below the window. For the first time, it was full of cars. A sign of *outside*. Other people. They might help me get away.

"Is it visiting day? Can my boyfriend come?"

She had a good laugh at that, showing her awful little teeth. "Visiting day? That's a new word for it. There's a tasting, for new season products, at the cellar door."

"Dairy or meat?"

"We are a dairy, dear."

The way she said *dear*, it made my skin crawl.

"Though if you want to try it, at four months, the foetus has a texture like snails baked in their shells. At six months, it's more like octopus. It's not until they're born are they as firm, yet supple, as veal."

She watched me, a nasty little smile skipping on her lips, waiting for me to snap.

Maree's voice talked in my head. *Stay cool, my ghoul.*

"Nice one," I said, showing my teeth.

Into the factory on level two cleaning reusable milk bottles, relabelling them, filling them, and sealing them. Stirring ginormous vats of cheese with long wooden paddles, adding ingredients—vegan rennet and salt, herbs and culture—by hand. Checking the cheeses as they ripened in the cellar, with their faint scent of vomit, which often made me go for a real one.

Level two also housed the canning factory. *Mama's Own* canned meat.

"I ate this as a kid." I turned to Maree. "You never see any animals round here. This shit is made of our babies."

Maree shook her head and laughed. "You're nuts."

There were all different flavours of milk—vanilla, caramel, strawberry, chocolate—but it all looked the same except for the packaging. Vanilla had a smiling blonde, caramel a picture of a slender tanned lady, strawberry a picture of a redhead, and chocolate had a lady with rich brown skin. I'd never liked milk, but this kind seemed weirder than usual when I held it up to the light. Watery on the most part, bluish almost, but the cream was super thick.

Maree was always there by my side, keeping me on track, or keeping track of me, slowing down as she got bigger, then heavily pregnant and puffing with swollen feet, about to pop.

"Not long now," I tried to comfort her, as she struggled up the stairs carrying a box of bottles, lighter than mine. The look in her eye, when she turned back, was devastation. Eyes wide and teary, jaw pulled back like she'd been punched in the mouth. I had brought up what we never talked about: the day they'd take her baby. "I'm sorry," I said. "I didn't—"

She put down her box. When she rose, her fake smile switched back on. "It'll be good to have it out. I'll feel so much better."

She sounded so bright I would have believed it if her eyes

weren't glassy pools of woe. The pain of it, of her losing her baby, made me sick. It would have made me angry once. What had happened to me?

"I'll miss you, if you're gone."

"Huh?" Her eyebrows rose in alarm.

"Just for the days you're gone, I mean." I reached out and twirled one of her perfect ringlets around my finger.

"It's a nice time, after giving birth. I'll put up my feet, relax. After my last baby—"

"This isn't your first?"

She wiped tears from her eyelashes. "It's my third."

"But, why would—? How—?"

"Just *promise* me you'll be good while I'm gone." She cupped my cheek in her hand. "Then I'll see you again."

Love warmed her sad eyes. I needed her, too.

"Why would you get pregnant again when you know what's gonna happen?"

"For the colostrum. That milk you make, at first. That's platinum." She licked her lips, thrall in her voice like she was talking about a superfast sports car. "The best money can buy."

"What for?"

She turned. "Let's put these bottles away."

"Maree, I *need* to know, especially if you're about to disappear, before I go nuts and try to break out through a wall. Where does the milk come from? Where are the animals?"

Worry lines creased her forehead. "You have to find out some time. And it's best if I show you. But we have to get permission. And you gotta promise me, you'll take it okay. That when I'm away, you'll be good. Because I *really* like you. Promise?"

"Um…" How can you promise all that?

"Otherwise, I'm not doing it." She folded her arms and raised her chin, like a snob.

"Maree—"

"Nup."

This was weird. "'Kay, I promise."

The landing, like all the stairwells in this place, had an old-fashioned black phone with a springy cord. She took the receiver off the hook and dialled some numbers. It was in-house only, no outside lines. I'd tried every combination for a dial tone and always got a fuck-off sort of *bleeeep*.

"Can I take Amber to level one?" she asked. "She's ready."

Probably not. Level one. I'd never been past the double doors, unlocked with keycards. Black-clad G-maas stood either side. Almost all the women went in and out of there several times a day, even Maree. Only the newer ones, like me, didn't. Not until after we'd had our first babies.

"Thanks." She hung up the phone and turned to me. "Remember what you promised. Let's go."

Brigit, on the door, smiled and waved us through.

Whatever I thought I'd see, on level one, it was not this.

Rows of women in armchairs, naked from the waist up, with suctioning machines attached to their breasts. Their faces docile, eyes vacant. From the pumps drawing milk from their bodies, cables flowed up through the ceiling, into the factory on level two.

"Welcome to The Barn," Maree said. "Three times a day, we're… milked." Her pitch rose on the last word, as though she could barely believe it either. Her brown eyes met mine, seeking understanding, insisting I be okay with this.

Along the far wall, women lay in beds. Unmoving, unconscious. They were wasted, ancient, wrinkled skins draped over skeletons. Only their breasts were plump on otherwise wraith-thin bodies as the continuous flow of white milk surged through the clear lines. Their jaws hung open, slack, with feeding tubes disappearing into dark, toothless mouths. Their eyes were open, but they did not see.

"Who are they?"

She screwed up her face. "The cows. They take a lot of care. I've been a milkmaid for them. It's the worst. Washing, redressing, turning 'em. Changing colostomy bags."

"But why are they like that?"

"They're the ones that wouldn't settle. The runners. The *fighters*," she said.

Like me.

"Are they drugged?"

"We can't take drugs." Her eyes widened. "Would tarnish our milk. We're Vilque Organics, top-shelf product. They take 'em to Surgical and cut up their brains so they can't do much of anything. They don't even mutter in their sleep. And they never leave here for tropical Grandmother Island. Just milked dry. Before coming in here, I read that if you're brain damaged like that, you're really happy. But they're trapped, locked inside their own bodies."

"And Vilque milks them dry."

"Non-stop. So, naturally, they're some of the biggest producers." She sounded *proud*. "Sometimes they wheel one out, on tasting days—"

"You know this is all so fucked up, right?" I dug my hands into my hair and pulled.

She gently moved my hands down by my wrists, then held my face in her hands, a frown on her brow, voice low. "Amber, you promised," she hissed. She raised her nose a little. "I can't afford to know that it's fucked up, and neither can you."

But it was. The most fucked up thing I'd ever seen.

Baby, if you can hear me, and I know you can, you have to come find me. One day, far in the future, find out what's going on. Baby, be smart. Be clever. Be careful. Don't end up in here. Come and tear this place down. Burn it to the ground, even with us in it. Death would be better than this.

The next day, I lay in my bed. Another day when the car park filled below. A tasting day. I missed Damo. I missed Zarraffa's ristrettos, ice cream on buttermilk cookies, and walking barefoot in the park. Grass is cool-soft in the shade, or crunchy and warm in the sun.

"Are you okay?" Maree waddled in and offered me an egg sandwich.

I leant up on an elbow, shaking my head. "When the car park

fills up, who are they? Fiddlesticks said it's a tasting."

Maree sniggered. "Oh, of sorts." Her tone was dirty. She leant close and whispered, her breath smelling sweet, of strawberries. "Some men don't like their milk cold, pasteurised. They like it fresh from the tit."

That took me a minute.

"Some...like to pretend to be babies." She smirked. "This one guy—"

"We're whored out?"

"No. We volunteer. Yeah, the men pay. But that's how you make babies, dumbo. And pay for your ticket to Grandmother Island. There's babies there, you know. Real families. You can talk to kids at the beach, in the parks—"

"But the men, don't they care? Don't they want their babies?"

"If you get pregnant, they don't let you go again till the baby's out."

"And you didn't tell the guy about it?"

"They never put me with him again. Can't say I was sorry, the nappy-wearing freak."

"They kept you away from him because you might've told him. And he mightn't have liked not knowing where his kid went. He might've helped you get—"

"God, Amber, for a snarky bitch, can you be that dumb?" Her eyes shone with love and sadness, resignation. She threaded her swollen fingers through mine. "They'll never let us out. Those men come here for milk and a kinky fuck. You think they'd help us?"

Nope. And even if one would, I wasn't going to let some weirdo drink milk from my boob.

*B*aby. *I want to tell you about your dad. I want to tell you about your mum, too. I flunked English at Bethania State High, but did good in maths and cooking. I worked at Yatala Drive-In, selling drinks and food at the shop. Doubled the profits in the first week, with new donut deals and discounts.*

Your dad, Damo, went for my cola spider and double donut combo. Two weeks later, we made you at Mount Gravatt lookout. Some things don't take long, hey.

He'd broken up with his ex and didn't want anything serious, but he was a good kisser, yeah, he was. Alone at the lookout, late, I rode him like a cowgirl, under the Southern Cross, on the bonnet of his car.

Maybe that's not the sort of thing you're supposed to tell your baby. But you should know you are the child of a great love. Hot and magnetic. On fire.

We weren't boyfriend and girlfriend, not yet, but we'd catch up nearly every night.

I wonder if he missed me.

If he worried about what happened.

What my parents told him when he come to pick me up, Sunday night.

He probably has a new girlfriend, by now. I guess I do, too. Maree is sweet.

Bub wouldn't come out. Smart kid knew what a fucked-up place this was. Two weeks overdue, she was staying put.

"They'll come for you soon," Maree whispered, dark circles under her eyes, biting her lip as I ate my cereal.

She was different. Losing her last kid kind of broke her. I'd held her while she cried all night. Kissed her salty tears. Maybe I was to blame, for making her face reality. I tried telling her jokes and massaging her feet, slipping her extra bits of chocolate, but she was permanently a little bit dead inside.

When my day came, the nurse approached with two G-maas. Brigit was one. The other tickled the taser on her belt.

"Induction time. Come with us to Surgical."

Maree was tearing up, her bottom lip quivering.

"I'll be okay, love," I said to her. "Be good. Come see me, after."

I rose, nodded to the nurse, went waddling behind her on swollen feet. In the surgical ward, I was given a blue gown with a slit up the back that showed my arse. As instructed, I sat back on the bed, spread my legs, and the nurse reached gloved fingers inside my vadge. She rubbed some gel deep up the end.

"Ow."

"This will get labour started. Save your moaning. By the time we're done, you'll feel like a ripped pin cushion."

"Why are you so mean?" Brigit asked.

"Would you rather me lie and tell her that it won't hurt, when it will?" She looked at me. "Relax, you won't feel a thing."

With a long hook, she reached up inside me. A pop as she broke through the skin of my amniotic sac. Fluid flowed out of me onto the bed. A needle dug through the skin on the back of my hand, into my vein, and she attached a drip which led to a bag of liquid.

"Hold on for the ride, contractions are coming." She patted my arm.

I could feel my heart beating fast, my throat tight. This was going to be bad.

Labour hit. Waves of pain, crashing like a storm, hitching up my uterus muscles and thinning them out, shoving bub down. I gripped the bedrails, moaning through contractions.

Bub descended, enormous, ripping me in half. Then it was out, crying, on the bed. I reached for it, but they cut the cord, scooped up my baby and whisked it away. Love split and exploded in my chest like a starburst, growing exponentially.

"Give it to me!" I cried. "I want my baby! I need it."

I struggled to get up, but they held me down. I needed to get that crying mouth to my breast. It cried. *Wahhh, wah-hah. Mummy,* it seemed to say. *I need you.* I needed its humid weight in my arms, its burning outrage for being torn from a safe womb, from warmth and love, into a fucked-up world. I needed to comfort it at my breast.

"Down," ordered the nurse. "The afterbirth is coming."

"I need my baby," I cried.

She patted my shoulder. "It's going to a better place."

"You make it sound dead!"

"A home. It will be fine," she snapped. "Better than you."

"Is it a boy or a girl?" I asked.

She shook her head. "Sorry, love. It's a girl."

"What's wrong with it being a girl?"

She just stared at me, my blood smeared across her cheek.

That night, the chaos had settled into a miserable ache. They served me veal for dinner. I cried with Maree, silent tears, holding hands, both of us staring into space.

Baby, I'm still talking to you, even though you're gone. You're far away. Not dead. That's the one thing that'd kill me. Can you still hear me? We have a connection, you and me. If you could ever hear me, maybe distance doesn't matter.

I have faith in you, baby. That you're better than my parents, better'n me. Each one that comes after has the chance to be better. Be great, baby, and strong. Win. And if you can come back for me, we'll burn this place down.

"**D**elivered, at last." Fiddington strolled into my room just after sunrise. She'd kept her distance lately. "Ready to become a productive part of our community? Hmm, you should have eaten your dinner."

"Would you have eaten it, if it could've been your kid?"

She sneered. "It was soy protein, idiot. You think we would waste real meat on you? That we could get away with killing babies?" She squeezed a wrist inside her other hand. "As if no one would notice. People *care* about babies. Their whole life lies ahead of them."

It was single mothers like me that they didn't care about.

"So, are you going to settle down and plug in?" She nodded to the expressing cups hanging on the wall. "Or do I call the surgeons and have you unplugged?" She mimed pulling a cord out of the back of her head.

I didn't know you could hate someone—something—so much, and still do it. Hating her, hating myself... I took the cold metal attachments in my hands. I pressed the hard plastic around my nipples. They took my breasts like hungry mouths, squeezing my engorged glands painfully.

"There." I clenched my jaw as they began to suck…to suck the life out of me.

As revolting as it was, it also felt good. Horrible, yet pleasurable. It wasn't just my milk. It was me being consumed. Swallowed.

Lips smacking, around me.

Gulp. Sigh.

Those sounds. That was me going up those pipes. Product. Profit.

Fiddington smirked. "Good girl. That colostrum, precious stuff. Every mil worth a thousand pennies. You can pay off your board-debt and save for retirement on Grandmother Island."

Even she couldn't look me in the eye.

We'd waved off the oldest G-maas and some cows two weeks ago. Sent them on their way in a minibus. Two days later, a truckload of *Mama's Own* meat rolled in, ready to be canned. A coincidence. Right.

Fiddington thought she'd won, but this wasn't over. It was never going to be over. Not until I'd burned this whole place down. One day, bub would come back for me. I'd told her every night. I'd sown those wishes, like seeds, into her dreams. I'd keep talking to her. Somehow, she'd hear me. She'd make a better world.

Being a woman was hell. This place had taken the worst and distilled it. Birth is pain and loss, blood and mess, but at the heart of it—*birth is hope*. These things attached to my tits, they might be sucking the life out of me, but I would never give up. Not while my heart still beat.

ENVELOPES

MATT TIGHE

The little girl from the end unit is riding her plastic tricycle on the footpath. She is really flying too, hitting the uneven joints in the concrete hard enough to make her head jolt and her pigtails whip up and down.

Renee smiles at her absently, but most of her attention is on the pale blue envelope she has just found in her letterbox. It has her name on the front in big, hand-printed block letters with too much space between each one.

R E N E E.

No last name. No return address, no stamp. She stares at it, one hand on the swollen curve of her belly.

No one has her address, and no one sends real mail these days anyway, not that this looks like real mail. Renee only checks for discount coupons. The old-style metal letterboxes lining the footpath are by far the nicest thing about where she now lives. The units behind her are a line of low, blind faces, any character they may have had long gone, leached away by the sameness of all the different lives within. It dulls Renee in a strange way when she looks back at her home, at her neighbours' homes, and tries to think of what will come next for her. But the letterboxes near the footpath—she likes them. They stand straight and bright and true on their little posts like something out of an old television show, where children run home after school and people smile at each other.

"Slow down, girl! You are going to hurt someone."

That is Renee's neighbour, Miss Emily, who is suddenly there and glaring at the tricycle rider. That's how she likes to be addressed, with the "Miss" and the "Emily". She is thin and hard and altogether unpleasant. Her hair is a grey perm that looks clamped to her scalp, and her skin is tight with age, almost translucent. She is in her nightgown, as she always seems to be, and is standing next to the lush rosebush that grows in the narrow rectangle of garden bed between her letterbox and Renee's.

Technically, these little bits of garden are common space, but everyone knows about Miss Emily's rosebush. She acts like all the common space is hers, although this yelling is new. Probably it's new. Renee hasn't been here long enough to be sure.

Renee turns away from her frowning neighbour and tears the envelope open. There is a crisp ten-dollar note inside, along with a single sheet of blue paper, the same shade as the envelope. There are more words printed there, short and succinct and strange.

For the next envelope, scream an obscenity right where you stand.

"What have you got there?" Miss Emily asks.

She has left her eyeballing of the girl and moved close. Too close, right next to Renee's letterbox, where she can peer at what Renee is holding.

Renee almost tells the old lady it is none of her business. Actually, she almost tells her to fuck off, but she bites her tongue. Renee is new to the units, and now that Jaimie has left, she is very aware of how alone she is. Just her and her swollen belly and those sharp pains she has been having. There may come a time in the not-too-distant future when she may need help, even from someone she dislikes.

Besides, the note is just some sort of scam, or weird marketing thing, or someone's obtuse attempt at YouTube fame. She holds it out, and Miss Emily bends forward to peer at it.

"Huh," she says, and then spins quickly as the tricycle flies by. "Get off the footpath, you stupid waste of a child!" she snaps, so suddenly that Renee jerks back a little. The girl jerks too, and almost comes unstuck. She swerves, and Miss Emily cries out, high and sharp, an emaciated bird of prey screeching an alarm. "My roses! You little bitch!"

The bush was never in any danger, but the words are enough—

too much—for the girl. There is a flash of wide, brimming eyes and a quivering bottom lip as the girl dismounts and runs for her own unit. She leaves the tricycle in the grass by the footpath.

"God, you didn't have to be so..." Renee starts, and then falters.

So what? Bitchy? Vile? She is suddenly angry, maybe even furious on the girl's behalf. It was excessive, even for the sour old woman, but Renee doesn't know how best to respond. Miss Emily doesn't give her a chance to figure it out. She sniffs in the direction of the vanquished child and then walks off. As she disappears through her own front door, Renee reads the note again.

Ten dollars is ten dollars, and ten dollars is a lot right now.

What a nasty old woman.

She draws in a deep breath.

"Fuck!" she screams, trying to ignore the initial flush of embarrassment, the worry that someone will appear and admonish her. But no one comes, and she thinks again of Miss Emily screaming at the little girl. "You old fucking bitch!" she screams, the ten dollars clutched in one hand, the handwritten note in the other.

This time, she doesn't worry. This time, something tight unknots inside her. She is flooded with frustration and fear, and more anger too, anger at where she is, at what is happening to her. She doesn't care if Miss Emily can hear her.

It feels good to scream.

Renee wants to drive to the coffee shop and spend the ten dollars on a caramel latte and a muffin, even if she isn't sure that her rust-bucket car would make it. Instead, she puts the money in the big jar on top of the fridge, the one labelled "Baby". The one that is still mostly empty.

Then she looks at her phone for a while. No missed calls from her parents. No calls from friends. No calls from Jamie; not that she is hoping for any from him.

The unit smells of his cigarettes and a hint of mould, but the rent is paid for the next month, and Jaimie's disappearing act means she has all the furniture, even if it is mostly rubbish. She still needs so much stuff, though. God. A mountain of things. A cot, a change table. No, a change mat would be cheaper. Baby clothes. Nappies. What else? She doesn't even fathom.

She should have known Jaimie was a waste when he held off so long before letting her move in. She should have known he wasn't really in it with her when he kept saying they would get all that stuff later, that they had plenty of time. Now he is gone, and the stay-away money her father gave her is nearly gone as well, and they won't give her shifts at the stationery store anymore. The last time she called, Tony the assistant manager told her to stop. That it wasn't *dignified*, as if a pimple-faced twenty-year-old in a fifty-dollar suit understood what that word meant.

Renee looks at the ten-dollar bill in the jar again.

For your next envelope…

The baby shifts, and a star-bright flash of pain shoots across her abdomen. It is there and gone before she can even gasp. Maybe it's one of those Braxton things, that sound like nothing more than extra cruelty piled on top of a shitty situation.

She will have to get down to the midwife clinic.

And get food. And do laundry, and go online to see about benefits. Why hadn't she done that already? She has to do something. She has to do more. More, more, more. Fuck Jaimie. Fuck her parents. Fuck Miss Emily, the nasty old piece of work.

She wants to scream again, but she doesn't think it will make her feel any better this time.

It is the next morning. Renee sits at the kitchen table, the new envelope fresh from her letterbox next to her plate of dry toast. This envelope is burnt orange, the colour of the bile her father no doubt tastes whenever he thinks of his daughter. *If* he thinks of her.

R E N E E.

In one hand, she is clutching the one-hundred-dollar bill that was in the envelope. One hundred won't go far, but there will be no more dry toast today. In the other hand, she holds the note that was with the money.

For the next envelope, smash the girl's plastic tricycle.

"This is sick," Renee says aloud. "It has to be some online prank."

Something being filmed, perhaps. She wonders if she is going to be caught on the internet doing something nasty.

But that would mean destroying the girl's toy, and that sounds too much like something Miss Emily might do. She tells herself that, even as she is doing the maths. Ten becomes one hundred. Could there be another? Would it be a thousand? That's food. That's a cot, and a pram if she is careful. It is a baby seat for her tired and rattling Corolla hatchback.

It doesn't matter. She can't do it. But she decides she will get her muffin after all.

Renee doesn't get much further than her front door. Her stupid car sits in her allocated space, looking oddly canted due to one very flat tyre. She tries to bend down to look and gets another of those shooting pains across her abdomen, like a belt of broken glass cinched tight.

"Fuck," she whispers, and stands up straight, breathing deeply as the pain subsides a little.

There might be a spare tyre in the back of the car, tucked away somewhere, but she'd have to work out how to change it, and she can't even move properly. She'll have to call someone. There goes her hundred, and probably more.

She blinks away sudden tears. As she turns to go inside, she sees the tricycle sitting in the grass near the rosebush. *For your next envelope…*

As soon as the soft fade of dusk is gone, Renee goes back outside. The tricycle is still there in the pale light of the street lamps. Ten became one hundred. Maybe the next envelope would have a thousand dollars in it, a gift from some perverse little god of envelopes and grey morality.

It's sick. Someone is probably recording her. She stares at the plastic toy, and tries not to feel her back aching, her feet aching, her bladder twingeing already even though she just went to the toilet. She tells herself the baby is not moving, and there are not little ripples of almost-pain around her belly.

She won't do it.

She tries to ignore the emptiness that is the unit behind her, as well as the gnawing emptiness inside her that is one-part hunger, three-parts the dried husk of hope.

She won't do it.

She walks back to her ailing and now undriveable Corolla and opens the boot. She can't see a spare tyre, but there is a tyre iron, dusty and spotted with rust. She picks it up.

She won't do it.

She walks back and grunts as she kneels on the grass, ignoring her own racing heart and the pull of her misbalanced body trying to tip her forward. There is a flash of pain behind her navel, but she doesn't straighten. The units are quiet, and the street is empty. The tyre iron is heavy.

She swings it.

The front wheel shatters like the cheap, sun-faded plastic it is. It probably would have broken in a week or two anyway. Swinging the tyre iron is suddenly so much easier than everything else, especially thinking.

She hits the tricycle again, hitching in her breath because she is big and uncomfortable and kneeling on the ground, not because she is suddenly flushed and sure.

And hits again, giving a little cry up to the night as the thing inside of her uncurls again, releasing her pain and rage.

"Ah!" she gasps with the next swing, and the next, and the next. "Ah, ah, ah!"

The thud of the metal bar jars her arms, and her belly tightens in a rippling wave that is both pain and the promise of pain to come. And further down, between her legs, she is hot—hot in a way she has not been since Jaimie. The tricycle is in fragments, splinters, but she keeps swinging, the thudding of the bar running up her arms and down her body. Frantic. Hard. Sure. She is grunting, soft expulsions of air that hurt but feel good too.

Fuck, she wants to scream. *FUCK!*

"Ahh!" she finally whisper-sobs instead, as the rage and the heat and the pounding all burst inside of her, and she drives the tyre iron into the ground. Her folded legs tremble, and she leans forward until her forehead touches the cool grass, and the hot tears run down her cheeks.

It is done.

Renee wakes to blood. Not much, but more than she thinks could be called "spotting". Her back aches, and her forearms are sore, and her abdomen is weirdly tight, even for the balloon it is. She showers and dresses slowly, using the plastic chair she has put in the bathroom so she doesn't have to bend too much.

Her bloodied underwear goes in the wastebasket.

She needs to visit the midwife clinic or the doctor. Maybe the emergency room. She could use the hundred and get a taxi, but she needs to also get the tyre on her car fixed. And she needs groceries. And the baby stuff. All those things, but it is really just help she needs.

Instead of thinking about any of that, Renee goes out to her letterbox. The short walk stretches out some of the tightness that loops low around her front, and by the time she gets there, she is not considering the hospital or clinic anymore. It will be okay. A bit of blood is common enough, she knows that, and last night was…eventful. She doesn't need the shards of plastic scattered in the grass to remind her of that.

There is another envelope. This one is a dark red, the colour of clotted blood. It is thick and heavy, and without thinking, she puts one hand on the letterbox to steady herself.

"What is it this time?"

She snaps her head around, and the fading tightness in her belly returns, almost like a cramp. Miss Emily is too close again, peering at the envelope in Renee's hand. She is holding a gardening hoe across her body, almost hugging it.

"It's nothing," Renee says, breathing out slowly, willing the pain away. She puts the envelope down by her side.

Miss Emily sniffs and then points at the smashed tricycle.

"People are horrible. They just need a chance to show it." Her gaze drifts down Renee's front, slow enough that it feels like a thin, bony finger tracing a line along her abdomen. "Most deserve what they get."

"No, they don't," Renee says, and as she speaks, her own gaze shifts back to the smashed pieces of tricycle. The envelope is heavy in her hand. Ten became a hundred. A hundred could become a thousand. "And you wouldn't know what anyone deserves, anyway."

"Because I'm just an old fucking bitch?" Miss Emily asks, and smiles.

It is a hard smile, a knife slash across her face. Miss Emily doesn't wait for a reply. She turns her back on Renee and, after a few steps, she is hoeing at the soft ground around her roses. She is fast, stronger than her age and thin frame suggests, and she rams the hoe down to tear out small chunks of dark earth and weeds, over and over.

Ah, ah, ah! Renee thinks, and flushes.

Renee sits in the kitchen with the red envelope on the table in front of her. It is thick and heavy, and surely holds the thousand. She hasn't opened it.

R E N E E.

Ah, ah ah.

People are horrible, given the chance.

Renee almost picks up the envelope, but grabs her phone instead.

She doesn't want Jaimie involved anymore, doesn't want him in any way, really, but her arms still ache, and her belly hurts again, and the envelopes are scaring her.

Because…because she wants the next one. And the one after that.

I need help, she wants to text.

I don't want to be a horrible person. She can't text that.

Finally—*I need money. For the baby.*

She waits at the table for a reply. And waits.

There is no reply. There is nothing but the empty unit, the shadow of pain deep inside her, and her thoughts.

And the next envelope.

She rips the flimsy thing open. The wad of folded hundreds she pulls out is both heavy and not heavy enough. The red sheet of paper tells her what to do.

For the next envelope, your neighbour's rosebush.

A thousand could become ten thousand. That's all the baby stuff she can think of and more besides. Maybe a better crap-box of a car. Maybe she could even move house.

She doubles over suddenly, pain screaming through her but then receding, gone as quickly as it came. Something is very much not right, and she has to take care of it. She will. Of course, she will, but first...

Fuck her parents. Fuck Jaimie.

And fuck Miss Emily. It's just a rosebush, and the old bitch deserves it.

It is late enough that little girls and old nasties should be sound asleep. There is a deep ache that thrums across Renee's midriff and all the way around to her spine, and she thinks she may be bleeding again. She will check after. Spotting is nothing to worry about. Neither are pains—she is carrying a damn person around, after all, and she has been exerting herself. But she will call a taxi or something anyway, and get herself to the hospital for a check-up. Soon.

In the pale glow of the street lamps, the letterboxes are grey memories of their daytime selves, while the row of units sits behind her, squat and black and bloated, staring blankly with curtained eyes. Beyond the frame of her own letterbox, Renee can see pieces of plastic—barely visible remnants of the night before. She wishes she couldn't see them at all, because it is too easy to also see the girl with bouncing pigtails, her eyes wet with tears, her mouth trembling.

People are horrible. They just need a chance to show it.

It is enough to make her hesitate, but then she sees Miss

Emily's hoe. It is there, right *there*, lying on the grass next to the bush. Renee can't recall if her neighbour left it behind, does not even know if Miss Emily usually puts it away somewhere, but now it is like a sign.

Ah, ah, ah, she thinks, and does a stupid half-bend-squat to pick it up. Her back screams and there is a shifting inside her, down low, that makes her legs tremble.

But the hoe is like the tyre iron, heavy and certain and ready, and she is suddenly sure she can take care of this quickly. Then she will take care of herself and the baby. She will take herself off for a check-up and some rest, and then she will look forward to the next envelope.

She steps closer and swings at the base of the bush. The stem shakes, and the leaves shiver in the dim light, but it is not like the brittle sun-faded plastic of the tricycle. The stem gives too much with the strike, and Renee's arms are far from fresh. She is exhausted already, and that tightness is closing in around her swollen belly like a tide of hot, black water.

She sobs and swings again. The hoe was there, it should have been perfect, a sign, but it is not right for the job. Nothing would be; nothing is right for a pregnant woman with sore feet and aching breasts and something wrong about the tightening in her lower abdomen, and she is crying louder now, ashamed and frustrated and so *angry*.

Angry at her parents. At Jaimie. At that nasty bitch next door, with her hard smile and her lingering gaze. But angrier at herself. Why has she left everything so late, telling herself nothing was wrong, not really, doing nothing until she has to grasp at some strange note in the letterbox like it is a lifeline and not a noose? Why is she doing this?

She drops the hoe and grabs at the rosebush, one hand around the thick stem and one around a large branch. Thorns puncture her skin, pinpricks of pain that ramp up her anger into something incandescent.

"Fuck!" Renee screams and shakes the bush. More leaves fall, a shower of them, and the bush finally shifts slightly. "You bitch!"

And then there is a deep thump that reverberates from her

side all the way through her body, driving the air from her. She falls sideways and hits the ground hard, instinctively twisting so that she lands on her side more than her front, but there is still a horrible sense of compression inside her. That tightening around her front blooms into a tearing, wrenching agony.

"Ah!" she screams and rolls fully onto her back.

Something has let go, and there is wetness between her legs, and heat. Far too much of both—this is not spotting. The pain is ripping through her, a ravening thing that has been pent up too long.

Miss Emily is standing over her, a silhouette against the street lights.

"Help!" she gasps. "Miss Emily, help me."

There is no response, and that is wrong, more wrong than what Renee has been doing, more wrong than even the pain.

Miss Emily steps forward, and the weak illumination from the closest street light falls across her. She is holding the hoe. Renee realises that Miss Emily has hit her with it. Obviously not with the blade—because there would have been so much more damage—but there is a sharp icicle of pain in her side, and Renee is pretty sure at least one rib is cracked. Any other time, that pain would have been all she could focus on. Now, it barely registers.

"You horrible girl," Miss Emily says. "I understood you doing what the first envelope asked. I certainly saw no lasting harm doing what mine asked, and yelling at that stupid girl on her tricycle. I had wanted to yell at her for so long anyway."

She takes a small step closer.

"The next was more of a problem. It wanted me to make your car undriveable. I wasn't going to do that, not even to someone who called me what you did. But then I saw you last night, smashing that girl's tricycle, and I realised you don't deserve the money."

"You fucking bitch!" Renee screams. The rage floods back, piercing the pain for a moment. "I'm losing my fucking baby here!"

Miss Emily flinches a little but then smiles that hard, sharp smile of hers. "Do you know her parents accused me of doing it? They stood there on my doorstep and told me they would have gone to the police if they'd had any evidence. Her mother said I was an old bitch that should just die. I didn't tell them it was you, though. Because I'm not horrible." She bends down slightly, her eyes dark. "I'll help you. My last envelope said to make sure you don't hurt my roses, and I guess I've done that."

Miss Emily has been getting envelopes as well. It must mean something—Renee tries to think, but the pain rips through her again, obliterating everything, tearing the dark night, the envelopes, the universe itself into tattered remnants. The pain lasts for an eternity, which is only a moment. When it eases a little, Miss Emily is still standing over her, unmoving, unmoved.

Renee bares her teeth in a snarl and kicks out.

Her foot connects with Miss Emily's thin shin just below the hem of her robe. There is a *crack*, and the old lady screams as she staggers sideways. Her damaged leg folds and she goes down hard, her head connecting with Renee's letterbox. There is a hollow metallic clang, almost like something from a slapstick comedy, and the letterbox itself slews sideways, hanging from the pole as if it is the real victim in all of this.

The old lady is lying close by with the side of her face pressed to the ground. The one eye that Renee can see is open, but the lid is fluttering spasmodically. The thin, papery skin at her temple has torn loose, and in the poor light, the side of her cheek is black with sheeting blood. The collar of her robe is wet and sodden with it.

"Uh," she grunts at Renee. "Uh, uh."

"Ah!" Renee screams into the old woman's face, as the pain rips through her yet again.

What she thought had been agony before was nothing. This, *this* is an ocean of pain, a deep and bottomless world in which nothing but nightmares and horrors can thrive. There is wetness between her legs, more wetness, God, so much of it, so far beyond what should be, and the pain is going to destroy her. She needs to get up. She needs to help Miss Emily, help herself, help the baby.

There is a low sound above her head, the sound of something sliding through the canted letterbox. A moment later, there is a heavy thump as an envelope falls to the ground.

It is black, midnight-black in the weak light, and thick. As thick as a wad of ten thousand dollars. Her name is written on the envelope in stark, white, block letters.

R E N E E.

She needs to get up. Her phone is inside. She needs to help Miss Emily, and call an ambulance for herself. The pain tears through her anew, and she screams again. God, she screams so much, so loudly, and now there are voices, lights coming on across the road and in the units behind her.

Neighbours are coming. Help is coming.

And the next envelope is right there. There will be the money. There will also be the next note, asking her to do something awful. Ten thousand could become a hundred thousand, she thinks, as she looks at Miss Emily's open and blankly staring eye.

And Renee knows. She understands.

People are horrible. They just need a chance to show it.

Renee reaches for the envelope.

FLESH OF MY FLESH

BEN MATTHEWS

*Whoever eats of my flesh and drinks of my
blood remains in me, and I in them.*
—*Jesus Christ, John 6:53-58*

Once your prey dies, how successfully you can dress it
depends on your skill with a knife. Killing, that's the easy
part: *Wham! Bam! Thank you, Ma'am.* Or, when you hunt deer:
Blam! Wham! Thank you, Bambi. A skilled hunter can skin and gut
a deer in less than five minutes.

What's the rush?

Because the instant it dies, your prey starts to cook. Its blood
roasts it from the inside out. Organs broil. Bowels ferment and
expand with gas. Body heat creates the perfect breeding ground
in the deer's corpse for the necrobiome, the microorganisms of
decomposition. Body heat, stagnant blood, and dead meat; the
perfect breeding ground for hundreds of millions of bacteria.
Breeding faster than rabbits, the bacteria fornicate, feast, and
spoil the meat you worked so hard for.

To save it, you need to cool the corpse as quickly as possible.
Cool it from the inside out. You need to drain the blood and split
open the body like a Rorschach print. *Tell me, now, what can you
see?* Preparing a dead deer like this is called "dressing game".
Remember, a skilled hunter will dress a fully grown deer in
less than five minutes. Most people can't dress themselves that
quickly.

I can only pray that Andrew Sutton can dress game fast enough that the meat doesn't spoil. But Sutton is not a hunter.

And I am not a deer.

Sutton has an advantage. I am willing. I let him drain my blood while I'm still alive. Most of it is in a bucket, on the floor of his purpose-built cool room. The rest swirls around me in the bathtub. A Van Gogh of pink paint spreading across the water's surface. There's more blood in the water than in my veins. My heart pumps fumes. The only thing keeping my head above water is that I've hooked the base of my skull on the lip of the bathtub.

Lying in the cold, pinkish water, I stare at the ceiling. Listen to Sutton preparing for the task that lies ahead of him.

There's a documentary about hunting that's playing somewhere in the house.

Sutton sharpens his knife.

Shick!

The hunter speaks back to a question I do not hear.

"There's nothing cruel about hunting. I'm a predator. It's prey."

Shick!

"It simply is."

Shick!

"Hunting is a victimless crime."

Shick!

Shick!

Shick!

How did the cannibal introduce himself?
It's nice to meat you!

You can find anyone online. Find anything. Find anyone willing to do anything.

The hard part? Not getting caught. Nothing spoils a meal like the boys in blue knocking on your door at dinner time. Luckily for me, Sutton is all over it.

VPN.

Blocked search engines.

Throwaway emails.

Burner phones.

When it comes to computer security, Sutton wrote the book.

It's easy to forget that about psychopaths. Just because they're twisted, just because they get off on torturing victims or eating human flesh, doesn't mean they're careless. Sutton, my psychopath, my genius.

I can learn a lot from him.

At first, it's just like online dating.

"What do you do?"

"I do blah-blah-blah. How about you?"

"I'm a blah-blah."

"Great. How long have you yada-yada-yada?"

And so on and so forth.

You must do it. After all, you can't trust anyone without sharing a few tasty morsels about yourself. Without serving up your very own candid canapés. "I'll eat yours if you'll eat mine." *How else do you get to know me? How else can I trust you?*

With Sutton and me, it's different. We skip the entrees. I need the main course: I need to know the reasons behind his deepest, darkest desires. He needs the main course: me.

We're starving.

I send him photos of my body with incision lines sketched in permanent marker. He sends me a burner phone and deletes our online profiles. The phone signals no more flirting.

Forget: "Do you like long walks on the beach?"

I ask, "How do you know you want to eat someone?"

"It's my dream. It's been my dream for as long as I can remember."

How can you trust someone if you don't know their secrets?

I'm running out of time. Sutton is desperate. He spills his guts. I don't. *Time enough for that later.*

"If I don't get to eat someone soon, I'm going to kill myself. I can't go on like this." He's chewing his lip over the phone. *Does it taste good?* "Whatever I do, all I can think about is what other people would taste like. This morning, I was in the lift with a guy who had been jogging. The sweat was dripping off him. I don't think he showered the previous night. His flavour filled the lift. If I wasn't holding my briefcase, if I didn't press my other hand up against the wall, I would have caressed him. Pushed him against the side of that tin can and sucked the sweat from his flesh." Sutton swallows deep. "The longer I try to fight the urge, the worse it gets. I need this."

I get it. I really do. Except I don't tell him. It's easy to forget that while it's a craving felt by a psychopath—even a mixed-up, muddled-up madman—he's not an idiot. I can't afford to scare him off. You only need to see the canapés when they are served. You don't want to know how they are prepared.

I need Sutton. Sutton wants me. Good enough. Beggars can't be choosers.

Meals can't be picky.

I am running out of time.

What do you need? Not a whole lot.
Water, shelter, food.
Sutton won't die if I don't let him eat me.
Water, shelter, food.
Sutton won't die if he never fulfils his lifelong ambition.
Water, shelter, food.
Sutton won't die. But I will.

Sutton's ultimate dream, the cannibal's dream, is a joke. It's not even about eating human flesh. Not that he, or any other cannibal, knows that. If they did, they'd all be vegetarians. If you think it's about the meal, you might as well think going on a date is all about your meal too. It's the same for the cannibal.

It's not the meal that matters. For the cannibal, it's about choosing a partner to share your body with. Or, more specifically, to share their body with you.

Beneath it all, under the flesh and bone, under the cold cuts and sweetbreads, the cannibal only wants a companion. To know they have devoured another is to know that from this moment forwards, their meal has become part of their body. From this moment forwards, they will never again be alone.

It's not water.

It's not shelter.

It's not food.

Sutton doesn't need this.

I do.

I need Sutton.

I need Sutton to do this.

Otherwise, I'm dead meat.

"**W**hat do you think it will be like?"

"Think of a lemon," Sutton says. "An enormous ripe lemon. Yellow as the sun. Bursting with juice. So perfect you can smell it. So sweet and sour you can taste it in the air. Now, imagine you are sawing into it with a knife. A frosty lemon zest, a citrus mist, fills the air and fills your senses. Can you taste it?"

"Yes."

"The idea of cooking and eating human flesh has the exact same effect upon me," Sutton says, swallowing deeply, "ever since I learned about cannibalism."

When life gives you lemons...

How can you trust someone if you don't share your greatest desires with them?

Sutton learned about cannibalism when he was eleven. In the pages of an encyclopaedia, he found an article about a tribe in Papua New Guinea. A tribe that believed in demonic possession.

A tribe that believed the only way to rid a person of demonic possession was to kill them and eat them. *Wham! Bam! Thank you, Satan!*

"When I read it, I was overpowered by the scent of hot, not-long-dead flesh as it was cut, prepared, and roasted in the tropical heat. I could feel the fats and juices on my tongue. I knew then that, until I could taste it myself, I would never be happy. I need it."

You want it.

"I've never been able to look at another person without needing to taste them. Bite their flesh, savour their odour. I thought sex would make it better, but it only made it worse. If I don't do this… I…I can't go on. I know that."

You want it.

"Are you hungry now?"

Sutton groans into the receiver. "More than anything."

His words don't convince me. His tone does. *This is a man who truly believes in his perverse fantasy.* The story of consuming tropical human flesh has him quaffing great mouthfuls of saliva. I can almost feel it flecking my face through the phone.

This is the one. The one to be one with my flesh. To carry me within him.

Beggars can't be choosers. Meals can't be picky.

I am running out of time.

Pablo Picasso said, "Learn the rules like a pro, so you can break them like an artist."

How you dress your game is up to you. Until you're an artist, follow what you're told in your hunting magazines. Listen to the experts who write columns in hunting blogs. Copy the professionals who make video tutorials online. If you ruin a deer's corpse, you can go out and shoot another one. *Blam! Wham! Thank you, Bambi.* With a human body, with my body, there will be no second chance.

Sutton memorises the steps to prepare my corpse once I'm "gone". Drones through them, day after day, reciting them like the

"Our Father". His tools are laid out on the kitchen table:
  Field-dressing knife
  Bone saw
  Hatchet
  Heavy-duty pruning shears
  Tarpaulin
  Buckets
  Meat hook.

When I exit the train station, Andrew Sutton leaps out of his car. His eyes are bursting from his head. He shakes like he's got kuru.

"I can't believe you're here!" Sutton clenches his arms around me, folding his chin into my neck. He smells delicious, with a heady aroma of sweat, adrenaline, cheap soap, and woody cologne.

"Hi," I croak.

"Are you okay?"

I nod. The motion almost makes me fall over; I am that light-headed. *I am starving.* Plus, cannibal etiquette demands that the meal doesn't eat any food for eight hours preceding their consumption. An empty stomach keeps the meat clean. Fresh. There's nothing worse than eating someone who tastes like burgers and chicken wings.

"You look amazing."

I glance around the station. "You are sure the cameras can't see us?"

"Not well enough to get a decent image. I write the codes for those kinds of cameras. They are trash."

I nod.

Sutton tastes my unease. "Come on, I'll drive you home."

I follow him out of the station into the cool night, affecting an easy stroll. If you saw us, you would see just a normal pair of guys wandering to a car. Sutton doesn't look like a murderer.

I am no lamb.

Sutton opens the door of his sedan for me. Once he's settled behind the wheel, he turns to me and sighs with contentment. "Did you want air conditioning? Or I can open a window." He turns on the air conditioning and opens a window.

I shake my head.

"Sorry," he says, and hands me a thick fabric bag.

I put it over my head, and tie it shut. *You can't be too safe.* Then I recline the chair and lie back. To anyone driving past, Sutton would look like an ordinary computer programmer driving home after a dull workday. Not a man about to fulfill his wildest dream.

"You can sit upright if you want," he says.

"I don't think that's a good idea."

"Oh, yeah, no, you're right. I can get you some water? I didn't bring any...uh, I can pull over at a service station—"

"And leave a record of where we've been? I'm fine."

"Uh...okay. I have lots of fresh water at home."

I'm running out of time! I rub my belly to suppress my hunger. It doesn't work. I keep rubbing.

"I can't believe you're here." Sutton's voice trembles. When I don't reply, he goes on, "I deleted all our internet history after you left your home. Canceled your VPN. You've destroyed your laptop?"

"Mm-hmm."

When Sutton speaks again, he sounds hurt. "If you...you know, if you don't want to, then...then I understand. I won't make you do anything you don't want to do."

"I want this."

"That's what they all say," he says, dejected. "If you've changed your mind...if I'm not what you expected...I can drop you back if you don't want to. We can stop at any time."

"I know." I press my hand between his legs. "Pull over."

Afterwards, we drive in silence. If you want someone to trust you, let them have sex with you. Andrew doesn't ask me to put the bag back over my head. He sucks his bottom lip where I bit him. Now I'm the one trembling. *I can't wait much longer.*

I can feel the love radiating out from Sutton. It's wonderful. After less than an hour, we arrive at his house. I could describe the abode to you, but why bother? He's fucked me. It's time for him to kill me.

S utton serves me up a bottle of moonshine, to make my "passing" more palatable. I take a few hair-scorching swigs before we get started. It makes my hunger worse. Drains my remaining strength. I steady myself against the table.

"Too strong?" Sutton says.

I shake my head.

Your prey is ready. Waiting. So, where would you start? Sutton, he wants to start the same place all the others do: the penis. *And you don't think it's a sexual fantasy?* The psychology of his choice is interesting, but you can't eat psychology. I don't care. Let him have his fun. I'm halfway through the bottle of liquor now, and my limbs feel like sunshine. I kiss him on the mouth, remove my trousers, and steady myself against the kitchen table.

Cutting off a penis is harder than you'd think. It might look like a sausage, but there isn't a sausage on the earth that can withstand as much abuse as a penis. *Have you seen what guys do to them?* When Sutton gets down on his knees, with my flaccid member between his lips, I know he won't be able to bite through it. *Let him have his fun. I promised him this. Didn't I?* Oh, I can't remember. It doesn't matter. If he wants it, he can have it.

Sutton smiles, bites down hard. My cock crunches like a stick of celery. It falls from his lips, still attached. He didn't even break the skin. A blue line of teeth marks rapidly fills with blood. The pain is exquisite. Sutton blushes. *Bite off a bit more than you could chew?*

I've underestimated him. Remember the pruning shears? I didn't. Sutton squats down before me, shears in hand. He clamps his teeth on my cock and leans back. Stretching me as tight as possible, using two hands, he snaps the shears shut, and topples backwards. He stands up and opens his mouth. It's empty. Sutton cackles with glee, clapping his hands together.

It's almost scary.

I stagger to the chair we prepared, leaning forwards so my stump squirts blood into the bucket. It's not a big bucket, it doesn't need to be, you don't have that much blood inside you.

A fully grown male contains about five litres of the stuff.

Sutton stirs his finger in the rapidly filling bucket and sucks it clean. "You are delicious." Saliva sprays onto my face. "Absolutely delicious."

I lower myself onto a chair, positioning myself over the bucket. *You don't want to waste a drop.*

When the hole between my legs starts to congeal, when the bucket cannot hold another drop, Sutton helps me to the bathroom. My vision is blurry, my bloodless limbs are as functional as putty. Sutton has run me a warm bath. I fall sideways into it, and he needs to position me on my back so I don't drown. Even my insatiable hunger quietens down in respect of the moment.

It's time to die.

Bleeding out in a bath filled with warm water is the closest thing you'll ever find to heaven. Imagine the warmest blanket, the softest bed, the most complete fatigue you've ever felt. Lying in that bath, bleeding out from the hole between my legs, I relax in my own personal Nirvana.

I can't feel my pulse. My vision is failing.

A blurry image kneels beside the bath. It's Sutton. Something long and silver glints in his hand.

"I love you," Sutton says, his mouth full of saliva.

I try to speak. My lips fail to respond.

It is time.

He stabs the knife through my throat. Drags the sharpened steel across the bones in my neck. Sutton stabs me so hard he knocks my head from the edge of the tub.

Shloompshsh!

I slide beneath the surface of the water.

Don't worry, it doesn't hurt.

Not anymore.

Now, it's all up to Sutton.

If he fails, I'm deader than dead.

Sutton lays my corpse on the kitchen table. Spreads my legs so that my knees are over the edge, exposing my genitals — what remains of them — and anus. The more you can open up the corpse, the easier you can "open up" the corpse. This is how you dress game.

Step One
Cut the anus out. Take your knife and cut around the orifice, like you're cutting a circle around a hole in a piece of cardboard. This way, the anus remains sealed, a natural drawstring for the — now detached — colon and bowel. Next, you want to cup the colon in both hands, and push it up inside the pelvis as far as you can.

Sutton gets in as far as his elbows, shivering in delight.

When you're up to your elbows inside the pelvis, place the colon in the bowl of the pelvis. You need to get it out of the way to make the rest of the dressing easier. Then pull your arms out slowly. If you're taking notes, underline <u>slowly</u>. Slowly, pull your arms out. One at a time. If you move too fast your arms create a vacuum, and you've just made a big hole in the corpse, so I'll let you work out what will happen. So, slow and steady, slide your hands out.

Slathered in visceral fluid and blood, Sutton stands back. He's flushed with excitement. Tears of joy run down his face. In his belly, hunger must be flickering.

Step Two
With the anus out of the way, bring your knife up through the top of the hole you just cut in the pelvic floor. Slice towards the ceiling until you hit the front-most part of the pelvis: the pubic bone. Or, more specifically, the pubic symphysis, a joint where the left and right pubic bones meet. You don't need to worry about the genitals. If you haven't worked it out yet, the

penis is overrated. You can pretend it's not there, a flaccid little piece of skin that vanishes once you shuck the skin off the corpse. Without the skin, the testicles flop out of the way. If you want, cut them off and save them for later.

This is exactly what Sutton does, clipping the testicular tubes like he's pruning rose stems.

Plop!

Plop!

He drops them into a jar of marinade and places them in the refrigerator for later. *Waste not, want not.*

Now, move up to the chest and make a very superficial cut at the base of the neck. Start in the sternal notch, the egg-shaped depression where the throat meets the ribcage. Gently, like you are giving the corpse a giant paper cut, slide your blade over the sternum. Continue down the belly, over the belly button, and stop at the pubic bone.

Then, return to the base of the sternum, where the ribs join and the abdominal muscles start. Very carefully, sink the tip of your blade one centimetre into the abdominal muscles. It only needs to be deep enough to work your finger through. Now, make a hook with your finger and pull the abdominal muscles outwards, up towards the ceiling. This creates a "tent" as you lift the muscle sheet off the intestines and bladder. This is vital, to avoid cutting innards. Remember, it's hot in there. Tight. The bladder is a bulging water balloon, and the bowel is full of fermenting gastric juices and bacteria and shit.

Keep pulling upwards with your finger, and run the knife along the incision you made before. Keep going until you reach the pubic bone again.

Done right, the abdominal muscles will unzip as smoothly as a jacket.

Step Three
The Rorschach Inkblot.

Take your bone saw, and saw through the pubic symphysis. The pubic bones should now appear like bone handles, perfect for you to grab a hold of, one in each hand. Now, wrench them apart.

Back up to the top, use the bone saw to cut through the sternum, and secateur the ribs on each side, in line with the armpit, and wrench the ribcage open like a book. *Tell me, what can you see?*

Step Four
Take your knife again, cut through the diaphragm and, reaching as high as you can up into the throat, cut across the trachea and oesophagus. You can't miss them. Now, the entire gastrointestinal tract and cardiopulmonary system is little more than a giant worm coiled inside the corpse. Grab a tight hold on the trachea and pull down hard towards the pelvis. Maintain your grip as it tears away and keep pulling. The heart, lungs, and entire gastrointestinal system should pull free like you are birthing a calf. You can dispose of the organs, but Sutton, my best student yet, will not waste a thing.

Beggars can't be choosers. He squeezes the bowels into a bucket, clearing the tract, and then deposits all the organs in another bucket filled with a dilute alcohol solution.

Waste not want not.

Done right, done with love, this entire process is divine.

Sutton, weeping with relief and delight, carries the broken butterfly of my carcass—it's a carcass now, a body prepared for consumption—to the meat hook, arranging me like a bloodless, écorché Christ.

Before my carcass is even cold, Sutton strips a long, slender piece of meat from my thigh. With garlic cloves, virgin olive oil and sea salt, he sautés it in a fry pan, slavering over the red flesh with thick lashings of yellow fat. It produces an aroma so perfect it pains him.

What does it taste like?

It's fattier than beef, but not as greasy as lamb.

More bitter than veal, but sweeter than pork.

More tender than beef, and it doesn't taste like chicken.

Even if he could describe the flavour, Sutton's mouth is too full to answer.

His meal flows down his throat. With grease all over his face, before he finishes swallowing, Sutton's back inside the cool room, cutting more meat from my thigh. If he feels any misgivings, any visceral unease, he doesn't show it. Why would he? He's never eaten human flesh before. To him, this hunger and excitement is all new. He cuts another strip and returns to the pan. No ingredients this time. Just meat. He barely manages to wait until its cooked before he wolfs it down.

After two more helpings, little remains of my right thigh, and Sutton's stomach bulges, gurgling when he moves. Sutton sits back at the kitchen table and belches. *Does he feel satisfaction?* Not for long. Within seconds, hunger is clawing its way up his throat. No, not hunger. He's not hungry. He's starving. Astonished, he staggers back into the cool room.

There is a price to pay for getting what you want. Sutton got what he wanted. It's time for me to take what I need.

Sutton slurps down the last mouthful of broth from his enormous cooking pot. It's not even down his throat before he convulses in the agony of starvation. My starvation. Clutching at the kitchen table for support, Sutton grabs the handle of the pot and dumps out a thick waxy sludge of hair, fingernails, teeth, and bone jelly. He scrapes all of it across the table and into his mouth, swallowing in great heaves.

He licks the table clean.

There is nothing left of me.

Nothing in the jar of marinade, a shattered green muck on the floor.

Nothing in the bucket that contained my gizzards.

There aren't even the excreta he squeezed out of my bowels. He has eaten everything.

Driven by desperation, Sutton grinds his tongue across the wooden tabletop.

When he arrives at the pot, lying on its side, he mounts the table, pushes his head inside, and licks the steel clean. Deep, wet glugging sounds reverberate throughout the kitchen. When he's polished the last smear of fat from the pan, he throws the pot across the room. Weeping, he rolls off the table. He doesn't bother to brace as he hits the floor. Hits it with a sound like a mud patty. There is no pain on this Earth that compares to his insatiable appetite. Rolling onto his back, curling up like a kidney bean, he tries to defend himself from the pain within. His bony arms can no longer reach around his distended belly.

Ping!

A button pops off his shirt. A purple mass of distended gut protrudes from the newly made hole. His belly looks like a suitcase of shapeless purple-grey leather. It bulges with angular points. Threatens to burst. Hot red stretch marks glow, jaguar's scratches. If you pulled his jaw down and shone a light in the back of his throat, you would see hair and skin bobbing behind his uvula. You would see his epiglottis flapping like the seat on an overflowing toilet bowl. How can he still breathe? And still, the hunger burns. And I'm all gone. Used up. Consumed.

It doesn't get any better.

Suttons screams in agony.

You can't do anything about the pain. The hunger that exists outside of thought. Outside of anything that was once human. I should know. It's this hunger, this demand to be destroyed and remade, broken down and born again, that *is* me.

Don't pity Sutton.

Pity me. I am nothing. Less than nothing. A hole.

Don't pity vampires, they can feed on victims.

Don't pity zombies, they have brains-a-plenty.

Pity me.

Me, all I can do is search for people like Sutton.

Sounds funny, but you can't make people eat you.

Don't pity Sutton. I gave him what he wanted.

Don't pity Sutton. He will only suffer this once. I have suffered, and will suffer, for all eternity.

Sutton wails, curled up on the kitchen floor. A child's sculpture of Gluttony: a bulging, bulbous belly, stick limbs, and a tiny bald head.

Sutton's mind twitches. Senses something within himself. Can feel me starting to move. Feel the strength I'm drawing from him, as his system digests everything I am. I've been devoured, and now I'm returning the favour. His cells absorb me, and I them. I can taste his suspicion as my thoughts begin to push him aside. I suppress his panic. It's only wasted energy, there is nothing he can do, as my cells rapidly infiltrate and overwhelm his.

How long does the mind take to break? Not long. A skilled hunter can dress his game in less than five minutes. I press upon Sutton's mind. Like the yolk of a fried egg rupturing beneath the tines of a fork, he yields. I surge forward and seize the throne. Sutton is extinguished. He who dreamed the cannibal's dream, who dreamt of making me part of him, has become one with me. It is his flesh that has become my flesh. He shall live on within me. The flesh of my flesh. The blood of my blood. Another disciple. I stand in Sutton's body, my body, and massage my receding belly. My familiar hunger already burns there. No, not hunger. You wouldn't call this hunger.

I am starving.

TWO SIDES OF A COIN

ROBYN O'SULLIVAN

I live a quiet life, these days. In a little studio near Flagstaff Gardens on the edge of the Melbourne CBD. It's a busy location, crowded, relatively easy to stay under the radar. Though I do have one noticeable quirk.

Whenever I make a decision, I have to flip a coin. Always. About everything. Will I go to the café or a pub? Should I go to work or stay home? Take a bus or the train? Get a bike or a scooter? Be kind or mean? Give or take?

I flip the coin and act on the outcome. Every single time. But it can't be just any coin. I only use the very old one that's always in my pocket. I found it when I was in England. It's my talisman. Heads or tails? I trust them both, even though they're absolute opposites. Like good and bad. Or right and wrong. Or guilt and innocence.

No, not the last set. They seem to be opposites but, in real life, there are lots of situations where they could merge or overlap. As a matter of fact, the more I think about this, the more I'm convinced that the distinction between guilt and innocence is, in many circumstances, hazy. So, strictly speaking, they're not opposites. At least, not in the same way as the two sides of a coin; they can't even see each other, let alone merge.

I've actually been pondering this conundrum for a while now. Ever since the day I went to prison.

I was working in England at the time, as an editor in the London office of an international publishing house. On a three-month secondment from the Australian branch in Melbourne, I provided the "antipodean voice" on a travel series they were publishing.

I'd been to a professional development course for work. One of those touchy-feely gatherings where you're supposed to bond with your colleagues, understand each other, enhance working relationships… It was held at a conference centre in an old manor house in rural Hampshire. Beautiful place with all the trappings necessary for an authentic olde-worlde experience, alongside up-to-the-minute requirements for twenty-first century business clients.

There was a bit of trekking through wheat fields, with a compass and scanty map. Some meaningful games. A lot of building-blocks stuff. And a shitload of drinking in the bar, which was open to the locals at night… I swear, by the time we left, I had a week's worth of hangovers piled up.

We were at this PD course for five days. It was intense. I had resolved to keep my wits about me but, in the end, I succumbed to the psychology. Found myself "connecting" with Ralph Blight. But he wasn't someone from work. I met him in the bar the first night. He was a local.

"Haven't I seen you somewhere before?" he said.

"I doubt it. I'm from Australia."

"Well, I know a pretty face when I see one."

I laughed at his pickup line. "Not very original. But I'll talk to you anyway."

We chatted, and it sort of grew into a nightly thing. To tell the truth, we didn't really have that much in common. But there was some kind of shared…I don't know. Can't really put my finger on it. We just seemed to click somehow. Anyway, on the last night, Ralph told me about the farmhouse where he lived. In a nearby village, it had been in his family since Tudor times.

Being a bit of a history nerd, I was intrigued. "You have my full attention. Tell me more."

"It was a reward from the village elders for the original Ralph Blight, who was a prodigiously successful witch hunter."

"Really? Oh, you're joking."

"Nope. Good old Ralph cleared the area of anyone associated with the black arts and turned the villagers back to godliness."

"Incredible. How did he do it?"

"Accused them of witchcraft, then drowned or hanged them."

I shuddered. "That's horrible."

"I know," he said, shrugging his shoulders.

He sounded a little glib. I wasn't entirely sure I believed him.

"An interesting ancestor," I said, lamely.

He laughed. "Thanks. And there's been a Ralph Blight in residence ever since."

"So now you live in this farmhouse that's…what…more than five hundred years old?"

"Yes. Well, it's actually two cottages cobbled together. One is original and the other was added about two hundred years later. By another Ralph. He had ten children."

"A prodigiously successful family in more ways than one."

He invited me to stay the weekend. Curiosity aroused, I accepted. Dodgy, I know. But it sounded fascinating. I figured it would be relaxing, too. And I needed to unwind after the PD.

The next morning, I got a taxi from the manor to the farmhouse. A hairy trip, combining a speedy driver with narrow, winding roads where two cars can't even pass each other. By the time we pulled up at the farm gate, I was definitely queasy and feeling a bit off balance.

Dragging my suitcase, I headed up the narrow driveway. Like a country lane, it meandered into the distance, both sides lined with field grasses. Oak trees formed an arch of green overhead. Utterly beautiful.

About half a mile in, there was a lake. Its banks were not circular but irregularly shaped, and edged by trees with weeping foliage. A couple of punts were tied to a jetty, and a mouldering statue of a Greek goddess stood nearby at the water's edge. I couldn't help myself. I walked over to the statue and ran my hands over her. Though weather-beaten and crumbling, she was mysteriously spellbinding.

And then I saw it.

A thin, curved piece of metal. Jammed into a cleft in the folds of her robe.

A medal? A coin? An offering to the goddess maybe? Or had it been hidden and then forgotten? I pulled it out and examined the worn surface. On one side was a barely-distinguishable crowned head with what appeared to be a Tudor Rose beside it. The lettering around the edge was damaged, but the name "Elizabeth" was clear. A shiver ran up my spine. Turning it over, I saw a coat of arms with the date 1565. This was real! When I placed the coin on the palm of my hand, my fingers instinctively closed over it. Without hesitation, I put it in my pocket.

Yes. I took the coin.

I knew it was thievery. But I *had* to have it.

Grabbing my suitcase, I returned to the driveway and kept walking. A bit further on, the driveway opened out into a glorious garden filled with fruit trees, lavender bushes, artichokes, peonies. And behind it all, this long higgledy-piggledy farmhouse, like a backdrop. It was wonderful. A magical place.

Ralph came towards me across the grass, arms outstretched. He gave me a bearhug—which I wasn't expecting—then gestured expansively.

"What do you think of the place?"

"I love it!"

"Come on in, allow me to show you around my humble abode."

We entered through a heavy timber door that bore the marks of its age. Ralph led me into the living room, pointing out the casement windows and broad fireplace, then on to the rustic kitchen.

"Look at that cooking range. It's fabulous!" I exclaimed. "And the hearth tiles. They're lovely. Is it all original?"

"No, there have been updates and replacements along the way. For example, my father put those tiles in, but they are still old. Victorian, I think." He ushered me on. "And through here is the original part of the house, the Tudor dwelling. Mind the low doorways."

He should've mentioned the staircases, too. They were unbelievably steep.

Ralph showed me to my room, which was not near his. Thankfully. When I said we clicked, I didn't mean romantically. Surprising? Maybe. He wasn't bad-looking—tall with dark eyes and prominent features—but it was a different kind of connection. Something, perhaps, otherworldly or fey? Not exactly rational.

Anyway, he left me to settle in. My room had old timbers, like you'd expect in a Tudor house. They were eaten away and shrunken. And they had symbols on them, too. An arrowhead—or maybe a chevron—and three short lines. I'd have laid bets those walls knew some secrets. I kept looking around. Outside the room, there were other marks carved over the doorway. A sort of daisy inside a circle. I traced the lines with my finger—

A jolt up my arm!

A scene in my brain!

The bank of a river. A crowd of heckling bystanders... A young woman strapped to a dunking chair that's hanging over the water. She's in a long dress and a cap. A man in a tall, black hat stands close to the river's edge. He points at the young woman, accuses her of being a witch.

"You have given birth to a babe; dare I call it that? It had six toes on its left foot. And a red birthmark on one side of its face. A heinous disfigurement," he pronounces. "Was that not enough?" He gestures to the baying crowd, goes on. "Your husband has since gone missing, believed to be cursed. What have you done?"

He pauses. The heckling intensifies.

An older woman steps forward and identifies herself as the midwife who delivered the babe. "A girl child, born one moon cycle too early," she says. "I saw the deformities. True signs of birth from a witch's womb. And I saw the mother attempting to hide the marks of witchcraft. She smothered her newborn infant."

Weeping, the young woman cries, "My child was stillborn, and my husband ran away."

The man in the tall hat loosens a rope at the end of the timber beam that's attached to the chair. She plunges into the water. Her head disappears below the surface. The man waits, counting to thirty, then forty, before he hauls up the chair.

The young woman emerges. Spluttering. Coughing. Gasping.

The scene faded…

Confused, exhausted, I stumbled to my bed to lie down. My skin was tingling, my brain wired. I couldn't fathom what my mind had just done. I closed my eyes.

The scene returned.

My eyes shot open, but it continued to play.

The young woman in the chair. Her cap gone, hair loose. Water dripping from her clothes.

The man repeats the charge. "You are a witch, and you gave birth to a witch for the purposes of sorcery," he says, harshly. "You would do well to confess that you killed your child and bedevilled your husband. Then God will forgive you."

Sobbing, she pleads with him. "You must believe me. It was a stillbirth. I wouldn't…I couldn't smother my own child. And I did nothing to my husband. He abandoned me!"

Nearing hysteria, she continues to protest herself innocent of these wild accusations, begging for her life. The crowd calls for the dunking to proceed. The man crosses his forefingers and holds them up in front of her face. He then extends one hand. And in his palm? A silver coin.

The young woman cries out when she sees it. "That's mine! You stole it from me."

The man slowly closes his fingers over it. "Nothing belongs to the one accused of witchcraft."

"Please, please give it back," she begs wildly. "I need it to pay the priest, so he'll bury my child in hallowed ground."

The man laughs.

She pleads again, this time trying to control her voice. "If you spare my life and return my coin, I'll leave the village and bury her elsewhere. I give you my solemn promise."

"The promise of a witch has no value," he says, and releases the rope that holds the chair.

She plunges into the water. Screaming. Choking. Drowning.

She? No. Oh no, not *she*. It's me.

The young woman is me.

The scene vanished abruptly. I was on my bed in the old Tudor house. Jumping up, I went out of my room and stood, panting, mesmerised, staring at the carving above the doorway.

I heard footsteps on the stairs.

Standing close behind me, Ralph murmured, "It's a daisy wheel. A witches' mark, carved as a protection against witches."

I turned. And looked straight into the face of my accuser. The same dark eyes and thin nose. High forehead and jutting chin. The only thing missing was a tall, black hat. I realised instantly that he knew who I was, too. Had he recognised me that first night at the bar? And lured me here?

I pushed him away. He stumbled and grabbed the stair railing.

Then the bastard crossed his forefingers and held up his hands. Right in front of my face.

That's when I remembered the coin I'd taken from the statue. I pulled it out of my pocket and brandished it.

Ralph looked surprised. "Where did you get that?" The expression on his face turned to anger, though the tone of his voice was measured. "I know you found it here. I would suggest you give it back."

"You can't have it. This coin is mine."

He lunged for it.

I had to stop him from taking it again.

I shoved hard, both hands into his chest. He went backwards down the steep, narrow stairs. He broke his neck. Once more, I was the accused. Convicted of manslaughter. Again, it was me who was punished. Sentenced to prison.

But this time, I survived. And this time, the coin is where it belongs. With me.

My life these days is nothing like it was before I did time in prison. I served five years, followed by three on parole, living in a flat above the fast-food outlet where a job was arranged for me in London's East End. After completing my parole, I was deported back to Australia. Free, at last. But it didn't feel as good as I'd imagined. Everything about me had changed. I was a convicted criminal, forty years old, homeless and childless. I couldn't go back to where I left off.

Now, I don't have any contact with family or my old friends. I no longer work in publishing. I never travel outside my home city. I abstain from alcohol.

And I know how important it is not to take risks or leave anything to chance. So, because I can't trust my own instincts, I always make decisions based on a flip of the coin. I have faith in my talisman; it will always land on the correct side. My coin will make sure I'm never again in a situation that could trigger visions about events of another time and place. It will protect me from circumstances where I might cross paths with someone who lived another life centuries ago. This talisman is a shield against the past and the future.

The two sides of my coin are lucky.

WE HAVE CHILDREN NOW

ANTHONY O'CONNOR

Trent had just about finished pissing in the potted cactus when he heard the voice, low but insistent, saying his name through the screen door.

"Trent?" And then a little louder, "Is that you?"

Stuffing his still-dripping prick back into his grimy jeans, Trent turned towards the sound, plastering a smile across his stubbly face. The same toothy grin, charming in its wolfish way, that had opened so many hearts and legs over the years.

Without even a hint of embarrassment, he said, "Yeah, it's me, hey. How are ya, Gaz?"

"It's Gary now," came the rather prim reply.

"Gary. Righto."

The screen door opened with a panicked shriek that made Trent wince, his nerves still jangled from the previous night's excesses, and he smiled blandly as his old mate stood revealed.

They hadn't seen one another in eleven years, and Trent's impression of Gary was that time had not been kind. Oh sure, his friend still had a full(ish) head of hair—unlike Trent's own hairline, which wasn't so much receding as desperately fleeing his tall forehead as if from a war zone—but Gaz (sorry, *Gary*) looked aged in a way that was less obvious. His edge bevelled by suburban mundanity, perhaps. The way he dressed now, like a smart/casual Mormon, spoke of a crushed spirit in Trent's opinion. It was hard to believe this was the same guy who once sold ecstasy in goth clubs and regularly wore a dress when he went out on the pull. Looked good doing it too, Trent had to admit. The bloke had killer legs.

This guy, however? Looked like he made regular noise complaints to the police before 9:00pm, and no one could see his legs beneath those tan slacks.

Grim shit.

Still, Trent was here now. Might as well make the most of it.

"Good to see you, Gary." Trent reignited that killer smile and was gratified to see Gaz give him one in return, albeit a rather beige version.

"You too, Trent. Come on in."

The inside of the joint was another slap in the face. Looked like it had been designed by someone's nan. Framed pictures of dreary-looking holidays, numerous ugly pets and…was that a framed *doily*? Who the hell would frame a doily? Unless it was some kind of "break glass in case of a terrible taste emergency" situation.

Trent managed to turn his chuckle into a cough when Gary glanced at him curiously.

"Nice place," Trent lied with practised ease.

"Thank you. We like it."

Gary led Trent through a dimly lit living area into a more spacious dining room. And there, sitting at the table smiling radiantly was Tansy, aka the real reason he was here in the first place.

"Trent," Tansy said, voice still a husky purr after all these years, "it's so good to see you."

"You too, Tansy," Trent said.

He wasn't lying this time.

To be honest, Trent was a little shocked to get the invitation at all. He hadn't spoken to either Gary or Tansy in over a decade, and it would be fair to say they had not parted on good terms.

The details were fuzzy, but he did vaguely remember a screaming match on the street at some ungodly hour of the morning, fists being swung with uncoordinated but passionate fervour, and a promise from Gary to Trent that the former would kill the latter if they ever met again.

Or maybe it had been a promise from Trent to Gary?

Either way, it had been a messy time, drug addled and sexually charged like most of the events from that bygone era. When passions ruled and responsibilities were nasty things that happened to other people.

Yet look at them now, Trent reflected.

There was Gary resembling the manager of a Christian rock band, and here was Tansy, a woman never far from Trent's detailed and specific sexual fantasies, dressed like a dowdy hausfrau. Or perhaps, as an ex-goth, that should be a "Bauhausfrau".

Although, to be fair, she pulled it off. Her dirty-blonde hair (no longer the various synthetic shades of red, purple and green that he remembered so fondly) was thick and hung messily around her shoulders. And although the oversized white blouse she wore was a little loose on her body, her natural curves—accentuated by age—were still very much present.

"You look great, Tansy," Trent said, a little more lustily than intended.

"Oh, stop it," she said, laughing, "I'm a fat old mum now."

"You're anything but fat—" Trent started to say before he stopped, stunned. "Wait, *Mum*?"

Tansy nodded, smiling, but it was Gary who answered.

"Yes, that's right." He spoke in a tone with just a hint of imperiousness. "We have children now."

It all started to make sense to Trent. The clothes, the decor, the uptight attitudes, these were the changes that occurred when people decided to breed. When they abandoned their principles, sold out and became normies.

He'd seen it a dozen times or more. Watching with dismay as artists and musicians and generally awesome people became full-time breeders, obsessed with feeding schedules and nappy changes and fucken *Bluey*.

It was as sad as it was predictable.

"Oh," he said, attempting to inject a little enthusiasm into his voice. "Congratulations?"

Gary and Tansy shared a look and then started laughing softly.

"Told you he wouldn't be impressed," Tansy told her husband wryly.

"Right as always," Gary responded with a little less affection.

"Don't worry, we're not going to ask you to hold them or anything," Tansy assured Trent, an ironic smile teasing her lips.

"No, it's fine." Trent found himself inexplicably trying to play diplomat. "I'm just surprised, is all. I didn't see any baby pictures in the hall and…well, you know. Youse were never keen on that sort of thing back in the day."

That was putting it mildly. In those years when Trent, Gary and Tansy had been a tight-knit, downright incestuous group of friends, they'd listed breeding as one of the signs of severe mental illness, along with "subscribing to organised religion", "believing in political institutions" and "wearing slacks".

Everyone changed, it seemed. Usually for the worse.

Christ, I need a drink, thought Trent.

"Hey, I brought some wine," he said, holding aloft the cask of lower-tier goon he'd flogged from the bottle-o on the way over.

"Lovely," Tansy enthused lightly. "I'll get pouring while Gary finishes dinner."

After a couple of glasses of wine (from Gary's supply, as the goon had been deemed unfit for human taste buds), Trent was beginning to feel better about the world. Specifically, the domesticated world he found himself ensconced so unexpectedly in.

Oh sure, Gary was still a bit of a buzzkill, although the dinner he cooked smelled delicious, but Tansy almost seemed like her old self. Her conversation sparkling, her eyes bright and alive with mischief.

As Gary was opening the fridge to grab something (and crikey, there was a lot of meat in there!) Tansy moved a little closer to Trent at the dining room table and said in a soft voice, "You know, I still sometimes think about that time. You know. With the three of us."

And Trent knew. Good Christ, he knew.

Eleven something years ago, he and Gary (Gaz then) had been testing the latest batch of pingers he was going to sell to scene kids at the clubs. This was back when they called it ecstasy and not Molly or fucken MDMA. Back then, the late '90s/early 2000s this would have been, the drug was proper potent. It wasn't a "pleasant vibe" and a quick dance; it was like being deliciously beaten up by a massive teddy bear...and a "microdose" was when you only took one.

Anyway, they'd been snorting lines of the stuff, listening to music, knocking back beers when Tansy had come home from whatever ghastly corporate job she did to pay for her drugs and, to a lesser extent, rent and food. It seemed to young Trent that she wore that office outfit really well, and he told her so, much to her delight. Tans quickly caught up to the boys with pills and grog, and then she and Gaz started going at it, pashing and groping and whatnot.

Trent wasn't offended at all. Half their luck. He'd vacate the premises and maybe pop down to one of the bars where a skinny, lank-haired, gothy-looking bloke with impressive cheekbones like himself might be appreciated. Perhaps even rooted. The night was young and so was he.

But as he moved to stand, Tansy's hand, pale with thick black nail polish immaculately applied, had settled warmly on his thigh.

"Trent," she'd said, "you don't have to go. Does he, Gaz?"

Gaz looked from her to Trent and back again, a grin crossing his wide features. "Nah, you can stay, mate."

And then he'd leaned over to kiss Trent lightly on the lips, tongue flicking out like an uncertain whisper. Half turned on by the gesture, and half trying to impress Tans, Trent had responded passionately to the kiss, cupping Gaz's face and pashing him firmly.

"Fuck," Tansy whispered, clearly very turned on, and she quickly inserted herself in the action, stripping off her restrictive office wear, and from there? They flowed together. Like a symphony, like poetry, like a question that finally had an answer.

It had been magic. Oh sure, it was partly the drugs, but it was just one of those perfect moments. Unexpected and unrehearsed, truly passionate and unforgettable.

Literally. God knows, Trent had tried to shake the memory

that seemed to cast a shadow over the many sexual conquests that followed. And it had been even worse when he and the couple had parted ways, making hanging out with mutual friends wrenchingly awkward.

But that night, that one night that had turned into a long, spontaneous weekend of joyous experimentation… It had been one for the ages.

Trent noticed a not entirely unpleasant—but socially frowned upon—stirring in his jeans and stood, muttering, "Where's your dunny, Tans?"

"You sure you don't want to use a different pot plant?" Gaz asked, with an eyebrow raised. "I've got a fern or two you could water."

Trent stopped for a second, embarrassed, but then his old friends burst out laughing and everything was okay. Tansy directed him to the toilet and he chuckled his way down the hall and up the stairs.

After voiding his bladder, snooping in the medicine cabinet (nothing worth flogging, sadly) and giving himself a quick key bump of some biker-grade goey to keep him perky, Trent ambled back through the house. He stopped at a closed door marked NURSERY.

Not just closed but locked, he found after trying the knob. He put an ear against the door, yet failed to hear anything from within. Apparently, Gaz and Tans had managed to create spawn that could actually shut the fuck up from time to time. Wonders never cease.

Sniffing back the last of the powder through his inflamed nostrils, Trent jogged downstairs to a table covered with food that looked great and smelled even better. He didn't have to fake enthusiasm as he tucked into the lamb roast; it was absolutely superb. Cooked to perfection and dripping with gravy and some kind of garlic sauce.

He hadn't eaten so well in years.

Halfway through dinner, a strangled yelp echoed from somewhere above. To Trent it sounded like a dog being murdered, but judging from the looks on Tans and Gary's faces, it was business as usual.

"Once more unto the breach," Tans sighed, standing and starting to undo the buttons of her blouse. "I knew I was living in a dreamworld when I put on something nice for once."

"They're hungry," Gary explained, somewhat unnecessarily, as Tansy ascended the stairs with weary purpose.

"How old are they?" Trent asked, not really caring about the answer, but enjoying the feeling of being full and a little buzzed from the various intoxicants swimming in his bloodstream.

Gary spoke softly. "Oh, they're still very young. Babies, really."

Trent was waiting for further details, but that rather non-specific statement was apparently all the answer he was going to get.

"Mate, deadset, the food is bloody delicious." Trent poured himself another generous glass of red. "I remember back in the day you used to burn 2 Minute Noodles, so this is truly impressive."

Gary looked shocked for a second and then started laughing. "I'd completely forgotten that! How do you remember this stuff?"

"Oh, you know, just stuck with me for some dumb reason."

Just then a cry of pain from upstairs startled them both into silence. A moment later, the nursery door opened and closed, and footsteps got closer.

"You right, Tans?" Trent asked.

"Yeah, yeah, all good. Bloody things are getting a bit bitey," she answered cheerily.

But when Tansy sat back down at the table, she looked terribly pale. Trent couldn't help but notice the blood stains on her blouse around her left breast, small but numerous.

"Cut yourself shaving?" he quipped.

Tansy winced slightly, clearly in pain. "They're hungry little buggers."

"Do you have any pictures?" Trent sat back in his chair. "I saw heaps of the pets and that, but none of the nippers."

This was, for Trent, a gesture of extreme magnanimousness. Of course, he didn't give a rat's to see any piccies, but he knew that request was like catnip to parents.

Gary and Tansy shared an awkward, almost alarmed, look.

"Oh, you don't want to see boring baby pictures, Trent." Gary laughed a little too hard.

"Let's open another bottle and move to the lounge room." Tansy suggested.

An hour or so later, Trent was feeling no pain. This evening had ended up being an unexpected treat. He was filled with an expansive, warm glow and a surge of affection for his former drug buddies.

Hell, he'd admit it, he loved these wankers.

"I just wanna say," he slurred, trying to sit up straight in the couch that seemed to be slowly absorbing him, "that I wasn't sure about tonight, but it's been bloody marvellous seeing youse both."

Gary and Tansy shared a look that seemed, somewhat inexplicably, guilty.

"It's great to see you too, Trent," Gary said, a touch stiffly.

"I was surprised to get your email to be honest," Trent admitted.

"We originally weren't going to send it." Tansy refilled Trent's glass and took a sip from her own. "But things got a little desperate."

What does that *mean?* Trent wondered vaguely, yet didn't let it detract from his good mood. Overthinking could be a vibe killer.

"The thing is, Trent, we were told we couldn't have kids at all, at first," Gary intoned, looking off into the middle distance.

"Okay," Trent murmured, curious as to the sudden change in conversational direction.

"It's true," Tans affirmed. "We tried everything. Spent a fortune on IVF. Spent even more on bullshit cures from our hippie friends."

"If I even *see* another fucking crystal…" Gary muttered.

"We had to find solutions that were a bit more…esoteric, I suppose you might say." Tans waved a hand vaguely.

"Oh yeah? Like what?" Trent was surprised to find he actually wanted to know. He sat up to avoid the increasing sensation that he was sinking, melting, into the couch.

"We had to go back to The Old Ways. Find solutions that predate current medical learning. Some that predate humankind entirely." Was it Trent's imagination or did Gary shudder after he said that?

And were the thick shadows behind him on the wall moving?

"It was worth it, though!" Tansy said brightly. "Even if parenting can be its own challenge." She absent-mindedly brushed at the bloodstains on her blouse. "I've been spending a fortune on new shirts."

"And of course, there are the sacrifices..." Gary sighed.

"Sacrifi...fiiizze?" Trent found he was having trouble speaking.

Might be time for another bump to keep me sparky, he thought idly.

"All parents make sacrifices, of course." Tansy picked up the thread. "Yours did, mine certainly did. It's the nature of the thing. The ones Gary and I have to make are just...different. Not better or worse."

"That's right. When you have children, things change, you need to step up. Become an adult. Do what's necessary," Gary intoned.

"And we have children now," Tansy said.

"Yes, we have children now."

When Trent next opened his mouth to speak, he found he couldn't make sounds come out of it. Point of fact, he couldn't close the damn thing or move it at all. His jaw just sort of hung there like a half-open drawer.

Paralysed, he thought as a twinge of alarm skittered around his mind. *I appear to be paralysed.*

"At first, we picked people that, well, wouldn't be missed," Gary continued. "There was the sex offender a few blocks over. Awful man. Completely unrepentant of his crimes and had a hard drive full of the worst stuff you can imagine." Gary pursed his lips distastefully. "When he disappeared, no one cared. Truth be told, it was probably a relief."

"Then there was the Nazi. White supremacist, whatever those loons are calling themselves these days." Tansy nodded.

"Again, nothing of value was lost there."

"Then there was the street person who kept harassing passers-by, including young girls coming home from school," Tansy murmured. "Neither of us felt good about that one, mind you.

We both vote Greens for God's sake, but he seemed a logical choice, even if we both passionately object to the stigmatisation of the mentally ill."

"After that, well, we sort of ran out of the very objectionable who were conveniently located and wouldn't be missed." Gary sighed.

"So, we had to expand our range to old contacts and acquaintances." Tansy knelt in front of Trent to tell him this, making eye contact, making sure he understood. "We know you're not a bad person."

"No, not bad. I have such lovely memories of you, of our time together. Back in the day, frankly, you stole our hearts," Gary admitted.

"And our rent money." Tans smiled, showing there were no hard feelings.

"That he did. A true larrikin you are, Trent."

I meant to pay that back! Trent attempted to say, but instead a tendril of drool poured from his mouth, landing on his shirt. Sticky purple strings trailed from his gormless gob.

"So, no, you're not a bad person. You don't do terrible things." Tansy patted his leg.

"But you also…don't do many, or any, good things either, mate." Gary gave a regretful sigh. "Still wearing the same clothes you used to wear in your twenties, still trying to act like the skinny lothario you used to be, still taking drugs. It's a little sad, you know?"

Tansy stood and moved closer, reaching down to wrap her arms around Trent's left ankle. "You ready?"

Gary took Trent's right ankle. "Ready."

"Remember to lift with your legs, not your back," Tansy admonished. "We don't want a repeat of last time."

Gary laughed. "Okay, okay."

Together, Gary and Tansy pulled Trent's legs until he was lying flat on the couch, sprawled out like a starfish. He looked up at the pair and couldn't help but remember the last time he'd seen them from this angle. At that time, they were naked and crawling up his body, stopping to cut lines of ecstasy on his chest and snort them slowly, pausing to kiss and lick and then work their way up and down respectively.

Trent found he wanted to share this important memory with them, perhaps stop them from…whatever it was they were doing, but all that came out of his mouth was more drool and a low, rasping sound.

"Did you give him enough?" Tansy wanted to know.

"Yes. I think so." Gary nodded, frowning.

"He always had a shockingly high tolerance."

"It's fine, it's fine. Come on, they'll be getting fussy. On three. One…two…*three!*"

The next thing he knew, Trent found himself being dragged across the musty carpet, head flopping back and forth, taking in lurching glimpses of this strangely conservative decor and his friends pulling him towards the stairs.

There was a skull-jarring THUNK as the pair pulled him up the first step, and then another as his loosely hanging skull was bumped anew.

THUNK! THUNK! THUNK!

Trent's eyes flickered for a moment and then rolled back in his head.

When Trent came back online, he found himself sitting in a chair in a room he hadn't seen before. Actually, "sitting" wasn't quite right. He was lolling in the cold metal seat, held tightly by leather straps around his waist, chest, ankles and wrists.

Gary was tightening the strap around his right ankle while Tansy stood off to the side, shooting nervous glances across the room where two bassinets sat like totems. Filthy ones at that; both baby beds were covered with stains of rusty brown and lighter red. The floor, too, was unkempt with broken toys, dirty towels and what looked like white sticks strewn around the place.

The nursery seemed singularly unadorned by anything that would delight a ruggie. No happy bunnies or smiling clowns on these walls, just drab paint peeling forlornly and a single naked bulb dangling like an incandescent hanged man.

And the smell. God, the awful bloody smell!

Trent jerked slightly as he coughed, more drool dripping from his mouth. And from across the room, in the right bassinet, came an answering gurgle.

Tansy spoke in a low, tense voice. "Hurry, Gary, Youngest is hungry."

"Done." Gary stood up, a light sheen of perspiration shining above his eyebrows. "Well, this is goodbye, Trent."

"Try not to resist Eldest, Trent," Tansy said sadly. "I think it's less painful if you just let it happen."

"Tansy, let's go."

Gary began to drag Tansy out of there.

"Oh, and try not to move when Youngest comes!" she exclaimed, halfway out the door. "He has trouble latching on!"

The door closed with an emphatic thud. Then came the sound of a deadbolt punching into place. Then silence.

For a few moments.

Trent had enough time to look more closely at the objects on the ground. Close enough to see that those sticks weren't sticks at all. They were bones.

And that thing he had taken for a sun-bleached ball? That was a skull.

Trent's mind began to race with explanations, and he seized on a pleasing one. Could this all just be an elaborate joke at his expense? Yeah, that was it. He had, after all, wronged the couple in various ways over the years, and maybe this was retribution. Any second now, Tans and Gaz would come through the door, laughing and taking pictures of him looking like a pork chop.

Any second now.

Any second.

The left bassinet started shaking, and a low humming noise filled the room.

A moment later, a shape appeared over the edge of the baby bed, round and wizened and gleaming. A tiny bald wrinkled head. Eyebrow ridges followed, stern and hairless, and then eyes themselves. Small, gleaming things that seemed to shine in the dim light.

They were looking right at Trent. A flat triangular nose followed and then a mouth that was curled up in a smirk that was far older and more knowing than it should be. The whole head, in fact, looked more like a miniature old man, leering eagerly at Trent with an expression that said, *I know something you don't know.*

Trent stared into those eyes and got hooked by the gaze, his whole body jerking as he suddenly felt trapped. Staring, unblinking.

The room began to swim, and Trent's mind began to churn, as if the piercing gaze of that ancient-looking baby (*Eldest?*) was running hooked fingers through his thoughts and memories, snatching at the juiciest morsels.

Dark reminiscences began to rise to the surface of his consciousness. Unbidden and unwanted, they played on the grimy palette of the nursery walls, projected from within. Black moments, like the first time he stole money from his parents to score, his eventual ejection from his family home at eighteen years of age, those six months where he lived rough and did things he never imagined he would or could, and that guy he beat up for no reason, just venting his frustration on that gormless face with fist and boot. The jobs he'd lost, the relationships he'd tanked, the opportunities he'd squandered, all of it came rising up in a flood, pouring over him in a frothing tsunami of shame and anguish.

And then, of course, there was the time he'd stolen $780.00 off Tansy and Gary. Not much these days, he supposed, but a bloody fortune at the time. He watched with mounting dismay as the younger version of himself snuck out of bed, his beard still musky from both of them, and quietly slid the notes out of the wooden box with the Ministry and Front 242 stickers on it. He'd loved them both in his way, but he had a demon to keep happy, that demon of need called addiction.

Tears were running freely down his cheeks now, and he made a soft choking sound at the back of his throat. He wanted to scream apologies to his friends, to everyone he'd ever hurt, even to that strange thing in the bassinet that now appeared to be standing up.

No, not standing. *Rising.* In an unnaturally smooth movement,

Eldest was ascending, revealing more of his wrinkly body, with its shrivelled, claw-like hands and feet, and a withered-looking penis. It kept gaining height until Trent realised with a dull shock that it was now levitating a good metre above the bassinet, still locking eyes with him and refusing to let go.

A thick, viscous liquid began dripping from Eldest's pores, glazing that misshapen body and seeming to give the being—because surely this was nothing human—a foul and discordant pleasure.

All of a sudden, Trent realised this thing, this horrible imp, was feeding on his guilt and self-loathing, gorging itself on everything he hated about himself. This revelation sparked a pulse of anger that gave him control for just a second, and he wrenched his gaze away from the levitating gloom magnet, closing his eyes firmly.

Eldest made a frustrated gurgle, but that wasn't what made Trent's blood run cold. No, what sent a spasm of terror through his body was the noises that came from the bassinet on his right-hand side.

Youngest.

The heavy grunting, the sloughing noise, the sudden meaty plop of something that hit the floor hard. And after a few seconds of silence, the moist puckering sounds of wet limbs dragging a body across the boards.

His breath punching in and out of his chest, Trent strained with everything he had, urging the cocktail of chemicals in his system to beat out whatever Tansy and Gaz had drugged him with. He managed to jerk his left hand and utter a low cough that sort of sounded like "Help," but beyond that, nothing.

And then the confusing tangle of sticky limbs that belonged to Youngest wrapped around his ankle and Trent screamed internally, begging gods he didn't believe in to save him.

He managed to keep his eyes closed as Youngest, who felt like a bulbous, cat-sized tube, worked its way up his body, leaving warm puddles of fluids on him as it squirmed its way towards his face. It fell a couple of times—

He has trouble latching on!

—but moved with a dogged persistence, making eager cooing noises that seemed, impossibly, to come from multiple directions at once.

Don't look. Don't look. DON'T LOOK.

Trent didn't open his eyes until Youngest slid up his chest and wrapped limbs around his neck. He couldn't help it; the eyelids just sprang open.

He was just in time to see Youngest unfurl itself to its full height.

In the final seconds of sanity, before anything resembling rational thought had been displaced by screeching animal panic, Trent found himself wondering how something so small could have so many mouths.

THE TENTH LIFE

PAULINE YATES

Sylvarnia crushes a handful of autumn leaves beneath a waxing moon and casts them into the air. The chilly breeze collects her offering and carries the debris south. Hitching up her robe, she follows the leaf trail, hobbling through the trees until she reaches the outskirts of the small town at the edge of her forest. Pausing, she utters an age-old passage from her lore, then runs her hands over her stringy, grey hair and down her bony body. Her wrinkles fade, and her skin turns smooth and flawless. Her hair changes to shimmering raven-black locks.

Tingling with youth she's not felt for years, she continues the hunt for her quarry. She must hurry. Her illusion spell is strong, but without Solomon and his magic to help her spell linger, time is short.

The leaf trail leads her across a field as barren as her belly, and along a narrow lane to the town's inn. Light spills from the stained windows, dyeing the cobblestones purple and red. Inside, raucous voices, drunk on mead and merriment, rise above a flute's melody.

Pushing open the door, she's greeted by stale ale, stinking snuff, and lecherous eyes that strip the robe from her body. Striding to the bar, she entraps the barman's attention with a gold coin plucked from her pocket.

"Mead," she says, in a voice sweeter than honey.

The barman pours a measure into a mug and slides it across the counter.

Dipping her fingers into the amber liquid, she sprinkles drops in a circle around her feet. The lustful gazes turn away.

Continuing her search unnoticed, she glides between the tables, stopping where three farmhands trade tall stories. Two are not to her liking: the first is thin-limbed with a shock of red hair; the second has broad shoulders and is of sturdy build, fine qualities, but his hair is old straw and his eyes are bland brown.

But the third man...

His hair is blacker than a moonless night, and his amber eyes sparkle with flecks of yellow, so like Solomon's. So alike, she wonders if her faithful cat has reached from beyond death's veil to help her find what she needs.

Moving closer, she strokes the man's head. Silky strands, soft like cat's fur, kiss her fingers. Circling around him, she admires his sturdy frame, then slides her hand down the front of his shirt. Her fingers snare in a tangle of black curls on his muscular chest. She imagines birthing a daughter with raven-black locks like her illusion, and amber eyes like Solomon's. Or a son with strong arms and broad shoulders, a future prince of her forest. Satisfied, she leans towards the man's ear and whispers her desire.

He startles at her chilly breath and whips his face to hers. She catches him with a maiden's smile. Mesmerised by her beauty, he places his hand in hers. Concealed by her spell, they leave the inn, unseen.

Hurrying now, for the moon grows tired, she returns to the forest and takes the man to a secluded glen. The breeze whips up her robe, teasing her impatience. Facing the man, she slips the robe from her shoulders. The dying moonlight illuminates her porcelain skin. Shadows cast from the trees enhance her curves. She slides her hands over her hips to incite his desire, then lies on the ground between the rocks and the tree roots, his for the taking.

Befuddled by her magic, the man throws off his clothes and ravages her body with lustful lips and roaming hands. Spreading her legs, she clutches his buttocks and pulls him inside her. She moves in time with his thrusting, arching her back to catch his seed. He stiffens and moans, then slumps against her, his oily sweat sticky between them.

She kisses his cheek, taking pleasure in the scratch of his stubble on her lips. Then she grabs his head and twists, snapping his neck. The forest swallows the crack of bones. The breeze sighs and falls still. Sylvarnia smiles at the man's dead eyes—a death for a life. Better his life than hers.

The moon dips below the tree line, stealing her light and her youthful appearance. Pushing the man's limp body off hers, she rolls him over, takes a blade from her discarded robe, and cuts out his heart. With a flick of her bony hand, she covers his body with a layer of rotting leaves, then dons her robe and scuttles through the forest.

The man's seed is warm in her belly, but time is shorter still. Reaching her mud-brick hut, she drops the man's heart into a small and rusting cauldron, adds a vial of her menses stored from many moons' past, then lights a fire and brews the concoction to a simmer.

Returning to the forest, she drops to her knees and claws at the soil. Six long and lonely months she has had to wait for the earth to free Solomon's bones; the spell to produce life where none will grow won't work without his magic. No maggots remain, but the soil is alive after consuming flesh and it coats her fingers, making them tingle.

Touching bone, she scoops away the muck and pulls out the skull, vertebrae, ribs, and a jigsaw of smaller bones that were once four limbs and a tail; all that's left of Solomon, her faithful companion. Nine lives were all he could give her, but there's time enough for one more.

"Pray your magic is as strong in death as it was in life," she says.

Cradling the bones like the baby she hopes to conceive, she takes them to the cauldron and casts them into the brew. Claws and teeth spit and sizzle. Bones bubble with froth. Using her staff, she stirs three times forward, three times back, until the rising steam turns black and the mixture is tar thick. She dips her fingers into the brew. Flinching, she hisses through crooked teeth as the icy spell scalds her.

It is ready.

Scooping out a handful of the tar, she lifts her robe and packs it into her vagina, pushing it deep inside to mix with the man's seed. Her tender flesh shrieks like the scream stuck in her throat; she must bear this agony in silence for the spell to work. Death mixes with life, making her swoon, but she grips the cauldron and crosses her legs to hold in the tar until the weary moon fades. When sunrise cuts the horizon and bleeds red across the sky, she collapses, curls like a foetus, and prays for life to bud in her barren belly.

Then she waits.

The days shorten, and the forest sheds its orange gown. The nights grow long, and despair as bitter as the winter wind chills her to the bone. The stench of rotting brew makes her gag, but she dares not discard it, for there are no more bones or menses to make a fresh batch. But as the months drag on, and her belly stays flat, the fear of remaining childless ferments into overwhelming loneliness, and the emptiness in her life since Solomon passed threatens to consume her.

She aches for his company. Without his rumbling purrs to dampen dark magic's whispers, nightmares plague her: the decaying man ravages her body with rotten lips and skeletal hands; the town's hounds sniff out her magic trail and bay for her murderous blood. Solomon with his watchful, yellow eyes would always stand sentry while she slept, and his absence is as heavy as the tar in her belly.

The thought of this spell not working—of never teaching a daughter the ways of her lore or bequeathing command over her forest to a son, of living alone for the rest of her days—leaves her as bleak as the clouds that blot out the winter sun.

But with the change of season, hope stirs with a fluttering in her belly on a night when the moon is full.

Casting off her filthy robes, she bathes herself in the glowing beams. The power of a new life blooming inside sheds years off her age, sloughing away her wrinkles and leaving her skin milky white, and smooth with youth. She did not expect this. The spell was not to renew her own life. Yet here she stands, with raven-black locks and porcelain skin, the same as she appeared after her earlier illusion spell. She presses her abdomen, worried she's taken life not meant for her. But as the snow melts and the sun warms the earth, her belly swells like a brewing storm, and the fluttering changes to impatient kicks.

She dares not hope, not yet, not even when the nesting instinct kicks in. Death can still snatch life. Has she not stolen a miscarried babe? Caught a stillborn mother's tears for use in her spells? Instead, she stirs the stinking brew with her staff to keep it alive, just in case. Just in case.

The first contraction is a thunderous roll that shudders through her body, dropping her to both knees. A lightning strike of pain in her pelvis peels a screech from her lips. Clutching her inner thighs, she spreads her legs and bears down. A clot of black tar drops on the ground, then a splitting pain, like claws, slices open her uterus, sends tremors throughout her body and makes greasy sweat, sticky like the tar, pop onto her brow.

Gritting her teeth, she thrusts her hand into her vagina and probes the birth canal for the head. Her fingers grab a sodden mass of hair. Bearing down again, she yowls through a final push and yanks the body free. Sylvarnia stares at her newborn in shock.

Trust Solomon to know exactly what she needs.

Lifting her babe, she gazes into smug, yellow eyes. His tail curls around her wrist.

She smiles. "Welcome back, Solomon. You've been missed."

BITTEN: A LOVE STORY

DANI RINGROSE

Shop doors snap shut, vomiting us out onto the footpath. Three children, mine, my responsibility. They keen behind me for food I have only just packed in a shopping bag. Like cuckoos, they open their beaks and wave their heads around on unsteady necks.

Like cuckoos, they will outgrow me some day.

Flickering sharp sunlight spears through frangipani and fig, sun at the height of its apex roasting my children. I have forgotten to smother them in sunscreen. Forgetful or disinterested. Sweaty, sticky skin and wriggly bodies; I get more on myself than on each child I am meant to protect.

Behind me, a soft sound of a fist hitting an arm. A yelp.

A sound of smacking footsteps on the path comes closer, a small hand penetrates the fist I have unconsciously balled up. Without turning around, I know which of my trio has punched another. Crazed eyes peek up at me. A cracked smile pleads for a mother's love. My vinegared lips stay shut.

I stare blankly ahead, not gifting a smile in return. My jaw slackens, weighted with misunderstood commands, unspoken instructions, unheard reprimands. A whirlwind of feet behind, and another child appears at my side. A middle child, keen to please both siblings but accepted by neither. There is a shove, and the child in my hand is tugged out of my grasp.

Why did I have a trio? There is no balance, no harmony, no equilibrium to this number. Our lives roil, a push and pull of energy. Their fights ebb and flow. At no time are all three happy and satisfied, and at no time am I happy or satisfied.

As we enter the park, eyes scan us. *Who are you?* they ask.

What do they see? Three children, interchangeable, with freckled spots and dusty hair. A sunburned mother, without her mandatory coffee cup. Shoelaces dragging in the dirt, kids stripped of manners and silence, making honking noises that intrude on the peace of the playground. Parents instinctively clutch at their own children to protect them. I have trained myself to ignore their eyes; I smother myself behind oversized sunglasses and scrolling Instagram feeds.

Two children explode away from my side, to climb on swing sets and swing on climbing frames.

The eldest remains. The child has not forgotten its hunger. Can I not be…alone, can I not disconnect? To unattach this child, I have to feed it first. So, we sit, on this corroded bench, under a scant amount of shade, and it gulps what I gift it. I pay no attention: chips chocolate crackers cake cherry carrot cheese: they all make a smacking sound as its yawning beak snaps at whatever I hand it. It chews, it swallows, it burps, it laughs.

It runs to push a sibling off a flying fox.

I am alone.

I yawn.

They have eaten me alive.

I am not myself any more. I saw them being born, I saw each of them being cut apart from my umbilical cord, but they don't detach. The cord tugs inside my womb still, this invisible rope connecting me to my children. It twangs like fishing wire, a hook caught in my flesh. It stretches across the playground, a telegraph wire only worthy of sending monotone, transactional interchanges to my children about when bathing needs to occur, or when they should stop hitting a sibling. The wire feels faulty at times; it only sends signals one way.

I try not to look down to acknowledge my rounded stomach. It revolts me. It is all deflated basketball, with none of the curve that is desired by others. Like offcut meat from the butcher, I am the discounted flesh. Distorted lines; the last man that penetrated me was the surgeon with his knife who carved my youngest from my belly. The curve of this scar mimics the roundness of flesh, a smug slash that smiles downwards at my feet. The balloon womb didn't descend after the last birth; it weighs here like an unanswered question.

I am bile and fat and gristle. I heave, yet I have nothing to give.

Why do I use the word "I"? There is no *I* in us. I only exist if they are alive. I am only valuable if I keep *them* alive.

The only things that see me any more are my three.

My parasites.

From the top of the play fort, one catches my eye, and a sour taste rises in my throat. There is hunger in its eyes. The invisible placenta tugs on my innards, and I cannot fight the urge to offer food.

With no grace in its legs, it parks in the dirt by my side. I make an offering from our shopping bag to it, but that is not enough. It wants mother.

Teeth sink into my calves. Tiny milk teeth, rounded white pebbles; the hunger is what drives its jaws into my muscle. I feel my skin puncture with the force.

It nibbles at my leg, my youngest. On its delicate chin, blood dribbles. The liquid descends further down its chin with every chew, every nibble. It is rhythmic. I lean back on the park bench and gulp at the hot air. Rather than wiping the mess from its face, instead I reflect on whether I'd taken my birth control before we left in a hurry.

Metallic haem iron on the breeze calls to my other two. Mother: she is ready to serve now. The placental wires and blood vessels join in the call, and throb with the urge to continue to feed them. The older two scuttle in, and with no baby teeth to inhibit them, they drive quickly into muscle. There is an ache, a mother's ache, with the drainage, the depletion. They sup, they suck.

I am chewed. I am bitten. I am mother.

Other mothers monitor our family feeding at the park bench, they shift from side to side. One squints, and her gaze reminds me of my own mother, ready with a sharp rebuke about what I am doing wrong. I try to make eye contact, but it is sieved through my tinted glasses, and all the parents look away, towards recycled rubber mats and their own satiated offspring.

One of mine lifts its head from my body. Exposed to the air, the bite quickly forms a crust, and the child moves on to another piece of flesh. The pulsing of my blood shifts to a new hot spot on my leg. All blood travels to this fissure, and I feel a sucking as liquids drain from my body. There are sharp points all over my legs now, bite marks in pale skin. The sharp beaks that pierce skin are sounding more demands.

This body has been for the taking for many years. I have fed others for so long I have nothing to give to myself. For so long, I have been nourished by the smiles of my offspring, their growing tummies, tiny milk breaths, salt in hair. This is not enough now. They have drained me of so much the letters of my own name have melted away, and instead they leave their ghoulish, sticky fingerprints on my breast where a name tag would rest. I yearn to pick at the melted, syrupy residue on their hands, to place it in my mouth and suck at the sugar and additives, but I take to those hands at home with scrubbing brushes and stern words. If I left my offspring behind in the park today, distracting them with an upturned bag of crumbled biscuits, scattered like birdseed while I made a quick getaway—would I feel anything then? Would my numbness dissolve with every step? Or would the return of any feeling be so overwhelming that some mawkish mother would find me doubled over at the first corner?

Other parents look at us, but they do not register through the haze. Mother is feeding; that is what mothers do. My body shifts; I spread slightly so they can feed better. My movements rattle the parasites, and they look elsewhere for nourishment. With eyes barely open, they seek the rest of my acres of flesh on offer, heads bobbing to graze indiscriminately.

I lean sidewards, dizzy with inertia, to inspect my wounds.

One wiggles to my breast, expecting the richest of nourishment. I cannot look, but I expect my youngest to be the culprit, foraging for fatty milk. It scratches at my chest, slashing at cheap fabrics, and gnaws at a teat. No milk ducts work, yet blood and plasma rise to the surface, pulsing erratically into its needy mouth. I feel a pulling inside me, moving along my nerves, from my breast to my womb. There is a crying out from below, a calling or a summoning. The cry asks for their embrace, to dissolve them into my heart. The cry calls them back home, to the safety of the motherland. To the impossible return of my life before they existed.

Another child, hunting calcium, pulls and picks at a nail, and when that becomes a fruitless pursuit, places my thumb in its mouth, a pacifier. I try to shake it, limp-wristed, wheezing for air, but I am forced to sharply intake the air instead. The child bites, sucks hard, and by flooding it with saliva and immature enzymes, softens the nail. With a rip of its cuckoo neck, the nail becomes its next meal. What's left is a bed of pink meat and bubbly flesh; exposed nerves electrify with these unending dry winds. Momentarily satiated, its head bobbles sideways, and eyelids shut.

My hand rushes to my mouth, as though the infantile gesture of sucking my injured thumb will fix it. It stings and I gasp, clamping my jaw down. So tight that my shoulders raise, my neck begins to vibrate from holding the tension, and one hand wraps around the other in mock prayer.

I try to inhale—and can't. I have bitten into my own thumb; to try dulling the pain, I have created more. I wrench my hand back and gasp. At my own blood pasted everywhere. At the two teeth embedded. I claw, I pick, I scrabble at them—a molar, an incisor—I twitch, I pluck one off like a boil, and let it roll on the ground next to my foot. Rustling and subsequent crunching tell me that one from the trio has found it. I am too tired to be happy at the sight of it scrounging for mother's food in the dirt. I pull the other tooth out of my thumb, and hold it out in my flat palm, the same way you would feed livestock.

My own eyelids sag, drowsy with the weight of oxidised blood. Through slitted lids, I plead with the remaining playground parents: *They are eating me alive.* None register in return, although a father momentarily skips a beat at the glistening red flesh of my inner thighs. He is conflicted: the moist skin, the drowsy mother, the blood clots. The clots are a step too far.

Scabs on my legs form as he watches, and an itch throbs up

my nerves. I reach to scratch my calf, but instead find myself picking at rusted skin, prising the newly formed crust from my leg. I inspect it, coin-shaped, copper-scented. I lick it. Desperate to satiate myself, the rusty sharpness makes my mouth water. The father looks hopeful for a palatable morsel, and I briefly consider offering my skin to him. A head bobs in from my side and bites the crust from my hand, and with nothing more to offer this man across the playground, he swallows the leer he had proffered, and turns away.

The middle one reacts to my movement. It has not completed gorging, yet, and twitches its nose for further sources. A tongue flickers, seeks salt. It rasps against my exposed neck, suckling at my sweat that has appeared in the sultry afternoon. Hairs get caught in its mouth—I can hear the crunch and chew of my follicles—and its gag reflex stopping them from going any further echoes damply in my ear, like a Madonna and child sharing a secret. It spits out the hairs down my back.

It's with this gagging noise that you notice me.

You don't see the caring mother; you don't see the sacrifices I'm making. You see the mess they're making, the pretty parkland they're desecrating, the lolly wrappers and the blood, and we sicken you. A misshapen incubator, my hatchlings continue to gorge while you watch.

I want to ask you for help. I want to ask. I want to make a noise. Would you want to help? Are you a mother? Can you help me be a good mother?

What's worse than anger? Disgust? Your judgement?

Your indifference.

Your cold, dirty indifference as you exhale slowly, loudly, and walk on.

I loosen my waistband, and a fresh stretch of flesh appears for the eating. I cannot hear the playground now over the gluttonous chewing and ravaging. The dirt stuck to their palms mingles with my wounds. This is the meat they have come for. The domed lid that housed them; the abdomen that they shape-shifted and enlarged. The scars they caused with their births, they now tear open savagely. Here is the good meat. Here is the fat that nourishes, here is the gristle that binds families together. Here is the blood that brought new life into the world. Take all of it.

The trio is indistinguishable now, their faces painted in red, eyes closed, ratty hair matted with clots. My arms gather them in, like a poor mimicking of angels' wings. I press them close.

I press their faces in harder, and harder, organs slipping against their foreheads, one by one, harder, smothering them in muscle and flesh and love and blood. When their legs stop kicking, I place a red kiss on top of each head.

GRIZZLE

JASON FRANKS

The baby wasn't crying for his mother, because he'd only known her for a handful of minutes. Blake hadn't cried for her either in the three weeks since Sally had been gone. Or if he had, he didn't remember. Blake was tunnel-focused on the child. Bereavement was a disused station he'd left somewhere in the daylight far behind, barely glimpsed through the smoky windows of the insomnia express.

The owl-shaped nightlight glowed orange. Orange meant the temperature was good for the baby. Its clock showed 1:22am.

Blake hadn't been sleeping. He'd just been lying there, dazed, which was how he spent most of his time when he wasn't fussing over the infant. Blake and Sally had painted the baby's room together, but the child had never slept in there. He had installed the baby's cradle next to his queen-sized marital bed the day he'd returned from hospital.

Three weeks ago, Blake had found himself alone in the hospital suite with newborn Andrew lying blinking in his crib. Blake hadn't known what to do with the infant while he waited for someone to bring Sally back from theatre. He took out his phone and tried to get a selfie with the boy, but the angle down into the transparent plastic crib was too difficult. He didn't trust himself to hold the baby and snap a photo one-handed.

Thirty minutes later, a doctor arrived with the news that Sally wouldn't be coming back. A midwife materialised in the doorway as soon as the doctor had vacated it. The baby looked cold, she said, and spirited Andrew to the nursery to put him under lights.

Not long after that, a different nurse came and turned him out of the private suite. Since Sally was not going to be recovering there, the cleaning staff would prepare it for another new family. Blake hadn't known how to react, so he didn't react at all. They shunted him to the public hospital and admitted him as a boarder into a ward with two new mothers. After a couple of days of "parent crafting" lessons, the hospital subjected him to a brisk storm of paperwork and then discharged him. Blake had no idea what he had signed. He couldn't remember driving home. The next thing he knew, he was carrying the baby capsule into the house, with Sally's duffle bag full of toiletries and her new-mother maternity clothes slung over his shoulder.

And now, in his cradle, Andrew was still swaddled up tight, lying on his back, squalling, with his face turned away. Blake sat up and rolled his legs over the side of the bed.

A succession of nurses and social workers came to the house to check on Andrew's health and to teach Blake how to feed and care for the baby. The only acknowledgement from any of them about his wife's death was an off-hand comment that he needn't worry about breastfeeding.

Blake's friend Erica, a maternity nurse, had messaged him continually for almost a week about "wrongful death". The hospital was covering its arse, she said, and he needed to talk to a lawyer. But it was too hard to think about, so Blake had stopped looking at his phone altogether. He already had his hands full.

Andrew's squalling intensified. Blake unlatched the safety hasp and started to rock the cradle with his left hand while he rubbed at his own temple with the right. The hinges squeaked. The glowing owl looked on.

Blake couldn't recollect Sally's funeral, but he did remember their last conversation. No, their last argument. Sally had screeched at a nurse, who had fumbled three attempts to find a vein for the oxytocin drip. "If you think that's painful," he said, "you're really going to enjoy the main event." When Sally replied that he was going to be a terrible father who would probably let their child die of neglect, he smirked and shrugged. When she wished him a miserable and early death, he said something stupid about hormones and laughed. Sally went back to screaming.

The rocking motion did not diminish Andrew's crying, so Blake hitched the safety hasp again and lifted the infant from the cradle. He held him to his chest and swayed with him in his arms, one hand supporting the baby's head. The child was warm, his forehead soft against the stubble on Blake's cheek. After some minutes, Andrew settled, and Blake put him down again. He lay back on his own bed and looked at the ceiling.

Every particle of his body was weary. He was tired at the subatomic level.

The house creaked as the temperature fell a couple more degrees. The owl's dull radiance dropped from orange to a sallow yellow. Blake heard the vertical blinds shift as the heating breathed back on.

Suddenly, the bed was no longer comfortable. Blake sat up. In the nightlight's small radius, his shadow bled across the carpet. He touched Andrew in the cradle to make sure he was still breathing, and then padded to the kitchen, his bare feet slapping on the floorboards. He didn't need to turn the light on. It was only a few paces, past the laundry and the three steps down to the entrance hall.

In the kitchen, Blake fumbled around with the steam steriliser. He pulled the components from the drying rack and laid them on the counter. The steriliser was a plastic dish filled with stands and flanges to support all the baby paraphernalia that needed to be cleaned. Blake added water to its base and arranged the collection of bottles and teats. The bottles had been in the drying rack beside the steriliser—he'd already cleaned them, but now he wanted to clean them again. Why else had he got out of bed? He set the dome cover onto the steriliser and put it in the microwave to run another cycle.

When the turntable started, Blake looked away from the microwave's inner light. He couldn't hear Andrew over its noise, so he went back to the bedroom to check on him, where he found the baby snuffling quietly. The sight of the unmade bed made Blake feel light-headed, so he lay down on it, legs hanging over the side. He knew the microwave would rouse him soon, but he didn't know if he could get up again. The owl was still yellow. The blinds continued to flap gently over the heating duct.

Had he told the office where he was? He must be well past the end of his two weeks' paternity leave. When had Davis and Trina come around? Last weekend? They would have told the office what was happening, probably. Blake remembered their visit.

"You're doing so well, mate," Davis had told him.

Davis spoke easily, but Trina couldn't keep the pity from her face.

"House looks clean," she said. "You keeping fed?"

Keeping the house clean was easy for a man who didn't sleep. Meals…he wasn't sure. Definitely, he ate when someone stopped by with a food package. That was most days.

Sally would have been disgusted with him. "This is what I have to do to get you to pick up the broom? Give birth to your spawn and die?"

Blake wished his mom was here, but she was dead and buried back in the old country. Not that she would have been much practical help—she'd had a maid to look after the house for most of her adult life—but he didn't need her to cook or clean. He just wanted to be around someone who wouldn't judge him.

The house creaked so loudly he wondered if one of the roof timbers had snapped. Blake didn't flinch, but he could feel his hair pricking up. He turned his head towards the cradle. The nightlight shining on the slats cast stripes of thick new shadow on the sleeping infant. Slowly, he blinked, moved his head. The darkness boiled away, curled up into some dim, hovering threat he couldn't quite see.

Fatigue smothered out the moment of fear. He really needed some sleep. Maybe in the morning he would put Andrew in the capsule and go find a chemist, look for some melatonin again. Last time, the pharmacy assistant could only offer him the "homeopathic version". Blake knew there was more melatonin in tap water.

Blake's eyes were closing, but he knew he couldn't take his eyes off the cradle. The shadows would come back if he stopped watching.

The microwave chimed, and he rose as if on strings. Andrew snorted and fidgeted in his sleep, though not strongly enough to shake free of his swaddling.

The microwave chimed again. Blake looked towards the kitchen, then back to the cradle. He was hot, now that the heating was really working, but for some reason, the nightlight had dropped to blue. Broken already. He and Sally had bought it at a warehouse sale the week before Andrew was due. The microwave chimed a third time.

In the hallway, Blake noticed the laundry door was open. Usually, he kept it closed because the room was drafty, but sometimes, if the heating was on, the difference in air pressure would suck the door open. Blake went into the kitchen and the microwave chimed again, just as he reached for it. The sound made him flinch.

Annoyed at the machine, Blake yanked open the door with one hand and grabbed the steriliser with the other—but he'd forgotten how hot it would be. He snatched his hand away and the steriliser fell to the floor, splashing scalding water over his bare feet. Bottles and soft plastic attachments bounced across the tiles.

"Fuck!"

He knelt down in his wet pajama pants and fumbled around in the light of the open microwave, collecting the pieces by feel. He stacked them up on the steriliser, and put the device on the counter. He would definitely have to run another cycle.

"Fuck, fuck, fucken, *fuck*."

The puddle of water spread from the kitchen out into the hallway.

"Just…fuck."

The laundry door was all the way open now, but he barely noticed as he went through it. The floor tiles were cold on his feet, but mercifully dry. He opened the cupboard, wrestled out a mop and bucket.

That was when he heard the sigh.

Blake was confused. Had *he* been the one who'd sighed? He didn't think so. He'd been about to, but he still felt full of air.

Blake stepped back, drew the mop and bucket towards him, and closed the cupboard door.

Sigh. There it was again.

Blake cast around to locate the source of the sound. There, on the floor, sticking out of the three-inch gap between the broom cupboard and the rack shelving, was the outline of a foot. A woman's foot. As he watched, the outline bubbled into three dimensions and filled itself with flesh, as pale as laminated plywood.

Blake inhaled sharply and gripped the mop handle. The bucket rattled on the tiles. He didn't want to, but he leaned over so he could better see into the gap.

Sally was there, sitting with her knees to her chest. The geometry of the too-narrow space could not confine her shape. She was still wearing the green hospital gown. Tubing from the epidural curled around her legs. Her head was down. Dark locks that had escaped from the medical hairnet were plastered against her face.

Sigh. Sally's loose hair moved with her breath.

Blake made a constricted, croaking sound as he tried, and failed, to breathe. He didn't know if he was trying to inhale or exhale. His equilibrium wavered, and he had to lean on the mop to stay upright.

She wasn't real. He hadn't slept. She couldn't be there. He was dreaming. It wasn't Sally. It was someone else. She was something else.

Blake's legs were cold inside the wet pajama pants.

Sally raised her head to him, but her eyes stayed closed. "Blake."

He didn't know what to say.

"Blake." It was more breath than whisper. "You forgot me already."

"I didn't."

"That thing about the cleaning. That's the first time you've thought of me in three weeks."

It wasn't true. Not exactly. He was working hard not to think about her. Not to have to deal with her death.

Sally opened her eyes. They were the same colour as the owl, and just as radiant.

"Your eyes are blue," he said.

"Three weeks dead, and you've already forgotten the colour of my eyes." Somehow, she squared her shoulders in that confined space. "You never loved me. Do you even love our boy?"

He had bent every strand of his will and every chain of molecules in his body to staying vigilant, to keeping Andrew safe and warm and alive. Even though the owl had gone blue. Was that love? Or was it just a semblance of that emotion, a pantomime act by a hollow man, trying to hold onto the only thing of value he had left?

Sally drew upright in a strange uncoiling motion, sidling out of the narrow gap between the cupboard and the shelving as if she was emerging from a hallway. Blake let go of the mop handle and took a step back.

Sally maintained the distance between them, hips swinging, though her feet barely moved. Her arms hung and the backs of her hands twitched. Another tube was there, drooping from a forearm bruised by the nurse's failed attempts to find a vein. Dry. There was blood on her gown. Black stripes, which had dripped down her legs. But the blood was dried and cracking. There was nothing wet left inside her now.

"He's just a thing to you, a possession. Same as I was."

Blake started to reply. He wanted to ask if she knew Andrew's name. He couldn't remember who had chosen it, or when.

Instead, he said, "You were everything to me, Sally." It sounded like the cliché it was. He didn't know if he meant it.

"*You* are everything to you," she said, advancing.

Blake scrambled backwards into the hallway. He set his foot down on a slick spot from the steriliser spill and felt his balance going. Blake swung his arms to steady himself, took another step back, but there was no floor there.

There were only three stairs down to the entrance hall, but his feet were tangled and he didn't know what to do with his arms. There was an impact, and something cracked near the base of his skull.

Blake's head was tilted at an angle he didn't like, directed so could see up the three stairs. One of his feet was on the second step, but he couldn't see where the other lay. There was no pain, but maybe that was just the adrenaline. Maybe it was something worse.

Sally stood at the top of the steps, hands hanging in front of her. Tubes dangling past her knees. Sweat-soaked hair in her face. The gown covered the wound from her C-section, but he could imagine it there, stitches bursting over crusty black flesh. Sally's eyes were dark now, but he didn't think that was the right colour either.

"Useless." The sound was guttural. The first proper vocalisation this version of her had made. "Just useless. You let me down, as usual, and now you've failed the baby as well."

She turned her back and returned to the laundry, dry tubes dragging on the floor behind her.

He couldn't see into the bedroom from where he lay, but the light cast by the owl reflected down the hallway, shining brighter than ever. Shining red.

In the bedroom, Andrew began to grizzle.

THESE BLOODY LANES

LEANBH PEARSON

Surrey Hills, Sydney, 1920

The night is rich with the foetid stink of night soil, rotting garbage and old blood. She throws back her head, basking in the moonlight. It's a night for hunting. The witch shifts. The bones of her hands crack, splinter and reknit into long, terrible talons. She screams in pain as the fangs force through her gums. Long tendrils of bloody spittle hang from her split lips. The goddess within her snarls in wordless triumph.

A feast is nearby.

Loping, quick strides carry her silently down the narrow lanes of these labyrinths of butchery. Shadows melt deeper into the darkness, but she scents the houses she seeks. The ones of rot, fear and blood. The first terrace house is lit by the dim glow of an oil lamp from within. Voices carry through the thin stone walls; pleading, sobbing, met by impassive, unvarying replies. Lamashtu will feast tonight.

She leaps the wall with claws scraping sharp against the stonework. Dropping onto all fours in the dark courtyard beyond, she crouches and lifts nostrils to the air. Here, the ripe smell of fresh blood rises and, beneath it, the older clotted blood that lines the rusty garbage cans beside the back door. No waiting.

She barges through the door, flinging it back against the wall and breaking old hinges.

A girl—barely a woman—lies in a blood-soaked dress upon the makeshift operating table. A man turns, glaring with shock and indignation, the foetus still gripped in his black rubber gloves.

Hunger rolls through her and she pounces. Those talons slice the butcher's jugular vein and spray the walls with crimson. She falls upon the foetus in unholy need. Blood pools thick and clotting on the floor as she satiates herself. Lost to the taste of blood and flesh, she's unaware as the girl staggers away from the house.

Sydney Hospital, 1920

I walk along the rows of beds. The hem of my grey skirt swishes against the blood-spattered and rusty bed frames. The stench of infection and rotting wounds makes me gag. Sydney Hospital is a convict-built sandstone series of buildings with interconnecting narrow corridors. The oldest hospital in Australia, it is still a place where the poor and sick end up. Some recover, but many more are treated without hope by the surgeons and medical men who can do little for patients in these overcrowded and unsanitary conditions.

A miasma of disease and death clings to the Open Ward, and I try not to look at bloody and bandaged wretches in the rows of beds.

I quicken my pace towards the closed doors of the private Women's Ward directly in front of me. These frosted glass doors offer a modicum of privacy but also assure the patients within are kept from public view. Beyond the doors is the domain of male medical doctors, who determine the lives of the women seeking aid after botched ministrations from the "backyard abortionists" that plague inner Sydney.

I will not avoid these women. I step within the ward, and the doors swing shut behind me with a sullen creak.

Within, the Women's Ward is lit only by weak sunshine straining through the grimy windowpanes. Beds are arranged in a semicircular pattern with a large empty space in the centre of the room where dust motes now spiral.

Before the war, the *Poisons Act of 1905* made abortive drugs like ergot and rye only available by prescription. The *Police Offences*

Act of 1908 drove abortionists into illegal operations, sought by desperate women who either lacked the ability to care for a child or had no desire for the pregnancy at all. The terrible result was a rise in botched abortions from anyone with training. After undergoing these illegal procedures, desperately ill women now rely on Sydney Hospital and an unknown fate.

Surrounding me in Sydney Hospital are the victims; these women our post-war society deems fallen, sinners, beyond redemption. These are the forgotten women shut away from view. I need to hear their voices because no one else will.

Someone seeks vengeance on the abortionists, and they know exactly where to find their prey. The newspaper reports of recent violent and bloody murders of pregnant women, their babies and the abortionists, caught my attention. I am one of a few with knowledge that society would deem wicked, and a vice. A person with specialised occult training. Some might call me witch.

Sinner.

Lilith.

I am some and none of them. I am now the only one who can recognise the summoning of an ancient goddess meant to wreak revenge against those who have wronged a witch. Does the summoner know the goddess can't be subverted to anyone's will? The lanes now run with gore and blood, and Lamashtu feasts on women, men, and babies alike. Some of these women around me have likely seen the witch or worse—Lamashtu possessing her body.

I know what I'm hunting. There's a part of me that wants to shirk this duty and close my eyes to the truth. But I can't. Lamashtu the demon goddess is powerful and can possess the weaker will of a mortal. There's an unknown witch on the streets I'm to sworn to protect and worse still, her summoning of Lamashtu allowed the demon-goddess to possess her body. These streets will continue to bleed unless I can find the witch and banish Lamashtu.

I turn to the first whey-faced woman in one of the beds. Her ash-blonde hair is mostly drained of colour, nearly white, and a fever-halo of perspiration stains her pillow. She looks as poor as any wretch I expect to find here.

"You're no nurse." Her voice is gravelly from disuse.

"Why do you think that?"

"You look at us and don't shrink away. You *see* us. None of the nurses even look at us. Sin might be contagious."

I move to her bedside. Her body is wasted with thin, stick-like arms protruding from beneath the sheets.

I say, "Tell me how you ended up here."

"You're one of those Women's Society snoops, aren't you? Trying to moralise about us poor sinners prone to vice?"

"Nothing of the sort. I'm seeking the murderer now stalking these lanes. Not one of the Razor Gangs, mind you, I know the witches in their employ. No. This one is killing not just abortionists but the women and babies too."

Her eyes narrow as she scrutinises me and weighs up whether I am lying. Her pale tongue licks at bloodless lips. Finally, she speaks.

"I'd been too close to full-term when I'd gathered enough coin to pay for what needed doing. She might've been a nurse once, but years of liquor had made her hard-looking. After she finished her work, she dropped my child into a bucket like it was rubbish. She pulled me from the table and pushed me out the back door into the lane beyond, already mopping up blood and fluids; getting ready for the next poor girl."

She closes her eyes, as if she can't bear the images that flash through her memory.

"Go on," I say.

"I saw the one you're asking about. I thought I had a fever already when she climbed over the brick wall. Her face was twisted by teeth, big as a lion's choppers, and her hands were long claws. Shouting erupted from that awful house I'd just escaped as that monster took the body of my child and tore it apart. I ran. Too desperate to escape that nightmare, I didn't notice the blood pouring down my legs. It didn't matter if I outran her or not. She only wanted my dead baby and the abortionist who ripped it from me."

"Did you know the murderer? The woman?"

"Wasn't no woman, I can tell you that straight up. It was

inhuman, whatever it was."

"You don't expect me to believe you, but I know what you saw was real."

"You believe me? Just like that?" Her fever-bright eyes shine from the depths of bruise-dark orbits, and blue veins snake across her pale skin. She's not got long left in this mortal plane. "You some gullible fool? Or unnaturally unafraid?"

"I can't make recompense for the wrongs done to you," I say. "But your story isn't the first of its kind I've heard in this room. I'm no fool, and I'm certainly afraid of the thing I'm hunting. Do you remember anything about what the witch was wearing?"

"She's a witch then? What does that make you? A witch-hunter? Another witch? Her clothes were like any flapper from George Street. But mark my words, a finely-dressed monster or not, her eyes burned like hellfire."

"I'm going to find this witch who's summoned that demon you saw, who is possessed by it. I'll find her and stop her."

"She did this on purpose? She let loose that horror on the women of Razorhurst?"

"The witch might be like yourself and fell victim to a botched abortion. Whatever her story, she's summoned something in vengeance but can't control it, and it's gone berserk."

"Let me give you some advice, gal," she says. "Don't go talking too much like that around here or they'll lock you up in Callan Park with the insane."

I understand her meaning. I've overstayed my welcome and dredged up her traumas.

"You and these other girls don't deserve the horror you've endured," I say. "You deserve a choice over your own bodies. It's a choice that men have taken from us since returning from the war. We had freedom—just a taste of it—but we're being forced back into the spaces and roles men decide for us."

She sneers. "Bah, I know I'm not going to live. Preach your suffragette nonsense somewhere else. If this witch has brought destruction and death to Razorhurst, I'm not sure we don't deserve it."

I leave the Women's Ward with the words of the dying woman

echoing in my mind. I'm not sure she was wrong. Razorhurst is ruled by cruel and ruthless gangster queens. Now Lamashtu chooses to cleanse these streets with blood. I have to stop her. She's drawn the attention of the press—and police. My protection and employment by Razor Queen, Kate Leigh, is to keep police away from Surrey Hills and its nest of laneways filled with thieves, prostitutes, sly-grog owners, and drug dealers. Whoever this unsanctioned witch is, she'll meet brutal justice of her own making.

I linger long on the streets tonight. I patrol alongside many of Kate Leigh's lookouts, and we exchange a few quiet nods of acknowledgement. I'm as well known in these parts as the Queen of Razorhurst herself. A few whispers in the right ears in dark alleys, and word will spread I'm looking for a well-dressed woman who looks more at home at one of the high-rolling gambling rooms than in this neighbourhood.

It's late in the evening before I return to my lodgings. I'm no closer to knowing how this witch gained the knowledge and skill to summon such a powerful goddess.

But there is a good reason the ancient Mesopotamian magicians feared Lamashtu.

Surrey Hills, Sydney, 1920

I wake the next morning to a roughly torn piece of paper slid under my front door. I approach with caution, already conjuring a defensive hex but as I get closer, there's no residual malice or taint of another practitioner's handiwork. The paper is probably just a note.

I slide it free from where it's been wedged between the bottom of the door and wooden floor. Flipping it open, there's a hasty scribble of unfamiliar handwriting.

> *Kate Leigh's Witch,*
> *You asked for any sighting of a strange woman in those lanes the abortionists use. I saw a dark-haired woman in a sequin dress. Loveliest thing I ever damn seen. She wore these most scandalous heels. I would've thought her a high-*

class lady except when she looked my way, embers burned in her eyes. Reminded me a little of you. Beware her. She's dangerous, that one.
Violet.

I'm not sure if I like being "Kate Leigh's Witch" but better that than any of these girls know my real name. There's old power in the knowing of true names. Why, even this working girl goes by the incredulous name of "Violet". I doubt she's anything so sweet or innocent.

I'm not going to dismiss her advice though. Tonight, I'll stalk these awful mazes of lanes and hunt for the practitioner whom Lamashtu now embodies. Kate pays me handsomely, and I'll take down the practitioner before any more scrutiny turns towards Kate's patch.

Twilight is falling as I start my search through the labyrinth. Each row of terrace houses backs onto narrow dirt lanes, and empties a filthy sludge into the gutters. It's a squalid mixture of night soil, piss, vomit and blood. These are the poorest areas of what's known as Razorhurst.

It's the domain of the Razor Gangs ruled ruthlessly by proclaimed matriarch, Kate Leigh, owner and protector. In return for her patronage and protection, these people of Razorhurst kindly return the favours whenever Kate finds herself up before the magistrate on her latest charges. I was unlikely to encounter anyone of good intent on my hunt tonight with the exception of the only female police officer, Lillian Armfield, who often patrols these dark and shadowy lanes looking out for the girls.

It's an absolute warren in here of uneven streets, shadowy lanes, thieves, and prostitutes looking for business. I've chosen a loose-fitting shirt and wide-legged pants for ease of movement, and pinned my long hair in a chignon with a baggy hat covering it. I can't let this witch get any loose strands of my hair to work a hex against me. If I am even half right in the hunger that drives Lamashtu, the witch who is nothing more than a vessel for the goddess will be hunting tonight.

These may be her hunting grounds, but they're also my streets to protect.

The stench of burning flesh and bone where these backyard abortionists run their trade draws me like a lodestone. There is no way a fiend like Lamashtu can avoid this offering.

I hide within the shadows of an overhanging wisteria to give both protection from sight and also scent, as I don't want Lamashtu distracted by the smell of a witch. We all have a tell-tale signature to our magic, and something as ancient as Lamashtu will know I'm here. I want her to focus on her hunt, and then I can spring my trap. From where I'm hidden, I can keep watch over several backyard gateways that lead into known abortion houses.

A nervous girl fidgets as she walks down the laneway towards me.

She's a strawberry blonde with a pale complexion, clutching her small handbag tightly against her stomach as if showing proof that she can pay for what needs doing. She's checking a scrap of paper and the numbers of the houses as she walks.

Pity swells in me for this girl, but I don't move from my post.

She shoots a quick glance up the filthy lanes and darts into one of the three houses I was watching. The back gate slams shut, and I grimace at the echo. The whiteness of her dress is visible for only a few moments before the darkness of the house's back door swallows her up.

I lean against the wall behind me and cross my legs at the ankles, preparing to wait. My hands reach into my pockets and check again the ritual items I've got with me.

There's muffled conversation from inside the house where the girl has gone. The volume rises into a small argument as whatever price the abortionist first offered now seems to have doubled. The girl's voice is high-pitched and desperate. In the end, I know—as good as the abortionist knows—that she'll pay whatever he asks just so that the pregnancy and this horrid night will be over.

The argument must surely alert any of the local patrolling police, but the streets are eerily quiet. Anyone who makes a living in these streets knows a nastier predator when they see one.

Lamashtu is coming.

I'm hit almost like a blow by her presence as all my nerves are on fire. The air tingles and crackles with the power of the ancient goddess as she stalks down the centre of the dirt lane. The grime of the day still bears the dried blood of razor fights, but this woman treads the lanes in her finery and her dark hair flowing free. Any doubts I might've had that this woman is the embodiment of a goddess of violence and savagery flee when I see her eyes, burning like twin fires in the darkness.

The argument from inside the terrace house grows louder. The goddess increases her pace and with it, she shifts. Her hands snap and lengthen into talons, and her jaw pops as unnaturally long fangs pierce her gums. The visage of the witch is gone, consumed by the goddess possessing her, revelling in her horror and glory.

A door slams, and shouts echo from within the darkened yard. I see a flash of the white dress of the girl who's been within for only minutes. I can't reach her in time. I already know, even as I push away from the wall. Lamashtu leaps with inhuman speed over the terrace enclosure and into the darkness of the garden beyond. My heart pounds as I run. There's a terrified scream cut short by the horrid gurgling of blood filling lungs and throat. I dash for the gate to the terrace garden, pulling free from my pockets the ritual items I need to constrain Lamashtu. I know I'm too late even as I shove the gate open.

There are more screams and curses from within the house, and the clattering of thrown furniture as Lamashtu takes her vengeance on the abortionist too.

The dead girl is at my feet. Blood spreads in a wide pool around her and trickles down the slope towards the lane outside. What is left of her body is a mess of meat, viscera and ever-spreading blood. The foetus, torn from her body, is discarded by the back door.

I'm overwhelmed and terrified by the violence and destruction around me. I'm too late to save the girl, too late to save her unborn child. The sound of another feast comes from within the house—I'm too late to save the abortionist. I turn my focus to restraining Lamashtu before any others die tonight.

"Lamashtu." My voice is strong with the power of my magic behind it.

Inside the terrace house, the sound of tearing flesh and slurping of blood pauses. The goddess is listening.

"Lamashtu. You have no power here. I call you forth, daughter of the Sun, demon goddess of the night. Leave the body you inhabit and wreak no more carnage here."

A snarl like a lion erupts from within the house. The inhuman form of the goddess bursts through the remains of the shattered door, leaping over her meal, the butchered remains of the abortionist.

I pull the two simple but effective candles inscribed with ancient sigils from my pocket. Willing the power within me, flames spark from the candle wicks.

Lamashtu doesn't even stop. She barrels into me, and together we sprawl into the dirt and blood in the yard with the corpse of the girl beneath us. The candle flames scorch Lamashtu's flesh, and I break that candle and toss it aside. It lands with a hiss into the blood surrounding us. In this blood Lamashtu has spread, I scrawl the banishing sigils from the ancient Mesopotamian sorcerers.

She roars, and there's a sharp scrape of her claws against my flesh.

I push the second burning candle into her skin and recite the banishment curse. These are ancient words, powerful magic inscribed in cuneiform tablets and spread throughout the old world.

I whisper the last words of the banishing spell as my blood from the many cuts Lamashtu has given me mingles with that of the dead girl beneath me. There is power in the blood of Lamashtu's victim and, together with mine, it binds my spell tighter to Lamashtu. I break the second candle and, with it, end Lamashtu's reign of vengeance and violence throughout Razorhurst.

The power of the banishment spell works through me. Lamashtu towers over me and for a terrible moment I think the spell won't work. Then it pulls her back to whatever immortal realm such a terrible goddess inhabits. The body above me transforms, with Lamashtu's elongated limbs and claws retracting and the mouth of fangs pulling inward until the body shrinks in on itself, leaving only the witch behind.

She stares down at me, the sudden absence of Lamashtu's possession stunning and confusing her. She rolls away and looks around at the horror of the yard. Blood pools in congealed patches. Torn and half-devoured flesh lies in visceral heaps.

"You're an unregistered practitioner," I say, panting. "A witch without enough sense to understand the power of what you summoned. You're responsible for the murders of innocent lives and a contagion of terror. Perhaps you didn't know that once you summoned Lamashtu she would take possession of your body, and you would have no control over her. A goddess like Lamashtu is not to be taken lightly. This is my only warning. If I catch you practising any form of magic in these streets again, it will be Kate Leigh that you deal with next, and nothing happens in these streets without her say-so."

The witch looks at me with eyes still wide with shock. "You work for a gangster?"

"We all work for someone, and we all owe our lives to some-one. Right now, you owe your life to me. *Never* make me need to call in that debt. I'll do it without remorse. Now, get out of my sight."

Her dark hair is a wild tangle of sticky blood and gore. Even so, I snatch a few strands as she runs from me. Better to have insurance for the future if the witch ever practises magic again.

My shoulders twitch with the unseen gazes of gangsters waiting in the lane beyond. A crew to clean up the horrible deaths and wash the blood into the gutters. I turn, but none of those hardened men will meet my eyes. They know the power that women wield and, in turn, I owe Kate Leigh a talk.

I leave the abortion houses behind me. A breeze lifts up from the harbour bringing the unpleasant smells of the Razorhurst slums with it. Behind me, Kate's crew are hosing out the terraces and yards. These lanes run with blood, but I hope it's for the last time.

LEACH/LEECH

ROWAN HILL

The babies howl, and the cut where they were torn from my body burns even in sleep. Scored, seared, cauterised, raging blue light flickers like a strobe against my eyes and I blink awake. Across our current population of birthing mothers, there was a third of a chance for failure, a C-section critical. But I guess twin blessings meant all bets were off. Drugs were parcelled and my babies were extracted, screeching new lungs with dusty air. I blissfully couldn't remember a thing about the traumatic surgery or even arriving home. There was once a fuzzy memory of a nondescript nurse, instructing with a dull voice that it would take six weeks to heal, till that burning below my belly subsided. But that memory has long since dissolved.

One of them wails again. Higher, panicked, upset at my delay—*where are you!?*—and I roll in bed like a great, groggy worm for the clock's angry red numbers. The twins had given me two hours of sleep. Better than nothing? Another burst of crying, an explosion of sound, and I scramble into a new blue robe. A throwback in maternity styles, it is still tight with baby weight.

"Yes, yes, darlings, Mummy is coming," I call, rushing the short distance between our rooms.

What is the point of even having a nursery if I never leave it? I'm sure there is a point. "Sleep when the babies sleep," they say. Oh yes, good luck with that. Surely a man said that once upon a time and thought his voice sounded knowledgeable.

Their room is dim, twin cribs pushed into the corner, and I run as a woman possessed, their cries intolerable to maternal ears. The cherubs, my cherubs, are still pink and squishy from the womb and have escaped their swaddles. Chubby arms flail wildly, eyes and foreheads scrunched tight, as if fearing they would never eat again, and I reach for them, cooing in soft tones.

"Shhhhh, okay my loves. It's okay, it's okay, I know, I know. Oh, you're so hungry. So hungry." By the time we settle into the nursing chair, my darling boy, my first son, is nearly fidgeting out of the crook of my arm. "Shhhh, darling, just hold on."

My night shirt is pulled and stretched beyond repair, so much so that I now call it the "anytime" shirt, though I can't remember anyone laughing at my joke. I arrange the babies alongside my breasts to feed at the same time. Both little mouths maw the air in anticipation.

They latch. Little clamps painfully tighten, the hard gums with developing teeth unerringly aiming for the tenderest, rawest part of each breast, and I flinch in that first agonising moment. But after another, the pain eases, melds with a different sensation of cathartic pain, and together we three mould into the rocking chair.

Fluid, milk, life, *whoosh*es from my breasts, and it is a release to bestow. I hear it, them, suckling. Now their faces lose the impatient flush, and I can only stare at them, still sleep-groggy. The thread-thin scars around their hairlines, evidence of the doctor's metal forceps, remain. There is little hope they will disappear.

But still…it is a sin to call them adorable, my children are far beyond that. I brush their soft heads. They are captivating, ethereal. Blessings. Children are blessings, and we had waited so long for them. So long and now I would do anything, give anything, for these two bundles of miracle. Love swells my heart three sizes too big for my body.

The rocking chair is old and squeaks on the apex of every rock, but it is soothing after all this time of nursing. A familiar, discordant rhythm with motion.

An explosion rocks the house slightly, dust shimmering from the cement ceiling, and both babies wince but stay attached to eat greedily, concerned only with their hunger.

"Shhhhh, shhhh, it's okay. We're inside, it's okay," I whisper, glancing out the grimy window.

A mushroom head of dark, billowing clouds plumes on the far horizon, pre-dawn light casting it in shades of dirty rose. Maybe the next city over? Far enough for us to stay but perhaps close enough to make me a refugee with newborns.

I rock a little harder, press into the balls of my feet a little more. Using the familiar, ugly squeak to reassure my bundles of joy that everything is the same. Babies need routine. Nothing has changed.

"Shhhh, it's okay. Mummy is here. We're all safe in our house. All safe and warm with full tummies," I coo.

It's a lie. I am starving. But my loves take comfort because their eyes, always closed, un-scrunch and their faces relax. I would love to see their eyes. Why haven't they opened yet? Together we rock like three figures on a calm sea, just us three. Words fall from my mouth in short mumbles, sleep deprivation catching up to a new mother. Wasn't sleep deprivation a form of torture? Why does no one mention that? "You will literally be tortured." But it is in the name of love.

Through hooded eyelids, I look at the two angel faces, now asleep, pressing against my bruised breasts. Little mouths gaped, black holes for ingresses, smears of breast milk on their lips. I understand why no one bothers with horrific stories of new-motherhood torture. Because new mothers wouldn't care. They behold their babies with rose-coloured glasses and declare, "I'll take it. More, please." They would protect them from war and terror and even let them suck life from their flesh. Happily.

A noise, a clatter downstairs, draws my attention from their sleeping faces, and with the gentleness of a bomb diffuser, I lay them in their cribs. Rumbling outside touches the house like a far-off thunderstorm, a white noise for ambience. How long would the invasion continue? It can't last forever.

I creep out and downstairs to the kitchen. The grey concrete floors are cold. The house is down to its barest bones, marrow sucked dry. A chair here, a table there. War and famine dictate what one can live without. I am stopped short by the basket of food sitting atop the kitchen counter, larger than those before. A smorgasbord. A large jar of synthesised honey, fresh salmon, a loaf of bread, paillards of beef, potatoes in a bag. Calorie-rich food. Food for a breastfeeder. For all my fatigue, my sleep-, audio- and sensory-deprivation, the isolation, all the hardships of a new mother, my mouth still has the energy to water at the sight of food. Gush with saliva.

But why didn't my husband stay? See the babies, check if they are okay? We prayed for children for so long, and when they are finally given… The front lines are endless, but I can't recall the last time we spent the night together. A meal. A conversation. What was it like to talk to another adult? To have thoughts beyond sleep, breastfeeding, nappies? Repeat. Always repeat.

No, I am being selfish. He needs to do his part for the war, and I am doing mine. I'm lucky he still thinks of me amidst war and galactic terrors. Provides so I can care for our offspring.

Without hesitation, I pull the salmon from its packet and eat it raw. It is synthetic, obviously. Fleshy pink, bland and unremarkable, but the exquisite texture of fat alongside scales remains. Oil slicks my fingers and makes the fish so hard to hold I eventually push it against my mouth, remnants of my teeth gnashing through the occasional fishbone, tearing sinews. Unseasoned. Tasteless. Exquisite. I eat the whole thing, the entire fillet undoubtedly intended for two or three meals. Meant to be rationed in these times of scarcity.

But there is really no other time. No other time guaranteed for food, a future in limbo. I sit in the only chair and lay forward on the table. The fish uncomfortably slides down my oesophagus. My belly, still bulbous from carrying and creating two children, gurgles in anticipation. What else is in the basket? Potatoes sound nice, but will take time to cook on my tiny flame grill, and I am so tired. Always tired.

An animal shrieks, and my sleeping head shoots off the table. An animal? In the house? The baby cries again and I snatch two potatoes from the basket. One is for my pocket, the other I bite into like an apple of old, bounding up the stairs.

"I'm coming! Coming, darlings!" I call through bites and quickly return to their room.

My daughter, light of my life, stops crying once she hears me, her tiny chin quivering, threatening to wake her brother if I don't attend to her absolutely right now at this second. Chewing the last of the small potato and forcing it down, I pick her up. Her dirty nappy is immediately noticeable.

"Shhhhh, it's okay, little girl, I've got you. I'm here. Let's go to the table, huh?"

The changing table is beside the only window and a wave of nausea, a tsunami of exhaustion, sweeps over me as I lay her down. How long had we been doing this? The names of days lose meaning when there is no rest to punctuate them. No weekends for Mummy, and I reach for the window to steady myself.

"Oh darling, I think we're going to have to give Mummy more rest, huh?"

Maybe if they sleep in my bed? I open her nappy and frown. Meconium? The black poop of a newborn? Shouldn't that be all done? I look to her angel face, feeling her forehead for a fever, some symptom of malady. Where could I even go for medicine if she is sick? But she smiles for the naked, free feeling, the pink thread scars behind her ears tug at her new skin.

A woman screams, wild and frenzied, and forgetting my daughter I peer forward, my fingers prying the blinds apart. Across the desolate street with the broken blacktop, a woman, dressed in a bed robe, runs from her house. Her arms clutch a writhing bundle against her unsecured breasts as she sprints with bare feet down the busted footpath. She screams again, a harsh cacophonic note, glancing over her shoulder, and I follow her gaze only to immediately flinch away.

One of *them* leaves the black hollow of her front door. Have *they* broken through the frontlines and are in our neighbourhood? Seven feet tall and beige, spindly legs attached to a thorax, scuttling fast over torn pavement, the alien catches up to her, my poor, nameless neighbour, in an instant. Too fast. Its insectoid head with bulbous eyes shakes from side to side, fastidiously, as if reprimanding her. Silly female. A strange helmet materialises from one of its pincers, flashing blue inside, before the baby is extracted from her arms. She howls, lunging for the bundle, fruitlessly, and I nearly cry with her, my hand bridling my face.

A mother separated from her baby. The hurt, the unexplainable soul-splitting anguish. That could be us. I can't watch, and let the blinds fall.

My daughter squirms and through welling eyes I weakly smile for her, finishing her nappy and blocking the woman's cries. "Shhhhh, shhhhh, it's okay, we're okay, we're safe and warm, darling girl."

Girl? It is certainly time for names. Hadn't I been waiting for my husband to help with naming? It is common in our families to name after grandparents. "Junior" and "Little"… Sounds good on any child, adorable. Heirlooms of the spoken word. Memories of humanity living in the children's very designations.

Beyond the blinds, the childless mother screams again, and her shriek is muffled as I imagine her being dragged back into her home. My body physically shudders in sympathy, empathy, foreboding, and I pick up my daughter, hugging her close. Hugging for my comfort. There is nowhere else to go.

"Shhhh, we're okay."

Another lie, of course, but we all lie to our children. Lying for their sense of security is the only good reason to lie.

She gurgles, a sound only babies can make to send mothers' hearts fluttering. Unfortunately, it wakes my son and he murmurs, stirs, and I know *that* sound. How can such little things consume so much? Feedings twelve times a day sounded crazy but has proven true. And now she is making the same mouthing movements.

Little mouths move in unison and I swear, I hear their internal monologues. *Mamma, I'm hungry, I need you.* I add that last part as I arrange my breasts for both to feed. It's nice to think they need me, specifically. Of course, it is me *specifically.* A mother for a baby. A bond. For us.

Little mouths search for my nipples, always sore and swollen, latching immediately and I wince again, my eyes squeezing shut on their own. Women's bodies are amazing hosts. They will suck up any fat, spare proteins, residual energy, sanity, and strive to make milk for their darlings. My body will ignore that I am tired, dishevelled, near breaking point emotionally, terrified of planetary invaders one day threatening my children, our lives, and will still have a biological imperative to make milk for my children. Sharp...gums?...bite against my tender areolas.

"Ow! *Ow!* Darlings, please, shhhhh, carefulcareful. I'm not a pin cushion."

I tuck my son beneath my arm for a better position. Oh, he has definitely grown. Evolved. My tired muscles recognise his extra weight. A sense of pride envelops me as he squirms, sucking more milk. I did that. I made this tiny, loving bundle grow. Healthy and strong, my body, my milk has transformed him. I did that. No one else. No one else could.

Once more, their little, puckered mouths go slack, falling into their milk coma. My breasts, my body, given reprieve. I stare at them indulgently. Chubby cheeks, smooth little foreheads, squashed ears. Oh my, mymymymy. Devotion, reverence is overwhelming. I would do anything for these babies. I would give them every ounce of my body if they needed.

But luckily, they are satiated, and once more I lay them gently down before shuffling back to bed and falling immediately asleep.

A high-pitched treble noise rattles through the house, and my body, tuned should the children need me, nearly jumps itself out of bed. I don't even need to see the clock to know there was not enough sleep. After days, weeks, maybe even months alone with the babies, there will never be enough sleep. There will always be a deficit. I will always be in the red. I have heard mothers only catch up on sleep when their children finally leave home. Even then, we will remain in stasis, a sleeper agent, alert should they need us. A mother will never have enough of what her body needs but will give everything it has.

My baby—my daughter—shrieks again. Holy shit!? Is that her? I race through the rooms. She must be in pain for such a sound to come through angelic lips. The room is dim, sunset goldens the nursery through the boarded slats, and I rush to her crib only to halt.

Black eyes stare at me. There are no irises, no whites, and her skin looks…painful. Stretched. She howls again, her eyes scrunching closed in fear, and my maternal instincts demand I pick her up. She is getting bigger, stronger in her squirming.

"Shhhhh, hey now, what's going on here?"

I sit with her, rocking, examining her closer. Her anxiety lessens with the motion, calm resuming her face, her eyelids still closed. Prying and poking her soft skin, I wonder what I saw in the gloom. Hallucinations of a fatigued mother. We rock, both tired. She must have had a nightmare. Could she sense the turmoil raging outside? Am I not lying well enough? Is the outside world worming its way in? Sneaking through the erratic screams and caustic winds, creeping beneath the doorways? Shaking the house's cement bones with a distant explosion, a gunshot, a scream, a cry? I am doing my best, but maybe it's not enough.

The rocking motion, the faint squeak, the warmth of my baby hugging my chest sends us both to sleep.

The same kind of night but another night. Clacking, high heels on wood floors, wakes us in the chair. My son wriggles at the intrusion, a great giant baby I now struggle to hold. No, nooooo, I could cry. I swear he just fell asleep.

"Shhhhhh, babybabybaby, sleepysleepy time. Back to sleeeeep."

He squirms, his eyes always closed before stilling and retreating into his milk coma. How many times have I watched them fall into sleep, envying and thankful? Such a strange emotion. The scars around their tiny faces linger, stretching with growth and age. His chubby little skin is firm, bulging, protruding.

They are changing, growing up. It is beautiful and horrible. My newborns are leaving and turning into real babies. And for all the hurt and pain and stress and exhaustion they caused, for all the weight I lost, literally sucked of life and vitality, for the constant swelling and hurt in my breasts, for all the blood seeping from my areolas, I didn't want it to end.

Another clatter of heels, feet spiking the floor downstairs. Every muscle in my body tenses.

"Shhhhh, shhhhh."

I lay him down and creep from the room.

Clack clack.

Oh God, oh God, please, please, let them sleep through whatever is downstairs. Don't let them wake to see whatever is here. Clearly the front lines had broken, the sporadic screams were too frequent. It has been weeks, more, since anything was announced through the neighbourhood speakers. We're obviously losing if the enemy is behind the lines, scouring dilapidated houses for hostages, if that's what they're doing. I cinch the loose bathrobe tight and gently pad downstairs, freezing on the midway landing to gasp.

My heart sticks mid-beat.

Spindly olive-green-beige legs walk behind the dividing wall. Why are they here? It must be to do with my husband, they've somehow discovered he is infantry. Retribution? Against us, our babies? It seems negligible to target one family in a worldwide war.

I peek around the corner; a leg moves deeper into the living room. Shit! Shit! What do I have? What is left in my shell of a house? A plank of wood, splintered and fraying, is on the floor beside the front door. A remnant from boarding up the front windows to make the house seem abandoned. Before we knew they would breach the front lines, weaving through the suburbs, as insidious as ants searching for sugar.

Leaving the protection of the stairs, I pick up the short piece of wood. It's not much, but if they even so much as try to come upstairs, I swear to whatever deity remains, I will swing with wild abandonment.

Clack, clack, clickclickclick.

Oh Jesus, that's how they talk, isn't it? It's strangely familiar. Fucking insectazoids. Just let them try. Just let them fucking try to lay hands, paws, claws, whatever the hell they have, on my children. They have no idea what lengths a *human* mother will go to, to protect her child. Their *clacks* move through the house, coming around the living room and into the kitchen's other entrance. I glance around the corner, my heart a lump behind my tonsils.

There are two. Bulbous heads nearly touching the ceiling, attached to long thoraxes held aloft by four spindly legs. Standing over my kitchen table, one holds a small machine in his claw. A bright, neon-blue light beeps erratically, and the aliens "talk" while scanning my breakfast.

Exhaustion suddenly floods my body and I wobble, the movement spotted by the intruder in the kitchen. From behind, a pincer grabs my raggy hair, nail scraping my scalp with its messy mum-bun, earning a brash scream from my dry lips. Jesus, God, there are *three* of them in my home. If I scream loud enough, will someone hear me? Help me? I know there are other women, other mothers in these rows of houses. But they would do what mothers had to, protect *their* children. Stay hidden, fearing their own safety.

No, it's only me and this piece of wood.

My hand swings wild, hitting something soft and malleable.

Clack, clickclickclick, clack.

One of the monsters scampers past, its claws tapping on the stairs.

"No! *NOOOOOO!*" I screech, yanking my body towards the ascending alien only to be held still by more pincers on my neck. "No! You bastards! Take me! *TAKE ME!*"

The wood is stolen from my hand, painfully ripped away, splinters lodged deep in my bony fingers, and the scanner is brought out again. They hold me still by my scruff. Its flickering strobe shines over my body, the beam narrowing until it stays still on my lower belly. The blue abruptly changes to green with a melodic beep. I struggle harder.

Above, my babies scream. Wild cries. Unworldly howls that force every atom in my body, millions of years of maternal evolution, to fight harder against this alien's hold.

They're murdering my babies.

"YOU BASTARDS, YOU BASTARDS. THEY'RE JUST BABIES."

I scream through tears, and with a great heave, I pull forward, scalp and hair ripping away as I stumble through the narrow hallway. Pain lances everywhere in everything. But what is a little more? I have been in pain since having my beautiful children. In my gut where they were extracted with sterile forceps, in my breasts where they gnaw milk from my body, in my eyes that are constantly open, my wrists that strain from holding their growing weight, my back from bending over constantly to pick up their demanding little forms. And my heart, where I gave half of it away. What is a little more from my scalp?

I reach the base of the stairs, hear an unfamiliar caterwaul. Descending, the alien holds my babies, one in each disgusting arm, and I *lunge* for them, the breath in my body erupting in a violent, territorial, leonine scream. An unyielding bracket of alien arms grabs my soft body from behind, but I am close enough to lay a hand on my son, a finger desperately pawing at his ear. It hurts to choose, unfathomable.

"Just give me him, they are nothing to you, they can give you nothing," I plead, my voice hoarse and dry.

My son's ear slips off his scalp, his skin stretching away with my pawing fingers, and the plea sticks in my throat, bile rising.

My struggling body freezes mid-fight, mid-air.

The scanner emerges again and this time, I watch, a terrible dread curling the same gut where I grew these babies. Once more the blue light passes over them, and I squeeze my eyes shut against the blinking neon beam. Memories flash, spark against the black behind my eyelids.

Blinding lights and surgical tools.

The beam focuses on their tiny bodies before flashing green. They squirm with wraith-like cries.

Clack, click clack. The imposing aliens speak between themselves, ignoring the only human in the room, as I shrink inside myself. Retreat into something unfathomable. Pincers poke my children who wriggle in discomfort, wanting, *needing* their mother. Howling for the only person they have. My arms clutch my stomach and that curling knot of terror, watching pincers reach for my daughter's face, pinching her ear, tugging it hard.

Her tender baby skin peels away, and sobs burst from my hollow chest. My hands press against my heart as it fractures and melts. The aliens, the invaders of Earth, the conquerors of my home, peel skin off my son and daughter. Their baby flesh rips at the seams, a mask. A Halloween costume. Detaching to reveal sinister, brown-shelled bodies. The black eyes I once hallucinated beg for me. Maws with tiny mandibles search the air for my breasts.

Larvae grown into nymphs. Nymphs on their way to adolescents.

My son, the larvae, warbles a strange cry. No longer cooing. My motherly instincts fail, cascading like dominoes.

I finally find my voice. "What…what have you done to them? Where…where are my children?"

These, these *things* can't be my children, the loves of my life, the ones I would have given everything and *anything* for. The aliens *clackclickclack* at me again. Those damn clacks with their damn machines.

"WHERE ARE THEY?" I scream, still caged in the alien's grip.

The alien holding the *things* masquerading as my children begins to leave and scuttles out the door. I break free. A pincer reaches for me and I dodge, chasing after my children, leaving my house for the first time in months since giving birth. Since being implanted.

My bare feet run over the broken cement, cool wind brushes my bleeding scalp, and I scream and curse. From the row of drab houses across the street, many blinds in upper windows twitch aside. Faces of more scared women, clutching their own children. Nothing but women, hiding in assigned houses, caring for their young. Designed to love them. Grow them. Two aliens intercept just as I am about to reach the kidnapper, lifting me easily. Screaming and flailing are my only defences, and I cry to the other women for help. They do nothing. No, that is not true. They watch.

Dragged to my house, a strange, recognisable helmet emerges. Blue light flashes, and I writhe and twist, trying to avoid them placing it on my bleeding scalp. Inside and away from the terrified eyes of neighbours, my struggling body is laid out on my own table. Stretched and bound. Harsh fluorescent lights, bare bulbs in the ceiling, glare in my eyes, the headset attached firmly.

FLASH, FLASH, FLASH.

A blinking cursor rests against my brain. Envelopes it. Blue light. My babies. Gone. My loves. Never. Assigned parasites, buried in the womb, in my body, inserted as a wasp buries its young in the protective shell of a beetle. I loved them as my own. They weren't my own, but they were.

FLASH, FLASH FLASHFLASHFLASH

A harsh cry breaks the dark, my C-section scar still burns with a strange numbness as I roll in bed. Pre-dawn light glints through the gaps of wood planks at my window. My groggy eyes blink awake towards the clock. It's early, too early for normal people to be awake. But not mothers. Mothers are not normal people.

My son cries again, his tone panicked, wondering where I am. My body hurls itself out of bed and I cinch my robe tight. I lost more weight than I thought after pregnancy, a stroke of luck some would say. But I feel too thin, like maybe I will one day stretch and be nothing.

Rushing between rooms, there is enough light and I come to his crib. Wasn't I just here? With how much he ate last feeding, I was hoping for at least two hours of sleep. He is only a few days old, but the drain on my body feels weeks, months, years in the making. One thing they do not tell you about pregnancy is that you can lose hair, and a breeze of cold air passes over the bald spot I have accrued from giving my nutrients to my child.

I pick up his newborn body, his eyes still shut, crying for something he knows not.

"Darling, shhhh, shhh, Mummy is here. I got you."

He cries as we settle into our rocking chair together. My right breast comes out of the feeding shirt. It feels fuller, and his nuzzling nose and gawping lips search the naked skin in the half-light until he finds my nipple. I flinch, strangely accustomed to the amount of pain made by breastfeeding.

But after a moment, it subsides and we rock together, a gentle quietude settling over the room, separate from the chaotic world outside. I look at him, so perfect. The most picturesque baby in the world, like he had been designed only for me.

I would give anything for him. I would give everything for him. I would die for my child.

THE GREEN WOMAN

RACHEL DENHAM-WHITE

The men of our village are disappearing.

It started slowly, but soon a pattern built up in a rush of frantic phone calls and midnight searches. Each and every evening, the next victim would walk out their back door and vanish into the rippling curtain of trees. The next day he would be back, sitting peaceably at the kitchen table or the foot of the bed, as if nothing had happened.

The vicar was the first reported disappearance, then the butcher's partner, then the librarian. I watched my elderly next-door neighbour plead with her husband as he walked towards the border of their property. She slapped his face and tried to drag him back inside, until he shook her off and left her crying brokenly on the ground. He was unhurried but deadly focused, each step as calm and measured as the walk up to the executioner's scaffold. It was only after her husband vanished into the dark that I ran out to help her. Our slapdash search lasted well until midmorning, and we found him lying awake in bed on our return. His pyjamas were pristine, but black dirt was caked beneath his toes.

The police chief and the doctor were routinely called after each midnight flight, but my neighbour was given a clean bill of health.

"Nothing to worry about," the doctor reassured, grinning widely as he packed up his black bag. He shook his head at our frantic, feminine worry. "Probably just stress-induced sleepwalking. It's very common during the darker months of the year."

I swear, I wanted to believe him. But then I saw his eyes.

It took me until that moment to realise how much danger we were in.

We were a small but proud community, cut off from the outside world by acres of ancient land. The cottages were full of elderly farmers, ready to sit still for their last few years after a lifetime of labour. The quiet tread of time amongst the trees suited them. Modernity may pursue its hectic dash of progress, but no matter what scratches we made to carve out our little homes and the village shops, we knew we were in borrowed territory. The woods owned us.

I always found it comforting. Like every other child, I had climbed my share of trees, dammed my share of streams, got perilously close to lost in the thicket of trunks. I always made it back. I felt as though I could rely on the forest, the indemnity of its graceful, cyclic life. We'd had our share of odd disappearances over the decades, tourists and the like, and we told ourselves it was fine. Every stretch of unmarked land demands its tithe.

But now it was actively taking from us.

The men who returned were identical in nearly every way. But we still glimpsed the subtle differences. A sickly, greenish cast to their skin, and the whites of their eyes. A stuttering motion when they blinked, as if they were still learning how to do it and hadn't quite mastered the skill. A head cocked, as if they were listening to some strange melody that no one else could hear. And they never slept.

I heard it from the postmistress, as she muttered hurriedly over the counter to a gaggle of frightened customers. None of the men had slept since the night of their disappearance. They just sat bolt upright in bed, cross-legged, naked or clothed, and stared out of the window at the ripple of shifting branches.

Our number was worryingly few, and most of the villagers were old, tired, and couldn't be expected to help. The police chief, the doctor and the vicar had all been among the first to go, neatly excising every pillar of the community. The stolidity of routine had been wrenched away, eaten by a land that we had once trusted. The best the remaining couples could do was lock their doors, cross their fingers, and pray it would not hit them next.

I, on the other hand, didn't have any kind of religion.

I had sworn to myself I never needed anyone else's company, real or imaginary. School and a couple of whirlwind years at university had been more than enough time spent tapping my fingers in irritation against the press of people. I'd be crammed in by the ever-present "thereness" of human bodies, buoyed along and surrounded, but always left behind. As I got older and became a grown woman, I was still too intimidated to ask anyone out, too afraid to flirt, immersed in my terror of people, which flooded my body and sealed my mouth with a film of ice. It was simpler to just give up.

All throughout my life, I had gazed at the women I admired from afar. When I felt brave enough, I imagined pouring out my soul to them, each word fuzzy with tenderness or gilded with desire. I wrote them sonnets with my blinks, and composed arias with the pattern of my breaths. Sometimes, it got so bad that I imagined them as strange, beautiful gods, looking down on me from some unknown plane.

It became too much. I returned to our small village to write and craft and make art, and even if I scraped by on my shoestring budget, I was cut off from the world, which suited me. Mostly.

Years passed. I kept to myself, all throughout my twenties and a good way into my thirties. I moved back with the intention of being safely alone, and life certainly felt easier. Sometimes, I could even shake off my own guilt of how terribly I still wanted! Not just to feel someone else's affection, but to gift every ounce of love my heart had in it. There was the ever-present yearning to make someone—anyone—happy, but I had no idea how.

The days were quiet. No lovers, no friends, few conversations. The only person I'd ever felt comfortable around was my grandfather. And as he lived only a couple of roads away from me, I knew it was just a matter of time until the woods reached him too.

Dusk was settling on the trees in a violet haze when I pulled into Grandad's driveway, and I saw his distant form treading towards the forest. I jumped out of my car and ran after him, screaming his name. When I reached him, I shook at his shoulders and clicked my fingers in his blank face, but his eyes didn't even flick in my direction.

I stood frozen, looking at him with indecision as he walked on. The cool night breeze was a distant hush against my exposed skin, yet my panic thrummed and bubbled and swept away all sensations of touch. Part of me wanted to grab Grandad's arm and haul him back to the house, but I didn't dare wrestle with him. A bad fall could put him in hospital for weeks.

Dread warred with an agonised shame that I'd been too late. But I wasn't about to let this unknown trance sink its claws into him. Resigned, I picked up my pace and followed my grandfather into the forest.

We walked for a long time. Hours, maybe even half the night? The glitter of the moon never changed. I stayed a few steps behind Grandad, and if I screwed up my eyes, I could just about pretend that this was one of my childhood walks. How many times had I followed him along bridle tracks, a little girl in bright-red wellies? I would search for fairies and brownies among the leaves, or convince myself I could see Pooh and Piglet darting between the great oak trunks. Grandad was always content to let me dream.

But now, everything felt like a dream. It was *far* too quiet. No birdsong, no wind, not even the rustle of animals. My phone had no signal. It felt like time itself had stopped. We could be walking across an untouched stretch of wilderness that existed before humanity had even begun. Or perhaps, after it ended. A lush, verdant, and lonely blasted heath.

I called his name, not expecting an answer.

Silence.

The nagging voices in my head were incessant. *Why wasn't I running back to my car to call the police?* But I had a terrible feeling that if I took my eyes off Grandad, even for a few seconds, I'd lose him forever. There was this half-baked notion in my mind that if I followed for long enough, I could fight whatever was calling him. After all, I'd known this whole time that ending this nightmare was up to me, hadn't I?

Hadn't I?

My grandfather stopped dead.

We had reached a circular clearing, almost the size of a football oval. To our left was a great rockface of jagged stone, reaching higher than the tree canopy. Directly across from us, faint in the distance, two willows had grown together. From base to boughs, they formed a twisted arch. If I tilted my head, it became a hungry mouth, a silent scream, the open maw of the unknown. My stomach plunged. Everything in this glade shrieked of menace.

Suddenly, Grandad sprinted forwards. I gasped as he flew headlong towards the arch, running faster than a man half his age. I knew there was no way I could catch up, but I followed him desperately, calling his name in a plea for him to stop. As I neared the far side of the grass clearing, I saw that it wasn't a pointed arch at all. It was oval-shaped, tall, and almost perfectly symmetrical, grown from two sprawling willow trunks that had sagged together like toppled giants. I gave one last belated cry as my grandfather disappeared into the opening.

I stopped with a jolt, staring between the trees. The hole had completely swallowed him up. He was simply no longer there. No shadow, no faint movement. Just gone. I turned on my phone torch and shone it into the opening but nothing penetrated. The darkness glared back at me, matte black and solid as granite.

My nervous swallow felt loud enough to echo across the clearing.

Lifting the torch higher, I saw the roots that twisted up and across the trunks of both willow trees. No, roots upon roots, growing over each other in bundles that started on either side and disappeared into the opening: four long bunches, and one shorter one. Almost like fingers and thumbs.

BOOM! The night broke open with a sound so loud it could have been an exploding bomb. It thundered through my whole body, ricocheting from my feet to my eardrums. I felt the earth judder. The sound continued, deep and ragged at the edges.

It was moaning, I realised with horror. A long, slow, ecstatic moan.

I dropped my phone and looked up, up, up into the tree canopy, desperately trying to find the source of the noise.

Two huge golden eyes stared back at me.

Screams tore up my throat. Sobbing, I fled back towards the cover of the trees. I tripped, stumbled, flung myself onwards, frantically swimming through the night air. Glancing over my shoulder, I saw the eyes still trained on me. Too big, *far* too big. So huge I couldn't figure out where the face even started. Adrenaline fired in my veins and my feverish half-thoughts propelled me to the cliff wall.

If I'm high enough, I can see what the hell it is!

I slammed into the rock with a grunt and pulled myself up, scrabbling for handholds. My nails tore on the rough stone. I reached and pulled and pushed and shoved, forearms straining, muscles bunching under my skin. At one point I slipped and for a second, I dangled from a single hand, but I threw my body upwards and clung to the rock like a lizard. Slick with blood, my fingers scuttled across the cliff face, until finally, I reached the precipice and dragged myself up with one last wrench. My body hit level ground with a thud that knocked my lungs flat, but I pushed myself around on my stomach to stare at the clearing below.

Like a stereogram, two images superimposed themselves on my vision. I saw the glade and…the creature.

My mind processed the creature in fragments. Hair. Chest. Stomach. Thighs. Pubis. Nails. To see was to disbelieve. My brain fishtailed in frantic contradictions. *Real. Not real. Real. Not real.*

The giant, naked woman was sitting, leaning with her elbows pressed against the ground to support her back, and her head thrown back in ecstasy. The legs were spread wide, with her hands holding open her elongated vulva, creased, furled and enormous. But her flesh was wood. She grew right up out of the forest floor. Hundreds of trees conjoined and twisted together in huge striations to form the ample curves of collarbone, buttock, calf, and her enormous, straining belly. Her hair was made of hundreds and thousands of leaves — oak, beech, ash, elm, rowan — fanning out in elaborate spirals of green. If I squinted, I swore I could see her chest rise and fall. The moaning faded into silence.

I stared at her, willing her to go away.

And sure enough, between blinks, she faded back into the night. Maybe she was still there, but my mind refused to recognise the dark patch of forest as anything but ancient trees.

But she had stared...into me. In those brief few seconds, those eyes had filleted my soul and laid it out in neat segments, separating my loves and desires, my needs, hatreds, and fears. She saw my loneliness. She understood. I had felt her compassion, a soft bloom on my skin.

I hated her for it.

I sat on the cliff's edge, pressing my scraped hands against my shirt to staunch the flow of blood. The pain was a distant prickle. Eventually I would have to climb down, but I didn't even want to think about stepping back into the border of dark greenery.

What was she?

A distant memory surged forward. A heritage site, an old Norman church crumbling under the weight of centuries. The candy-coloured, stained-glass windows contrasting painfully with the ponderous stone. I sat alone in a pew, my worksheet resting on my lap as the other students clustered in their own groups, pestering the tour guide and the teachers. I was staring at the grotesques carved into the upper buttresses, and one stood out apart from the rest. An impish face gurned at me over its elongated, spread labia.

The tour guide had called her a *sheela na gig*. A fertility spirit.

I stared at her for minutes at a time, and slowly, the mischievous smile seemed to stretch into a grimace of agony. Why was she there, trapped with all the other pagan demons? She might have been a goddess when the church was carved. And after the weight of all these centuries, what was she now? A trickster, a jokester? Or a more corrupting influence? Perhaps imprisoned in granite and turned into a lusty old hag, a shameful monster.

An outsider.

Sightless eyes bore into my skin. I couldn't help but feel sorry for that small, stone carving...

And now, as I looked out over the forest, I realised that none of my fantasies even mattered. Why was I concerned with fictions? Nothing like that giant creature could possibly ever exist! I wasn't remembering moments that I'd thought were long since forgotten. I had hallucinated the giantess out of fear, stress, and pure exhaustion, and that was it.

But no. Wait… I'd known as soon as my eyes found her burning golden ones that she wasn't going to let me go. No amount of scrubbing could pare away the feeling of her gaze.

I…I *needed* to know why she had looked at me—

No! I slapped down my emotions and pulled myself upright. This monster had taken a member of my family and countless other men from our village. We weren't going to get them back. The best thing I could do was get away from the forest as fast as I could, and move away, never to think of this nightmare again.

It felt like an eternity, but eventually I staggered out from the tree line and back to Grandad's house. I passed over the luxury of a warm shower and sat at the kitchen table, waiting till the sky lightened. And when that thing that pretended to be my grandfather returned, I shot it through the head with his own hunting rifle.

That night, I returned to the trees.

I had found the axe in the tool shed, propped up against a stump of wood Grandad used for splitting logs. It was old, with its cherry-red handle worn to a whitish pink with use. The axe felt staged in my hands, like a child's attempt at playing soldier with a toy gun. I carried it awkwardly. But there was no way I could take the rifle. What would a chamber of bullets do against her?

As far as I knew, I was the only one who had seen this creature and lived. Something in me felt duty-bound to avenge my grandfather and all the others lost. Or at least, I knew there was something driving me forwards. A dark and burning pull, flowing with a rhythmic susurration that felt as simple as breathing. I told myself it was anger.

My feet remembered the way better than my head, and all too soon, I was walking across the clearing. I tilted my gaze skywards, searching for the eyes that had pinned me as securely as a butterfly under glass. Nothing. Just the blank glare of the moon. But if I strained, I swore I could hear an undercurrent of breathing. Maybe she slept, dreaming of bodies and blood and a stranger's eyes.

I halted and stared into the great chasm of her genitals. The wood was carved—or maybe it had naturally grown—into creased folds above and around the vulva's opening, and strands of weeping willow made a shaggy patch of pubic hair. My heart pummelled, but I imagined it pumping fury through my veins, smouldering under my skin in a pattern of dark lacework.

Gripping the axe till my knuckles turned white, I stepped into her.

All light vanished, as quickly and neatly as turning off a switch. I turned my head, but the darkness never even flickered. I knew in my gut that I could turn right around and walk in the opposite direction, but I would never find the opening again. The pull told me there was only forwards.

I placed one foot in front of the other, again, and again and again, trying to follow a straight line. I kept my elbows pinned tightly by my sides, holding the axe in front of me and wishing I could fold in on myself until I took up no space at all. Everything in me reviled from touching her.

The passage vibrated with far-off whispers. I screwed up my face, listening so hard that it almost hurt, but I couldn't extricate a single word. Just the wet feeling of breath echoed in my ears.

My foot slipped. I threw out one hand desperately, and my palm pressed flat against solid wood. I caught myself with a huge, huffing gasp of relief, until I felt the surface pulse.

It was warm.

I wrenched my hand back with a strangled shout. I had *felt* it move, a ripple under my fingers, rising and falling like a delicate ribcage. I reached out, and realised with my arms outstretched that my fingertips could graze the edges of the passageway. Biting down curses, I forced my feet to move.

Onward. Inward.

The air got closer. Sweat built up in beads and trickled down the sides of my face like tears. The wooden walls began to grow damp, then clammy, then velvety, until the pads of my fingers sank into a spongey substance that gripped me back. I could feel my throat rise and clench, nausea clogging my airways with hot revulsion. There was a smell too; the deepest nose-wrinkling, stomach-churning, cloying tang of dead, growing things.

Tighter.

Gelatinous ooze seeped through my shirt, sticking my hair to the back of my neck. Sweat ran between my breasts. The walls constricted, pulsing and twisting. I angled my shoulders to the side and crab-walked. One hand was firmly hooked around my axe, longing to thrash and pummel with the haft, batter my way through. But no. Slow and steady. One step at a time. Claustrophobia champed at my brain, but the pull was deeper, so strong it almost seemed external to my body. I rasped a lungful of air that felt as solid as treacle. A glistening, invisible cord seemed to be wrapped around my ribs, yanking me. I fell into it, rife with savage need. With want.

Forwards. Forwards. Always forwards.

Up ahead, my light-starved eyes caught a flicker of movement. I gasped as the passage pressed inwards. Slime glued me in place for a second. My body writhed. I imagined the walls seeping over my outstretched fingers and up my arm, pulling me deeper into its embrace. Syrupy wood growing over my torso, tendrils infinitesimally pressing into my skin. My back prickled. I would be entwined so close! The tendrils would encase me, grip my spine and slowly branch into my brain, growing inch by careful inch. Loving every surface of my body…

I clutched at the siren song, using it to wrench, rip, heave. The patch of light was near enough to touch. With a slither and a scream, I fell through the narrow opening.

It took a long time for me to slow my breathing. When I finally looked up from the ground, my eyes adjusted to the sight of a gigantic cavern. Illuminated by a soft golden glow, I could just about make out the walls and floor, made of the same dark wood as the passage. But this cavern was covered in moss as thick as a shagpile carpeting, with dark tendrils bisecting the greenery and twining like veins. The smell of mulch was so strong that I had to breathe through my mouth. Even then, bitterness coagulated on my tongue.

I lifted my axe. The call had dwindled, and now that I saw just how big this thing was, my plan seemed even more impossible than before. But I no longer cared. If this was her womb, then I was going to smash up as much as I could reach. An amateur hysterectomy. I was going to make sure this thing never spawned another changeling ever again. I was going to make it *hurt*!

Green and gold light glinted off a speck in the distance. I stepped forwards but froze as my foot crunched against something brittle. I looked down. My boot had shattered a femur.

As my eyes adjusted further, the field of white ridges swam into view. Bones stuck up from the ground in ragged spikes, fragments of spines and arms and legs and pelvises recognisable in the gloom. The closer I moved towards the edge of the wall, the more whole the bodies became, until I could see shreds of muscle and skin, and even a severed arm. The skin was mummified, clinging in dry whisps to the bone, with spatters of rust where the tendrils had sucked it dry.

For now, I could see the tendrils that stretched and cradled the bones in a gross embrace. I saw where each man had fallen, and I shivered as my eyes picked out discarded shoes, glasses, wallets. The speck of green-and-gold reflected light turned out to be a watch dripping from dangling fingers. No clothes though. They would have needed their clothes; none of the men had returned naked. I imagined each victim calmly taking off his pyjamas or nightshirt, folding them in a neat pile for later, and then laying down while tendrils crowded around him to begin the feast.

The roots were getting thicker and thicker, bundling over each other in huge ropes of fleshy sinew. I gazed at the place where they conjoined and as my eyes travelled upwards, I saw clusters jutted out from the wall like bulbous, parasitical growths. Like seed pods.

Inside the nearest bulge in the murky green, I saw a distorted shape lying in a foetal position. Tendrils clung to the pulsing skin of the pod, and as I peered closer, I saw how each doppelganger had been created. How liquid flesh crept over every notch of the wooden skeleton.

I made my decision right there and then. Hefting the axe over my head, I sent it smashing towards the pod with all my strength.

Something snatched it out of my hands.

Looking up, I saw the tendrils snaking above my head, whipping back and forth like reeds in a high wind. One of them held my axe, and as I gazed in terror, I saw it rear back and fling it into the ground just next to my feet, embedding the blade so deep that only an inch remained. The floor pitched with a cracking groan.

I yelped and ran back towards the entrance, but vines snaked around my arms, wrapping tight. I hung with my feet scrabbling against the wooden floor and tendrils twining around my wrists, forearms, torso, neck. The more I struggled, the tighter they clung. Each sinuous rope was smooth, but twisted hard enough to raise welts and I cried out in pain as my whole body smarted.

Suddenly, I felt a terrifying lurch as my feet flailed and hit nothing but air. My stomach dropped. There was a burning pressure against my arms, as the vines began to lift me higher and higher, up, up, up, towards the ceiling. My legs pedaled in empty space. I was screaming fully now, throat raw with blind panic, thrashing against my restraints and finding no release. In fact, more and more vines wrapped around me, slithering with dry rasps against my skin. My body was completely immobilised and suspended high above the wooden floor, shaking, and incongruously heavy as gravity pulled me hard towards the ground.

I don't know how long I pleaded but eventually…something changed.

I heard her voice.

Like the tinny spiral of shrieking at the barest edges of my hearing.

Like the deep, wet pulsing of breath before a scream.

Like the silent roar of fear and terror and the animal howl at the end of the world, I heard her singing.

It unmade me. Unknit me. I came apart in her hands with a cry that might have been pain.

I saw through her eyes. I breathed with lungs made of wind and stretched with trees that grew with the turn of the Earth. I heard the choral mutterings of a thousand, thousand tiny beings that lived and died within me. I sucked raw marrow. I conjured blessings. I existed, apart and withheld.

I came back to my own body, and suddenly I understood why she had called to me.

She gave and she gave and she gave. She yearned with every fibre of her being to spread love, and desire, and wild untamed passion, her instincts honed by generations of deep worship. Her very image had once been protection, clutched in sweaty fists and pinned by desperate eyes mid-scream. And yet, her flock had slowly blown away like leaf skeletons on the breeze until nothing remained. No more offerings or temples or totems. Just silent, distasteful contempt.

Until me.

A young girl, whose *want* spilled over like sacramental wine through cupped hands. And then she had known that she was not alone.

Those empty bones down below were nothing but vindictive trinkets. Food and entertainment as she helped to remake the world. But oh, she was so lonely. All she needed was someone to love her. No matter how many centuries it took.

And she knew—had made sure—that I would have eventually gone to her willingly.

WATER IS THE WOMB OF THE WORLD

MATTHEW R. DAVIS

When I take my first step into the sea, the chilly bite of the brine sends a shock right up my spine to the back of my skull, and for a moment, it feels like starting awake from a bad dream. The kind of dream where it seems perfectly reasonable to clamber out of bed at 3:00am in a blind panic, drive straight to the nearest beach, and stand at the water's edge in nothing but a pair of old briefs and the baggy Black Sabbath tee I've slept in for five years.

The moon is a widening eye, as unable to believe what it's seeing as I am to be doing it. The sky is dusted with sugar-spun clouds, teeming with an audience of stars. My eyes are turned to them as I take another step into the creeping wash, the sea plucking possessively at my feet. I don't look down. Some things are best left unseen.

There's not a single rational thought in my head, though a part of me is documenting this insanity with a cool detachment. Images burn bright as suns for a split second and burst; voices break in my brain like the waves around my ankles; words streak across the roof of my skull. I reach out and grab these: *Water is the womb of the world.*

I can't tell if that's my thought or one I'm remembering, but it rings true. Life on this planet began in primordial seas that pushed our distant forebears onto the shore in a slick of salty afterbirth; water is the mother's milk that sustains us. And we ourselves are around seventy percent water, which makes wombs of us all.

The perfect place for something to grow.

I knew from an early age that I didn't want kids. My parents heard it enough as I grew up that they didn't push the point, unlike others who asked the question and received what was, to them, an inconceivable answer. *You'll change your mind one day*, they'd say, and *When you meet the right person*, and even *You can't just live for yourself, you know*. Like my feelings on the matter weren't as set in stone as my sexuality—like I wasn't perfectly happy living my life for the only person who could truly lay claim to it. Like arguing otherwise wasn't the most patronising thing I'd ever heard, which, since I'm a woman, is saying something fucking profound.

Therefore, I never expected to get involved in kid stuff. When I was first invited to a baby shower, my horror-loving mind got all literal and pictured a hail of infants falling from the sky to break open on the ground like fat red raindrops. The truth of the matter was much less appalling, and by the age of thirty, I knew these events well.

My sixth and final baby shower was thrown by Kristin and Cunneen Quigley, and notable for many reasons. It was my first queer shower, my first double-header since both partners were expecting, and it ditched the usual "cuddly baby" imagery in favour of a spooky goth theme. Consequently, it was the most fun I'd ever had in celebrating the imminent arrival of screaming hellspawn, because it gleefully literalised that angle. Whilst the guests snacked and chatted, the playlist threw up a death-metal version of "Baby Shark" and Fantômas covering the themes from *Rosemary's Baby* and *The Omen*. How could I not love women whose minds worked in such weird and wonderful ways?

The shower was held one Sunday night in the Quigley carport—attached to the side of the cream brick house they'd bought after their wedding, windowless and fully enclosed, long enough to fit two sedans nose to nose. The cement floor was softened by rugs for the food tables to stand on, the cobwebs amid the rafters joined by streamers of ebony and teal and pumpkin and absinthe. The food and plastic chairs were clumped up the back end, the front reserved for another table bearing gifts to be ceremoniously unwrapped. A twinkling silver banner declared WE LOVE YOU LITTLE STARS. Though the Quigleys attended their ultrasounds, they had no interest in the birth genders of their children and were intending to raise them pretty much the same in any case.

Our hosts made for a striking couple. Kristin was short and round and blonde, the kind of cutie you might assume to be just a bubbly office manager who never forgot a colleague's birthday — until you noticed the Baphomet sigils tattooed on the backs of her hands and followed them up her sleeves to realise she was inked all over. She favoured dresses like tonight's choice: a white number scattered with purple flowers and black skulls, cut low for cleavage and high for thigh. Cunneen, also heavily tattooed, was tall and rangy and forever clad in black jeans and metal tees, less femme and more pagan punk. She wore her newest midnight denim, a ruby nose stud, and a Paradise Lost shirt two sizes above her normal. Both were eight months pregnant and carrying tight, bulging bellies that must have made kissing a tactical exercise.

I was peckishly perusing the laden table and deciding where to start when Kristin appeared at my elbow and threaded her arm through it.

"Dig in, mate. Eat, drink, and be merry!"

"I better behave myself," I said, "or people will think it's a three-way baby shower."

Kristin laughed, a constant and charming sound. I became uncomfortably aware of my arm's proximity to her rounded belly and slipped free on the pretext of grabbing a paper plate. As the playlist served up Magic Dirt's "Babycakes", I foraged for vegan rolls and cheese cubes and meat-free samosas. Kristin followed as I roved around to the dessert section, which boasted chocolate ghosts and cookies cut in the shapes of stars. I paused to stare at the centrepiece: a three-tiered tree of fat cupcakes glistening in silver liners, each decorated with rich blue waves of topping and marked with pentagrams drawn in white chocolate.

"Try one!" Kristin urged, and I dutifully tasted the nearest.

The cupcake was stuffed with rich, creamy filling that made

me feel instantly fatter, and a woman appeared on my other side to watch me with interest. She was perhaps fifty-five, her hair a tousled mop of mercury-dashed black atop a six-foot frame that reminded me of a genial scarecrow. Her earrings were a cascade of silver stars that almost reached her shoulders, and she wore a long blue dress that clung to her spare curves like water.

"Delicious, aren't they?" Kristin prompted. "Jenny made all the desserts. She couldn't just help us get pregnant, she has to be an awesome caterer, too."

The older woman, Jenny, smiled as I took a second bite to avoid making conversation—my Aquarian nature waxing gibbous, perhaps, but I also felt feckless and raw beside her broad-spectrum competence. Kristin and Cunneen's fertility specialist, friend, and now caterer, she had made herself indispensable throughout the paired pregnancies and become a beloved honorary aunt.

"Filling, aren't they?" she asked, as I licked the last of the cream from my lips.

"Very. My belly already feels as big as Kristin's."

"I'll take that as a compliment!" Jenny crowed. "Were you planning on having children?"

God, this fucking question. "No, not ever. Maybe I saw *Alien* too young, but pregnancy always seemed like body horror to me. Total Cronenberg."

Remembering who I was talking to, I sucked in an anxious breath and turned to Kristin with a lemon-suck look, but she just laughed. "Babe, you don't know how right you are! I don't even recognise my tits anymore. Tell you what, this kid had better be worth it."

Jenny reached past me and placed one gentle, almost worshipful palm on Kristin's belly. "Your children will shine brighter than anything in this world."

"You're just saying that because you want to take the credit."

"Oh, absolutely!" Jenny laughed. "I've put a lot of work into these two. I'm not saying you should name them Jenny and Duckworth, *but…*"

"Knowing these guys," I interjected, "they're probably thinking Asmodeus and Lilith."

Kristin mock-slapped my arm. "No goth clichés here, thanks!"

Cunneen called her wife over, which left me standing awkwardly with Jenny. I gestured with my plate to indicate I was going to go eat, and she placed another cupcake on it before waving me away. *You've got to be kidding me,* I thought, and assumed that if she couldn't get me pregnant, she would settle for getting me fat. Then guilt kicked in—why did I always think in binary terms when it came to body size? Thin/good, big/bad? Perhaps being weighty would feel too much like pregnancy, and whilst I was happy for my friends, the last thing I wanted was to carry another life within. I remembered what I'd said to Kristin and pictured Samantha Eggar in *The Brood,* lovingly licking her external womb. Shit, I really had started watching horror movies too young, hadn't I?

I'd come solo tonight, as usual, but most of the other attendees were coupled up. Marieke and Tran were also married and raising a child; Buckley had transitioned since I'd met them and now wore a full beard, their partner Fern femme as ever; Travis was a thrash drummer whose none-more-metal image was at odds with his wife Kittie's anime look. Tonight, Travis had traded rocking a stage for rocking the pram that held their six-month-old Maeve, who wore a cat-ears headband to match her mother's. I took a seat beside them and watched as Kittie leaned forward to coo over the child. Maeve caught my eye and stared back with that infant goggle of utter incomprehension, then broke out into a beautiful smile that I couldn't help but return. No, I didn't want kids of my own, but I was more than happy to play the cool aunt.

My gaze wandered back to Kristin and Cunneen, and I wondered how their children would turn out. They'd be bright and keen and decent, I knew that much, because my friends were. They'd undergone partner IVF, which meant each was implanted with a fertilised egg from the other, and so the kids would have a biological connection to both mothers. They'd worked hard to start their family, and I couldn't help but imagine what the pair would've thought ten years ago if someone had told them how things would pan out.

They'd met when Cunneen started hanging out with Kristin's

social group, a crew of occult-loving goths who revolved around a dark son known as Seyden Lecker. They were a hedonistic bunch, transgressive in the way youth understands it—drugs and bloodletting, clubbing and casual sex, heresy and ritual—and they followed a kind of homebrewed Thelemic philosophy established by Seyden, who fancied himself a hot cosmic prophet in the debauched vein of Aleister Crowley. Kristin had been one of his primary lovers, but she didn't get it together with Cunneen back then. Her future wife haunted the fringes in the last days of the group, which broke up in a clearly acrimonious fashion that Kristin glossed over in her telling with a rare fake smile. She moved to Perth for a job and only crossed Cunneen's path again five years later, at which point they fell almost instantly in love. Whilst neither seemed to practise even casual occultism, the past visibly echoed through them: they bore matching tattoos on their forearms, *LOVE IS THE LAW* on Kristin's right and *LOVE UNDER WILL* on Cunneen's left, so that the full quote was formed whenever they held hands.

I found myself gazing at the latter half when Cunneen eased herself down into a chair beside me, wincing as she tried to get comfortable.

"Having a good time?" I asked, an insipid question.

"I am tonight, yeah. Haven't been sleeping so well."

"Par for the course, I guess."

"Just another perk, right? Wish someone had told me about the dreams, though."

I was more able to engage with esoteric subjects than the rigors of pregnancy, so I asked her to elaborate.

"Well…last night, I dreamed I was lying in bed—and then it was a waterbed, and then it was just water. Everything was dark, like I was floating in a sensory deprivation tank. My belly lit up from inside like it was the sun, and it kind of *was*, and me the insignificant galaxy around it. The light started levitating and I went with it, floating up into the sky. I was expecting to give birth right there in mid-air, but I guess it wasn't time. I just woke up instead. I didn't tell Kristin about it. I think she's been having some strange dreams too, stress-related stuff about the baby."

"Okay! Well, I'm no expert, obviously, but maybe you subconsciously know your baby's gender, and so—"

Cunneen slapped her hands over her ears. "Spoilers!"

"'Neen, you were about to give birth to a *sun*."

"Yeah, but that can still go either way," she said, and then she produced another Thelema quote as if to reinforce their past connection with the cosmic. "*Every man and every woman is a star.*"

Soon, the time came for the opening of presents. We moved our chairs down to the front end of the carport to form a ragged phalanx across from the gift table and its welcoming silver banner. Fat balloons bobbed and danced on either side, inflatable bats and ghosts anchored at the ends of their strings by a small fist of wood—more favours from the ever-thoughtful Jenny. Maeve grizzled and settled as Kristin and Cunneen turned off the music and took their places before the table.

"Thanks for coming, everyone," Kristin began, as Cunneen settled for punctuating her speech with heartfelt nods. "It means so much to have you here with us tonight. This has been a long, hard journey for us, and we really appreciate your support. We're looking forward to many more years of friendship with you all.

"Now, those of you who've known us longest will agree that we *never* would have seen this coming back in the day! I wasn't into the idea of having kids, partly because of a former partner who was weirdly pushy about knocking me up, and Cunneen never really thought it a possibility. But when we got together, everything seemed so achievable, so *limitless*. After a while, we turned to each other and went, *Well, what about…you know?* It was no longer an idea, but a dream—and what do we do with dreams? We make them a reality."

Kristin paused to link her hand with Cunneen's and gaze up into her wife's eyes. I'd never seen a couple so clearly in tune and in love—moments like this were so pure that witnessing them felt like intruding upon an act of intimacy. My eyes dropped to their arms, to the Thelemic couplet formed by their held hands, and I wondered what Seyden Lecker would think of this outcome. I never met the dude, but I would've bet good money that his Sade-meets-Crowley schtick had dried up by now and left him stacking shelves somewhere, pot-bellied and balding. Or maybe he was putting his narcissism to good use as a rising member of the One Nation party. Who could ever tell?

"We honestly couldn't have done this without Jenny Duckworth," Kristin continued, gesturing in my direction, and I realised the woman was standing a few feet behind me. "We met her by chance when we weren't even thinking about having children, but she saw something in us, and she gave us her card and said, *When the day comes...* And so, when we decided we were ready to start IVF, we turned to her. And she's been not only an exceptional fertility specialist, but a good friend and miracle worker. We owe you so much, Jenny. Thank you!"

We broke out in a spontaneous round of applause, and I turned to witness the woman's response. She wore a thin smile, serious eyes fixed on the pair as she clapped herself.

"Anyway, without further ado, let's get cracking on the unwrapping!"

Cunneen unlinked herself and reached for the biggest gift. From Travis, Kittie and Maeve, it proved to be an absolute bounty of baby wipes.

"Trust me, you're going to need them!" Kittie called as we dutifully applauded.

Travis nodded wearily and added, "Baby wipes will be your most precious resource. Even more so than sleep."

I watched the expectant couple unwrap the next few presents, wondering if mine would seem less practical or welcome than this parade of cute onesies and linens and heating pads. Sure, the selection of baby books I'd bought had appeared on their gift registry, but I couldn't help feeling left outside the inner sanctum of mums and mums-to-be. I hoped they'd remember me as they read to their kids and appreciate my gift of knowledge, of enlightenment.

The table was heaped with scraps of torn wrapping when Cunneen passed a curiously tiny gift to her wife. Kristin looked in vain for a card, then shrugged as she picked at tape until the paper unfurled like a dawn flower and fell to the cement floor to reveal the content. It appeared to be a clear plastic cup with a red screw-on lid. I recognised at once what it must be—if not what it could mean.

"Is that what I think it is?" Cunneen asked.

Kristin nodded, frowning, and revolved the container to read the label affixed to its side.

"Oh, get fucked," she said.

We sat, bemused, and waited for the punchline.

Kristin's blue eyes blazed at us. "Is this someone's idea of a joke? Because let me tell you, it's in pretty fucking poor taste."

Cunneen read the label over her shoulder and visibly flinched. She rested a protective hand on her belly as Kristin thrust the item toward us, presenting the damning evidence—and yes, it certainly appeared to be a sperm donor cup.

"Well? Anyone want to own up?"

We exchanged baffled glances, disturbed by our host's anger. No one spoke.

Until—

"That…is from *me*."

I twisted in my seat to stare up at Jenny Duckworth, steepling her hands in what might have been prayer or a villainous flex.

"But…*why*?" asked Kristin, flabbergasted, and "What does it *mean*?" queried Cunneen.

"I wanted you to know who was responsible for your great fortune. His contribution was kept in there, frozen, for five years before I used it to fertilise your eggs."

Kristin wilted as if she'd been stabbed. Cunneen held her wife upright and, huffing with wrath, glared at Jenny.

"Are. You. *Seriously*. Telling me…that the sperm you used for us…came from *Seyden* fucking *Lecker*?"

Jenny allowed herself a sad smile. "My son."

I looked back and forth between them, stunned by what I was hearing. In a matter of seconds, this happy day had soured like milk in the summer sun. Kristin threw one hand to her mouth, looking fit to puke, while Cunneen's glare at their fertility specialist implied that if she didn't have to hold her wife upright, she'd pounce across the carport, pregnant or not, and deck this woman.

"Well, you must be just *itching* to tell us your diabolical plot," she said instead. "Go on, then. Explain why you've implanted us with your own grandchildren."

"You remember what Seyden was like," Jenny declaimed, "the things he sought, wished, dreamed. He longed to ride high among the stars, and if he couldn't do that, well, he'd bring the stars down to earth instead. And he found a way! But you were already gone. You all abandoned him, left him a prophet without a church. He *needed* you, Kristin. The way he'd bonded you to him, preparing you, combining your essences… It had to be you that bore his child. To make it *more* than a child. But do you know what happened next?"

Kristin swallowed hard and closed her eyes to the answer. "He died."

A chill rippled through the small crowd.

"Yes, he did. Leukaemia. Which at least gave him time to leave me a sample of his seed for future use. I'd already been working in the fertility field for years, which just goes to show how fate works out sometimes. He'd been very specific about the recipient, so I kept tabs on you, Kristin. I engineered that 'accidental' meeting in the wholefoods store. I charmed you. Gave you my card. And I waited."

"You evil cunt!" Cunneen shouted. "Why pick on us?"

"I'm *telling* you—it had to be Kristin. The intricate, intimate rituals she and Seyden performed together… Oh, that face! What, don't you like hearing about your gay wife indulging in torrid practices with a man?"

"She's bi. And she already told me everything, you sick witch."

Jenny cackled as if to confirm the accusation. "Good! I want you to remember my son that way, deep inside your woman. It'll help you remember that your children are *his*. Anyway, I wasn't sure that the plan *needed* to involve you at first, so I experimented. You'll notice the cup is empty. I only needed a single sperm for each of you. Aren't you wondering what I did with the rest?"

Cunneen winced. "*Really* trying not to think about that."

"I fertilised another woman first, a couple of years ago. It… got messy. I realised his seed would only successfully take root in you, Kristin, so I waited. And you came to me, just as I planned—wanting *two* babies! Partner IVF meant I could plant his children in both of you. Later, I found a…*tasteful* use for the remainder of his legacy."

The rest of the party echoed my stunned silence. No one dared break into this strange scene.

"Why are you doing this, Jenny?" Kristin wailed, wan with betrayal. "Why even tell us at all? Do you hate us that much?"

"Oh, I don't hate you, dear. One doesn't loathe the loam, one tends it. But I couldn't bear for Seyden's achievement to go uncredited—nor mine, I suppose.

"The time draws near, and your children are growing stronger. Even now, they *shine*. The light is coming off them in waves. And together, we grant you this celestial boon."

Jenny lifted her hands and curled them closed in a movement that looked eerily like a pair of eyes shutting.

And the lights went out.

Tran's startled yelp was the loudest, and others echoed it, but silence fell when we saw what hovered before us in the deep dark.

Patterns had been hidden on the balloons, invisible by light but incandescent blue in the pitch black. Upon each was traced the traditional shape of a star, but their five points seemed to flicker and shift, constantly changing in number as I watched in mesmerised awe. I considered a hidden projector, but some long-dormant instinct insisted this surreal spectacle had no such mundane cause. The incomprehensible forms danced in my mind, dazzling all reason, and then those stars shot forward toward us.

One seemed to flash right through me, and I curled up as a stabbing pain tore downward through my innards, as though my stomach had just dumped its contents into my uterus. The agony ceased almost as fast as it began. By the time I straightened up, the lights had cut back on.

Stunned faces stared back at me with dilated eyes, guests reeling in their chairs. Kristin had staggered against the gift table, and Cunneen was fighting a slapstick battle to keep her from falling. I turned and saw the kitchen door closing as Seyden Lecker's mother departed, and I slumped back in my seat feeling like a lump of raw dough that'd had one of her star-shaped cookies stamped out of it.

Before the questions could begin, our hosts hurried into their house and hid behind a closed bedroom door. Fern and Buckley angrily popped the bobbing balloons, Kittie and Travis fussed over a smiling Maeve, and I stared at the silver banner whose message had turned mocking: WE LOVE YOU LITTLE STARS.

My sixth and final baby shower was over, and I had never been so glad to know that I would always be alone in my body.

Kristin and Cunneen didn't contact me for a while, and that was fair. They had more pressing concerns, and I don't think any of us were ready to try and unpack the baggage Jenny had dumped at their feet. I only found out they'd given birth together when they posted a Facebook status about it, and since they requested a period of solitude whilst they adjusted themselves and their babies to this new reality, I didn't see them for three months. And then it began to seem a bit weird.

I sent them a message asking when I should drop by. When no one replied, I decided to turn up unannounced.

Cunneen looked less than thrilled to find me at their door, though her embrace was, if anything, firmer than ever. She led me into the lounge, where a haggard Kristin met me with a gaze that would've been startled if she'd possessed the energy for it. We made stilted small talk as they changed nappies, and I got the strangest feeling that my friends were carefully curating their words as though speaking before an audience. Then they sat their children upright on their laps, and I met Stella Maris and Adam Astra Quigley for the only time.

The babies regarded me with an intent sense of personality I'd never before experienced in someone so young—a self-possession, perhaps, the ultimate realisation of the precociousness I'd wished for them. I introduced myself the way I would to any adult, and as one, they raised their stubby little fingers to me. Ignoring a gnawing unease, I smiled as warmly as I could manage and gently clutched their tiny hands in mine.

Everything flashed an intense white for a single frame, and the ghost of that stabbing pain returned to haunt my insides, but it was all over by the time I fell back onto my rump. Kristin and Cunneen tried to look concerned but could barely muster a raised eyebrow between them. Stella and Adam *grinned* at me, and all at once, I'd seen as much of these babies as I could stand. I made my hasty farewells and left my friends to their strange new existence.

I didn't seem to sleep at all that night, just lay in my bed and stared at the back of my eyelids forever. But when strange and incandescent stars began to burst through the blackness and burn in my brain, I found myself starting awake as if shot. It was 3:00am, and the room was as dark as the depths of space, and when my hands brushed down my front, they found a belly hard and tight with child.

I screamed and snapped my bedside light on. The nightmare didn't end. I was heavily pregnant, almost full-term. I began to hyperventilate, and my breathing made me think of Lamaze classes I'd never taken, and I wished for wakefulness to wash this horror away. But nothing had ever felt so solid and real beneath my trembling hands.

Denial died, and I accepted this was nothing natural. My personal prejudice against fecundity meant that I was fastidious in my sexual habits, never allowing so much as a drop of pre-come inside me, and anyway, I could never swell up this fast in a matter of hours. I considered a phantom pregnancy, even a vile and rapacious tumour, but—*I knew*.

I scrambled out of bed in blind panic, acting on some deranged autopilot. I didn't think, *couldn't* think, just stumbled through my flat and grabbed my keys and left the door open behind me as I fell into the car. Some vague part of me understood my destination and what was going to happen once I reached it, and I sobbed hysterically as I drove, but not for a second did I turn from my path.

It led me to the beach.

And now I'm walking into the sea, the chill waves breaking around my calves, and I barely feel present even as sensation wracks my underdressed flesh. My mind is a storm of static, and I believe I'll never think straight again. This, however, strikes me as a short-term problem, because the water has reached my waist and I'm not stopping. If the burden I bear is aware of the danger, it gives no sign other than a dull warmth that shields my womb from the fangs of the sea.

The sand shifts beneath my feet and I fall forward, my face smashing the waves apart, and then I'm sinking below the surface, my legs dumbly kicking for purchase and finding none. I've walked off a shelf, and the drowning dark is so, so cold, and this is what I want. I am nothing, nothing but water, and water is the womb of the world.

And my mind finally clears enough to admit the implacable truth. I didn't come here to kill myself; this is not my will at all. This is not an end. This is a beginning.

I can't see anything, but I know my belly has begun to glow. My thrashing hands fall on it and feel a deep heliacal heat. And as the water breaks around my face a second time, allowing me breath and passing me into the clutches of the air above, I blink my eyes free and see the spreading sky embracing me. My womb is a shining, blinding sun and I am rising, burning, rising. There is no pain, just an intense and singular contraction that drives my legs apart as I levitate higher above the ocean, and I can't hold my head up to see my burden born. I stare at the stars scattered across the night sky like spectators, like siblings, and as a molten universe pours through me, I can no longer tell which are billions of years old and which are mine.

IN WAR WITH TIME FOR LOVE OF YOU

CAROL RYLES

They've gathered in the ship's galley, Cora staring into her coffee and Alice discussing calculations with Frankie and Saul. Cora wants to contribute, but she's too numb to think about anything except home. She floats to the viewport to contemplate the stars, lurches sideways in zero gee. What she would give for the luxury of gravity!

Saul brings her back to the now. "Cora, the modifications are ready."

"We can't guarantee it will work," Frankie adds, frowning.

Saul rewards Frankie with a glare. "Whatever the outcome, there's nothing to lose." He outlines the pros and cons in his usual over-the-top detail, waving his hands for emphasis.

When at last he's done, Alice repeats what they've already discussed. "Let's not forget, the decision is ultimately Cora's." Her words are precise, objective. She's given up wearing her uniform and is the last of the four to do so. Her civvies are crumpled. Her hair is untied and drifts above her face.

Cora wishes she could sleep through everything, but that's not how reversals work. Besides, facing one's mistakes is better than ignoring them. "I want to go ahead," she says.

Frankie shrugs. Saul grins with triumph. They both flip away from the bulkhead, perfectly at ease with being weightless. When they're no longer there to distract her, Cora returns to the viewport, tries to locate the distant pinpoint of Sol, but it's so far away it could be any one of millions. She wonders if she'll ever see Eric again. She imagines living and reliving the past, learning and unlearning what should never be encountered.

The Skłodowska drive thrums into life. There's no acceleration—no semblance of gravity—only a hollow whine that smacks of defeat.

"Back we go," Alice says, lifting her chin.

Saul's voice is confident through the comm node. "Forcefield initiating. Three, two, one..."

For several tense seconds, there's nothing. Then abruptly, the boundary between the inside and outside consolidates. Beyond the viewport, the stars remain visible, unchanged. *At least there's that*, Cora thinks. The air whooshes. Time within the ship pauses, shifts into reverse, and Cora closes her eyes against wave upon wave of dizziness. Next comes bewilderment as entropy impossibly rewinds.

Any other time, she'd laugh at how smoothly her heart goes from bumpity-bump to bump-bumpity. Her body tingles as her blood retraces its flow. A scratch ends with an itch. So much for the Second Law of Thermodynamics, she thinks.

Saul opens his mouth and his words literally emerge from Cora's ears. "...nuw, oot, eerth."

Ridiculous, unintelligible, laughable. But Cora has heard it before and her brain immediately untangles his meaning. "Three, two, one..."

She's thinking about what comes next when Frankie and Saul float backwards from engineering. Saul grins in response to Frankie's shrug.

It worked! Saul did it! present-Cora thinks, feeling much like an observer as events uncoil as hazily as they did in real time. Meanwhile, her past self remains oblivious, as if every thought, every action, is new. *I'm Schrödinger's cat*, present-Cora thinks, *existing in two timelines at once, both thinking and unthinking, remembering the future, awaiting the past.*

Her chest tightens in anticipation of what's to come, the sleeplessness and exhaustion from a loss that no mother should have to face.

The body bag, sealed in the freezer with the emergency rations...

"I want to take her home," past-Cora says, not wanting to close the freezer door, because once she does, she'll never be able to face it again, and her baby will continue this journey alone.

Time unwinds even more hazily after that. Present-Cora floats from the galley to her quarters, to the bridge, and then back, both dreading and embracing the memory of what's soon to unfold. *I can't*, she thinks, backing into sick bay, but it's too late to change her mind, too late to do anything but go with the flow.

She floats down to the med-couch, straps herself in and curses its non-functioning software. "Those fuckers who attacked us. They could have at least spared us this."

Her belly is soft, empty. She wishes she'd given birth in her quarters.

Forty-Eight Weeks Earlier: Departure

Cora stepped into the space elevator's foyer, felt oddly unsettled, then stepped back out. She met Eric's gaze and his returning smile told her he understood her indecision. They'd said their goodbyes already. Last time had been hard enough. Would this time be different?

"I've already lived my year of glory." He glanced upwards, through the enviro-dome to the pale Martian stratosphere. "Now it's your turn."

She nodded, unwilling to disagree. Explorers were destined to explore. The rest of her life would come later.

In the half-day it took for the elevator to reach Spaceport II, she sat in the café with the team, going over procedures. Eric had given her an antique book of poetry, and when she kept it in her pocket, he didn't feel so distant. Occasionally, she'd peer through the Plexiglas floor to watch the Tharsis plains receding beneath. The elevator's nano-lattice girders stretched down like aerial roots into the spindly forests of Valles Marineris. As the elevator ascended, Cora couldn't help but think: Why leave the world that was not only home, but also an extension of herself?

To quell her misgivings, she shifted her attention to the drone reports from previous decades. Lazuli: an Earth-like planet orbiting the red dwarf Kepler 186. It was statistically too hostile to support life, yet Lazuli's biosphere had already been confirmed by FTL drones. What xenobiologist would pass up the opportunity of studying that?

All doubt disappeared when the elevator reached its summit. As she and the rest of her team floated through the sky-bridge to the docks, Cora's gaze drifted beyond its viewports to the teardrop hull of the *Amelia* against a backdrop of stars.

"Magnificent," she breathed.

"I still can't get my mind around how it works," Alice, the team leader mused. "Quantum physics. Artificial gravity. Seemingly impossible. Weirdly, counterintuitive."

"I could explain the nuances of quantum entanglement," Saul said, and Cora wondered if he would launch into one of his protracted lectures. Instead, he added, "If you have a few extra years to spare."

Frankie laughed. "I fully accept how we're slaves to physics, but when we mess with the quantum, how can we be certain it won't mess with us?"

"Most physicists believe macroscopic life is destined to go with the flow," Saul said.

"And you?" Cora asked.

"From an engineer's perspective? Anything's possible."

Cora adjusts the med-couch restraints, relieved to be alone as Alice heads for the cargo bay. She wishes she'd brought her poetry book to at least have a piece of Eric with her. Spherical air scrubbers float out from a bulkhead, whirring in zero gee. As they move in close to hover near Cora's face, teardrops float down from their orifices. Blood clots like rosebuds taint the air with their coppery smell.

Then Alice is back again, her magnetic boots click-clicking their strange backwards gait. She swivels and there in her arms lies Molly, achingly small and lifeless. Zero gee is hard enough on adults; harder still on developing foetuses. Cora knows she must weep, but not yet. Not until her body stops trembling, and her emotions feel real again instead of the empty coldness that has taken their place.

Cora looks to Molly, determined to imprint every part of Molly's ruined perfection in her memory. Lemur-like eyes bulge from a round, puffy face. Fingers limp and spidery, like beached anemones. Clubbed nails, twisted toes, immature lungs too stiff to breathe. Cora would do anything to bring her back, and here she is attempting it.

She sucks out a breath, draws the baby close, skin to naked skin. For a long time, there's nothing so promising as a heartbeat. Then Cora eases her grip, and Molly's sunken chest rises with a barely perceptible exhalation.

Cora wants to scream, shout, sob, curse, but holds it in because no child should have to leave or enter the world hearing that. Minutes pass. Hours. Molly's body warms. Her chest rises, falls, and her skin turns from white to blue to pink.

Impossibly and wonderfully, she stirs.

Thirty-Six Weeks Earlier: Transition

Eight weeks out from Mars, excitement reigned. The *Amelia* had reached the outer edge of the heliopause, sufficient distance from Sol to initiate its transition to FTL. Only Frankie and Saul had experienced interstellar travel before, yet even they expressed wonder.

The crew of nine gathered in the galley by the rear-facing viewport.

Saul poured them each a glass of champagne. "Disconcerting, isn't it?" he said, glancing to the shrunken disc of Sol.

Alice's glass clinked against his. "And also exhilarating."

"It's both," Frankie added. "Cosmos and dreams. A glorious embrace."

Everyone stared at her, and then at each other. Frankie, their narrowly-focussed engineer, had suddenly waxed lyrical.

"What?" she asked, her face colouring.

"Mars-Frankie and Space-Frankie are two different people," Saul said.

Even Frankie laughed at that.

Caught up in the moment, Cora added, "Meanwhile, Mars is but a speck of dust. An invisible red dot."

The sentiment reminded her of a passage in her grandmother's journal. Fifty years before Cora's birth, her grandmother, Mary, had written: *I envy my descendants. The experience of seeing one's world from afar would be at once miraculous and terrifying.* Those words had etched themselves into Cora's soul from the moment she'd read them at the age of ten. Now here she was, further away than even her grandmother had envisaged.

"Three, two, one..." Saul raised his glass again. "Zero!"

The forcefield shimmered on, transforming the ship and its crew into the equivalent of quantum entities—both particles and waves—no longer beholden to the laws of physics at the macroscopic level. Beyond the viewport, the cosmos disappeared. The Skłodowska drive hummed. Cora gasped with surprise. She'd expected to feel a slight disorientation, despite Saul outlining the reasons she would not.

"In that instant, we'll be in two places at once," Saul had explained at their briefing. "Beyond Sol's heliopause and also beyond Kepler 186's. Then, when the forcefield retracts, we'll revert to single entities again, magically delivered to our chosen destination."

Both impossible and possible, Cora thought, sipping her champagne, then putting it aside just in case. Her queasiness of late was slight, more likely due to months spent in space than anything to do with hormones. And although her menses were light, they'd remained doggedly regular. Her hand strayed to her belly. She and Eric had taken the standard precautions. If sperm and egg had managed to meet, her uterine lining would have been too hostile for a blastocyst to implant. But what if it had? What if, after all these years, she'd finally conceived?

Saul's voice broke through her thoughts. "Three, two, one, zero..."

The forcefield retracted. Beyond the viewport, the distant glow of a red dwarf smouldered against a background of unfamiliar stars. All around, glasses clinked.

"Welcome to Kepler," Saul said.

Molly smells sweet and new, a welcome contrast to the sour odour of blood and sweat permeating sick bay. Cora holds the fragile body to her breast. She wishes time would cease to exist, and death could be cheated. If praying would help, she'd beg to be spared the inevitable loss. Her rational-self understands she's reliving the past, but her emotional-self reacts exactly as it did before the reversal.

"The deformities are as we suspected," Alice says, gravely. "I'm so sorry."

Molly lets out a reedy cry, and Cora fools herself her baby may well survive the long haul back home. She'd need therapies of course, and years to reverse the damage from gestating in weightlessness. But at least she'd live.

Optimism plunges Cora deep into the reversal. She fears she'll not have the strength to carry on. Then, slowly and heavily, her knees bend. Her feet push hard against the med-couch, tensing her in the restraints. Her legs part.

"You did so well," Alice says.

Alice opens the sealed container. A veiny, meaty placenta oozes out from it. The gory mess flips, and the umbilical cord twists and turns in graceful eddies. Blood torrents from the air scrubbers. The placenta squirts toward Cora's vagina, slips inside and fills it with a squelching, sluggish warmth.

Twenty-Two Weeks Earlier: Arrival

Two months in from the heliopause, Frankie parked the *Amelia* into low orbit around Lazuli. Up close, the planet's biosphere was as lovely as drone images had suggested. Its pristine seas appeared as welcoming as Earth's, and its violet-tinged landmasses were as delightfully exotic as the terraformed plains of Tharsis.

They orbited for days, celebrated the presence of life in its many forms. Remote analyses described an ecosystem in perfect balance, undisturbed by the influences of anything resembling technology.

"Time to go planet-side in person," Alice said. "Grade three respirators and bio-suits will suffice."

Protocol dictated that Cora should be amongst the first five, but instead of heading to her workstation to prepare, she could only stare ahead. Her stomach felt queasy, her hands and feet unusually cold.

"Are you okay?" Alice asked. "You look pale. This time, I'm not suggesting you check in with the med-couch, I'm ordering you to."

Cora swallowed. "Copy that."

She headed to sickbay, and reassured herself that her fear of being pregnant would soon be dismissed. Her last period had been a month ago. And although her stomach had grown a little, so had everyone else's. Too much space food, and not enough exercise. Nothing but a typical case of work-related obsession.

"How do you feel?" the med-couch asked as she lowered herself into it.

"Reasonable."

The scanners zoomed in close. Her skin tingled.

The AI's voice slowed, a sure sign it was about to feign emotion. "Congratulations," it announced. "You're at sixteen weeks. The baby is healthy. Would you like to see?"

"What?" Cora's voice rose an octave. "Why?" Another octave. "How?"

Motherhood? Too sudden, too soon!

She drew her knees to her chest, hugged them.

Think. Breathe. Think.

"I sense you're not pleased," the med-couch said.

"Why would I be? I have work to do. I have plans. I'm not ready for this."

"If you'd not skipped your routine medical, you could have known before it was too late to abort. Fortunately, stasis is still an option for you."

"I'm well aware of that."

Cora closed her eyes. Denial had been a wonderful thing while it lasted, but now she had no choice but to face reality. Yes, she actually wanted this baby. But not yet, not now. Besides, not all pregnancies remained viable, so she'd left it up to her body to decide, if indeed her body should be given a say.

"Would you like to know the gender?" the med-couch ventured. "If it's not to your liking, there is time to modify."

Cora shook her head. "I'll let the baby decide for themself when they're old enough."

"You have a girl," Alice announces from her precarious position between Cora's knees, her face blood-spattered and weary.

As Cora slumps against the restraints, her joy that the pain is finally over gives way to detachment. She's vaguely aware of Alice un-cutting the cord, reconnecting mother to baby, returning them to a viable and living whole.

A brief smile tugs at the edges of Cora's mouth. Against all expectations, Molly lets out a reedy cry.

Cora has never felt so overcome with inconsolable dread. Molly floats limply towards Alice's outstretched hands. Why must babies enter the world on the brink of turning blue, teetering on the edge of death, needing only an intake of breath to escape it? Is the terrible memory of being forced from the womb etched into their subconscious, always present but never graspable?

"Breathe," Alice implores, lifting the oxygen mask away from Molly's face.

Fearing the worst, Cora shivers. Her love for this tiny being eclipses everything, even the stench of blood and sweat as it mists around them both. The stench gathers at the back of her throat, all dank and coppery. She tries to spit it out, but her mouth is dry.

The umbilical cord pulses. Molly floats up from Alice's hands, skin waxed in vernix, limbs too curved and too long. A cascade of blood and amniotic fluid spurts out from the air scrubbers, collides with Alice's face and she holds her breath to avoid breathing it in. Then almost as quickly, it coalesces into a globular whole that gushes into Cora's vagina. She gasps as her uterus cramps, hardens, loosens.

Molly surges towards the birth canal, feet first. Suddenly, she looks too huge to fit; and then, as if massless and formless, her legs and body slide in. Cora gasps with relief.

"The worst is over," Alice says.

Cora's abdomen is swollen again, obscuring her view of Molly.

Alice leans closer. "The head's out. Oh, the baby's awake."

She mutters something that could be important, but Cora can't grasp its significance. Not while the head has yet to force its way in; and certainly not while her lower half is un-stretching and un-splitting in cresting circles of pain.

It returns too soon, that terrible urge to pull, and Cora is not ready for it, doubts she will ever be. Molly's head is a cannonball intent on dragging itself inwards, transforming Cora into an organ of suction. She grunts and groans. Her body takes over and her guts heave as her birth canal un-stretches, millimetre by excruciating millimetre. She prays for it to stop, to slow down, to speed up and get itself over with. She tries to breathe through the pain, to do everything the antique birthing texts suggested, but her body is too human; *or perhaps,* she wonders, *not human enough.*

"I can't do this without gravity," she mumbles. "I need it as much as Molly does."

But gravity's gone, stolen, and the med-couch is as good as useless. She, Alice and Molly are alone. Her uterus must clench and unclench of its own accord, punishing her with agonies upon agonies upon agonies.

"Breathe, push, breathe..." Alice urges.

Each push is a pull, each contraction at once an aftermath and a prelude to torture. There's no time to rest in between. Her breath gasps in, heaves out. Her voice takes over and moans and moans and moans.

Thirty-Two Weeks Earlier: Expulsion

"**I** feel for you, Cora," James said, after celebrating his promotion to chief xenobiologist. "I thank you for giving me this opportunity to be one of the first to step on Lazuli."

Cora almost replied with, "It wasn't my doing," then stopped herself because the choice had been hers all along.

She'd opted for luck, and lost.

Cora watched the shuttle depart, and tried her best to not resent the tiny scrap of life that, in reality, had no choice at all. When the lights dimmed to simulate night shift, she wanted to keep working, but Alice ordered her to rest. Again, Cora blamed the baby, and admonished herself for not choosing stasis.

She tried to sleep, couldn't. She wandered to the galley, but the smell of food did little to offer comfort. To amuse herself, she headed for sick bay and put herself into the med-couch.

"Are you feeling poorly?" it asked.

"Poorly?" Cora chuckled. "Who taught you to say that?"

"How may I assist?"

"Show me the baby."

The sensors hummed, and the foetus's image filled the screen. Cora envied its serenity, oblivious in its liquid world of filtered light, its heartbeat a fragile counterpoint to its mother's.

"Analyse their DNA," Cora said. "Extrapolate."

"You wish to know their gender?"

"I wish to know my baby."

Slowly the foetal image grew until it curled up tight with chin on knees, thumb in mouth, and legs gently kicking.

"Continue," Cora said.

The uterus peeled away and the image continued to grow from infant to toddler to child, teenager and adult. A girl, with eyes like Eric's and a gaze that seemed part curious and fashionably ironic. Cora had seen that look before in an antique video of Grandmother Mary on Earth, star chart in hands, telescope pointing skywards.

"I'll call her Mary," Cora muttered before remembering her grandmother preferred Molly.

Her resentment paled. She no longer envied James for taking

her place. The first Molly believed that seeing Earth from afar would be miraculous and terrifying, and now Cora would at least be present and witness the excitement of discovery up close.

Miraculous? Absolutely. Terrifying? Not while there's—

Molly's image winked out.

The med-couch shuddered. "Brace!" it said.

A terrible shriek rose up from below decks. Cora braced as a mounting crush of g-forces pressed over her.

Alice massages Cora's shoulders, but her fingers transform muscles into ever-tightening knots. Cora screams, begs for the med-couch to flood her with analgesics, curses the fact it's no longer functional.

"Yes," Alice says. "That's true."

"It's a sign my cervix is fully dilated." Cora's voice is guttural, primordial, an animal's dirge, and she's trapped. "My feet. Curling!"

Breathe and pull.

"Nearly there," Alice says.

Cora groans and pants, shallowly, desperately, but her body is no longer her ally. The contractions come in waves, so close together there's no rest between, barely enough time to draw breath.

"If I had gravity on my side, I'd be done," Cora says. "Two centimetres may as well be two hundred."

"Your cervix is at eight centimetres. Two more to go." Alice eases gloved fingers into Cora's vagina.

She wants to demand that Alice hurry up and put Molly back, but her voice comes out in a wail, like something wild and wholly inhuman. "Get her out now, she's killing me."

A new contraction grips. The baby's head pulls backwards, and each millimetre of un-stretching feels like a metre, each agony as spiteful as the next. Her body wants the baby out, her mind wants it in. Reality exists in two states at once and she's a witness to her body birthing and un-birthing, pushing and pulling, bleeding and un-bleeding, and ultimately caught in an unending, excruciating state of *now*.

The contractions begin to ease, one good, one bad, and space further and further apart. When they no longer feel like a false alarm, Cora unstraps from the med-couch and Alice steadies her away from it. She and Alice have spent weeks studying birthing holograms, preparing themselves for what to expect.

Cora nods. "Yes, I remember that."

"Now your waters have broken," Alice says, "so things are speeding up."

Cora slips out of the med-gown and puts on her clothes, grimacing as her pants cling wetly to her buttocks. Frankie and Saul arrive from engineering and wish her luck. They guide her backwards to the galley and take her to her favourite spot by the viewport. She is about to strap herself to a seat, when an air scrubber zooms in and spits out a wash of pale amber globules. Faster and faster, surrounding her in a halo of wetness.

"My waters," she says, voice shaking with embarrassment, while at the same time thinking, *How ridiculous of me to get squeamish over amniotic fluid, especially after everything I've already seen.*

Frankie and Saul lurch forwards, holding their breaths. The globules coalesce into a watery cloud and Cora's belly hardens.

"Oh," she says as the cloud oozes into her crotch.

Her pants turn from wet to dry. Another contraction, stronger but bearable—a beginning. And, also an end.

Frankie replies with a rare smile. "I'm with you on that."

"I'm craving cake," Cora says." One of those Martian choc-cherry volcanos, with cream. I don't even care if it's frozen. I'm hungry."

She looks to the viewport, wishing she were home with Eric. But at five-hundred light years distant, she can barely pick out where home used to be.

Thirty-Two Weeks Earlier: Concept

"**G**ood news and bad news," Alice said. "We've restored comms. Drone footage points to an attack from Lazuli's north pole. We've lost propulsion and gravity. A power surge took out eighty percent of our food storage."

"What of the shuttle?" Cora asked.

Alice's voice hitched. "Destroyed, I'm afraid."

Five people lost! Disbelief vied with an outraged sense of injustice.

"Mars is sending a rescue ship," Alice added. "But they can't risk another attack, so it won't be venturing this side of the heliopause."

Cora considered the maths. "At this speed, our rendezvous will take years."

"Five years, four months and twenty-six days," Saul put in. "Unless by some goddamn miracle we can fix the Skłodowska drive. Unfortunately for us, whatever hacked into its software made certain that we—" He shrugged. "You get the gist."

No one needed to be told that the *Amelia* would be drifting towards safety at the sole mercy of inertia.

"We can't give up," Cora ventured. "Nothing's unfixable."

Saul looked askance. "We'll do our best."

The days passed with interminable sameness. Cora's pregnancy progressed. When Molly quickened, Cora could only mark the occasion with fear. She retreated to her quarters, to sleep, to memorise poetry and imagine she was home with Eric. Then, all too quickly, her confinement ended, and Cora endured the birth under the same barbaric conditions as her grandmother had.

In the weeks that followed, the crew barely left their quarters, except for Saul, who spent his waking hours in engineering, determined to restore the ship's propulsion. Rations were running low. Meals became snacks and snacks became nibbles. No one spoke of hunger, but Cora could see it in their faces, in that gradual thinning.

As the four met in the galley to discuss what they now referred to as the "end times", Cora floated at a distance, and escaped into poetry.

"In war with time for love of you…" she murmured.

Saul raised his eyebrows. Frankie stared.

"Shakespeare," Cora said. "Sonnet fifteen. It's about time's arrow and how it carries us towards death." She let out a weary sigh. "If only time could be rewound. Is such a thing possible in quantum physics?"

Saul creased his brow, thinking. "It's worth a try." Gradually, the tension around his mouth eased.

Frankie shot him an irritable glare. "If you're talking about repurposing the Skłodowska drive to create a loop, we can only return to the point where it failed, then progress to when we created the loop in the first place. What Cora will face is, arguably, unethical."

At first Cora didn't understand what she meant. But when the consequences sank in, she asked, "How many loops?"

"To get us to rescue? Several," Frankie said.

The transition date was set and rations were redistributed. Everyone enjoyed their first decent meal in weeks.

"How will it look eating in reverse?" Alice asked. "Will food leave our mouths reconstituted? Return to its packaging? Will we notice the paradox?"

"Like chewing one's cud," Cora said through the ghost of a smile. "In and out, out and in, back and forth, until rescue."

The same as birthing and un-birthing, she thought, wishing there was some other way.

The first loop returns to the attack. Time's arrow reverts to its natural direction. Despite what's to come, Cora remains secure in the knowledge that, beyond the forcefield, the *Amelia's* hull will continue its long slow haul to the heliopause.

She floats away from the med-couch. Her newly-diagnosed pregnancy is terrifying and unstoppable. Past-Cora fears for her baby. Future-Cora consoles herself with hope. The crew mourns for their colleagues lost in the shuttle. All too soon there's another birth, another death, a return to grief and a funeral. When everything seems hopeless, Saul proposes his audacious plan. If he's conscious on two levels like Cora is, she cannot tell.

"Inside each loop," he says, "our actions will be pre-determined. As for our thoughts: nothing is certain with quantum physics."

"Even in forward time?" Cora asks.

"Even then."

Frankie clears her throat. Her frown deepens. "Throughout the loops, you'll be subjected to three births and four un-births. All unstoppable."

"But not so cruel as death," Cora says.

"The final loop will end immediately after the attack," Saul adds. "The forcefield will drop, and the rescue ship will meet us."

Everyone agrees the choice must be Cora's. When they meet her gaze, their eyes betray hope, expectation and fear.

"If that's what it takes to save us," she says firmly, "let's get on with it."

Past-Cora is terrified of how it will feel. Future-Cora remembers she already knows.

THE STRANGER IN MY YARD

KAT PEKIN

There's a man by the truck.

I can see him from the window through the curtains. He's injured. Infected, maybe. I abandon the dirty dishes in the sink and duck down behind the counter. The closest gun is by the door, and I manage to get to it without making the floorboards creak.

"Mamamamama!" Charlie's calling for me. He likes to run the name together, and he's too young to know that's not who I am.

"Quiet!" I hush him.

But he's two, he doesn't understand context, and comes toddling out into the hallway. His small, round face looks confused. He sees the shotgun in my hands, and he wobbles a little on his feet.

I hold my hand up to him. "Stay there, baby."

I watch the man through the glass panel in the door. He didn't seem to react when Charlie called me. Maybe he didn't hear it. The man is stumbling. He's dressed in dark clothes. He looks like a scavenger. Maybe not infected. He's hugging his left arm close to his chest, but his right arm is covered in blood.

He looks ahead, towards the house, but he doesn't focus on anything. He looks towards my truck and the small shed next to the house. I haven't been away from here since the storm came through last week, so everything looks shabbier. He might think this house is just another abandoned property.

I have to catch him off guard.

He stumbles sideways into my truck and holds his arm upright to the sun. I watch him struggle to tear a strip off his raggedy pant leg, and use one hand and his mouth to tie it around a wound on his left wrist. It doesn't look like a bite. It's not haemorrhaging.

He's tending to a wound. He's fleeing something. A bad community? Other scavengers? He's a threat, whatever and whoever he is. I have to take him out. The kids are in here.

A voice whispers my name. "Rose?"

"Stay back," I warn Lexi, as I keep my eyes on the stranger.

He doesn't look well. I realise his clothes are quite bloody, and he's pale. He's probably lost a good amount of blood. He won't last long out there.

"Should we hide?" Lexi asks.

"No, don't make a sound."

I've taught her to rush them all to the basement when there's trouble, but this guy can barely stand up, let alone attack us. And if he thinks this house is empty, let him think that. If I leave him long enough, he'll just die out there. Hopefully, he wanders far enough away to not be a problem. If he drops dead this close to the house, they'll come in and eat him. Then one of the kids will cry and we'll get discovered and have to go running again.

"He looks sick." Lexi is at my side. She moves so quietly.

I don't like her looking at him. She's seen enough of all this mess, but the longer it goes on, the more it seems that this world will finally succumb to this last Covid variant. So, my desire to keep horrible things from her seems to be becoming an elusive and unlikely prospect. Lexi's only nine, but she acts older. Probably because of what she's seen.

"He won't get in," I tell Lexi. "Don't worry."

"Maybe he needs food?"

He has a backpack, but it doesn't look all that full. I see a couple of knives hanging from his belt but no gun or bow. He can't have lasted this long out there without a stronger weapon. He must have come from somewhere safe. He doesn't look starving, but he cuts a slender frame. He looks roughly my height and age. Maybe he's normally fast, but right now he's too injured. "We can't help him," I remind Lexi.

She looks at me with an expression that ages her another twenty years, almost like a withering look from a parent. Sometimes I worry she thinks that's her role in our little group, that she thinks she's a parent rather than one of the kids. If that's the case, it's my fault she thinks that way.

"Go back to the kids," I instruct her. "Make sure Charlie and the babies stay quiet. If they wake up, run to the basement."

"What are you going to do?" Lexi asks.

"Make sure the windows are locked in there," I tell her. "Read Charlie a story, but not—"

"Not one with dogs, I know," Lexi finishes, then she quietly leaves my side.

I bite at the inside of my cheek. Charlie laughs and barks loudly whenever he sees dogs in books. Lexi's the one who told me to stop doing it. He gets too excited, and it's tricky to calm him down.

The stranger falls. Actually, he slides down the side of my truck until he slumps in the dirt. He tucks his arm into his chest again. His hair is shaggy and dark. Maybe he'll just die there. Then I can drag him into the bed of the truck and dump him away from here. Maybe even without the kids seeing.

Then one of the babies starts wailing.

And the stranger hears it.

I see the second he catches it. His head flicks straight up towards the house. To me in the window. He sees me.

"H-Hey!" he tries to call out, but just coughs. His voice is gravelly and dry.

In the other room, I can hear Lexi trying to quiet the baby down. I think it's Phoebe. Her screech is quite piercing, much more so than Louisa's. And Charlie's babbling again. Now this stranger knows there are living people here.

"I-I'm not bit." He manages to push himself back up on his feet, but he still leans against my truck for support. I realise he's wearing a jacket and a button-down shirt. Three knives on the belt in the front, shirt untucked at the back. He could have a hidden weapon.

Fuck.

I unlock the front door and storm out with the shotgun aimed at him. I shut the door behind me, and a few seconds later, I hear the lock turn from the inside. Lexi is so damn fast.

The stranger sees my gun and tries to raise his hands in surrender. The injured hand that he wrapped with his pant leg won't go too high. He's roughly fifteen feet from me. The gunshot will be loud, but it will take care of him in a flash. And we can wait out any undead that the sound brings in as long as we keep to the basement.

"I-I have a—"

"You shouldn't be here," I growl.

He looks at me, squinting in the glare of the sunlight. "You got kids in there?"

I take a step closer to the veranda stairs. I can blow off his head from here. I lift the gun, aim it and close one eye.

"I gotta ticket!" he yells out. "I gotta sub ticket!"

I pause, just for a second. Then we stare at each other in silence. Now I know he's lying.

"There aren't any more subs," I say, and cast a quick look around.

Maybe he's playing for time and there's an ambush coming. Do I have time to kill him, grab the kids, and get into the truck before they storm my home?

"In my bag," he says.

He lowers one hand just enough to shrug the bag off his shoulder, and then he tosses it towards me. A dodgy throw, doesn't even make it halfway. I don't move. I don't know if he thinks I won't kill him or if he's just tired, but he collapses down on his backside, and his arms fall limp to his sides.

"Rose?" Lexi calls.

"Go back inside."

"I can hear them coming."

Dammit. The kids or the stranger or my yelling or a mix of it all have alerted whatever undead are lingering nearby. I have to get back inside; they'll get bored and move on if we're quiet enough. I'll have to rely on Lexi again.

"Lexi, get his bag," I tell her. I don't shift my aim from his head. "You move, I shoot."

He doesn't even blink as Lexi drags his bag back to my side.

"Front pocket," he pants.

God, what if he has a bomb? I reach down to pull Lexi back, but she's already unzipped the pocket and pulled out what looks like a folded passport.

Not official, obviously. It can't be. A good fake, I guess. Just one piece of paper pressed inside a cheap plastic wallet. The first thing I notice is the CVA insignia stamped at the top of the plastic. Why does it look official?

"Read it," I tell Lexi.

I can't afford to take my eyes off him. But now I can hear the moaning on the wind.

"Your CVA submarine will dock in Nelson's Bay on the ninth of July 2027 as per official military request," Lexi reads almost breathlessly. "The sub will arrive for Hadley refugees at 0600 sharp. Present this ticket to gain access to the sub and refuge from the mainland."

It can't be real. The CVA? The Covid Variant Administration? They're still around?

"I can take you," the guy pants. "I can take you with me, but you'll need me, or they won't let you on."

I can feel Lexi looking at me.

"Is this real?" she asks.

I found Lexi early on. She eventually told me her family got tickets for one of the last subs, one of those that never made it out. Most of the people on that dock were eaten alive. Lexi survived by climbing on top of a campervan. She broke a window, climbed in and stayed hidden. She said she'd been there two weeks when I found her. There was food and water, and anyone alive was staying clear of the docks. That's why I'd come searching inside the van. I must have looked a sight with Charlie strapped to my back and Louisa cuddled on my front. Charlie took an instant shine to Lexi, and Lexi carried him out of the van that day. She never once asked about Louisa's leg, so I never asked her why she was alone.

The growls are louder now. They're getting closer. Dammit. I have to take this stranger inside. He might die anyway. May as well try and see if this ticket is legit.

"Can you stand?" I ask the man.

I won't put down this gun. He grunts but manages to slide back up onto his feet.

"Take off your knives," I order.

He glances to the woods, where the growls are intensifying.

"Take. Them. Off."

He takes out each of the three knives and drops them in the dirt.

"Take off your jacket."

"Shit, I can't," he groans, but he does manage to shrug off his jacket.

It's not hiding any weapons. And his button-down shirt is so thin, I can see his chest through it and the bruises on his arms.

"Rose—" Lexi starts.

"Take the bag inside, lock the kids in their room. Now!"

She shoulders the bag and scurries off.

"Walk," I order. I keep a wide berth and circle around him. "Lift up your shirt."

He seems to get the idea and shows me that he doesn't have a gun in his waistband.

"Walk slowly."

He rasps a laugh and limps gingerly towards the house. It feels so wrong to have him walk in before me, for him to be between me and the kids. But I have the gun. He won't catch me off guard. I won't let him.

Lexi is waiting to lock the door once we come through. I direct him to our little living room, and he sinks down onto the couch. Lexi has already drawn the curtains, and I hear a muffled babbling from downstairs. She's taken the kids to the basement.

I stay standing with my gun on him. I see Lexi in my periphery doing something I shouldn't be surprised to see her doing. She's getting the stranger a water bottle. She even undoes the lid and hands it to him.

"Lex—" I go to warn her, but she's already handed it over.

"Thanks, kid," the stranger coughs.

Lexi takes the plastic passport from her front overalls pocket. "Where did you get this?" she asks.

"I was at a CVA refugee camp in Hadley." His voice is less

hoarse now he's had half the bottle of water. "Military run. They requested a sub for our community."

"Last I heard of Hadley, they went radio silent," I tell him. "We figured they were overrun last year."

"Running outta food," he says. "They wanted to feed who was there, not anyone new. They stopped broadcasting."

My stomach turns. "There are still people out here."

"I know," he says.

"We still need help."

"I know."

In the weeks following the declaration of an undead Covid pandemic, the government and CVA started shipping people out of cities onto huge submarines given the grandiose title of "Valiant Subs". It all seemed to go pretty smoothly to start with. Tickets were issued in plastic passports from local schools and churches and league clubs. All you had to do was wear a mask and not have a temperature to get one free of charge.

Then panic set in.

Rumours spread there weren't enough subs to cater for survivors, and that you had to pay to confirm a seat. People were paying for tickets on subs that didn't exist, showing up to the docks and causing a scene when they were denied boarding. I was with Vivienne and Charlie then, Louisa bouncing around in my sister's belly not quite ready to be born. We were listening to the panic on the radio on the drive back from Townsville. My sister and I weren't even going to attempt the docks. We had to try and make it back into Brisbane to find her husband.

We never found him.

Within a month, all the subs were gone, the CVA issued a statement that there were no more coming, and tickets like the one in Lexi's hand were worthless.

"Last week's storm flipped a tank through our fence," the guy continues. "Undead got in. I don't know what happened to the people who didn't die."

"How did you get away?" I ask. The gun is getting heavy, but I won't lower it.

"Ran." He drains the last of his bottle. "Figured I'd go back when they cleared out, but they never did. The sound brought more of them in."

Lexi hands him a second bottle of water. "How did you hurt yourself?"

"Broke into a car." He holds up his hand and starts to undo the pant-leg strap with his teeth. "Slept there a day or so."

"This date is tomorrow, right?" Lexi asks.

The man nods. "Figured I could limp my way to Nelson's Bay, but I fell running from those arseholes and landed heavy. I think I broke some ribs. And I tore my hand open again. Can't keep it clean."

He uses the contents of the second water bottle to wash off his hand. Lexi leaves again, and I know she's gone for medical supplies.

He flicks his chin up at me. "Your name's Rose?"

I nod.

"Max," he says.

Downstairs, I hear a little bang. A dropped toy? Then there's a cry. And then another. And another. Dammit, they're all upset.

The man gives me a strange look. "How many kids you got in here?"

"Shut it," I say over the gun. "Lexi?"

She runs through and drops a small parcel of clean bandages and disinfectant on the coffee table, then she hurries down to the basement. The wailing quiets after I hear her slide the metal door closed.

"How many?" Max asks. He leans forward and starts to tend to his wound with what Lexi has left behind.

"Five, including me."

"You're what, thirty? They all yours?"

"They are now."

He grimaces as he cleans his hand. "That truck outside work?"

"Why?"

"To get us to Nelson's Bay."

"Us?"

"They won't take you without me."

"Why not?"

He shifts awkwardly in his seat and uses his damaged hand to pull up the sleeve of his shirt. I realise what I thought was a bruise is actually a coin-sized scar in the shape of an oval. It has the letters CVA stamped in the middle of it. It's not a tattoo as much as a brand. It's still slightly red, like it's not more than a couple of weeks old.

"Gotta show this to get on," Max says. "Everyone at Hadley got one. The captain who organised the sub made sure this was a failsafe, so the right people got on."

My mind screams. "Right people?"

Max seems to know he's said something stupid. "From the Hadley camp, I mean."

"And what about people who weren't lucky enough to find a refugee camp?"

"I'm sure they'll take you anyway," he sighs, annoyed at me or in pain. Or both. He holds a hand up. "They see a pretty face and cute kids; I doubt they'll turn you away."

I feel like this is all a big scam, that I'm going to catch him in a lie. "Then why show me the brand?"

Max gives a tired shrug. "Guess I didn't want you to think I'm expendable."

I can hear the babies still crying. Not loud enough to bring in the undead, but enough to know that Lexi can't handle them alone.

"I won't hurt you," Max says.

He seems sincere. I've been wrong before. Yet there are more weapons in the basement. I can lock him out if I need to. And Lexi has his ticket, so if this is all legit, he can't leave without it.

Still, as I back away from him, I keep my gun poised. He doesn't move. Nevertheless, I don't take my eyes off him until I'm down the stairs and out of sight.

It was Phoebe causing the trouble. Sweet thing. She's the youngest, I think. Phoebe and Louisa are both under a year old. I untuck Phoebe from her bassinet and cuddle her close. She loves cuddles. She's the newest addition to our little group. She was born after the undead pandemic, of course. Like Louisa. But I found Phoebe thanks to her piercing screech. She had been left locked in the bathroom of a convenience store. I'd gone there for supplies. There was a zombie trying to bash through the door to reach Phoebe. I assume it was her mother, because she had left a note on Phoebe's car seat.

I was bitten. This is Phoebe. Please tell her how much her Mama loves her.

I'd thought she was hungry and that's why she was screaming, but she'd quieted down just a few moments after I scooped her up. She just likes to be held. It's impossible to get her to sleep unless she's in your arms.

Lexi is helping Louisa try to stand up. She's almost got it. She can hold it for a couple of moments, then she flops to one side. Her little expression doesn't change when she tumbles. It makes us giggle, which makes her laugh. Louisa's leg is completely healed, and she doesn't seem to need the missing right foot. The remaining part of her lower leg—a stump from the knee—is scarred, but the skin looks a healthy pink.

Charlie bangs some blocks together, which catches Louisa's attention, so she scoots over to him. Lexi crosses her legs and takes the passport from her front overalls pocket again.

"It looks like the one my parents got," she says.

"Lex—"

"Why would it be fake? Why would he waste time doing that?"

I can't give an answer because I don't have one. Instead, I attempt to reassure her. "We're still alive because we're careful. That ticket is dangerous."

"Maybe it's a way out?"

"Maybe it's a trap."

Lexi gives me that withering parent look again. "Why would he do it this way? Everyone thinks the subs are gone."

She's right, it's a weird angle if he's trying to trick us. If he knew we were here, he could have snuck up on us at night and not bothered with the theatrics of an injury and pretending as though he'd just stumbled upon our home. To plan this ticket thing would mean he'd have to have found an old ticket, a working computer, matched the font, and printed it out. I suppose that's not impossible, but why go to that trouble just to fool us? To what end?

Lexi smiles a little. "Isn't it worth trying at least?"

I'm surprised when I come back upstairs and Max is still there. I don't know if I expected a group of people waiting to pounce or that maybe he'd just steal our stuff and run. But he appears to have been in an uncomfortable sleep when I get back to him. My footsteps wake him with a start. His eyes watch my shotgun, which I'm still holding, while not aiming at him this time.

We stare at each other for a few moments. Then I speak first. "Okay."

Lexi and the kids come up behind me. She's holding the babies; Charlie is clambering up by himself. He sees Max, points to him, looks up at me and grins. Like he's spotted something amazing for the first time. God, he looks like Vivienne when he grins.

Lexi hands Louisa over to me. Phoebe can't really hold her head up yet. I prop Louisa on my hip and keep a grip on my gun.

Max nods towards me, to Louisa. "What happened to her leg?"

"She was born without it," I lie.

I don't feel like telling him how Vivienne tore it off the week after Louisa was born. That image is burned in my brain. My infected sister snatching her baby so violently it severed her leg at the ankle. Her mouth reaching to bite the newborn, then Vivienne's head exploding as I didn't hesitate to shoot. Charlie screaming. I thought Louisa was dead. She had to be; she'd lost her leg. And taken by her mother, no less. But she survived. Somehow.

One day, she'll ask me why her leg is gone, and I'll have to have an answer. Just like I'll need to tell Charlie one day that I'm his and Louisa's aunt, not their mother.

But I don't have time right now.

Max sits in my front passenger seat. I didn't want him behind me. The kids are in the back. Louisa is in the car seat, Charlie buckled in next to Lexi, and Phoebe in her bassinet behind the driver's seat. Unsafe, but this might be the last trip we have to make. Nice thought, that one.

I expected it would take me a while to pack, but it turns out we don't have that much stuff. Nothing really worth carrying. I hadn't got a lot of sleep the night before. I wanted us to be on the road before 5:00am, even though Nelson's Bay is only a fifteen-minute drive. I was up with Phoebe anyway, had her in the baby sling while I packed up clothes, food, and water. Max eventually passed out on the couch. He didn't cause any trouble.

Before sunrise, Lexi helped with the kids, and we were out of the house just after five according to our watches. Lexi and I both have them so we know we're on the same time.

Signs directing us to Nelson's Bay shine in the morning sunlight. Charlie gets excited whenever a bird flies by. At one point, he starts barking and pointing at the window. I see the flash of white-grey fur sprinting through the trees. Some kind of animal, but he doesn't care. To him, it's a dog. And this time, he can bark without me shushing him.

Even though I'm driving slowly, the road is such a mess that every time I clip the edge of a pothole, Max grunts in pain. He hasn't really improved since he appeared on my property. But he hasn't got worse. I suppose that's something.

I keep stealing glances at Lexi in my rearview mirror. She knows these roads. These are the roads that lead to the bay where I found her, and where her family died. She's purposely not looking out the window, and fussing over the little ones instead. I don't know what they would do without her. I don't know what I would do without her. Would I even have had the strength to take care of all these kids if she wasn't here with me?

Maybe that's why she wants this sub ticket to work out. So she doesn't have to be a parent anymore. My heart aches with realisation that I want that for her too.

We take the final turn for Nelson's Bay. I must have been going much slower than I thought, but we still have seventeen minutes until six o'clock.

The parking lot is littered with abandoned cars, strewn luggage and, of course, the dead and undead. More of the former than the latter. The few upright ones are barely vertical, and shuffle when they hear my truck. It's not like they can sprint after us.

We won't get out of this vehicle, Lexi and I already decided that. We didn't give Max back his knives. He's unarmed, but she and I are not. I park by the dock. There are no zombies nearby. We have a clear path to drive out. We can wait for now. We sit silently. The babies babble and coo. Charlie is playing with his seatbelt buckle. Lexi is resting, looking at the sky through the rear window.

"What happens if it doesn't show?" Max asks after a time.

I glance at him sideways. He chose careful words. He's asking if I'll kill him if the sub doesn't arrive, but he's being evasive, as if he doesn't want to scare the kids. Perhaps he had kids of his own. I don't know anything about him, and am struck with the realisation that I might actually want to know a little bit more.

"Good thing you were comfy sleeping on the couch then," Lexi pipes up quietly.

When I look at her in the mirror she's watching me, that parent-look again. This time, her expression is firm. Telling me what's going to happen by tone instead of words. How is she so clever?

I don't want to look at my watch because I already know it's past six.

After a few moments, Max speaks again. "You know why they stopped the subs?"

Lexi bites and asks. "Why?"

"They ran out of waterproof paint."

It takes me a couple of seconds to realise he's kidding. He's sort of half smiling, but it looks more like a grimace. I guess he's trying to lighten the mood. Lexi gives him a weak chuckle and rolls her eyes.

All I say is, "I didn't know they painted submarines."

I wasn't joking, but Max scoffs.

I rest my head back in my seat and stare forwards at the ocean. I hear moans on the wind. I know they're closing in and we have to leave. I know the time for the sub has come and gone. I know I won't kill Max because I would have done it already. And I know he knows that too.

I know I'll head back home, unpack all our stuff, and get back to our little life. There might be other refugee camps out there. Heck, all this started two years ago and we only just yesterday found out about the Hadley camp. There must be more. Maybe I can find them. For the kids, for Lexi, because this is my family now.

Then I feel the rumble from the ocean.

CONTRIBUTOR BIOGRAPHIES

EDITOR

DEBORAH SHELDON is an award-winning author and editor from Melbourne, Australia. She writes short stories, novellas and novels across the darker spectrum of horror, crime and noir. Her award-nominated titles include the novels *Cretaceous Canyon, Body Farm Z, Contrition* and *Devil Dragon*; the novella *Thylacines*; and the collections *Figments and Fragments: Dark Stories* and *Liminal Spaces: Horror Stories*. Her most recent books include the novel *Cretaceous Canyon* and the novella *Redhead Town*.

Deb's collection *Perfect Little Stitches and Other Stories* won the Australian Shadows 'Best Collected Work' Award, was shortlisted for an Aurealis Award, and longlisted for a Bram Stoker. Her short fiction has been widely published, shortlisted for numerous Australian Shadows and Aurealis Awards, translated, and included in various 'best of' anthologies.

Deb has won the Australian Shadows 'Best Edited Work' Award twice: for *Midnight Echo 14* and for the anthology she conceived and edited, *Spawn: Weird Horror Tales About Pregnancy, Birth and Babies*.

Other credits include TV scripts such as *Neighbours*, feature articles, non-fiction books (Reed Books, Random House), stage plays, poetry and award-winning medical writing.

Visit Deb at http://deborahsheldon.wordpress.com

AUTHORS

DMITRI AKERS is a writer and poet of the weird. He was born in Thuringowa/Townsville (Nyawaygi country) but has lived most of his life in Adelaide (Kaurna country). What interests him most is the nexus of the poetic, the folk, the hidden, the dreamlike, as well as the ends of reason, in weird literature. His poems and prose have appeared in *Penumbra, So It Goes, Midnight Echo,* and *Spectral Realms.* https://dmitriakers.com/

EMMA ROSE DARCY started out writing dark fantasy (not published anywhere, just noodling about) but in the last two years has switched to writing almost exclusively horror (published sometimes, yay). She shares her name with a famous romance writer who, when she finds out what this Emma Darcy has been writing, will be very upset. Emma Rose has a wife and two children, works in a library, does freelance digitisation work, and paints miniatures in her free time. Find Emma on Instagram @ofcoursethehorrors

MATTHEW R. DAVIS is an author and musician from Adelaide, South Australia, with over eighty short stories published around the world thus far. He's been shortlisted for a Shirley Jackson Award, the Washington Science Fiction Association Small Press Award, a Ditmar Award, and multiple Aurealis and Australian Shadows Awards, winning two Shadows for 2019. His books include the short story collection *If Only Tonight We Could Sleep* (Things in the Well, 2020), novel *Midnight in the Chapel of Love* (JournalStone, 2021), novella *The Dark Matter of Natasha* (Grey Matter Press, 2022) and flash chapbook *Bites Eyes: 13 Macabre Morsels* (Brain Jar Press, 2023), with a second full-length collection, a nonfiction music book, and a feature film novelisation confirmed. He shares his life with the artist Meg Wright, aka Red Wallflower Photography. Find out more at matthewrdavisfiction.wordpress.com.

RACHEL DENHAM-WHITE is an emerging writer living in Boorloo/Perth. In 2022, she graduated with her Bachelor of Arts (Hons), with her dissertation on the Postfeminist Gothic movement in the works of her favourite author, Angela Carter. She was a regular contributor to UWA's student magazine *Pelican*, and also wrote for publications such as *Damsel*, *Peach* and *CUB*. Since her graduation, her work has been featured in *Westerly* and the entertainment website *Seesaw*. She currently reviews books for *Good Reading* magazine. In her spare time, Rachel can be found playing DnD, reading and writing horror, eco-horror, Gothic horror and pregnancy horror, and saving up for her Master's degree in Publishing and Professional Writing. This is one of her first publications. You can find her online at https://www.instagram.com/raes_readingcorner/?hl=en

JASON FRANKS is the author of *Bloody Waters*, *Faerie Apocalypse*, and *X-Dimensional Assassin Zai*, and the writer of the *Sixsmiths* graphic novels. He works at the intersection of horror, science fiction, fantasy, and comedy, but he'll stalk a story into any genre. Franks's work has variously been shortlisted for Aurealis, Ditmar and Ledger awards. He lives in Melbourne, Australia, with his family and a brace of guitars. Find him online at jasonfranks.com

ROWAN HILL is a beach-loving Novocastrian who has lived a little bit of everywhere but still calls Australia home. A sci-fi horror author with a love of creature features and flawed women who occasionally murder, she has a wide range of publications and her next, *No Fair Maidens from Earth to Mars*, will be released with Trepidatio Press in late 2024. She can be found on her website https://www.writerrowanhill.com/

SAMUEL M. JOHNSTON is a Melbourne-based writer and audio engineer. He's recently completed a Bachelor of Media and Communications, majoring in Creative Writing and Literature with a minor in Advertising. He enjoys writing sci-fi and horror stories that involve otherworldly intervention, with some emotionally-focused character drama on the side. He's had multiple works published in Swinburne University's *Swine* and *Backstory* literary journals. His other creative projects can be found on his socials: @creativeman_sam

CAROLE KELLY lived in NZ and the UK before finally settling in Australia. Her early careers have included window dressing, debt collection, and working for the British Civil Service. After returning to her country of birth, New Zealand, she pursued a career as a complementary therapist focusing on remedial massage, Reiki, and medical herbalism. In Australia, Carole extended her allied health practice by moving into grief and trauma counselling and, after completing a Master's in Counselling & Applied Psychotherapy, she specialised in relationship therapy. Carole has been writing for most of her life but has been treating it seriously only in the last three years. Her first published work is "Cerelia", a dystopian post-holocaust fiction, which is included in the anthology *The Four Season Project*, released in 2022. 'Food is Love', Carole's second published work, is included in *Leaving Home and Other Stories*, an anthology published in 2023. www.blacknosugar.com.au

BEN MATTHEWS is a physiotherapist, born into a medical family. His mother is an Emergency Department nurse, and his father is a GP Obstetrician. Conversations around the dinner table have always been nightmare fuel, and as such, he's hardened to viscera and gore. Having always had a passion for reading and writing, he completed a Master of Writing at Swinburne University in 2021. He is a contributor to the *Killer Creatures Down Under: Horror Stories with Bite* anthology, and a finalist in *Dark Regions: Survive the Night* horror writing competition. He received an honourable mention for his flash fiction in the *Minds Shine Bright Writing Competition 2023* for the theme 'Storms'. When he is not writing, he is drawing, or riding his unicycle. He lives in Perth with his amazing wife who thinks horror stories are silly. You can find him on Twitter @benmatt322

An Australian writer, singer-songwriter, actor and rapscallion, **LILY MULHOLLAND** enjoys exploring the role of women in society through multiple genres and art forms. Her stories are grounded in the everyday struggles we face in discovering who we are and what choices we make in a mixed-up world. You can connect with Lily via her website https://lilymulholland.com.au or on Instagram at @lm_mulholland

ANTHONY O'CONNOR is a Sydney-based Australian writer of genre-bending movies and books. He wrote original screenplays for inner city black comedy *Angst* and blood-soaked office horror,

Redd Inc. (aka *Inhuman Resources* in the US/UK). More recently, O'Connor released the post-apocalyptic cult classic novel *Straya* (now in development as an animated feature) and spooky YA ghost yarn, *Emma After*. O'Connor is currently developing a horror film project *The Hum* and finishing his third novel, *The Human Teacher*. He regularly reviews film, TV and video games for various outlets including IGN, Flicks and FilmInk. You can find out more about his work at www.anthonyoconnorauthor.com and follow him on Twitter @clawtalk / Insta @antknee242

Australian author **ROBYN O'SULLIVAN** lives in a 100-year-old house on the wildly beautiful Bass Coast of Victoria. Her published works include short-story collections and a novella for adults, in addition to dozens of non-fiction educational books for children. In the past few years, Robyn has focused on writing short horror fiction and memoir, with pieces included in *Quadrant*, *Guilty Pleasures and Other Dark Delights*, *Blood and Thunder*, award-winning publications *Midnight Echo 14* and *Spawn: Weird Horror Tales About Pregnancy, Birth and Babies*, as well as *The Horror Tree*, *Trembling with Fear* and *The Night's End* podcast. Robyn is currently working on a creative memoir, whilst still dipping occasionally into the horror genre. Read more about Robyn on her website: http://robynosullivan.com

LEANBH PEARSON lives on Ngunnawal Country in Canberra, Australia. An award-winning artist, LGBTQI and disability author of horror and dark fantasy, her writing is inspired by folklore, fairytales, myth, history and climate. She's judged the Australian Shadows Awards, Aurealis Awards, is an invited panellist and member of the ASA, AHWA, CSFG, Australian Fairy Tale Society, British Fantasy Society, HWA, and SFWA. Leanbh has been awarded AHWA and HWA mentorships, was a Ditmar Awards nominee and winner of an HWA Diversity Grant and AHWA Robert N. Stephenson Flash Fiction Story Competition in 2022. Leanbh's alter-ego is an academic in archaeology, evolution and prehistory.

https://linktr.ee/leanbhpearson

KAT PEKIN is a speculative fiction writer living in the western suburbs of Brisbane, Australia. Her work has been published in numerous local and international anthologies, and her stories have won and placed in Australia-wide writing competitions. Kat works at a bookstore and spends her free time plotting tales and inventing characters. Kat has a passion for telling stories and creating worlds. She writes speculative/dystopian/post-apocalyptic fiction and enjoys delving into what life would be like if the world ended.

Facebook: https://www.facebook.com/kat.pekin
Twitter: https://twitter.com/littleton_pace
Tumblr: www.littletonpace.tumblr.com/

DERYN PITTAR is an award-winning author who writes sci-fi, fantasy, futuristic and contemporary fiction, plus a dash of horror. She enjoys the challenge of short and flash fiction and dabbles in poetry. She is published in many genres, including poetry.

The Carbonite's Daughter, a dystopian novel, was released in 2022 by IFWG Publishing. The sequel, *Quake City*, will be released August 2024. Her monthly newsletter https://iwriteuread.substack.com—will drop short fiction in your inbox. See her books at https://www.amazon.com/author/deryn-pittar-books.com and her writing videos at https://www.youtube.com/@virginniadeparte8500

DANI RINGROSE is an emerging gothic and body horror author from Brisbane, Australia. She is a middle-aged single woman with no kids, and leans into all the criticism society levies at her for it. She is in awe of every woman who chooses to raise kids in this world, and her friends with children are her heroes. She instead chooses to manipulate the minds of others' children in her role as high school Literature teacher. She is working on her first novel, set in the Blue Mountains. https://www.daniringrose.com/

CAROL RYLES is a Western Australian former registered nurse who fell in love with speculative fiction at the age of ten. Her stories often cross genres and have appeared in numerous anthologies including *Aurealis, Eidolon, The Year's Best Australian Fantasy & Horror*, BSFA's *Fission #3*, and *Of Gods & Globes #3*. Her fantasy/

sf/steampunk novel, *The Eternal Machine*, was independently published in 2022. She is a Doctor of Philosophy, a graduate of Clarion West, and a committee member of the Australasian Horror Writers Association. You can find more about her work at https://carolryles.net

EM STARR (she/her) is an Australian horror writer, whose work has appeared in lit mags and anthologies such as *Midnight Echo* and *Nightmare Fuel Magazine*. She lives in Melbourne, on Boon Wurrung land, with one husband and two naughty dogs. Get to know Em at www.emstarr.com.au

H.K. STUBBS is an Australian writer, journalist and creative producer who loves following stories and paths for the discoveries along the way and the surprise at the end of the journey. Stubbs's stories and essays have been published in *Apex Magazine, Nightmare Fuel Magazine, Kaleidotrope, Midnight Echo,* and in books published by GSFG, Black Beacon Books and IFWG Publishing (*Killer Creatures Down Under, Spawn, A Vindication of Monsters* and more). Her non-fiction appears in *We Are Gold Coast, Nevertheless* and *Binna Burra Art Nature Science Program*. She won the Aussiecon 4 short story competition with 'The Perforation.' Her story 'Uncontainable' was shortlisted for an Australian Shadows Award, and she won a Ditmar Award for Best New Talent. When not writing or caring for her kids, she's happiest rock climbing and exploring the mountains of South East Queensland. Follow her adventures and climbs on Instagram @helenstubbs, Twitter/X @superleni, and her blog https://helenstubbs.wordpress.com

MATT TIGHE lives in northern NSW, Australia. He is an academic with never enough time to write. He received the 2021 Australian Shadows Award for his short story "A Good Big Brother", published in the award-winning anthology *Spawn: Weird Horror Tales About Pregnancy, Birth and Babies*. He is a Ditmar and Aurealis Award finalist. His debut collection *Drowning in the Dark and Other Stories* is forthcoming from IFWG. His wife has asked him many times if he would like to write a story with a happy ending. He is thinking about it.

https://matttighe.weebly.com/

PAULINE YATES surprised herself by becoming an Australian Shadows Awards finalist, having work translated in Italy, and being mentioned on Ellen Datlow's 'Recommendations for Best Horror Long List', so she knuckled down and fulfilled her dream of becoming a novelist. She is the creative force behind the novel *Memories Don't Lie,* and has had her short-form fiction and poetry published in Australia and internationally. Her home is on a mountain in Queensland's south-east hinterland, where she lives with her family and adopted rescue pets. A magnet for local wildlife, she likes the birds and the bandicoots; not so much the snakes. https://paulineyates.com/